COMPLICATED LOVE

A BLACK LIGHT NOVEL

LIVIA GRANT

e-Book ISBN: **978-1-947559-95-0**

Print ISBN: **978-1-947559-96-7**

BLURB

Keeping two lovers in sync is hard enough.
Three is incredibly complicated.

Jaxson, Chase, and Emma may have officially bit off more than they can chew. Already running two wildly successful clubs in Washington D.C., they decide to expand opening Runway West and Black Light West in luxurious Beverly Hills, California. But there is no relaxing for the infamous threesome. With construction deadlines looming, staffing decisions to make, and multiple outsiders hitting on her men, Emma feels pressured into keeping a dangerous secret from them, breaking the number one rule of their unique relationship.

Can Jaxson, Chase, and Emma's complicated love survive all that life is throwing at them, or will the pull of outside influences cause it to fall apart forever?

CHAPTER ONE ~ CHASE

"*J*'m so excited to welcome our next guest to the morning show. I've known Chase since we grew up next door to each other in Huntington Beach. Welcome, Chase Cartwright!"

Chase took a deep breath and stepped out from behind the backstage curtain and onto the closed set stage of the Los Angeles morning show. He'd plastered his show-smile on before he'd left the green room. He was used to living in front of the camera.

He was, unfortunately, also used to women throwing themselves at him, although he had to admit this time felt different. Brandi Wittman, the longtime anchor of the regional show, had only told part of the truth. Yes, they'd grown up as neighbors, but she'd left off the detail that she'd been ten years older than him and had been his babysitter on many occasions before she left for college.

The attractive thirty-something anchor hugged him just a little too hard... a little too long... too intimate. When he finally extricated himself, he felt the full burn of her seductive glare. They were on live television, and he had a premonition, if she wasn't careful, Brandi was about to make a fool out of herself.

After pulling himself out of her embrace Chase moved to sink into the leather chair reserved for the day's special guest. While the star-struck host seemed distracted, he nervously reached for the steaming cup of coffee waiting next to him, hoping to fill the growing awkward silence by sipping for the fans watching.

Finally remembering she had a job to do, Brandi shook her head as if to clear the cobwebs and jumped into their interview. This was his third live appearance on TV during the weeklong PR push to advertise the upcoming grand opening of their newest dance club, Runway West. He was already exhausted and the club wasn't even open yet.

"So, I think I speak for all Southern Californians when I say welcome home. I've heard you finally moved back to the Sunshine State after living on the wrong coast for a few years." He tried not to cringe at her misguided attempt to be funny. She'd just pissed off anyone watching who loved the East Coast.

Chase smiled politely, keeping his voice steady. He didn't want his tone to betray his growing displeasure with the recent change in his life. "Yes, at least part-time. We still have homes in New York City and D.C., but we decided it would be fun to spend a chunk of the year on the other coast."

"And so, of course, you just had to purchase one of the most opulent properties in Beverly Hills and turn it into your new West Coast hub, right?"

"Well, you know what they say," he chuckled. "Go big or go home."

Brandi's flirtatious reaction was over the top for the tame morning show. "Go big, indeed. That's a perfect description of how I remember you. *Big*."

His burst of laughter was out before he could contain it. He tried to smooth over Brandi's misplaced innuendo.

"The gated estate we purchased is five full acres of prime real estate just a few blocks off the famed Rodeo Drive and not far from the Beverly Hills Country Club. We're almost done with the extensive renovations to turn the mansion into the premier entertainment destination in Southern California."

"That must have cost you a fortune. It's a good thing your modeling career was so successful."

He noticed the slight blush on her cheeks as she struggled to take his lead at refocusing the interview on the club. "Yes, Jaxson and I did quite well on the runway, and in print, and while we opened Runway East completely on our own, we did decide to collaborate with several investors in the lucrative Runway West project. We, of course, retain the majority ownership in the investment." He left off how much it cost just to soundproof and secure the basement level where the most private parties would take place. They wouldn't be mentioning *that* club in the public relations jaunt.

"So, are the rumors true?" She was back to her flirtatious banter.

"And which rumors would that be?" He grinned, casually sipping his coffee before adding. "There always seems to be an abundance of drama that swirls around us at any given moment."

No truer words had ever been spoken Of course, considering the public way they'd outed their unique relationship, he knew they had opened the door to the scrutiny.

"Well, feel free to set the record straight on any or all of the outrageous things printed about you. I'd love to get the scoop." She leaned across the short distance between their chairs to pat him a bit too high on his thigh.

"I bet you would," he snarked, patting her hand once before picking it up and clearly putting it back in her own lap. It was getting harder to contain the laughter he was suppressing at her expense. She was making a fucking fool of herself.

Brandi recovered with her follow-up question. "I'm specifically referring to the rumor you're building the next Playboy mansion. That you're planning on hosting sex parties and skinny-dipping pool parties." Before he could respond she tacked on, "If so, I hope my invitation is in the mail."

Chase smiled politely, careful to look towards the live camera feed. "Well, I'm sure Jaxson, Emma, and I will be christening the pool, and every other room in the house, if you get my drift. But I'm afraid the rumors are false about hosting sex parties."

She appeared annoyed at his continued insistence on using words like 'we' and 'us' and appeared outright hostile at the mention of his lovers' names.

He used her continued silence to add on. "What we *do* plan on hosting are parties for the rich and famous that will be free from prying eyes. We've made the decision to make the entire estate electronic free. Meaning all guests will be required to check their phones, cameras, smart watches, Fitbits... you name it. All electronics will be checked immediately upon entering the mansion. The only electronics will be our own private and high-tech security cameras meant to keep everyone safe."

Brandi finally started acting like the journalist she was supposed to be. "Why in the world would you create such a restrictive rule? Aren't you worried no one will come? After all, I don't know of many people who let their cell phone out of their sight for more than two minutes these days." As if to prove her point, she reached behind her back and pulled her own phone out to show the camera.

He smiled indulgently. "Maybe in ninety-nine percent of the country this rule would be business-suicide, but we're banking on a large portion of our targeted patrons appreciating the privacy we'll be able to offer."

Her sly smile was back. "And exactly what will happen behind closed doors that needs to stay so private?"

Chase chose his words with precision, careful not to cross the line between advertising their public Runway West venture and disclosing details of their extremely private Black Light West project.

"Well, we learned in D.C. there's a portion of the population that is always in the spotlight. Maybe it's because of their job or who they married, their athletic prowess or their sexual exploits. Hell, whatever the reason, every time they leave the house they are on display. Jaxson, Emma, and I know something about having to hide from the paparazzi just to go out for a pizza or take in a movie. It gets exhausting. Runway West is meant to be a safe haven where the rich and famous can let down their hair and just be themselves without fear of pictures showing up on social media within minutes."

"But surely there aren't enough people in that category to make your club a success?"

"That's the best part. There are even more people looking to have a good time, who'd also love to rub elbows with their favorite actor, model, rock star, athlete—you fill in the celebrity. Runway West will be the place for fans to meet their favorite celebrities in an intimate setting. There's just one hitch. We'll be making sure what happens behind closed doors will stay there. There will be no paparazzi allowed."

"Ooooh, this sounds like so much fun. I hope I'll get an invitation to visit the club."

"No invitation needed. Runway West will be hosting concerts, runway fashion events, and will be open three nights a week to the public. All you need to do is invest in the entrance fee or a ticket to one of the hosted events, sign a standard NDA, and you'll be in." Chase didn't miss her pout when he ignored her invitation to treat her like a VIP with a personal invitation.

"It all sounds so secretive. What will happen to someone who gets caught sneaking in their phone or talking about what happens there?"

Anyone who knew Chase at all knew he didn't have a mean bone in his body, but he used his acting skills to plaster on his most menacing smile. "Any violators will be publicly humiliated before they face a lifetime ban on returning."

LIVIA GRANT

He didn't miss Brandi's pupils dilating as she fidgeted in her chair at the thought of being publicly humiliated. Her voice cracked with her follow-up question. "Wow, that sounds deviously naughty. Now I know how the rumors started about the similarities between Runway and the Playboy mansion. I suspect there was a little bit of public humiliation going on there on a regular basis."

He shrugged. "I wouldn't know, but I heard rumors of my own that you happened to be a guest of Mr. Hefner's more than once before he passed away." Chase had done his homework and it paid off. Her bright red blush told him he'd struck gold. If he played his cards right, this interview would be trending on YouTube within the hour. "I see by your blush you understand the value of privacy. Maybe you should plan on visiting after all," he teased.

She finally recovered enough to glance down at the cue card in her lap before blurting, "You chose to have Cash Carter and the Crushing Stones play for the grand opening at your club in D.C. last year. Everyone is anxious to hear who will be headlining the opening of Runway West."

"You'll be excited to know you are going to get the scoop on this. We just got the deal finalized yesterday. I'm thrilled to announce we have an all-star lineup for the grand opening, starting with an exclusive poolside fashion show luncheon where none other than Randy DePaul will be showcasing his newest line of sportswear. Jaxson and I have invited some of the top fashion models in the world to be with us that day, and, of course, some of the biggest names in fashion will be on hand to help us open the outdoor venue.

"We'll then be hosting an evening dinner gala, by invitation only, in the grand ballroom. Cash and the boys have promised to attend, but the entertainment during and after dinner will be by Grammy award- winning artist, Diva Frost. And finally, I'm thrilled to announce our guests will be dancing into the wee hours to the live music of Divinci."

6

"You're kidding me! Both Diva and Divinci are filling huge stadiums. Why would they be playing in such an intimate venue?"

Chase grinned slyly. "They were just excited to be part of the biggest party in town." He carefully hid the real reason they'd signed on was they couldn't pass up the lifetime membership to Black Light. All three celebrities were kinksters who had played at Black Light D.C. in the past.

"Well, now I really do hope to be receiving that invitation. It sounds like an amazing night. When is the big date?"

"Two weeks from tomorrow. We'll have the opening for the general public the next night, and we've arranged for yet another headliner to take the stage that night. It promises to be a huge night."

He just hoped he would make it that long. He was exhausted, and knew that Jaxson and Emma felt the same. Truthfully, he couldn't wait for the whole damn opening to be behind them so things could get back to normal. Or at least as normal as things got for the infamous trio.

Brandi turned to speak to the camera. "You heard it here first, folks. Mark your calendars and let the fun begin! I suspect little work will be getting done between now and then with so many people distracted trying to figure out how to get their own personal invitation."

The anchor turned towards Chase, that seductive haze back in her eyes as she added "I'm glad we have a personal history, Chase. I may have to leverage our relationship to be sure I'm on that intimate invite list."

Just as Brandi's hand slid across his knee, Chase glanced past her towards backstage. Emma had left the green room and was watching from just a few feet away. He saw the flash of hurt as his lover watched another woman touching her man.

He knew what he needed to do. He loved Emma, and Brandi had just served up a lie too big to let pass. He swung and hit a homer.

"I'm sure Jaxson and Emma won't mind me skimming an invitation for my old babysitter. I think I was about ten when you left for college, right? I do have awesome memories of us playing PlayStation for hours when you came over." He delivered the blow with the utmost sheen of charm and a smile, picking her hand up off his thigh and turning the grip into a limp handshake as he added, "Thanks again for inviting me onto the show. I've had a great time."

Several seconds of awkward silence followed until he heard the producer yell, "We're clear," from the sidelines. He glanced up to see the on-air light was now off before reaching for the tiny microphone clipped to the neckline of his designer shirt.

He stood, holding the mic out to Brandi who remained stunned, slumped back against her chair. When she didn't take it, he threw it into her lap.

"A little piece of advice. Don't try to seduce taken men on camera. You only ask to be humiliated. At least now you know what the public humiliation punishment would feel like if you try to sneak electronics into Runway West. Good to see you again, Brandi."

He wasn't normally so ruthless, but nothing felt normal these days. Jaxson was grouchy. Emma was weepy. That meant he was stressed on top of everything else going on.

He stopped to shake hands with a few people as they rushed him off the set so they would be ready when they came back from commercial break. The closer he got to Emma, the brighter her eyes shone. It was something new he was starting to get used to. Tears were almost always in her eyes, and he hated it.

He smiled his best smile, the one he knew she loved. "Hey baby. How'd I do?"

"You did fine. Can't say I was impressed with Brandi."

"Yeah, well, I got the last laugh."

"Does it make me a bad person that I'm relieved she was just your babysitter?"

"Bad, no. Naughty, yes. And I think you need a bit of time spent over my knee as your punishment."

"As long as it's just the three of us, I'll even take the cane," she whispered against his ear as he held her close.

He pulled back just enough to look into her eyes. Emma hated the cane, yet he saw it in her eyes—she was serious.

"When are you going to tell me what's going on inside this lovely head of yours?" He tapped her temple gently. Not for the first time, he felt like he was losing her, and it scared the shit out of him.

"I'll just be glad when we get the new clubs open and all of the employees hired. We're too busy. We aren't spending enough quality time together."

She was right about that.

"Let's get going. If we hurry, we can get back to the house before Jaxson leaves for the day."

He held her hand, dragging her behind him as they rushed to the exit.

CHAPTER TWO ~ JAXSON

"*I* don't think you heard me correctly so let me repeat myself. We will be opening in exactly two weeks, with or without your help. I've jumped through legal, zoning, and financial hoops. I've already secured the grand opening entertainment and I've started hiring and training employees. If you think for one minute I can't fire you this morning and have another contractor on the ground by noon, you're fucking delusional," Jaxson warned their security contractor with a deadly calm voice.

"Don't threaten me, Davidson. We have a contract. You want to fire me, fine. But you'll still pay me every dime."

Jaxson chuckled. "You didn't have your lawyer review the contract before you signed it, did you?"

His response was met with silence, so he continued. "Listen up, George. I'm an honest businessman. I don't want to exercise my out clause unless I have to, but here's the deal. We *will* open on time. That means you're gonna have to get used to me having my boot shoved up your ass or you need to tell me right now if you're not capable of pulling it off on time and I'll find someone who can."

"Screw you, Jaxson."

"Is that a 'Yes, sir, I understand' or a 'You'd better find someone else'?"

His barb was met with dead silence, making the sound of the garage door going up pierce through the quiet morning. Jax smiled, relieved Emma and Chase were back so soon.

"Fine. I'll pull two other crews off the jobs they're on. I'll throw everything I have at your project, but you owe me," the unhappy contractor threatened.

"And I'll pay you every penny you earn. You really didn't read the contract, did you? I added a five-figure incentive to meet our aggressive timelines. You can take your wife on a nice vacation when it's all over."

"Fuck that. My wife is boning our insurance agent. I'll use the bonus to hire a lawyer and start divorce proceedings."

Jaxson stifled a chuckle. "Hey, whatever works for you. The point is I know I have high expectations, but I'm willing to reward those around me that can make it happen.'

"Fine. I'll clear my schedule and meet you at the job site this afternoon. I'd like to walk the property with you and make sure we're crystal clear on your expectations."

"Wise man. I hope to have my new head of security onboard by then. He can walk with us. It'll save me time to explain it all to both of you at the same time. Later."

Jaxson hung up just as he heard the door to the attached garage close. He'd been working at the kitchen island of the house they'd rented just a few blocks away from the new club. It was cramped, and in desperate need of renovation, but the location was convenient for the frequent trips back and forth to their new property. Still, he couldn't wait until construction was complete, and they could move into their newest home

He heard Chase and Emma chatting just before they rounded the corner. It still amazed him that his heart could actually ache at times when he caught a glimpse of his lovers. The physical twinges in his chest were happening more frequently in the last few months and the reason was no mystery.

He'd fucked up. He was in way too deep now to stop it, but he never should have set the insane timeline for the opening. It was pushing him, and everyone around him, to the brink and he fucking hated it.

Chase greeted him first. "I was happy to see your car still in the garage. We were hoping you'd still be home."

He didn't have the heart to tell his lover he was already late and needed to leave soon. "I wanted to congratulate you on your successful interview this morning. I'm glad I didn't go with you. I might have interrupted to bitch-slap Brandi if she'd pawed you one more time."

Emma threw her purse down on the counter with a huff before crossing to the coffee pot to grab a cup of brew. "Yeah, well, my palm was twitching there a few times, too."

Always the glue of their trio, Chase soothed them both. "I took care of it, didn't I?"

"I was so fucking proud of you. I think I've officially rubbed off on you. You cut her to the core at the end there, exactly how I would have handled her if it had been me." Jaxson didn't share that he'd cheered out loud at Chase's parting comments to his old babysitter.

A grinning Chase approached him, leaning in to hug Jaxson around the waist as he answered, "Yeah, well we do enough *rubbing* it was bound to happen." Jax felt the hard cock of his lover jabbing his hip, rushing blood to his own growing erection.

Cupping Chase's package through his dress pants, Jaxson groaned. "I wish I had time to take this bad boy out and play, but I should have left for the property already." Not for the first time, Jaxson stumbled on the description. He didn't know what to call the location of their newest venture. It was to be their home, but it was so much more than that. It was a gated paradise with gardens and pools, a grand three-story house with a full basement. It was, by almost anyone's standards, a mansion, yet he hated how pretentious he sounded using that word.

Chase wasn't to be deterred. The sexy blond's hands roamed lower to cup Jaxson's growing appendage just as an unexpected visitor joined them.

"I stopped by the mansion first, but when you weren't there I decided to look for you here." Lola paused momentarily, taking in the occupants of the kitchen. "Oh, I see you're being distracted. I thought you wanted to stay on schedule."

He'd hired Lola Garcia as his personal assistant for that exact reason––to stay on schedule. So why did it annoy the shit out of him to have her constantly lecturing him about what he was working on?

Maybe because he was the fucking Dom of their household and he didn't take kindly to women, or men for that matter, who imposed their will on his. *He* was the one who called the shots.

"I'm on schedule. I'm meeting people there after lunch."

"The two final candidates for head of security are waiting to meet with you now. I didn't like leaving them there together."

"Then why did you? I don't need you here." He didn't miss the evil looks he was getting from both Chase and Emma. They hadn't been thrilled with the addition of Lola to their West Coast team in the first place. Her continued appearances in their private space were putting additional strain on the trio.

"Of course you do. You need me everywhere. I already sent out the VIP invitations that we talked about yesterday early this morning. I also placed the order for the glassware and grand opening swag. They should all be here in a couple of days."

Lola's welcome efficiency balanced her annoying bossiness most days. "Excellent. You go back to the property. I'll be over within the hour. Let's push the interviews back to after lunch."

"No way, I'm not leaving without you. We have too much work to do," she lectured. She'd crossed the kitchen and was presently grabbing the coffee pot directly out of a stunned Emma's hands while reaching for a nearby mug and boldly stealing the last of the java.

He took a deep breath, much like he often did when working with his assertive Runway manager, Maxine Torres, back in D.C., trying to recognize her value to the process.

"I appreciate your diligence. I even appreciate your assertiveness, but there is one thing you've not learned yet, Lola," he declared. Extricating himself from Chase, he stood with his arms across his chest until she finally turned around to face him after fixing her coffee.

There wasn't a submissive bone in the assistant's body. She met his glare with her own steady look, even having the audacity to crack a smile at his continued gruff demeanor. He wasn't used to being challenged—not by Doms at Black Light and certainly, not by women employees.

"What is it I still need to learn?" she prodded, unaffected.

"I'm the boss. You work for me. If I tell you to go to the property to wait for me, I expect you to say 'Yes, sir,' and move your ass."

Her smile turned to a grin. "Well, then your expectations are stupid. I'm your PA, not your submissive. You pay me to get shit done, and I can't do that if I have to ask permission before every move I make. I'm not a child, I don't need supervision."

The woman had a serious death wish. If it were just his own ego on the line, he could have dealt, but Jaxson didn't miss the muffled moan from Emma. He glanced up as she was turning to look out the window above the kitchen sink, just in time to see the familiar tears in her eyes. His Emma was not happy. It didn't take a brain surgeon to figure it out, and that flutter in his chest came back stronger than before, this time because he had a growing fear that she was starting to slip away from him and Chase.

If he were a good Dom, he'd have them boarding a plane for a far-away destination where they could reconnect... talk... make love… fuck like rabbits. Not for the first time, he regretted that he'd set them on this insane schedule.

And he was wasting valuable time.

"No one in my life is a child, Lola, and while I appreciate how you get shit done that won't save you from getting axed if you ever speak in such a disrespectful tone to me or about my submissives ever again. It's clear you don't appreciate our lifestyle. Fine. I don't give a shit. But as my employee, I *do* expect you to follow orders when given. Now, take your coffee and go back to the club. I'll meet you there within the hour."

Lola's eyes dilated. She was having serious issues following orders. They played chicken, waiting to see who would flinch first. Wisely, it was Lola.

"Fine. I'll meet you there, but don't take all day," she huffed, hitching her purse higher on her shoulder and retreating without another word.

Chase broke the silence. "Wow, she's worse than Maxine. I can't believe you let her get away with that shit."

Even though he agreed with Chase, Jaxson didn't appreciate having it rubbed in his face.

"Listen, we're on an incredibly tight schedule. Making personnel changes at this juncture would put the opening at risk. We just need to get through the grand opening, then we can re-evaluate and make staffing changes if we need to." He paused, turning back towards the sink. "Emma, are you okay, baby?"

She didn't turn to look at him as she replied, "Yeah, just great." Her voice was pinched. "If it's okay with you, I'd like to go spend the day with Khloe over at her beach house. She and Ryder got back yesterday from her on-location shoot in New York."

As much as he hated when Chase and Emma weren't with him, he was relieved to know Emma could take a day off from the stress of the opening plans. He and Chase had both been worried about her for the last few weeks. The men couldn't put their fingers on it, but their Emma wasn't herself.

"That's an excellent idea. You've been working so hard on dealing with the financial end of things, you could use a day off." Jax paused before looking at Chase. "I'm sure you could use a day off too. You could go with Emma if you'd like."

"Oh no, you don't. You're not getting rid of me that easy. You need me to keep handling the deliveries and coordinating all of the vendors." Chase stopped and grinned at Emma's back. "Anyway, I'm sure the ladies would like an afternoon of gossip without us men hanging around."

Chase's assumption made Jaxson feel worse, not better.

"Wait a minute. I don't want them completely alone. Khloe has a lot of crazies still trying to get to her. I don't want Emma exposed to danger."

Emma finally turned around to add, "Even if Ryder is gone, Trevor will be there. One of the two of them is with Khloe at all times."

She was right. Jaxson acknowledged while the list was short of who he'd trust to protect his submissive, Ryder Helms and Trevor McLain were at the top of that list.

"Fine, but I don't want you to drive there yourself. We'll call you a car. Text us when you're ready to come home, and one of us will come get you."

Emma hadn't made eye contact with him since Lola had burst in. He watched her body language, picking up on her hugging her middle and rocking gently.

"Emma, eyes."

Several long seconds passed before she complied. The second her unique violet eyes met his, the ache in his heart stabbed.

"Come here, baby." He held his arms wide, relieved when she rushed forward, allowing him to hold her tight. Chase didn't miss his opportunity to move into their favorite position, stepping close to Emma's back and sandwiching her between the two men who loved her.

No one spoke. Words weren't needed. Every second that went

by, the trio got stronger as if being locked together like puzzle pieces had the power to refill their depleted tanks with love. They'd been too busy, allowing life to pull them apart. Jaxson hated to end their embrace.

"I promise you both. One week after the opening, I'm going to book us a long weekend away somewhere. Just the three of us. No talk of work. Just us. Naked, sleeping, eating, and fucking." He felt Emma hugging him tighter with his promise.

Regretfully leaning back, Jax took charge again. "Chase, you'd better change for the construction zone. Emma, go pack a small bag with your swimming gear. I'm sure you girls will enjoy taking a dip and maybe walking along the beach."

Emma clung to him until he had to almost pry her loose. Something was definitely wrong. He just hoped she could hold it together until after the opening when he could focus on something other than business.

Both men watched as their girl headed to their room to collect her swimming gear.

Once she was out of earshot, Chase mirrored his own fears.

"Something's wrong."

"I've seen it too. She's shutting us out. If I thought I could spank the truth out of her, I'd tie her down and wail on her ass until she told us the truth."

Chase glanced up, worry shining in his eyes. "I've tried to get her to open up. I've begged. I've tried to Dom it out of her. She's dug in."

"Do you have any idea about what's bugging her?" Jaxson asked, desperate for answers.

"Honestly, I don't think she likes California. It all started around the time we got serious about the West Coast project."

"It has taken up more of our time than I'd expected it to." Jaxson sighed. "And I fucked up rushing the opening schedule. It's too aggressive. She's gotten the short end of our time for the last few months."

"Don't blame yourself. You were honest with us. We agreed to the plan."

"*You* did. I don't remember Emma saying more than two words. I took her silence as consent."

"Oh no, you don't. She's been an active participant in the project, working up all of the financial models and setting the final budget. At any point during those crazy long working sessions she could have spoken up if she didn't want to pursue the project. Emma may be our submissive, but she's not a pushover. She's had no problem standing up to us in the past when we needed her to. Hell, that's one of the things that made us fall in love with her."

"I guess. I just wish she'd open up and be honest with us."

"You and me both. We'd better get going. I don't want the two security dudes to kill each other before we get there."

CHAPTER THREE ~ EMMA

"*E*mma! You're here!" Khloe Monroe flung the heavy front door of her Malibu beach house wide just as the driver brought the car to a stop in her circle driveway.

Emma grabbed her purse and the small duffle before exiting the car. Her pulse was racing, her nerves fried. She hadn't wanted to stay in the awful rental all day, and she certainly couldn't stand the idea of spending another day watching Lola pawing Jaxson or the gay interior designer hitting on Chase. All things considered, spending the day with Khloe had sounded like heaven until on the drive over, she realized she'd also be spending the day with Ryder.

There was a time when Ryder Helms had scared the shit out of her, but those days were over. It wasn't fear of the man that had her wanting to limit her time with Khloe's Dom and significant other. No, it was Ryder's eerie way of forcing the truth out of people. It had to be his CIA interrogation training, but the one thing she knew with complete clarity was people with secrets shouldn't spend time hanging around him.

And she had the world's biggest secret.

"I've missed you!" Khloe squealed as she hugged Emma close.

Emma hadn't felt like herself in weeks... hell, months. For a

19

brief moment, she leaned into her girlfriend's hug, allowing Khloe's genuine joy at seeing her push down her internal panic.

"I'm so glad you called me. I've been going crazy spending so much time in the chaos of the construction zone," she admitted.

Khloe released her, linking her hand through Emma's bent arm to tug her into the house. "Come on in. Trevor was just making us a light lunch. Emphasis on the word light... I hope."

Emma smiled as they entered the gorgeous home of the award-winning actress. She'd visited several times in the last year, but this was the first time without the guys. Her heart constricted as it did often these days each time she was forced to acknowledge how far apart their threesome had started to drift. There was a time she had almost felt smothered by their love. For two years, she'd had almost no private time because at least one of the men had been with her. Most of the time she'd loved it, but what a fool she'd been to not treasure their attentiveness more.

"Hello. Earth to Emma." Khloe' s voice cut through her internal angst.

"Sorry, I zoned out."

Khloe had turned, looking her up and down. "Is everything okay?"

She felt guilty causing her friend to worry enough, small frown lines popped up on the actress' forehead, so Emma forced a smile. "Oh yeah. I just haven't been sleeping the best and we've all been under a ton of stress trying to get everything done in time for the opening."

That was the truth. Not all of it... but the truth just the same.

Satisfied with her answer, Khloe turned and resumed the trek through her upscale beach house, headed towards the heart of the home—the mammoth kitchen with a wall of windows that opened out onto the pool deck with a view of the Pacific Ocean just beyond.

Her host spoke over her shoulder. "If you say it's stress, I believe it. I've heard that building a house is murder on a marriage. I can only imagine building two clubs *and* a home is triple the stress."

Emma forgot to answer. She was hung up on the word *marriage*. A word she was beginning to understand would never be part of her life. A few months ago, she would have said it wasn't important. That Jaxson, Chase, and she had an unshakable bond... a commitment... stronger than any damn piece of paper could ever be, anyway.

Lately, she wasn't so sure.

"Emma. It's great to see you." Trevor welcomed her as they rounded the corner to the two-story luxury kitchen. He was standing at the eat-in island, looking like a dichotomy of master chef and biker gang member as he chopped veggies.

She hustled around the counter to rush in for a bear hug from Khloe's tall, tattooed bodyguard and friend.

"Hi, Trevor. It's wonderful to see you too! You weren't here the last time I was over."

They peeled apart and he went back to his culinary tasks while they talked.

"Yeah, I had a few weeks off when Ryder was around. Now that he's been getting busier with his new business and having to travel more, I'm planning on being around more as well. Not to mention, things are heating up again with Khloe starting to shoot again."

Khloe was pouting as Emma joined her to sit on one of the bar stools opposite Trevor. "You guys do realize I'm an adult. I don't need babysitting as if I were a child," her friend complained.

Trevor frowned, scolding her. "You could have fooled me. Wasn't it just a week ago I caught you throwing your entire dinner down the garbage disposal while I left the room for two minutes to take a call?"

Khloe growled with frustration. "It wasn't the whole thing. I'd eaten more than enough. And anyway, you know I hate when you make such heavy foods."

"Khloe, it was a piece of lean steak and spinach."

"Yeah, but you smothered the spinach in a cream sauce."

"Enough! Until we can trust you to eat right, Ryder doesn't want you alone."

Khloe turned to her to ask, "Can you believe this shit? I bet Jax and Chase don't treat you like a baby."

The question returned Emma to her inner angst. "No, not so much anymore," she managed to respond.

"You're so lucky. I get that I need help when I'm on the road on location, or going into the set every day, but when I'm just hanging out at home between projects I would like a speck of privacy."

"Why? What is it that you want to do you can't do with me here?" Trevor probed.

Khloe leaned in to whisper, "For starters, I'd like to sunbathe naked next to the pool."

Trevor had good hearing and chuckled. "Hey, sunbathe away. Doesn't bother me." He grinned devilishly as he dished up the veggie omelets he'd made for the girls.

"Yeah, well it bothers Ryder," Khloe pouted.

"I can't help it if the bastard is too insecure to trust you."

Emma's stomach growled embarrassingly loud. She self-consciously grabbed at her tummy and apologized. "Sorry about that. I didn't eat breakfast this morning."

"See, and the world hasn't come to an end." Khloe glared at Trevor before leaning close to Emma to add. "They'd have me weighing three-hundred pounds if it was up to them."

Emma smiled indulgently at Khloe's dramatic exaggeration. She knew her friend wouldn't be happy with her, but she said what was on her mind.

"I know it frustrates you, but for what it's worth, you've never looked better. You were too thin last year. You look so healthy now."

Khloe took a tiny bite of the omelet before answering. "Fine.

I'll admit I took my starvation thing too far, but I put on ten pounds. I'm at goal weight. This is Hollywood. I can't afford to be fat."

Emma shuddered in the chilly air-conditioning, although she knew the real reason was she was hyperaware that being fat in Hollywood was a bad thing. Their move to Southern California may have brought better weather than D.C., but it also brought back her body-image problems, in spades. Every day, she was surrounded by women thinner than she was. More famous. More beautiful. More cutthroat and bitchy. Like Brandi. Like Lola. Women moving in on her men right in front of her eyes.

She took a bite of egg, trying to swallow down the lump in her throat with her lunch.

Khloe chatted on without noticing. "I can't wait for the grand opening in a couple of weeks. Ryder hates spending time in D.C. for some reason, so we barely get to go to Black Light anymore. I am so fucking excited that there will be a club out on this coast now."

That makes one of us.

Trevor had already wolfed his lunch down and was wiping down the counter as he muttered, "Yeah, like you need to go to a club with a playroom in the basement."

"Hey! You aren't supposed to know about that room!" Khloe complained, blushing.

"Yeah, right. Who the hell do you think helped Helms carry all of that heavy shit down there? Once again, he treated me like his lackey."

Emma noticed, in spite of Trevor's complaint, he was grinning. It was the nature of the men's relationship. It reminded her of brothers who fought but were always there to back each other up. In some ways, Khloe was as lucky as Emma having not one, but two men who loved her in her life. If only Trevor could find his own someone special since Ryder didn't like to share the same way Jaxson and Chase did.

"You ladies finish up. I'm gonna change and go for a run before it gets too hot. Emma, you're in charge of making sure this one eats her lunch." He thumbed in his boss' direction.

"Oh no, you don't! I'm not getting into the middle of this."

Khloe patted her arm. "It's okay. I promise to be a good girl for you."

Emma and Trevor chuckled together before he headed out. "I'll be back in an hour. Try to not get into too much trouble while I'm gone."

He was already halfway down the open staircase leading to the basement where he kept a room when Khloe shouted out, "Text me when you're almost back! I'll need to put my top back on." Only after she heard a distant door closing did Khloe turn on the bar stool and pin Emma with an intense glare. "Now that he's gone, *please* tell me you got to bitch-slap that slutty local newswoman this morning after she kept pawing Chase on camera. I wanted to reach through the screen and slap her myself."

Emma outwardly smiled at the serious look on Khloe's face while internally she focused on shoving down her insecurities.

"I didn't need to. Chase did a fantastic job of putting her in her place all on his own."

"OH MY GOD! I was cheering when he outed her as his old babysitter. And he did it with such charm."

"Yeah, I was so relieved. I wish he'd told me that before the interview started. It would have kept my blood pressure down a bit during the interview. The stress is getting to me."

Khloe took another tiny bite before asking, "The stress of the club opening?"

She took her own bite, using it as a reason to not look her friend in the face as she answered, "Yeah, it's insane."

"You should try my trick. When I have a particularly intense schedule for a few weeks, I pick a date in the future I know will be after things die down. Then on days when the stress gets to me, I focus on that date and how I'll be rewarding myself by getting through until then. I always schedule a full spa day to pamper myself." Khloe's eyes lit up as she added. "Let's pick a date now for after the clubs open, and I'll call and reserve us both an all-day pamper session at my favorite salon!"

Emma smiled, agreeing, "That sounds nice. Thanks."

But, she knew there would be no magic date that her stress would end. In fact, she'd decided it would be after the grand opening of the clubs her real stress would begin. There was no way she could add to the guys' plates right now, but there was an expiration date on how long she could hold it all together without letting things explode.

In that moment, as nice as it was to be here, she regretted spending the day at Khloe's.

As stressful as it was watching Lola try to move in on Jaxson for the hundredth time, in that moment Emma's heart constricted, fear gripping her that she was on the verge of losing everything that was most important to her and she wasn't there to stop it. And, like clockwork, the now familiar guilt crushed in, threatening to suffocate her.

"Hey, are you really okay? Something seems off today." Khloe was perceptive, but then again, it was near impossible to hide how in over her head Emma was. Her parents had started to pick up on it during their FaceTime sessions. Samantha had started sending her texts daily to check on her. She was lucky to have so many people who loved her in her life. She would need that safety net more than ever in the future, and yet as most were friends with Jaxson and Chase before she met them, the fear of losing her friends in the coming months weighed on her like a heavy blanket.

Emma finally managed a lame answer. "I'm fine. Like I explained, we just have a lot going on."

She was relieved when her friend let it drop. "You okay with us laying out on the deck while we catch up? My next project I'm playing an undercover DEA agent. We're filming in Miami and a small Honduran island. I'd like to not have to spray on my tan if possible."

Fifteen minutes later, the women had moved to the cushioned chaise lounge chairs on the patio overlooking the Pacific Ocean. The cool breeze coming off the water tempered the warm early April sun. The view was beautiful, but it couldn't erase how conspicuous Emma felt in her one-piece swimsuit. Seeing Khloe Monroe's perfectly proportioned, sex-symbol body in all of its naked glory as her friend took off her swim wrap was almost too much for Emma. Her recently filled tummy lurched, ready to expel its contents. She forced a deep breath and fought down the nausea.

"What?" Khloe asked innocently as she noticed Emma staring at her.

"Nothing," Emma answered as casually as she could muster, reluctantly removing her own swim wrap, throwing it on an empty chair with her duffle bag. She was grateful for her large sunglasses to hide the fucking tears that seemed to be lurking at all times these days.

"Actually, I'm glad the guys didn't come with you this time. I'd be mortified if they saw this."

Her friend turned, displaying her perfect ass, made even better by the crisscross pattern of raised welts across the actress' perfect globes.

"Ryder got a little carried away last night. I know he's a sadist, but I swear he does it just so I always have marks to prove he's the master of my body. As if I need tangible proof when he's not there."

The skin on Emma's own ass tingled, not from recent attention, but from the lack of it. She'd deny it to her deathbed, but the truth was she missed having her ass paddled. It had been weeks, hell, *months*, since the guys had taken the time to discipline her, or even give her a funishment. She should be happy, so acknowledging how much she missed the intimacy of their domination over her body was testament to how much their relationship had changed in the recent months.

Khloe was busy slathering on lotion as she chit-chatted. "It isn't fair that getting sun makes us look better in the short run, but it can do more harm in the long run. Fucking wrinkles."

Emma nodded, grabbing her own tanning lotion and absentmindedly applied the coconut-smelling concoction that made her stomach lurch, attempting again to evacuate the recently eaten omelet. Abandoning the lotion, she grabbed an ice-cold bottle of sparkling water Khloe had brought for each of them and took several swigs in an attempt to settle her tummy.

"I'm so jealous of your curves. I'd give anything for your boobs," Khloe observed as she stretched out.

"Oh no, you wouldn't. You'd gain ten pounds."

"It would be worth it if it was only in my breasts. It's the rest of my body I can't afford an extra ounce in."

"You're being dramatic again. You look perfect, and anyway, you have more talent in your pinky than half the people in the industry. I hate to agree with Ryder on this, but you really do need to worry less about your appearance. Didn't being nominated for an Academy Award this year prove that to you?"

"Yeah, well, I didn't win, did I?" Her friend shielded her eyes from the sun to peer up at Emma.

"Not this time, but you're young. You have a long career ahead of you."

"You sound like Ryder."

"He's a wise man. You should listen to him," Emma replied, lying out next to her naked friend, refusing to remove her own suit.

"Yes, he is, but please don't feed his ego. By the way, he told me not to let you leave until he gets here to say hi."

"Oh, he's in town then?" Emma tried to keep her voice steady. "I didn't think I'd see him today since Trevor was here."

"Yep. He and Axel are up to something. He doesn't talk about it much, and I've learned to stop asking questions."

Emma took another swig of water, trying to swallow down the anxiety, but resisted the urge to grab the mammoth beach towel she'd brought and cover herself completely to avoid looking at the rounded tummy and protruding boobs overflowing her too-small suit.

The silence stretched between them as the women laid prone, soaking up the sunshine. Emma was exhausted. She tried to relax enough to nap, knowing her body needed the rest, but her brain was her enemy. She looked out over the powerful ocean, feeling small. As Khloe napped next to her, Emma took the quiet time to think through her limited options.

Not for the first time, she doubted the choices she'd made over the last few months. She'd made one amazingly stupid mistake that had now snowballed into a big, fat, hairy web of lies that she had absolutely no way of extricating herself from without destroying herself and everything she loved.

Jaxson and Chase would never forgive her. She didn't know if they would be more upset about the lie itself or the fact she'd been hiding something so important from them for so long. Her reasons had seemed to make sense to her at the critical moment of truth when the first lie had popped out of her mouth. Now, over a month later, she knew she'd made a critical error.

Then things had been compounded by Jaxson's almost reckless pursuit to open the new clubs in an insanely tight timeline, all in an attempt to get grandfathered in on some city building codes that would be changing on May first. A deadline that, if missed, could cost them months and millions of dollars.

No, they couldn't deal with the added stress right now. She loved both men too much to add to their already full plates. She needed to carry this burden on her own until after the clubs were open. It was her contribution to staying on schedule, even if she hated the idea of spending any more time in California than absolutely necessary. In a few weeks, she'd have no choice but to come clean and pray the guys could forgive her.

Emma dozed fitfully, images of beautiful models and actresses pawing and kissing Jaxson and Chase interrupting any attempt at real rest.

She must have finally fallen into a deep sleep, because the feeling of her lunch coming up jarred her awake. Emma shot to her feet, throwing her hand over her mouth as she took off running towards the bathroom just off the kitchen.

She barely made it to the toilet in time to deposit the eggs Trevor had made into the porcelain bowl. Her stomach roiled even after she had nothing left to expel. She knelt on the cold tile, trying to remain calm as she self-consciously wrapped her arms around her waist, cradling her upset tummy. She reached to grab a handful of toilet tissue to wipe her mouth, spitting several times to try to clear the bad taste from her mouth.

Finally feeling like she might be done, she pushed to her feet, flushing the toilet as she grabbed more tissue to try to wipe away the streaks of mascara from her tear-stained face. Pushing her sunglasses on top of her head, she caught herself in the mirror. She looked like a hot mess.

Who was she kidding? She *was* a hot mess.

She turned on the cold water, cupping her hands and swishing her mouth clean. Spitting into the marble sink, Emma splashed more cold water across her face in an attempt to chase away the green hue she often had these days as she fought the frequent queasiness.

When she finally felt like she'd succeeded at putting herself back together, she opened the door to find Khloe standing guard outside. Her friend had thankfully put her swim wrap back on.

The women stood still, neither speaking until Khloe finally broke the silence. "I didn't know you had an eating disorder, too. Do you want to talk about it?"

Emma wasn't sure whether to be relieved or angry at her

friend's assumption. She forced a laugh, refusing to meet Khloe in the eye as she moved around her to walk back towards the kitchen, calling over her shoulder, "I don't know what you're talking about. I just didn't feel well. That doesn't mean I've got some disorder."

"Don't bullshit me, Emma. I'm the queen of eating games. We don't just throw up for no reason. I should know."

Emma had reached the refrigerator. She opened the mammoth, industrial-sized, stainless steel door, helping herself to a fresh bottle of sparkling water. "Maybe I'm coming down with a bug."

"Don't. Not with me. Please."

Emma refused to turn around, too afraid to let her friend see her eyes as she lied through her teeth. "I don't know what you're talking about. Really, the flu has been bad this season. I think I should go, just in case, so I don't accidentally expose you to it if I'm coming down with something."

Emma started walking back towards the wall of windows that formed the exterior wall of the beach house. She'd get dressed and find her phone to order an Uber. She felt like a coward running away from the truth yet again, but there was no way she could talk about this with Khloe before Jaxson and Chase. They deserved at least that much.

But she wasn't prepared for how upset her girlfriend was at being shut out. Khloe stormed around her to stand angry, hands on hips as Emma rushed to get dressed to make an escape. "What the hell is going on, Emma? You haven't been yourself all day today, and now this. What aren't you telling me?"

Emma reached for her phone, desperate to call for a car. The only problem was her hands were trembling so bad, she almost dropped the phone to the wood deck just before Khloe snatched it out of her shaking hands.

"I need that!" she cried as Khloe held the phone out of reach. She hated the sound of desperation in her voice.

"Not until you level with me. What's going on? Is this because of moving to California?"

Damn, how easy it would be to just go with the nugget of truth Khloe had served up. She was just so damn tired — physically, mentally, but especially emotionally. Tears sprang to her eyes, making it harder by the minute to dig herself out of the hole she was standing in.

"I don't like living here. I miss D.C.," she answered truthfully.

Unlike the men who had been too preoccupied to dig deeper into her frequent tears, Khloe looked like she had nothing better to do for the rest of the year. Emma felt the heat of her glare as she crossed her arms over her chest, waiting for Emma to continue.

She reluctantly added, "I'll be happy when the club opens and the guys are less distracted."

"You need to tell them," Khloe asserted.

Emma's heart rate doubled, unsure what her friend was implying. She asked cautiously, "Tell them what? That I want to go home?"

"That, and that it's causing you to struggle with an eating disorder. I give Ryder and Trevor shit for how they hound me, but I know they both do it because they love me. Jaxson and Chase love you more than life itself. Anyone who watches the three of you together for two minutes can see it. They may be distracted, but you need to get their help."

Emma reached out to snatch her phone back, unhappy with the conversation. "They're too busy right now. They don't have time to worry about anything else until after the clubs open. It can wait until then." Emma let her friend continue to think they were talking about bulimia, even though nothing could be further from the truth.

Khloe leaned closer, talking softer. "We both know they are going to lose their shit when they find out you kept something this important from them."

They were going to lose their shit no matter what.

Through trembling hands, she managed to get a car en route to her location as she ignored Khloe's continued staring. Emma pulled out her wrinkled sundress and threw it over her bathing suit, anxious to leave.

Panic was closing in. She'd been holding on by a thread. She needed to escape before she lost it. She tried to brush past her friend, but Khloe grabbed onto her biceps and dug in, painfully holding Emma in place.

"Ow! You're hurting me!"

"No, you're hurting yourself. Talk to me, dammit!"

The women's eyes met for the first time, and Emma saw understanding and empathy pouring back at her from Khloe's expressive glare. It was tempting. Having someone else to share the burden of the truth with.

"I can't."

"I don't want to pry, but this is something I know about. Please let me help."

"Sorry," Emma scoffed, "but you don't know shit about my problem."

"I've spent a damn fortune on counselors and therapy to work on my eating disorders. If my acting career ever tanks, I could make a living as a psych specializing in this area."

Up until this very minute, Emma had skirted the guilt by being able to say that she had told half-truths. She'd simply not included all of the details when the guys would inquire about what was going on with her. It was a thin line in the sand of accountability and truthfulness. With certainty, she knew to continue letting Khloe believe she had a disorder would be wrong on so many levels.

She took a deep breath before clarifying, "You're just gonna have to trust me, Khloe. I am not forcing myself to throw up because of a disorder."

"But if not that, then… " Her friend's question died in the air as excited surprise replaced concern in Khloe's eyes. "Oh my God. You're pregnant!" She'd shouted the words loud enough, the neighbors acres away had to have heard.

"Shhh. I think the guys heard that all the way in Beverly Hills," Emma complained.

"Why didn't you tell me right away?" Khloe bounced on her toes with excitement. "Chase must be beyond thrilled. He always loved kids. And I can't believe Jaxson even let you out of his sight. I would have thought he would have wrapped you in bubble wrap by now, refusing to let you do anything that might hurt you or the baby."

Emma looked away, too ashamed to look Khloe in the eye as she answered. "They have enough stress right now without adding to it," she hedged.

"What?! You haven't told them? Are you crazy?"

Tears flooded at hearing the words she'd been internally scolding herself with for weeks spoken out loud by the only other person, besides her doctor in D.C., to know the truth.

"I need... to go..." she choked out, trying to hold it together. She had to agree that being pregnant certainly messed with a woman's hormones. She felt like she was on an emotional rollercoaster these days.

"Wait. No. I'm sorry. Stay. You just surprised me is all."

Unwanted tears kept coming as despair threatened. This was supposed to be one of the happiest times of her life. She wanted to be happy. She loved the little nugget growing inside of her more than life itself, but would that be enough?

She was at the front door when Khloe stopped her again, this time by rushing around her to block her exit. "Don't go. Not like this. You're upset. Talk to me. Explain it."

She was tempted. She'd carried the load alone for over a month. She'd been tempted to talk to Samantha about it, but knew there was no way Sam would have kept her news a secret from Jonah, and once Jonah knew, it would take ten seconds before he called Jaxson.

Emma pulled a tissue from her purse and blew her nose, trying to calm down. Khloe waited patiently, refusing to rush her.

"I haven't told the guys, no. They are so busy with the clubs. We have to get them open before the first of May to avoid a bunch of expensive add-ons."

"Okay, but that doesn't seem like that important of a reason to me. Jax and Chase adore you. They worship the ground you walk on. This is something they are going to be extremely upset about not knowing. They are going to be fathers."

"No, *one* of them is going to be a father. The other is about to feel like an outsider," Emma added bitterly.

"No way. They will both love the baby no matter which one of them is the biological father."

"Of course they will, but my father warned me about this when we started this complicated relationship. He made it clear he wasn't going to be happy if his little girl wasn't made an 'honest woman.' He's going to be pushing for us to get married. There is just one hitch — three people can't get married. That means one of us would have to be left out. I refuse to do that to either of them."

"Of course you do. There is no way you'd intentionally hurt one of them like that. You could never pick one over the other."

"So, my baby will be a bastard. I'm coming to terms with that. It's not that unusual these days, but my dad will lose his shit. And what about Jaxson's plans to move into the top floor of the club? Won't that be a wonderful place to raise a child? I mean I love Black Light, but it's hardly the kind of place I want to raise a baby. This will change everything with our relationship."

"Stop. You're getting way ahead of yourself. You shouldn't be dealing with this all on your own. Let them help you."

"Dealing with what on your own?" It was Trevor's voice booming behind her. He was back from his run.

The women's eyes met, and Emma silently begged Khloe to keep her secret.

Khloe went into award winning actress mode. "Emma is upset that the local newswoman keeps hitting on Chase. I told you about it this morning, remember? I've just been telling her she needs to talk to Jaxson and Chase about how upset she is."

Emma mouthed her silent 'thank you,' before Khloe pulled her into a hug.

Her friend whispered into her ear, "I don't like this. I'll keep your secret for now, but you need to talk to them soon."

"I will. I promise." She couldn't say more. She was choking on emotion. She needed to get the hell out of there. Needed to go somewhere where she knew no one. Where she could be alone to just think and get her head back on before going home.

The Uber driver honked from the driveway. Emma pulled out of the hug. "I gotta go." With a final smile, she flung open the door and rushed to the waiting black sedan, only letting herself release the pent-up tears when the car had safely pulled out of the drive on the way to nowhere.

CHAPTER FOUR ~ CHASE

"*D*on't worry. I can guarantee one hundred percent compliance with your security protocols. My team is the best in the business."

Chase had to stifle his laugh at the blowhard sitting at the other end of the makeshift conference table. He could feel Jaxson's growing agitation with the way the day's meetings were going. Lola had hired the most expensive recruiting firm in the region. They'd promised to endorse only the strongest candidates to fill the top positions for both clubs. So far, each applicant they'd met was more disappointing than the last.

Jaxson pinned the would-be head of security with a stern glare before asking, "And just how do you propose you'd go about that considering I haven't shared even one of our security protocols with you yet?"

The idiot was too stupid to realize how foolish his boast had been. "The recruiting agency shared your security protocols with me, of course."

"Really? That's interesting since we didn't share our plan with them either," Jaxson said.

For the first time the interviewee, Rob Starr, hesitated. "Well, I mean, it's a club. How unique could the procedures be compared to the other half a dozen clubs I've run?"

Chase reached into his briefcase, pulling out the half-inch thick manual they'd created the year before at Black Light in D.C. They'd created the handbook after a serious security breach nearly cost them the entire club within a month of opening.

He tossed the book into the middle of the large sheet of plywood they'd put across two sawhorses to create a table. "That's how unique the protocols can be. That's our security binder for just one of our clubs on the East Coast."

The candidate, realizing he had over promised, tried to discredit Chase next. "Well, sorry, but I'm the only security professional in the room. I think my experience weighs a bit more when talking about security procedures than a book created for a club thousands of miles away."

Chase ground his teeth in frustration at the asshole's condescending tone.

Jaxson countered, "And as the owners of the club, I think mine and Chase's extensive experience in choosing our key staff weighs a bit more than yours. You're dismissed."

The surprised look on the guy's face before he started to argue back was priceless. "Now, wait a minute. You're making a big mistake." The idiot in the immaculate suit and neatly cropped hair continued, "Mr. Rivera promised me I was a shoe-in for this position and that it would come with a six-figure base and monthly bonuses."

"Mr. Rivera is a minority investor. Extreme minority." Jaxson chuckled. "He can't promise jack shit, particularly when he didn't even bother to pick up the phone and call me with his dubious recommendation. Now, please leave. We have more people racked and stacked, waiting for their chance to be interviewed."

As the blowhard shot to his feet in a huff, Chase couldn't resist getting in his own jibe. "And just a piece of advice for your next interview. Don't ever guarantee one hundred percent success of something before you've even reviewed the job responsibilities. It just makes you sound like an idiot."

He caught Jaxson nodding his head in agreement out of his peripheral vision just before Lola leaned into his Dom's other side, placing her hand intimately on his forearm before whispering against Jaxson's ear, "This is the best candidate. You need to reconsider."

Chase gritted his teeth again, this time to stop from commenting. He had originally thought Emma was exaggerating when she'd complained about Lola's aggressive pursuit of Jaxson. Now that he'd opened his eyes and paid more attention, Emma was absolutely right.

The bitch needed to go as soon as the clubs were opened.

Jaxson wasn't deterred in the least, answering her quiet comment with a loud, "My mother could do a better job at keeping our clubs safe than that pompous jerk. If that's the best California has to offer, then we're in some serious trouble." He yanked his arm out of her grasp, making Chase want to cheer.

"Well, I don't know if we're going to have any new candidates in time to meet our timeline. The only other guy here for security isn't qualified to lead the team. And don't forget we're still looking for the club manager."

Chase silently added 'and a Dungeon Master' to Lola's running list of hiring needs. He was seriously beginning to doubt they would make their cutoff dates.

Jaxson was every bit as stressed as he was. Chase couldn't remember seeing his longtime friend and lover as agitated as he had been in the last few weeks. His naturally dominant Dom had become downright grouchy about how things were going. Normally the jovial one of their trio, even Chase was having a hard time staying positive under the tense conditions.

Still, he was worried about Jaxson who hadn't been sleeping well. Chase pushed down his own anxiety, knowing Jaxson needed him to be the calming force he often was.

Chase slipped his hand into Jaxson's lap, stroking down his Dom's thigh and back up again. He leaned close enough to talk softly into Jaxson's ear. "Take a deep breath."

Jax turned, their gazes connecting and, had he been standing, he would have toppled over from the hardness staring back at him. Jaxson was in a dark place. Contractors and construction crews worked around them to turn the already gorgeous private residence into one public and a second private club as Chase let his hand move to Jaxson's face, gently stroking the day old, and sexy-as-fuck, stubble on his best friend's clenched jaw.

He spoke gently, letting the love for the remarkable man flow out. "I mean it. Everything will be fine. This is just work shit." With relief, Chase could feel Jaxson's jaw unclench as he internalized Chase's encouragement.

"We can't open without a fully staffed and trained security team. All I can think to do is fly Blake out and put him on temporary assignment out here until we can find someone full-time."

Chase hated the twinge of desperation in Jaxson's normally confident voice. "You know that's not an option. He's only a few semesters away from getting his criminal justice degree. He can't leave D.C. midterm."

"You think Daniel could handle it?" Jaxson asked, grasping at straws.

Before Chase could answer, a voice interrupted their private conversation. "Excuse me, Mr. Davidson. Mr. Cartwright. I'd like to help if I can." The deep voice came from a few feet away, the speaker's accent thick.

The men turned in unison, looking to match a face to the sound. On the surface, the candidate was dressed appropriately for an interview—black slacks, white button-down shirt, and grey textured tie. Having spent years on the runway and in front of fashion cameras, Chase honed in on the details that told him just how uncomfortable the guy was in that tie.

He had earlobes with stretched holes, piercings in his right eyebrow and left nostril, and colorful tattoos bright enough to be seen through the thin, off-the-rack white shirt, with tendrils of what looked like an ink octopus sneaking out from the wrist cuffs. By the time Chase finished his assessment, returning his gaze to the guy's face again, the dude was smiling.

"I know. I may not look like Mr. Corporate America, but I'm fucking good at what I do."

Jaxson probed, "And what exactly is that again?"

Only then did the guy look down, grabbing a few sheets of paper and a small business card from the leather portfolio pad, moving closer to hand them to Jaxson.

"Miguel Martinez. I'm applying for the Head of Security position." Chase wasn't impressed until he added, "Ryder Helms is the one who recommended I apply."

"How the hell do you know Helms?" Jaxson questioned.

The guy looked uncomfortable before eventually answering. "Let's just say our fathers were part of the same family up in Santa Rosa."

Chase knew just enough about Ryder's history to know not to ask the candidate any personal questions. The guy's use of the word 'family' was clue enough.

He had almost forgot Lola was there until her shrill voice interrupted from behind them. "This is a waste of our time."

Jaxson cut her off. "You're right. Chase and I can handle this. I'm sure you have something more important to be doing somewhere else in the club."

She huffed before turning to leave. They could hear her heels clicking on the marble flooring as she stomped away.

"Let's continue. What kind of experience do you have?" Jaxson asked, reaching out to take the guy's resume, glancing over it as he answered politely.

"Well, for starters, I've been the head of security at The Office, our... clubhouse for almost eight years. It's a mixed purpose location, based on the time and day. We also have some rather unique security concerns, similar to what I understand you might be facing." The guy chose his words carefully.

"And just what exactly did Helms tell you about our unique security concerns?" Jaxson pressed, obviously agitated that Ryder might have shared info he shouldn't have with a non-member.

"Not much, but enough to know I'm interested in the position."

"I see. I have it on good authority Helms is compiling his own crew of security personnel for his new business venture. Why would he send you my way? Why not hire you himself if you're so good?" Jaxson's question was spot on and Chase turned to the man to see how he'd answer.

Miguel smiled broadly. "I just got married." He paused, holding up his left hand proudly to show them the gold wedding band as if they were playing a game of show and tell. "It's why I'm trying to get a better job and distance myself from The Clubhouse a bit. Ryder's offer would have had me traveling out of town, and even out of the country, for long periods of time with little to no forewarning. That isn't a good fit for me right now."

Jaxson looked up, an unreadable glare on his face. "We're not looking for someone who needs a nine to five. Working here will be the antithesis of that on the days the clubs are open. We also plan on hosting events on other days. Hell, even when we're closed, we'll need twenty-four seven security in place."

"Do you mind me asking some questions?" Miguel inquired.

"Shoot."

"What is the security budget per month?"

Jaxson glanced at Chase for support before answering. "I'll get that number to you if we hire you. Emma handles the budgets and finances. She has the day off."

"Okay. Have you worked up your staffing model yet?"

Crickets.

"Do you at least have any personnel hired yet?"

"We have most of the key positions filled with the exception of Security and the Club Manager. We've had four guards rotating through security shifts since we closed on the property. They seem to be doing an okay job, but I'll let the head of security decide if they want to keep them on or replace them with their own team."

Miguel nodded, looking back and forth between the two owners. Chase liked his easy confidence as he assured them, "It shouldn't take me more than a couple of days to work up the staffing plan. We may need to use a few rent-a-cops for the first few weeks until we find the right permanent team members. From what I understand we'll need to choose wisely. Privacy and anonymity for our guests will be critical."

He was saying all the right things. He was light-years better than the last asshole, but he was also being presumptuous. They hadn't given him the job yet.

Before they could seal the deal, Jaxson's phone started vibrating on the plywood. Chase assumed his lover would let it roll to voicemail. He was wrong.

"Hey, Helms. I see you're sending me your castoffs."

Chase loved seeing the first genuine smile he'd seen in weeks on Jaxson's lips as he gave their friend shit. It didn't last long.

"What the fuck are you talking about?!" Jax shouted.

A knot turned in Chase's gut the second Jaxson's smile turned to a dark scowl. His lover sought his gaze as he listened to Ryder shouting so loud, Chase could hear the mumbled reverberations.

"Stop! You're not making sense!" Jaxson bellowed.

Chase hated only being able to hear one side of the conversation. He moved closer to try to hear some of Ryder's commentary and Jaxson changed the call to speakerphone. Ryder's tense admonition echoed off the walls of the grand foyer they were standing in.

"You guys need to get your heads out of your asses and quick."

Jaxson's dark mood was back in spades. "I don't have the first clue what you're talking about, and I don't care. Put Emma on."

"That's what I'm trying to tell you. She left."

"That's not possible. I told her to stay put and we'd pick her up when we were done."

"Well, that was before things blew up."

"WHAT?" Jaxson screamed into the phone.

"Relax. I meant figuratively. Not physically. Wait. Are you telling me she's not there yet?"

The knot in Chase's gut exploded as he intruded into the conversation, "What time did she leave there?"

They could hear Ryder putting his hand over the phone to muffle his conversation with Khloe before he got back on the line.

"She left at least three hours ago, probably more like four. I was gone all day. I knew right away something was wrong when I got home."

"What are you talking about? Is she sick? And if she is, why the hell would she leave?"

"You need to talk to her about it, man," Ryder cautioned.

"Well, I'd love to, except she's not here!"

Chase could hear the panic in Jaxson's shout, and his imagination started to run wild. The paparazzi were relentless. The kooks were everywhere. He could count on one hand the number of times Emma had gone anywhere without one of her lovers or at least a security escort. The thought of her out in the unfamiliar city… on her own… needing them…

Jaxson pressed for more information, "What aren't you telling me? Did Khloe and Emma get into an argument or something?"

"Not exactly."

"That's not an answer. Put Khloe on the phone," Jaxson demanded.

"No."

"Excuse me? Emma is missing and you're refusing to help me figure out why the hell she left against my orders?"

"Khloe can't help with that. Like I advised, you need to sit her down the second she gets home and not let her out of your sight until she tells you the truth of what's going on in that pretty head of hers."

Chase's hands shook as he pulled his own phone out. She hadn't called — or texted. While Jaxson yelled at Ryder, he pressed *SEND*. His favorite picture of the three of them filled his iPhone as the call rang and rang, eventually rolling to Emma's cheery voicemail asking him to leave a message.

Fuck that. He hung up. His fingers trembled so much that it took several tries to get his *CALL ME RIGHT AWAY* message sent. The bubble was green instead of blue.

Fuck. Her phone was dead.

Tears filled his eyes, but he wiped them away. He needed to hold it together.

Jaxson wasn't doing much better. When Ryder ended the call, repeating that the men needed to talk with Emma as soon as possible, Jaxson lost his shit, picking up his phone and throwing it against the wall closest to them so hard that it shattered into pieces.

Chase rushed to him, hugging Jax as hard as he could from behind. He could feel his lover's erratic heartbeat pounding so hard under his palm that he worried Jaxson might have a heart attack. His Dom was several inches taller than him, so he went to his tippy toes to get close enough to try to soothe Jaxson's anxiety by talking softly against his ear. "Take a deep breath, baby. You won't be able to help her if you keel over from a stroke."

"No sense... never disobeyed... not like this. Something's wrong." Jaxson was short of breath.

All of that was true, but Chase wasn't going to say that out loud. "Well, there's a first time for everything. I'm sure she's just having fun shopping and lost track of time," he answered, praying it could be true.

"You're a terrible liar. Emma doesn't like shopping. You feel it like I do. Something big is wrong. This is my fault. She hasn't been happy for weeks. I knew it, but I figured I could get to the bottom of it after we opened because I was too damn busy to spend time figuring it out. Now I don't have the first fucking clue where to look for her. And I'm a dumbass and blew up my phone. Christ, what if she's trying to call me for help?" Jaxson's voice cracked with emotion.

"Mr. Davidson, sir. Maybe I could help."

It was Miguel. He'd come to face the two men, concern for a woman he'd never met pouring from his eyes.

When neither of them answered, he continued. "Do you have a tracking app on her phone by chance? If not, if you give me her credit card numbers, I can see if she's made any purchases today. Maybe we could track her down that way."

Jaxson stood frozen, uncharacteristically unhelpful in a crisis. Chase pulled out his phone to look up the credit card number Emma used, handing it over to the guy who didn't even officially work for them yet.

Miguel pulled a laptop out of the leather satchel he'd brought with him. Within minutes he was punching Emma's card number into a program. All around them, the construction guys who had been hard at work prior to the distraction now milled about in small groups, watching the drama from a safe distance, glad for once that Jaxson wasn't upset with them.

Chase released Jax and started pacing, making semi-circles behind the guy trying to dig up a lead... any small clue that would solve the mystery.

"The last charge to the card was at eleven nineteen this morning. Looks like an Uber driver."

"That can't be. That was..." Jaxson looked at his designer watch before finishing his thought, "Fucking four hours ago! It's like she barely stayed at Khloe's house."

Miguel was the only calm voice of reason. "Traffic is insane out there. She could just be caught in a jam."

"She doesn't have a car. She should have called if she wanted to leave," Jaxson groused.

Chase hated to add more bad news, but he knew it was important. "I think her phone is dead. It went to voicemail when I called her a few minutes ago."

Jaxson reasoned, "If this was D.C., we'd at least have a few places to check. Fuck! The only possible place she could be is back at the rental. Let's go." Jaxson took off at a jog towards the front door, and Chase was about to follow when he ground to a halt.

"Don't just stand there. You're hired. Your first job is to help us find and protect Emma."

Miguel leaned down to grab his bag before nodding. "Yes, sir. Let's go."

CHAPTER FIVE ~ JAXSON

"*E*mma! You here?" Jaxson shouted into the empty rental house. He'd made the normal ten-minute drive in less than five, luckily not getting pulled over along the way.

The lights were off. Exactly how they'd left them six hours before when he and Chase had left for the mansion.

He felt it. She wasn't here.

He'd almost talked himself into thinking he was overreacting in the car. He'd been so sure she'd be here. He'd refused to consider the alternative.

Vaguely aware of Chase rushing past him to head towards their bedroom, his lover clearly hopeful Emma was there taking a nap, Jaxson didn't have the heart to dash his hopes. Chase would find out soon enough the bed was empty.

He'd been pushing down his own subconscious warning signals for weeks. He'd made reckless decisions and put his family at risk. And that is what Chase and Emma were to him... his family. He'd put business ahead of them. Worse, he'd dragged them into the same insane schedule he'd signed himself up for. No one had held a gun to his head making him expand from two to four clubs. No. His own ego had done that.

Ryder's words haunted him. Gnawing at him that, at the present moment, Helms seemed to know more about what was bothering Emma than either he or Chase did. That was simply unacceptable.

"She's not here," Chase lamented incredulously.

Only then did Jaxson become aware they weren't alone. "What's her cell phone number?" Miguel had followed them, and he was sitting at the kitchen island having swished aside the piles of paint palettes, fabric swatches, and mammoth books of carpet samples. On the one hand, Jaxson wanted to rail at the interloper for being so presumptuous, but considering the security guy was taking charge at a time when he felt paralyzed, he instead felt grateful for his help.

Chase rushed to Miguel, giving him the additional information he needed. Emma's date of birth, driver's license number, recent photo. Damned if the guy wasn't compiling a missing person's report on the only woman to ever hold Jaxson's heart.

Relieved he wasn't needed to help Miguel, Jaxson collapsed into a cushioned chair on the fringe of the kitchen. He leaned forward, putting his elbows on his knees and his head in his hands. He ran his fingers through his own hair, yanking hard enough to hurt. Normally a sadist, not a masochist, he felt the deep need to punish himself for being a dumbass.

His mind kept racing to all of the evil things that could be happening to Emma, but he wrangled for control, forcing himself to remain calm and think through the recent clues he'd had to how unhappy his baby girl was.

He'd lost track of how many times he'd seen tears in her eyes for no apparent reason. He hadn't missed that she seemed to carry a portable pack of tissues with her wherever she went these days, often dabbing at her eyes.

What a fucking asshole you are, Davidson. She needed you, and you worked late instead.

He pushed aside his guilt, remembering how many times Emma had not felt well recently, often laying down for short naps. At first he'd thought she was using her naps as euphemisms for wanting the men to come to bed for a little afternoon delight, but the few times he'd gone to her ready to play mid-day, she'd actually been sound asleep. He should have driven her to a doctor the first time it happened, but he was always running late for some meeting, or on the phone with an investor, or some other unimportant task he allowed to suck up every waking moment until there'd been little left for the people most important to him. What if she were really sick?

He only half listened to what Chase and Miguel were working on. "I'm accessing the L.A. County law enforcement database. I'll run her driver's license there to see if she's been in an accident or been reported in any incidents."

Jax didn't want to know how the hell Miguel had access to a secure system like that, he was just grateful that he did. They only had a few more hours left for her to turn up and explain herself before he'd have to call the police and get their help. He dreaded making that call since their help would also come with public scrutiny on their already unconventional relationship, but they wouldn't rest until she was home safely.

Chase was pacing, his phone in his hand as he texted her over and over again, hoping for a different outcome.

Jaxson jumped out of the chair as soon as Chase's phone dinged with an incoming text. He rushed to Chase, only to find out his lover had texted Khloe. He leaned close to read the screen.

You need to talk to Emma. This is her secret to tell.

"What the fuck? What secret?" Jaxson demanded.

Chase looked up at him, fear evident. "She's not happy. I think she's planning on leaving us."

The words were a punch to his gut. He wanted to argue how ridiculous they were, but considering the signs, he couldn't come up with an alternative.

49

"Then we'll need to make her happy again, won't we? As soon as we punish her for this little stunt. The second I see her I'm going to hug her so tight she can't breathe and then I'm going to paddle her ass so hard she'll have trouble sitting for a month."

Chase shook his head. "I think that'll be a mistake."

"Well, I'm the Dom of this family and there's no way I can let her blatant disobedience go without a punishment, and you know it."

"Jax, you can't spank her into happiness."

"No, but I can damn well spank her into common courtesy—into simple observance of our long-standing rules. She knows she's supposed to have one of us or security with her at all times in public. She agreed to have her cell phone on and charged in case she needs us. And I told her explicitly to stay at Khloe's and we'd come pick her up, yet she left almost immediately."

Like he had at the club, Chase reached out to stroke his arm, doing his best to keep Jax calm. The problem was, Jax had a front row seat to the worry in Chase's caramel brown eyes. He may not be able to help Emma at the moment, but he sure as hell could do something to make Chase feel better.

Jax reached out and yanked Chase into his arms. The men clung to each other. As much as he loved holding his lover, he knew both men desperately missed the woman who was normally sandwiched between them. The clean smell of his lover's mint-scented hair products helped calm him.

Miguel kept working as the two men clung to each other, unsure what they could even do to help, but bringing comfort to each other.

"Bingo. Her credit card just took a decent hit. Looks like she took one hell of a joy ride. She just paid a taxi tab over two hundred bucks."

The men rushed to look over his shoulder at the screen.

"Does it give the location of the cab?"

"Unfortunately, not. Just the cab company and the taxi

number. Let me see if I can get into their database to track down the right medallion number. If I can t get in, I'll have to phone there and do it the hard way."

Chase said what Jax was thinking. "Once we find her, you'll have to fill us in on how it is you have access to all of these private computer systems."

Miguel looked up, briefly stopping his mad typing to add, "I'm pretty sure you don't want to know. Plausible deniability and all that."

Jax growled, "Maybe we don't want to hire someone with such questionable moral fiber."

Miguel actually chuckled. "Bullshit. I'm exactly the kind of guy you need on your team. I'll always be able to get you info you need under the radar."

"Right now, I'd appreciate you finding out what the hell is going through Emma's head," Jaxson grumbled.

"Sorry, I won't be able to help there, but I hope to at least locate her head. The rest will be up to you two."

Chase's phone rang. He answered it without even looking at the screen. "Emma?!" he shouted.

Jaxson couldn't hear who was on the other end, but he knew from the look on Chase's face it wasn't their girl.

Chase ran his free hand through his shoulder-length hair in frustration. "You're gonna have to deal with it. Send the rest of the candidates home and reschedule them for tomorrow." He held the phone to his ear, but Jax could tell Chase was more interested in watching Miguel work his keyboard.

Jax approached his lover who mouthed the word *Lola* to him, and he held out his hand for the phone.

Chase handed it over, relief in his eyes as Jaxson moved the phone to his ear and caught Lola's bossy ramble continuing on, unaware the listener had changed.

"You need to handle whatever drama you guys have going on with your little girlfriend. I need Jaxson back here immediately.

We have more candidates for club manager still waiting to meet him."

"First, Emma is more than a drama or just our girlfriend. She is our family. And no, I'm not going to leave Chase to deal with this on his own. Reschedule the interviews for tomorrow. Stay there until the construction crew is ready to leave and then lock things up. There should be one security guy who stays behind on duty."

"Jaxson, we have tight…"

"Stop. I know the timelines. This is my decision, not yours. You work for me. Follow orders." He was about to hang up but added, "Oh, and get me a new iPhone. I'll get it in the morning. And alert everyone at the house that if Emma shows up, keep her there and call Chase's phone immediately. You got it?"

"I don't like…"

"Yes or no?" He didn't fucking have time to be nice. Or patient. He needed compliance.

"Yes, *sir*." Lola's response was total sass, but he ended the call. He'd deal with her later.

He was reaching to hand Chase his phone back when he heard it — the quiet click of the front door. From the relieved excitement on his lover's face, Chase had heard it too. The men turned together and rushed towards the front foyer.

Jaxson had known he was upset, but it wasn't until he rounded the corner and caught his first glimpse of Emma standing just inside the door that he realized just how shaken he was by the day's events.

It was so much more than Emma's short disappearance that had him reeling. It was her blatant disobedience. Her keeping secrets. His guilt. It all crushed him until he stood frozen in the entryway, watching as Chase rushed to their love and scooped her into a bear hug so tight Emma squeaked.

Fucking tears pricked his eyes, but he willed them away. He had to be the strong one, although his heart ached with a physical pang as he watched Chase's joy. But when Emma's gaze met his over Chase's shoulder, the pang in his chest exploded.

She looked so lost, it slew him. His feet moved on autopilot, desperate to touch her. Emma was normally the center in the trio's sandwich hugs, but Jaxson hugged Chase from behind, his left hand wrapping around Emma's waist, and the other into her hair, finally linking the threesome together where they belonged. He crashed his lips to hers with an animalistic possession. It was his childish attempt to reassert his dominance, trying valiantly to chase away the feeling that he was losing control.

Only the wetness of Emma's tears pulled him out of the punishing kiss. He felt like an asshole when she had to gasp for air as he released her mouth.

Still, they clung to each other, no one saying a word for a long minute. It was Miguel's voice that broke the silence.

"I'll head out, now."

Jaxson finally released his lovers, stepping away to call out to Miguel who was opening the front door behind Emma. "Hold up, Martinez."

The stocky man turned to look back as Jaxson approached, his hand held out.

"Thanks, man. I don't often turn control over." He paused before adding, "I'm glad you were here today. You're exactly the kind of man of action we're looking for."

He smiled a crooked smile. "No problem. You do know Mr. Cartwright already hired me, right?"

Jaxson glanced back at Chase who had the decency to shrug his shoulders. "He's the guy for the job. And we needed his help."

"Agreed." He wasn't upset Chase had made the right call. Still, something nagged at him as he turned back to his new head of security. "Leave your info with Lola. Pick your team, but I have final approval on all staffing decisions. We'll work out the rest of the details tomorrow."

"Yes, sir, Mr. Davidson." The handsome Hispanic man smiled.

"It's Jaxson."

Just before Miguel turned to leave, he nodded towards Emma and Chase. "Glad we located Miss Fischer."

Jaxson nodded, closing the front door after their newest employee left and locking it. His hand gripped the doorknob as he took several calming breaths before turning back around. For the first time in years, he felt unsure of himself... as if he were barely holding himself together, like a steady wind would make him crumble. He leaned forward, resting his forehead against the cool wood of the front door as his mind raced to make sense of the afternoon's events, letting the relief Emma was safe calm him.

Emma's quiet "I'm sorry" was ridiculously inadequate for the hell she'd put the men through. As mad as he was at himself for letting things get so out of control, at that moment, all he could think about was her role in the day's shitshow.

Jaxson spun around so fast Emma flinched, burying her face against Chase's shoulder.

"You need to cool down," Chase cautioned, hugging their girl protectively.

"Whose side are you on? Ten minutes ago you were just as frantic as I was!"

"Since when do we take sides?" Chase snapped.

Fuck. He was right.

Jaxson ran his hand through his hair nervously. "That's not what I meant and you know it."

"The only thing I know is she's shaking like a leaf. We need to go in, sit down, and talk." Chase hugged Emma harder, speaking softly against her ear. "We were just worried, baby. Let's go snuggle and you can tell us what's going on."

When Emma didn't start moving towards the living room, Chase bent down and scooped her into his arms. Jaxson watched as Emma wrapped her arms around his neck, burying her face against Chase's shoulder intimately, clearly feeling safe with the switch of their trio.

Watching his lovers comfort each other, for the first time in their almost three-year relationship a hint of jealousy threatened to poison Jaxson's already precarious thoughts. He pushed it down, knowing intellectually it was ridiculous, but recognizing it as just another sign of how out of whack things had gotten in their complicated relationship.

Still, as he followed behind them irrational anger bubbled through his veins, infecting him as surely as a virus. Months of crushing stress mingled with the day's events resulting in an almost out-of-body crescendo of emotion he had no idea how to contain — let alone shut down. A quiet voice in his head begged him to storm out and not come back until he was back in control, but the louder fury won the day.

"As much fun as it is to watch you two snuggling, we have a few more important things we need to be doing right now."

Neither Chase nor Emma answered him. Both staring at him with a healthy dose of fear in their eyes, making him feel like a line had been magically drawn between them. Him on one side, them — together — on the other.

He fucking hated it.

Fine. He was the Dom. It was his job to be the bad guy when the occasion called for it. "Emma, come here."

Her teary eyes widened. She glanced at Chase, deferring to him for advice. He hesitated, but finally nodded. "Go ahead, baby," he whispered as he helped her to her feet.

Emma approached him slowly, stopping just out of his reach. She was taking shallow breaths, unable to look at her Dom.

"Eyes," he ordered. It was an order he'd given her hundreds of times before in the throes of passion or in a D/s scene, yet today it felt different. It *was* different. Their unshakeable bond had a crack in it, and by God, he was going to figure out why and glue it back together. "Were my instructions earlier today unclear when I asked you to stay at Khloe and Ryder's until we picked you up?"

"No, Sir," she whispered, looking away nervously before remembering he'd ordered eyes and snapping back to his gaze.

"Why did you leave then?"

She opened and closed her mouth several times, but no words came out.

"Emma, I'm waiting for your answer."

"I… don't… know."

"Fine. Let's try an easier question. Where have you been all afternoon?"

She hesitated, but eventually answered. "I went to the beach. I wanted to be near the water." Finally, a truthful answer from her.

"And the private beach at Khloe's wasn't good enough?"

"I… needed to…" She paused so long he didn't think she'd finish her sentence. Finally she added a soft, "think."

"Think about what?"

Silence.

"Why did you turn off your phone?"

"I didn't. It died. That's why I took a cab instead of an Uber. I couldn't use my app to call a car when I wanted to come home. I had to flag a taxi."

"Christ, do you know how many terrible things could have happened to you out there? With no phone? We've been fucking frantic."

"I didn't mean to worry you. How did you…" she stopped mid-sentence, silenced by his scowl.

"How did we know you'd left? Oh, that was one of the highlights of my day. I loved getting a call from Helms telling me to get my head out of my ass. Talking about needing to get some fucking secret out of you. I wanted to argue with him that we don't keep secrets from each other, but it was a little hard to make the case for that when I had no fucking clue where you were when he called!"

"Ryder called?" she squeaked.

Why was she suddenly even more afraid than she had been seconds before?

His instincts demanded the next question. "What are you keeping from us, Emma?"

Her eyes widened, but she stood silently.

"What's wrong?" Jaxson pressed again.

"Nothing," she finally answered, this time a bit stronger.

Chase stood, approaching as he tried to reason with her. "Talk to us, baby. It's clear you're holding something in. We can't fix it if we don't know what it is."

"This isn't something you can fix."

"So, there *is* something wrong," Jaxson reasoned, his anger growing again. "You just lied to my face on top of everything else." Patience wasn't something he had a lot of even on a good day, and today was definitely *not* a good day. "Maybe you won't tell us what's bothering you, but I sure as hell can tell you what's bothering me." He stopped long enough to widen his stance, crossing his arms over his chest aggressively before continuing. "I have a submissive who is refusing to trust her Dom with a secret she apparently had no problems sharing with Khloe and Ryder. That same submissive expressly ignored my instructions, putting herself in danger in the process, and scaring Chase and me half to death. Particularly when we couldn't reach said sub on the phone she is never to leave home without. We had to cancel the rest of the interviews! People who had taken time out of their day to meet with us for a job were sent away, and we lost a valuable afternoon when you know damn well time is short."

"Oh, believe me, I can't forget how valuable your time is. Lola reminds me of it every five minutes."

Jax wasn't sure who was more surprised by Emma's sassy outburst — him or her. She never spoke to him with that tone of voice. *Ever.*

She had his attention.

"Is that what this is about? Lola?" When she didn't answer, he tacked on. "For crying out loud. You can't possibly be jealous of Lola!"

"I'm not jealous." He almost called her a liar, until she added, "I'm angry."

"Angry? Why the hell would you be angry I hired someone to help us?"

"Because you let her treat Chase and me like shit. You've never let anyone else do that. I've heard you put so many people, including Spencer, in their place if they try to do that. Why not Lola?"

Jaxson had to push down his natural inclination to demand she use a respectful tone of voice with him as her Dom. He didn't want to do anything to stop her from talking now that she'd finally started to share, even if he hated what she was saying. "Lola is good at what she does."

"Bullshit. She's a bitch." Emma crossed her arms across her own chest, mimicking his defensive stance.

As much as he hated her insubordination, he'd take the spark of anger in her eyes over the fear he'd detected minutes before any day.

Chase, the peacekeeper of their family jumped off the couch, placing himself between the two of them as if he might need to referee. "Everyone stay calm." He turned towards Jaxson to add, "But Emma is right. Lola is a bitch and she needs to go."

"Oh, for crying out loud. Are you two so insecure that you can't deal with her for just a few more weeks until we get the clubs open?"

Emma harrumphed. "Are you so blind you can't see what she's doing? Between her and the damn designer always hitting on Chase and, hell, even the news anchor chick this morning pawing him on live television. Forgive me if I'm a little tired of feeling like a spectator in your lives." She'd rounded on Chase halfway through her rant.

"I handled Brandi," he defended.

"Oh really. If the situation had been reversed, the guy who did that shit to me would be in the hospital right now."

Jaxson growled, "Damn straight. So this is the big secret? You're jealous?"

A strange cocktail of emotions flitted across Emma's gorgeous violet eyes.

"Yep," was her snappy reply.

He knew in his gut they were barely scratching the surface of what was bothering her, so her quick lie as she looked into his face was the final straw.

"So, if I fire Lola tomorrow, everything will go back to normal around here?"

He saw her breath hitch. She swallowed hard. Her tears were back, and still she lied again. "Yep."

"Enough! Don't insult me. I know damn well you're hiding something. Tell us. Now." He felt like an asshole, but his patience was gone.

He noticed her head shake ever so slightly. She had dug in. Well, he could dig in too.

"Fine. You won't talk, then we'll move into action instead. Strip. Lay over the back of the loveseat with your ass in the air. You'll take your punishment now for disobeying and putting yourself in danger. Maybe you'll want to talk after I light your ass on fire."

Chase turned towards him. "I thought we agreed, you can't spank her into happiness."

"That's not my intent. I'm going to punish her into compliance. We have rules. She agreed to the rules and she broke them. Period."

"Jaxson..." His name was a plea from Chase.

"Am I still the Dom of this family?" he shouted, angry his decision was being challenged yet again.

"Of course, but..."

"Help her get into position. Then kneel on the couch facing

her and hold her hands tight. She's going to want to reach back before I'm done," he warned.

Emma hadn't moved. She stood frozen, looking between the two men as they uncharacteristically disagreed with each other. Only when Chase turned and walked slowly towards her did Emma's tears spill over.

An eerie silence filled the room broken only by tiny sniffles from Emma as her nose ran and the rustle of her sundress and bathing suit being discarded to the floor.

As always, the sight of her curvy body he loved so damn much sparked the start of an erection. He willed it away. Despite the fact they hadn't made love for several days due to sheer exhaustion at the end of each day, now was not the time for sex. Maybe after he'd disciplined her, then he could rectify their dry spell by fucking her hard from behind. He'd order Chase to fill her mouth with that thick shaft of his. Maybe then, everything could get back to normal.

He was a prick for feeling excited seeing her laid out before him. Her pink pussy peeking out from between her legs. He needed more. "Legs wider. Let me see all of you."

The loveseat back was low enough that with her legs wide, she was at the perfect height to raise her rounded ass high in the air.

"Please, Jax. Don't do this." This time it was Emma asking him to stop. "This isn't going to help."

"Maybe it won't help you, but it sure as hell will help me." He reached to unbuckle his belt, pulling the two-inch thick leather free so fast the end snapped in the air with a crack. Emma flinched.

He moved into position and before he could second-guess his decision, pulled his arm back and delivered a full-power strike across Emma's ass. Her gurgled cry told him he was getting his point across. Before his eyes, white skin turned to pink and finally red across the swath of punished skin.

The second lash was a bit lower, overlapping with the first

enough to make her want to stand had Chase not been holding her hands. He was used to tears during a punishment scene, but her choked sob tore at his heart. But he pushed through his reticence, desperate to regain control.

The third strapping brought a howl of pain like he'd never heard from Emma before. She was his experienced submissive. She'd been on the receiving end of harsher discipline sessions than the current one so her reaction was alarming. Chase felt it too because he looked up, tears streaming down his face as he silently begged Jaxson to stop.

All hell broke loose when the fourth strike connected with Emma's ass. It was as if it finally broke the dam Emma had constructed between them.

"Puppies!" she shouted.

Christ. In almost three years, she'd never once used her safeword. He froze, unsure how to proceed. He stood stock-still, watching as things moved in slow motion around him. Chase moved around the couch to help her stand, yet she collapsed into his arms like a wet noodle. He saw his lovers' mouths moving, but the ringing in his ears was so loud he couldn't hear what was said.

Chase shouting got his attention. "Get a bottle of water from the fridge." Chase was the one giving the orders, now.

Jaxson moved to do as he was told, listening to Chase trying to comfort Emma as she hiccupped.

She'd safeworded. It was a blow to his ego. He had never felt so distanced from his lovers. He had always prided himself on being the kind of Dom that was in tune with his submissives. That he had no clue why she'd stopped him drove home just how much trouble their family was in. For the first time, he contemplated the possibility Chase was right. Maybe Emma was so unhappy she was planning on leaving them.

The scene that greeted him when he returned with the water only made him feel worse. Emma was sobbing. Chase was hugging her close, his own tears streaking down his face, and Jaxson felt impotent to fix it.

He held out the water to Chase, unsure if Emma even wanted him near her. Stepping back, he gave them space, jealous Chase could comfort her where he clearly frightened her.

As if he could read his thoughts, Chase looked over Emma's head to lock his gaze with his Dom. Jax almost wept with relief when Chase silently mouthed *I love you* to him before reaching out his hand in a silent invitation.

He was a man used to being in control--the one everyone depended on. But he was bone tired and feeling lost. He let Chase's calming nature pull him back from the edge.

Jax fell to his knees, crawling the few feet between him and the couch holding the two most important people in his life, relieved when they both wrapped arms around him, pulling him into their tangled embrace.

The trio didn't speak, didn't even move. They simply clung to each other until he could feel the chinks that had wedged between them slowly being filled with love. He didn't have a clue how long they stayed intimately linked before he finally worked up the courage to voice his fears.

Pulling back so he could see her eyes, Jaxson broke their silence. "I know you haven't been happy lately. Please, don't tell me you want to leave us."

He was relieved to see a tiny smile play on her lips as she answered. "No, you aren't going to get rid of me that easy."

Chase got in on the action. "So what is it? And don't tell me this is all about Lola."

"It's not all about her, no. It's..." she paused.

"Then what?" Jaxson cut in, impatient to get to the bottom of what had her upset. "Are you sick?" He prayed silently that she didn't have some deadly disease.

"Not exactly."

"Then..."

Emma cut him off with two unbelievable words. "I'm pregnant."

His breath caught. *Did he hear that right?*

"You're…"

Chase finished his started question with an excited "…pregnant? As in having a baby?"

Jaxson's brain was overloading—misfiring.

"But how…?" She was on birth control. They hadn't even discussed her going off.

Chase wasn't bothered by the details of how the miracle had happened. He was grinning through his tears as he pressed Emma with questions. "And you took a pregnancy test over at Khloe's? Is that why she knew before we did?" Chase didn't even stop to wait for her answer, adding on, "This totally makes sense now why she wouldn't tell me your secret when I talked to her."

The thought of being a parent terrified Jaxson. He'd had the worst example of how to do it in his own father. It was easier to focus on the logistical details of how it had happened rather than how this little bombshell had just changed their lives forever.

Chase was oblivious to the growing distress in Emma's violet eyes. Jaxson pressed forward on instinct. "You didn't take a pregnancy test today, did you, baby?"

She hesitated, but her tears had stopped. In fact, Emma looked better… stronger… more like herself than she had in weeks. He had a premonition he was going to hate what came out of her mouth next.

"No, Sir."

Chase was still too exuberant to realize Jaxson and Emma's visual connection was telling a silent story.

"How long have you known?" he pressed, and Chase finally stopped to pin Emma with an expectant look.

"A while…"

"How long?" Jax asked forcefully.

Emma raised her chin, locking their gazes defiantly just before she destroyed him with two little words. "Valentine's Day."

He flinched as if she'd slapped him. Eight weeks. She'd kept the holy grail of secrets from her men for almost two fucking months. His mind raced, finding it impossible to grapple with all the implications of Emma's explosive news. Memories from the last two months flashed through his brain, all of them now tainted with the knowledge Emma had been lying to them the entire time.

The room was suddenly too hot. He felt sick to his stomach. He needed air. He needed time to think.

Jax pushed to his feet and rushed to the kitchen island to retrieve the keys he'd thrown down when they'd arrived. He didn't dare open his mouth to even tell them where he was going for fear he'd puke on the kitchen tile.

It didn't matter anyway. He didn't have the first fucking clue where he was going to go. He just knew he couldn't stay there.

CHAPTER SIX ~ EMMA

*E*mma pushed down the anger she felt at herself. She had totally botched what was arguably supposed to be one of the biggest and best days of her life. She hadn't expected the guys to be home before her, so she hadn't been prepared to be confronted.

Since she was a little girl playing with her baby dolls, she'd always known she wanted to be a mother. True, she'd put the idea to the back of her mind since beginning her relationship with the men she loved more than life itself. It had been too complicated to contemplate adding a baby to their mix.

But if she were honest with herself, holding Sam and Jonah's little peanut, Natasha, had changed things for her. Seeing Jaxson and Chase holding the infant had opened her eyes to the possibility of them being fathers and it had been hard to put it out of her mind since. Intellectually she knew her memories of holding Natasha had nothing to do with her getting pregnant just weeks later, but she worried she had sub-consciously set things in motion for it to happen anyway.

Now, fear gripped her. Jaxson had left. What if he couldn't forgive her? What if he was so against being a father he'd walk away, particularly if they found out the baby was actually Chase's. Considering their almost daily sex romps, it was a fifty-fifty chance either of the men was the biological father.

Lost in her own worry, she almost forgot Chase was still there. More guilt.

She was still in his arms, sitting on his lap, but where he'd been comforting her before, he had gone stiff. As she looked at him, she found him staring off into the distance, his jaw rigid.

She reached out to stroke his scruffy cheek to get his attention. When he turned back towards her, she wished he hadn't. Jovial Chase rarely got angry, but it happened. She'd just never seen his anger directed at her before. She hated it.

"I'm so sorry."

"Why? What the hell made you wait so long to tell us?" Desperation permeated his voice.

"I never meant to hurt you. I just needed to get used to the idea of being pregnant before I shared it."

"Eight weeks? It took you eight fucking weeks? Christ, the whole night of the Roulette event, while you were on the stage with me, you knew? Way back then?"

"I'd just found out. I was freaking out. It was why I was in the bathroom so long before we went down."

"You should have told us."

"We were already running late. And I needed to get my head on straight first."

"Fine. After the event. The next day. Hell, the next fucking week. Any time would have been preferable. I deserved to know I'm going to be a father."

"We bought the club within a few days after that. The schedule has been insane ever since. I've tried. I really have, but it just never seemed to be the right time. And then I panicked. I mean, I don't know for sure if you or Jaxson are going to be a father."

Anger changed to fury in Chase's beautiful eyes. "Are you fucking kidding me? It doesn't matter whose sperm won the goddamn race, Emma! Both Jax and I will love the baby like a father, no matter whose DNA she has."

She didn't know what to say, so she uttered nothing.

Chase didn't suffer from the same affliction. "You shouldn't have kept it a secret."

"Yeah, well, it isn't my only secret."

She saw a spark of fear in his eyes before she quickly added, "I hate California. I just want to go home to D.C. Everyone here seems so fake here, so judgmental. They're all model thin with their perfect beach bodies. It's only going to get worse, too, as I keep gaining weight."

"Don't you dare let Jaxson hear you saying that. You're already in so much trouble without adding putting your body down into the mix."

"I'm not putting myself down. I'm stating facts." She was relieved to see a Chase smile light up his face again.

"Are you kidding me? You are going to be the most gorgeous pregnant woman ever." He finally touched her again, placing his palm over her tummy. When he looked back up at her, she saw tears in his eyes. "You really have a baby in there?"

"Believe me," she chuckled, "it's taken me some time to get used to the idea, but yes. I talk to him or her all the time, telling them about their daddies."

"Do you know yet if it's going to be a boy or a girl?"

"Oh goodness, no. I haven't been back to the doctor since I found out I was pregnant. It's another reason why I knew it was getting time to tell you guys. I should probably be making another appointment soon. It's just…"

"What?"

"I want to go to my doctor in D.C. I want to go home. I want things back to the way they were, just the three of us." She dared to say it. "I wish we'd never bought the new clubs."

"It will get better once we get everyone hired and open." He tried to comfort her.

"Are you sure about that? Jaxson is so angry all the time. He's different. I miss him." She looked back into his eyes. "I've missed you too."

"Emma, I've been here the whole time. I don't know what you're talking about."

"Bullshit. I may see you and Jax every day, but nothing has been the same since we moved out here seven weeks ago. You are both distracted. You go off to work every day and don't take me with you. Even when I go, I have to watch Ted hitting on you and Lola hitting on Jax. It's not that I'm jealous. I know nothing will happen. It's just…"

"What, baby?"

"I'm tired of being an after thought. We promised to always put each other first and when I needed you more than ever you guys left me on my own."

Chase winced at her harsh words. "You're right, and I'm so sorry. We both knew you weren't happy, but I think we both took you for granted, assuming we could make you happy again once we got the clubs open."

"Now I've fucked it up bad. What if Jaxson can't forgive me? Can we call him and check on him?"

Chase frowned. "His phone is broken."

"Broken? It was working this morning. It's almost brand new. What's wrong with it?"

"iPhones don't do well when they're thrown against walls."

"Oh shit. So that's my fault, too."

"Baby, none of this is your fault. I let you down. You should have been able to come to me to talk about all of this weeks ago. I hate you didn't feel like you could."

"I wish I had. Maybe then Jaxson wouldn't have deserted us."

"He'll be back as soon as he calms down. He doesn't do well when he feels out of control and today was a red-banner day of losing control for him."

Emma's stomach gurgled so loud Chase grinned. He placed his

hand back over her tummy before he added, "It's getting late. You need to eat some dinner. You're eating for two now." She was happy to see his smile, thankful it was impossible for cheery Chase to stay angry for long.

Emma was hungry, having thrown up the light lunch she'd had at Khloe's. She'd managed to keep a small ice cream cone down while at the beach that afternoon, but she knew her baby needed more to eat.

Chase pinned her with a knowing look. "It's all making sense now. Why you haven't been feeling the best. Why you've turned into a picky eater all of a sudden."

"Yeah. Well, the smell of some things sets me off, and I can't seem to keep anything too greasy down. And holy hell, do my boobs hurt."

"I'm so sorry we didn't notice all of these changes. I just thought you were taking longer to adjust to being on the West Coast. I'm such an idiot."

Chase spent the next hour pampering Emma—making her a healthy dinner from scratch, making sure she ate every bite, even when she complained she wasn't hungry. It was a preview of the months to come when he would be watching her every move. She'd spent just a couple of miserable months without his attentiveness and she would never resent it again.

It wasn't until after they'd showered together and got into comfy loungewear for a quiet night at home the bare reality of Jaxson's absence became unbearable for the couple. For Emma, any relief of finally having her secret out into the open was overshadowed by her Dom's reaction and subsequent desertion.

As if he could read her mind, Chase hugged her closer. "He'll be home as soon as he's feeling back under control."

"What if that never happens? Having a baby is going to change everything."

"He loves us way too much to let that happen. He'll be back."

"But when? I hate that we can't at least text him."

Chase leaned down close to talk to her flat tummy. "Your mommy worries too much, peanut. Your daddy Jax will be home soon." He laid his palm against her tummy, expression revealing his awe of the miracle inside. "Now, you look tired. Let's get you to bed."

"No way. I'm not going until Jaxson gets home."

"Emma…"

"Please, I need to wait up so I can see him as soon as he gets back."

"Fine," Chase shook his head in defeat, "you can lay out here on the couch with me, but you still need to get in a nap. You'll be able to hear him as soon as he gets home."

Despite being exhausted, it took what seemed like forever for her to nod off. Each time she would get close to sleep, her brain would replay how angry Jaxson had been when he'd stormed out of the rental house. When she finally did get to sleep, she was plagued with nightmares where Jaxson kept screaming at her.

Eventually the dreams jarred her awake. The room was dark with only one light over the kitchen island casting eerie shadows through the space. Emma was snuggled up next to Chase on the couch, where he'd finally succumbed to sleep as well. She picked up his cell phone that was lying on his chest, to see it was after two in the morning.

Renewed panic squeezed at her heart when she realized Jaxson had been gone over eight hours now. What if he never came back?

"I'm here, baby." His low voice from the chair opposite the couch scared the bejesus out of her.

Emma squinted, trying to get a glimpse of the man she loved with all her heart. All she could make out was the outline of his strong profile.

"Thank God, you came home. I was… we were so worried."

"This isn't home." He sounded angry. She wished she could see his face.

"It is for now. Where did you go?"

70

"Nowhere... everywhere." He wasn't making sense.

She wished she could get up to go to him without waking Chase. Then she decided maybe it was for the best that she couldn't see the disappointment in Jax's gorgeous eyes she loved so much.

"I really am so sorry. I didn't set out to..."

"Stop. Don't ever apologize again."

"But..."

"Emma... never again. At least not for this."

"Okay." She'd agree to anything if it would bring her Jaxson back to them. She was so relieved he had come back, yet the wedge that had been driven between them by her secret lie seemed more like a cavern now. She hated the tears that came, making the shadow of a man swim before her eyes. She loved the idea of having a baby growing inside her, but she sure as hell hated what the influx of hormones was doing to her mental state. Always on the verge of tears at the drop of a hat. She hated weepy women, and now she'd become one.

The tears came harder when she saw Jaxson push to his feet and stalk past his lovers without a hug or a kiss or even a touch. She heard his dress shoes against the hardwood floor in the hallway before he disappeared into their bedroom.

Emma slowly worked to extricate herself from Chase's embrace without waking him. As soon as she was on her feet, she chased after Jaxson, arriving in their room in time to see him packing a suitcase lying open on their bed.

Her heart broke into tiny pieces at the realization he was leaving — packing his bag for God-only-knew-where.

She had to fix this.

Emma ran to him, pulling at his arm to stop him from placing the pile of clothes from a drawer into the open suitcase.

"Please, don't leave me. I know you're angry and hurt. I made a mistake. I got scared. But I need you so much."

He yanked his arm free and placed the pile of clothes in the bag before turning towards her, grabbing her biceps with his hands and squeezing hard enough that it hurt. "I just told you not to apologize ever again."

"But… you can't leave. I won't let you." She sounded stronger than she felt.

"Baby, you can't stop me." He paused before adding. "Go wake up Chase."

Oh, God. He was going to talk Chase into leaving with him. The pounding in her ears grew louder until she felt faint. This was worse than him yelling at her in her dreams. She would die if they left her now.

She only stopped from toppling over because he moved his hands to her face, holding her so tight she couldn't look away if she wanted to.

It was cruel he could think of leaving because her skin vibrated where he touched her. Their sexual electricity was alive and well, yet he was prepared to walk away from her. God, away from his child.

"Emma. Stop. I'm not leaving."

"You aren't?"

"No, *we're* leaving. Not me. Not Chase and me. All of us."

She tried to internalize his words. Tried to calm her heart rate. He finally added, "Look at the suitcase, baby. Whose clothes are in it?"

She let her gaze move to the left where she could see the open bag. The entire contents of her underwear drawer was visible. She closed her eyes, taking a second to let the news sink in. He wasn't leaving them.

When she opened her eyes, his green pools looked like they were going to devour her.

"But it's the middle of the night. Where are we going?"

"It's a surprise. Now go. Wake up Chase."

"I'm already awake." Chase's voice comforted her further, but it wasn't until he hugged her from behind, turning her into the middle of their infamous sandwich that she truly started to calm. They clung to each other as they would a life preserver if lost in the huge ocean. She'd been drowning in guilt and fear for weeks so she welcomed their lifeline.

Chase broke the silence. "So where are we going at this hour?"

Jaxson pulled out of their embrace just enough to gaze down on Emma again. "Emma's not happy here. We're going to move to a hotel until the new house is ready. I'm taking us somewhere we can be happy again."

His reasoning was sound, but there was only one problem. And since she'd gotten into the current mess by holding in too much, she wasn't ready to repeat her mistake. Emma took a deep breath and professed what was in her heart.

"You're right, I haven't been happy here, but it isn't just because of the house. A simple change of location won't magically fix what's gone wrong these last months."

Jaxson sucked in a sharp breath. "Maybe not, but it's a start."

Chase was nuzzling her neck as he added his two cents. "It's too late to go anywhere tonight. I have a better idea about how to make each other happy." He moved his hands from her hips—his left moving up to squeeze her tender breast and she felt his right hand groping Jaxson's erection pressed against her tummy.

Emma was relieved when Jaxson took the bait with a chuckle. It had been days since they'd made love or even played at a D/s scene. That was like a lifetime for the sexual trio. Tonight, more than ever, she needed her men inside her, marking her as their own.

Her silk nighty was the first piece of clothing to go as Chase pulled it over her head in a quick sweeping move, leaving her in her panties. As soon as her breasts were uncovered, Chase had palmed each of them, squeezing hard enough to draw a pained groan from her.

"Our girl told me her titties are extra sore these days, Jax. I can't wait to have a bit of fun playing with these curves."

Jaxson had stepped back to watch Chase grope Emma. It hurt so good as Chase pulled and pinched at the tips that were protruding obscenely. Enjoying the view, Jaxson slowly started unbuttoning his designer dress shirt, pulling the tails from the waistband of his perfectly tight jeans before sending it to the floor.

His chest was defined... hard... sexy as hell as he moved to the buttons on his jeans, leisurely pushing them down over his boxer briefs until he could kick them off, leaving him in his own underwear exactly like Emma. She let her gaze drop to watch his magnificent cock as it sprang free of the confining fabric.

Sometimes, like tonight, his perfection took her breath away. She still didn't understand how she'd gotten so lucky to find not one, but two, gorgeous men to love her. What she had learned in the years since they'd met on that train from the south of France to Paris was the men were so much more than just good looks — more than money or fame.

No, what she loved the most about them were the private secrets only they knew about each other... the inside jokes and intimate vulnerabilities. Those were the glue that ultimately held them together. It would be those intimacies that had the power to repair the damage of the last few weeks, relegating this time to just a bad memory.

Jaxson's hands replaced Chase's on her body as he ordered their lover to lose his clothes too. She had a front row seat to the look of awe in her Dom's eyes as he fell to his knees before her. He reached out to cup her ass cheeks, still a bit tingly from his earlier belt lashes. At first she didn't understand what he was doing. It wasn't until he leaned forward, gently placing tiny kisses across her lower belly that the lump filled her throat.

Like Chase had hours before, Jaxson reverently paid homage to the tiny life growing inside her. When he looked up from his perch below, the tears in her strong Dom's eyes humbled her. "Are you feeling okay, baby? Are you feeling up to making love? I wouldn't want to hurt you, or the baby."

She ran her fingers through his hair, trying to reassure him. "We're both fine. We can't possibly hurt the baby having sex."

"Are you sure? I mean,...." He hesitated. "Oh, who the fuck am I kidding? There's no damn way we'd make it nine months without having sex."

Emma chuckled, relieved to see the smile playing on his lips.

Chase hugged her from behind. She could feel his naked erection already at full-mast, pressing against her. Jaxson released her ass to stroke Chase's hard shaft as his lips latched onto her left tit and he sucked hard. It hurt oh-so-good as she hugged her Dom to her breast. She could feel the wetness of Chase's precum as it smeared across her lower back while Jaxson continued to jack off their lover.

Chase's gasps for air as he groaned his pleasure stopped just as Jaxson's warm mouth left her body.

Their Dom was back in control as he barked his next order. "Grab the lube, Chase. We need to get our girl ready for us. Help her lose the panties."

She loved it when they called her their girl, and tonight, after the emotional day they'd all had, she needed it more than ever.

Jaxson grabbed her hand, pulling her along with him as he moved to the bed. He took a second to throw the forgotten suitcase on the floor before sitting down at the end of the bed. He tugged, pulling her to her knees before him as he slowly stroked the long cock she loved so much. He opened his legs wide, the only invitation she needed to lunge forward and take the tip of his shaft into her mouth.

By now, they all had every centimeter of each other's bodies memorized. There was nothing they hadn't seen, sucked, stroked, or fucked over the years, so Emma knew exactly where to lick the underside of his cock to trigger his guttural groan as she tasted the first drops of his precum on her tongue.

As was their rule for her, unless otherwise instructed, her arms were behind her back, hands clasped. She controlled the speed and depth of the blowjob with only her mouth until, like always, Jaxson eventually laced his fingers through her hair, using it as a handle to control the scene.

God, she'd missed this. His domination allowed her to turn herself over, to surrender to his power — his will. She adored him, especially when he jammed her face down until she held every inch of him in her gurgling throat as a few course pubic hairs tickled her nose.

She was getting light headed by the time she felt her panties pulled down and Chase's slippery fingers slathering lube at the entrance of her backside. It acted like a love potion, ramping up her own sexual need tenfold as her body recognized it was about to be pleasured.

Once Chase had prepared her, Jaxson pulled her from his cock as he gave his next order. "Hop on my lap, baby. It's time for you to go for a ride."

He helped pull her to her feet before yanking her to straddle his body, placing her knees on the bed near his hips. Always protective of her, he first ran his fingers through her spread lower lips to make sure she was ready for him, and found her dripping with need. Jax replaced his fingers, lining up his shaft and just as she was about to impale herself demanded, "Eyes."

She was a few inches taller than him in their present position, looking down into his deep green eyes, getting lost in the love she saw shining back at her. She waited for his order, but she didn't have to wait long for his, "Now!"

He filled her in one quick motion as he raised his hips and she lowered her body weight, crashing onto his lap, impaling herself so deep she felt the tip of his long cock crashing against her cervix. It was impossible to know where pain ended and pleasure began as their bodies slapped together hard and fast. He pistoned hard and fast until she was close to tipping into an orgasm.

76

And then it all stopped. She groaned her displeasure at the intermission as Jaxson held her against him as he lay back on the bed with her lying against his chest. The skin on skin heat felt wonderful. The angle of his possession had changed, touching new places deep inside her. There they lay, waiting for the third member of their family to line up his cock at her puckered ass and start to push in.

Emma's body craved their double penetration like an addict needed their next hit. It had been too long. As much as she adored Chase for proceeding cautiously, she wanted more. Her body hungered to be taken... controlled. Impatient, she started rocking in an attempt to take more of Chase in. What she got instead was a slap to her bare ass.

"You're not in charge, baby. Take what I give you," Chase warned.

She didn't appreciate the vibration of Jaxson's chest she was using as a pillow, as he chuckled at her frustration.

"Yes, Sir." Emma closed her eyes, focusing on the sensations as four hands roamed over her body, massaging and relaxing. Inch by inch, they filled her until Chase's body dropped over her, linking the three of them together.

The stretch hurt just right. Over her head the men must have silently communicated because they moved into motion, their bodies perfectly synchronized to bring Emma the ultimate pleasure. She cried out as their hard shafts plunged in and out of her in their dirty dance for three.

Chase reached around to find her swollen clit with his talented fingers, strumming her to her first of many orgasms for the night. She lay caught as the men she loved played her body perfectly, chasing their own explosion.

Their strokes grew erratic as they neared their peak. They'd built the fire back up inside her until she too was on the edge with them. She could feel Jaxson's heart pounding under where she laid her head, the sweat from their exertion making her slip around on his chest from the strong force of Chase's thrusts.

Emma cried out as unknown fingers pinched her nipples just as she felt both men releasing their loads deep into her body. Her core contracted, pulling them deeper until they all collapsed into a limp heap, crushing Jaxson at the bottom of their tangled pile.

The only sound left was their heavy breathing as each recovered.

"As much as I love having you guys close, you're squashing me," Jaxson finally complained under her.

Exhausted, Emma answered truthfully. "I don't want to move. Can't we sleep like this?"

Chase lifted off her, taking his softening shaft with him and leaving her feeling bereft. Jaxson's soft caresses as he hugged her close coaxed her closer to sleep. She lay languid and let the men pamper her, cleaning her with a warm washcloth and lifting her in their arms to carry her to the head of the bed where all three crawled under the covers, weaving body parts together until they were comfortably linked.

Emma was almost asleep when she heard Jaxson's voice quietly adding, "Sleep well, little peanut. Your mama needs her rest." She was sure it was his palm resting on her tummy where their baby grew.

CHAPTER SEVEN ~ CHASE

The smell of bacon roused Chase from a deep sleep. He didn't have a clue what time it was, but whenever it was, it was too damn early.

The trio had been up most of the night, dozing between sex romps, finally sleeping as the sun was coming up.

He hadn't cracked his eyes open yet but he knew it was Jax playing chef for the day because Emma was snuggled up to him, using his chest as her pillow. That suited him just fine, in spite of the fact that it was hot as hell in the bedroom.

His quiet morning exploded when Emma shot upright, crawling over his body, kneeing his family jewels as she rushed out of bed and towards the bathroom.

She'd tried to close the door, but in her rush, it was left ajar. It wasn't until he heard her puking that he rushed into motion behind her. He found her kneeling in front of the toilet, bent over as she tried to keep her hair out of the line of fire.

Chase hurried over to her, taking over hair holding duty as his other hand rubbed her back lightly, trying to comfort her. "Poor baby. I can't believe you've been dealing with all of this on your own. I should have been here holding your hair every fucking day."

When it seemed that she was feeling better, Chase stood to wet a cloth with warm water, bringing it back to wipe her face.

"You still look a bit green around the gills, baby."

"Yeah, well, I feel a bit green. Certain smells kill me. I'm gonna have to give you guys a list of scents that set me off. Fried or greasy food is at the top of the list."

"Wait. No bacon?" Chase teased. "That's not fair. Next thing, you'll tell us we can't go to KFC anymore."

Emma chuckled at his attempt at a joke. "Since we've never eaten at a KFC since I've known you, I think you'll survive."

Chase got serious. "Tell me the truth. How often do you get sick, Em?"

She flushed before letting him help her to her feet. "It depends. Some days I feel fine. Others, every little thing makes me nauseous."

She made it to the sink and started to brush her teeth as he took a whiz. They were just finishing up when Jaxson called from the bedroom, "Brunch is ready. Come eat."

"I'm not hungry," she complained as she wiped her mouth.

"Too bad. I'm sure the baby is." His pulse went up just thinking about the fact she had a child growing inside her body.

"You do realize the baby is about the size of a lemon right now, right?"

He placed his palm over her soft tummy. "It's a fucking miracle, isn't it?"

"Well considering how often we have sex," Emma grinned, "not really."

"Alright you two, time to come eat while it's hot," Jax called.

Chase turned to see their Dom had joined them. He was relieved to see a hint of a smile on Jaxson's unshaven face as he looked at Emma. He hadn't been sure what kind of mood their lover would be in today after his disappearing act the day before.

"Emma's tummy is especially empty. She just puked," Chase reported.

"Snitch," Emma complained under her breath.

Jaxson's smile was gone. "Wait, you're sick?" He rushed to where she was brushing her tangled hair into submission.

"Sick, no. Morning sickness, yes. I feel a bit better now that I've thrown up."

Jaxson looked worried. "Let's get you out to the kitchen and get some food in you. We have a lot to talk about."

Emma caught Chase's attention behind Jaxson's departing back. He prodded her, "What's wrong?"

She looked pale as she answered. "I'm not sure I'm ready to talk about everything yet."

He grabbed her hand to pull her along with him. "Everything is gonna be fine," he said, hoping he sounded more convincing than he felt, for Emma's sake.

Jax had clearly been up for some time. The island was full of food dishes to choose from. It also looked like he'd gotten every single pot and pan dirty in the process of preparation.

Chase released Emma's hand to hug Jax from behind. "You've been busy."

"Yeah, well, I couldn't sleep."

"Poor baby. I had no problems sleeping as soon as you two sex fiends stopped trying to ravage my body," Chase teased, reaching to pop a slice of bacon in his mouth.

"Holy shit! It's after noon already?" Emma asked in disbelief as she caught sight of the time.

Chase wasn't surprised. Emma had laid some heavy news on the men the day before. The kind of information they needed quality time to work through together.

Jaxson confirmed Chase's suspicion. "We're all taking a few days off. We can go anywhere you want, baby."

"You can't afford to do that," Emma protested. "We're behind on so many things. I don't want to be the cause of us missing our opening date."

"Fuck the opening date."

"But, it will cost us…"

"Emma… let it go. I fucked up putting so many things ahead of us. It hurt you. It hurt us all. I'm not going to do that anymore, which means we're taking a few days off to get reconnected. Understood?"

Chase loved the soft love in her eyes as their sub answered with a compliant, "Yes, Sir."

His stomach growled. "Pass the pancakes, Em."

By the time they finished eating their fill, things felt completely back to normal for Chase. It was as if the emotional rollercoaster of the last few weeks hadn't even happened. Unfortunately, he knew better. They may have skillfully avoided any hard-hitting topics while they enjoyed their breakfast, but a tense silence hung in the air.

Emma stood, picking up a pile of dirty dishes, ready to take them to the sink, but Jaxson stood and took them out of her hands.

"Oh no you don't. No working for you. You go lay down and rest, baby."

"I'm pregnant," Emma sighed, "not sick. I'm not going to lay around like a lump for the next eight months."

"Maybe not, but you've had a stressful few days. You go lay down on the couch. Let Chase and me do cleanup duties today."

She finally handed over the dishes, submitting to her Dom's request. "Yes, Sir. I am kinda tired, but only because you guys kept me up all night. Not because I'm *sick*."

Chase had grabbed his own handful of dishes and was working on cleaning up when he tried to shoo Jaxson out too. "You cooked. I'll clean up. You go rest with Emma and let me get this."

He was happily surprised when Jaxson didn't argue with him.

His Dom just put the dirty dishes down and grabbed the same hand Chase had held on the way from the bedroom and pulled Emma towards the couch.

It took at least thirty minutes for Chase to get things back in order in the kitchen. Turning the lights off behind him, he headed around the corner to the living room The lighting was subdued because Jaxson had shut all of the heavy drapes to keep out the California sun. As he got farther into the room, he saw Emma asleep on the couch and Jaxson sitting on an ottoman he'd pulled over. His Dom's elbows were on his knees, his hands clasped in front of him as he leaned close to their sleeping woman.

Chase's heart swelled at the sight of the two people he loved most in the world.

Jaxson sensed his arrival. "She's so beautiful when she sleeps."

Chase came up behind him to kneel on the ottoman, placing his hands on Jaxson's shoulders as the two men reverently watched over their shared love.

"We got so lucky finding her," Chase added. "Do you ever wonder what we'd be doing if we hadn't been in Nice that morning?"

"Sometimes, but usually when I do I end up wishing I'd beaten those punk kids that were threatening her to a pulp instead of letting them slip away."

Chase chuckled. "Always our protector."

He hated the quiet huff of incredulous laughter that followed. "Some fucking protector I am. I almost ruined our family by being a dumbass."

Squeezing Jaxson's shoulders as hard as he could to get his attention, Chase argued, "We are not going to do this."

"Do what?"

"Play the blame game."

"The hell we're not." Jaxson shot to his feet, pulling away from Chase's comforting touch to pace across the room. "I'm the Dom of our family. You are my responsibility. I failed you both."

Chase had known this conversation was coming. He said a prayer of thanks Emma would sleep through it. She had enough stress right now.

He crossed the room, stepping close to face his lover and friend. "I love you," he promised.

"I don't know why. I can be a real asshole."

Chase smiled. "Yes, but that's just one of the things I love about you. You are fierce. Protective. And you're one of the most fair and honorable men I've ever met."

"A lot of good that did Em." Jaxson's voice cracked as he added, "She needed me and I wasn't there for her."

A pang of guilt washed over Chase. "Yeah, you can't take all the blame there. I fucked up right beside you."

"Bullshit. I'm in charge."

"Don't do that." He didn't hide his aggravation with the man he loved.

"What?"

"Act like just because Emma and I choose to submit to you in the bedroom, and even in our everyday lives, we aren't adults. We are grown-ups who choose to submit because it makes us happy, just like being our Dom makes you happy. But that doesn't mean we check our brains at the door. You've lectured it a hundred times. The submissives are truly in control."

"In a scene, sure. But what we have is so much more than that."

"Exactly. You just proved my point."

"You aren't making sense."

Chase reached to touch Jaxson, needing their physical connection as he continued. "All I'm trying to say is that I am submissive because you are dominant. I am the ying to your yang. You know I'd played around some before we got together, but I'd never seen myself as a sub. Not really. Not until my insides started melting every time you took charge. You're the only one who's ever done that for me. Ever."

Jaxson looked away, but Chase could tell he still held his Dom's attention.

"We all make choices, Jax. I chose you. I love you. But I also chose to take our Emma for granted right beside you. I knew she wasn't happy, just like you. I let our daily routines that keep us so in sync fall to the wayside, right beside you. I let the interior designer and Brandi and even Lola disrespect our girl, right beside you. This is on *us*, not you."

"But…"

"Let me finish…" Chase took a deep breath and barged ahead. "And Emma absolutely should have fucking told us about the baby. I've never been angry with her before, but she fucked up big as well. She can tell me it was because we were busy, and that may be true, but that's a bullshit excuse. What if something had gone wrong with her health and we didn't even know about the pregnancy? She hasn't been to her doctor in eight weeks. She could be putting our baby at risk by not getting the prenatal care she needs. She should be changing her eating and sleeping, but she didn't. Hell, knowing that she's pregnant even changes the construction plans for the club. She should have fucking told us the night of Valentine's Day after Roulette."

"What do you mean this changes construction?" Jaxson looked alarmed.

"We can't very well raise a baby above a sex club. At least in D.C. we have the townhouse. And our apartment above Runway has a private entrance we can lock down. Our planned apartment here is just a hallway away from the grand entrance staircase. I don't think we'll want our baby just feet away from guests in our public dance club."

"Fuck. I hadn't even got that far."

"Well, unfortunately, that's not even my biggest worry."

"Great. What's your biggest worry?"

"Emma's father." The men's eyes locked. Chase knew Jax

understood his concern even before he added, "He's already put us on notice his baby deserves a ring on her finger."

"She has better," Jaxson argued. "She has a collar around her neck."

"Yeah, well that makes him feel worse, not better," Chase added.

"Robert knows how much we love his little girl."

"Yes, but he is also an old-fashioned dad who is worried about his only daughter. Em may be our baby girl, but he isn't going like this. He'll lose his shit if she has a baby out of wedlock. He's pretty much vowed that already."

Frustration overflowed from Jaxson. "Well he's gonna need to get over it, since we can't all three get married legally — and there is no fucking way one of us is marrying her and leaving the other one out."

The trio had already had this discussion in the past. It wasn't a new concern for them. The stakes just got a little higher now that there was a baby involved.

"I get it, though. He loves her. He doesn't want to see her get hurt," Chase reasoned.

Jaxson ran a hand through his hair nervously as he countered. "He can't possibly love her more than we do. I'd jump in front of a speeding train for her and I know you would too."

"Of course, so we'll just have to convince him we'll love her and our baby even more." Joy filled his heart at the thought of holding their child. "I can't wait to see our little peanut."

He could see the unusual insecurity in Jaxson's eyes as he answered. "I pray you're the biological father."

"Are you kidding?" Chase was shocked at his Dom's assertion. "It doesn't matter at all."

"Of course it matters. I don't want to pass on the asshole gene. My grandfather had it. My father has it in spades, and we've already established I'm a carrier." At least a smile played at Jaxson's lips at his observation.

Chase grinned. "I happen to love your asshole gene since you're usually using it to protect all the right things." His grin faded as he turned serious, trying to reassure his best friend. "You're nothing like your father, Jaxson."

Jax hesitated, looking a bit lost. "What kind of dad will I be with my father as my role model?"

"The absolute best kind, because you've seen firsthand what not to do."

"What if I fuck up?" Jax had started to fiddle with a stack of paint color chips to avoid looking at Chase.

While Chase hated that his larger than life lover was feeling insecure, he actually treasured these moments when Jaxson peeled back his protective armor and let Chase see the soft side that he let so few people get a glimpse of. "You will fuck up. I will, too. And so will Emma. It's what parents do. But we'll figure it out. You know how I know?"

Jax shook his head.

"Because we have more love between us than a dozen normal couples." He watched Jaxson open his mouth to argue again, so Chase added, "Yes, we got lazy. We got off track. But everything is going to be okay now."

Jaxson reached out to pull Chase into a tight hug, clinging to him as his voice warbled out a soft, "I don't deserve you."

"Oh yes you do." Chase melted into the loving embrace, reassuring Jaxson. "You deserve the world."

"You guys are making me cry over here." Emma's voice broke the silence.

He heard rustling behind him and welcomed Emma into their embrace when she arrived next to the men. The threesome clung to each other, letting their love shore up the shaky foundation they'd been stumbling on for the last months.

Jaxson finally broke the quiet by asking Emma, "So how many other people have you told?"

Emma pulled back so all three of them could see each other. "No one. I didn't tell anyone."

"You mean other than telling Khloe." Anger furrowed Jaxson's forehead.

"I didn't tell her either. She guessed and I'm a terrible liar," Emma defended herself.

"That's the truth." Chase chuckled.

"So how the hell did Helms know to call me?"

"Because Khloe is a terrible liar too, which is sort of ironic considering she makes a living pretending to be people she's not. And I'm sure it helps that Ryder is a freaking interrogation specialist."

"Fair enough," Jaxson agreed. "So, you haven't even told Sam?"

Emma shook her head before adding, "I knew she'd tell Jonah, then he'd call you guys."

"So, you were determined to hide the truth from us, the fathers of your baby?" Jaxson chastised.

"I said I was sorry. I really did think I was keeping it a secret for all the right reasons."

"Your judgment was wrong." Jaxson squeezed Emma tighter before he launched into a lecture she deserved.

"Never again, do you hear me? I accept Chase and I made plenty of mistakes too and for that, I'm sorry, but you need to put yourself and the baby first. No more secrets, no matter how busy we may seem, got it?"

"Yes, Sir."

"I want to drag you over my lap and light up that beautiful ass of yours to make sure you really do understand, but I'm not going to do that, at least not until I can talk to your doctor. I'm not gonna do anything that might put you or the baby at risk."

"You plan on talking to my doctor about spanking me?"

"Damn straight. He's gonna call the shots on what activities are safe and what needs to wait until after you deliver."

Emma had just turned an adorable shade of pink at the

thought of talking about their D/s relationship with her OBGYN when the sound of the front door opening just far enough to jam against the safety chain broke their intimate conversation.

"Jaxson! You left the chain on. I can't get in." Lola's shrill voice poisoned their private space.

Maybe Jaxson had the right idea about going to hide out at a hotel where no one could find them.

Jax caught Chase's eye. "Take our girl back to the bedroom. I'll be there in just a few minutes. None of us got much sleep last night. I think today is the perfect day to lie in bed and snuggle. I'll bring some drinks when I come."

His best friend may insist he had the asshole gene, but Chase knew the truth. Jaxson Davidson was a romantic, at least where his lovers were concerned. He couldn't resist leaning in to steal a kiss from Jaxson's sexy as hell lips before he reached for Emma's hand.

He called back over his shoulder, teasing, "Don't be too long. I'd hate for you to miss any fun."

He was just about to close the bedroom door when he heard Lola's voice in the living room, bossy as ever. He smiled, knowing she was about to be taken down a few notches.

CHAPTER EIGHT ~ JAXSON

*J*axson exited his rental car, stopping to take a sweeping look around the grounds of the estate, anxious to see what progress had been made in the three days that had passed since he'd been there last.

Three of the best, and yet most stressful days of his life. Being sequestered with Emma and Chase had been a slice of heaven, especially after the rough couple of months they'd had building up to their mini-break. They'd used the time to get used to the idea that they'd be parents soon. His lovers had somehow managed to convince him he was going to be able to handle fatherhood with flying colors.

Now, away from their calming influence, and the distracting sexcapades, self-doubt was creeping in again. He knew he had to get up to speed on all of the construction and interior design updates first, but he had made up his mind to give Jonah 'Cash' Carter a call as soon as he could get a few minutes of privacy later that day. Cash hadn't been prepared to be a father either, but he had somehow managed to pull off the whole parenthood thing pretty well — at least from the outside looking in. If anyone would understand what Jax was going through, it was Cash.

Considering the trio had still not told anyone else, not even their families, making the call to Jonah would be a big step.

Forcing himself to focus on work, at least for a few hours, Jax resumed his inspection of the grounds. The monumental fountain in the middle of the circular driveway was shooting water high in the air. The plumbing contractor had gotten it fixed and the landscape crew had already repaired the green lawn and shrubs surrounding it.

Continuing his inspection of the grounds, he was pleased the lawn and surrounding landscaping he could see from the front carport was all neatly manicured and trimmed. Colorful flowers now replaced weeds in the beds. In the distance he could see the groundskeeper directing the full-time staffers they had hired to care for the extensive property.

Pleased that things seemed to be under control outside, Jaxson headed towards the grand staircase that led to the two-story double doors that served as the entrance for Runway West. In the distance to his right, he noticed the concrete had been laid to expand the parking for the many cars they were expecting. The valet shed had been constructed per his instructions, just to the right of the main entrance. It would help camouflage the long handicap ramp they had installed to comply with building code.

He took a calming breath before opening the front door. A gust of air-conditioned air welcomed him along with the scent of the six-foot-high fresh flower arrangement on a new grand entrance table. They'd discussed needing something to help drive the traffic pattern of arrivals and departures and seeing it in place he agreed with the solution the interior designer had come up with.

"Oh good, I'm glad you got here before I left."

Jaxson turned to see the security contractor, George, headed his way along with two of his installation crew. When the men stopped just in front of him, he reached out to shake their hands. "Hey there. How are things going?"

"All done. We just finished programming the surveillance cameras and setting up the back-up schedule for the system this morning. I left a manual and a bunch of other paperwork for you, including my six-figure bill, in the security office with Miguel."

"That's fine, but I'm afraid you aren't done yet."

"Now wait a minute here, Davidson…"

Jaxson held his hand up like a stop sign. "I'm sure you completed the contracted work. That's great, and I appreciate how you were able to meet our aggressive timeline. I'll be happy to write the check for your bonus."

"So, then what…"

"I have another job for you."

"I don't know. We're behind on other projects."

"I'll make it worth your while." He had the guy's attention with his promise, so Jax continued. "I've decided to flip-flop our personal living quarters and the planned guest rooms."

"Wait. You mean you're moving into the pool house?"

"Yep. For the most part, everything you've done in both locations is still needed. I just want you to put an extra level of protection around the pool house, more surveillance and…" Jax lowered his voice and leaned in. "I want a fortified panic room installed as soon as you can manage it. You'll have direction over the construction crew for any heavy lifting you need."

George stroked his beard as he thought through the request. "If you can give me a few days to wrap up some other projects, we can be back over here in a week."

"Sounds good. Thanks." Jaxson felt better already just getting things in motion to protect the West Coast home he would share with his family at least part of the year. He suspected pushback from their fellow investors on the change, but he was prepared to spend extra capital to make it reality if it came down to it. There was no way he would bring Emma and their child home from the hospital to a room above the dance floor. Where every time they left their rooms they would be subject to running into strangers.

The men had separated, about to go their own ways when George called back to Jax. "I'd watch out if I were you. Ms. Garcia is in rare form today."

Jax nodded with a grin. "Thanks for the heads up, but she is about to meet her match."

"Now that I believe. Later." George barked a laugh.

Jaxson proceeded through the open spaces that would soon be filled with paying patrons. Unlike the wide-open glass and modern lighting in the original Runway, the Beverly Hills club's decor was more intimate. Patrons would be able to move between different themed rooms as they mingled, making it harder for them to be seen by the entire club, as was the case in D.C. It would also make it easier for patrons to slip into hidden nooks and crannies for privacy.

He made a sweep through the grand foyer, walking through the great room with its showcase fireplace and several seating options, and then through the mammoth library stocked with thousands of books patrons could enjoy during daytime events.

Just past the library was the game room. Guests would be able to mingle while playing billiards, foosball, any number of board games, and of course several friendly poker tables.

They had converted a second living room space into a dining room where intermediate-sized groups could gather. In essence, they were becoming a banquet hall of sorts. The upscale industrial-sized kitchen would be offering gourmet menu items as well as providing appetizers when the club was open. They had hired a full-time chef who would also book dinner parties up to twenty in the dining room and parties up to two-hundred could be accommodated by setting up banquet tables and chairs on the dance floor for special occasions.

One of the biggest problems they had had to solve when converting the private mansion into a public club was installing the restrooms they would need. Their interior design guru, Ted, had come up with the bright idea of converting the master suite had previously been on the main floor into several key spaces. His changes were critical to their success, and they had been working on the modifications the last time he was here.

They had first carved out spacious men's and women's restrooms. With the area left over between them, they'd been able to create the necessary club spaces.

First was the check-in room with lockers, not unlike the room before entering Black Light. They would call this room Staging. All guests would start in Staging and not be able to proceed further without first showing their entrance ticket or paying, and then locking up their electronics. If they needed to make a call or check email during their visit, they would need to return to Staging to do it.

Like in D.C., the room had doors at both ends of the long expanse, making it a wide hallway of sorts. Security would route all arriving and departing guests through this space and security cameras that fed into the spacious and private security office next door would capture photos of each patron.

He poked his head into Staging and was pleased all seemed in order. He then went to the next door that had a new sign reading 'Employees Only.' As Jaxson tried to open the door it banged into the back of a tall guy he'd never seen before. It took a few seconds for the occupants of the room to move away enough to make room to let him to push into the room.

Apparently, the Security Office was presently the heart of the operation as there were close to a dozen people crammed into the room where the walls were covered in flat-screen monitors. He had paid George's firm to install hundreds of security cameras on the property, some visible, but most hidden. Electronic keypads had been installed at almost every door in the building. The security system would be able to track the movements of all employees and restrict access as required. Keys and codes would be changed at frequent and random intervals to ensure safety.

Despite all of the security measures, one of Jaxson's lingering concerns with his security team was making sure they had trustworthy people monitoring the feeds. As he was absolutely certain they would be capturing salacious footage of public figures, he needed to make sure nothing recorded at Runway, or Black Light on the floor below, ever made it into the hands of the paparazzi or it would be on TMZ within an hour. And he was no fool. The resulting lawsuit would happen less than twenty-four hours later.

The group in the security office parted, making a path for Jax to walk to the far end of the room where their new head of security, Miguel Martinez, sat at a counter with computers coaching a couple of new employees. Knowing how much he had riding on the performance of his head of security, he'd had Ryder and Axe work up a full background check on the guy to make sure he was the man Jaxson wanted in charge. He'd been pleased with the outcome.

He was also relieved to see the person of the hour he'd been looking for was next to Miguel, just as he had requested.

Jax smiled as he realized most of the men in the room seemed to be crowding the exit, keeping their distance from the only female occupant. She looked up and broke into a smile of her own when she saw him.

"I've been resisting calling you. I knew you'd be over as soon as you could get here."

Jaxson felt better already, just knowing she was there. He hugged her just a little tighter than he ever had before as he greeted the temporary addition to the Runway West staff. "Maxine, I can't thank you enough for coming. I'm sure your husband is less than happy with me right now, but I do appreciate you being here."

"Yeah, Eric is pissed, but after I checked into the upscale suite you have me booked into, I have to say I'm feeling pretty good about the decision to spend a few weeks out in California. Maybe he'll appreciate me a bit more after he gets an idea of how much I do around home."

Jaxson made a mental note to send Eric Torres a gift to try to make amends for stealing one of Jax's most important employees away from her family for at least a few weeks. There was no way he wanted to lose Maxine's leadership in D.C. long-term. In fact, he was counting on her, not Spencer, to hold down the fort on the East Coast while the trio was in California part of each year. Still, getting her help as they tried to open the club on time was huge.

"She's already proven how smart of an idea it was to bring her out to help." Miguel piped up. "Maxine helped me look over the staffing sheets and made some suggestions I think will save us a chunk of change each month."

"That's wonderful, but that isn't even why I had her fly in."

"I know." Miguel grinned. "Can I watch? In fact, I know a few people around here that would pay good money to be a fly on the wall."

Jaxson chuckled. "Just stay focused."

"You're no fun."

"Yeah, well I never pretended to be fun." He turned to Maxine and asked, "You ready?"

"You bet. I can't wait to get up to speed."

Jaxson nodded towards the door. Maxine's high-heels clicked against the tile flooring as the security guards parted like the Red Sea to make way for them.

Once they were in the foyer Jaxson scanned the area to ensure they were alone. For added measure, he ushered her into a small alcove where there would eventually be a photo booth. It gave him the privacy he needed to prep Maxine. "So, do you have any questions before I take you in and set off the fireworks?"

"No, not really. You did a good job of prepping me over the phone, and the files and pictures you emailed over yesterday were a big help."

"Fine. Just remember, you are now in charge. Miguel will

handle security, but everything else will run through you first. I'm not dumping this on you. I'll meet with you as often as we need to, but I need to have someone I can trust in charge, especially when I'm not here."

"Got it. I would like to meet with you to review the action item list one more time and make sure I have them in priority order." Maxine pulled her trusty iPad out of her big bag. She didn't go anywhere without it.

"I'd like that. Let's get you introduced to the gang first, then we can go through it as a group. That way you can ask questions along the way."

It only took a couple of minutes to wind through another den-like sitting room where patrons could eventually come to chat away from the loud music if they wanted. He heard Lola's booming voice even before he could see the arched double-doors that marked the opening to the huge dance floor and main bar.

The previous owners had used the space for grand balls back in the day. The parquet flooring had been stripped and refinished to a shiny gloss. The two-story walls along the perimeter were made up of over a dozen expansive, arched, floor-to-ceiling windows. The sheer drapes had been installed since his last visit, bringing the room closer to opening night ready.

In the center of the room, there were a dozen banquet tables setup in a U-shape. Until the official Runway West business office was ready on the second floor, this had been acting as command central. Both Lola and Ted had set up shop on opposite sides of the U.

They were crossing into the room when Maxine placed her hand on Jax's forearm and motioned for him to stop. They stood silently near the doorway, undetected, listening to Lola who had her back to them. She was talking to a young woman with long black hair. The petite woman looked familiar, but Jaxson couldn't remember her name.

"I refuse to put up with incompetence. If you can't handle the job now before we even open, you're never going to cut it. I'd fire you right now if I could, but for some reason nepotism is ruling the day. It was unprofessional of you to bring your uncle into this discussion."

The young woman Lola was yelling at contained her temper, but retorted, "I didn't bring Uncle Kai into this. You did by screaming so loud this morning that he could hear you outside."

"So you say. I don't like being blackmailed."

"Oh for crying out loud," The shorter woman snorted. "Now you're just being ridiculous."

"Hardly. I'll be discussing this with Mr. Davidson the second he arrives. I'm sure he'll agree with me that you and your uncle both need to go this afternoon."

Jaxson highly doubted that. He'd heard enough.

"I'm here now, so fill me in." He resumed his walk into the room just as Lola spun with a familiar glare of superiority falling on everything she saw.

"It's about time. I was going to send out a search party for you. We have work to do."

"Excuse me?"

"It's after ten," she spat with disgust.

"Thanks for the unnecessary update," Jaxson deadpanned, sensing rather than seeing Maxine step up to his left as he turned his attention to the other woman standing in front of him. He held out his hand, adding, "Jaxson Davidson. And you are?"

The Polynesian woman had to step around Lola to take his hand. He appreciated her strong grip as they shook hands. "Nice to meet you, Mr. Davidson. Nalani Ione."

The name was familiar, yet he was grateful when she added on, "I'm your Executive Housekeeper. I look forward to working with you, Mr. Cartwright, and Ms. Fischer."

Her introduction unlocked the memory of a recent conversation with his groundskeeper. "Ah, it's nice to put a face with a name. You come highly recommended by your uncle."

"I'm not sure why we are taking recommendations from an employee who can barely get his own job done," Lola scoffed.

Nalani released his hand to turn towards Lola. "Maybe if people would stop changing the plans at the last minute, we'd both be able to finish our work."

Lola crossed her arms across her chest in a huff. "If you can't handle a bit of change, this isn't the right job for you."

Then Maxine spoke for the first time. "What is it that you've been working on, if you don't mind me asking?"

All eyes turned towards her as Nalani answered. "I have my team focusing on the first-floor public areas. The construction crews are finally done on this level in all areas except the men's room. I was trying…"

"And I told you that could wait. I need the second-floor north suite deep cleaned before the new furniture arrives this afternoon."

"But no one will be…"

"Not that I owe you an explanation, but the opening entertainer, Diva Frost, will be staying in that room starting tomorrow."

Jaxson jumped in. "Since when?"

"Since it was part of the negotiations of her contract," Lola added.

"I helped negotiate her contract." Jaxson worked to hold his temper. "At no point did I agree to house her at the mansion."

"I've had to handle the final arrangements all by myself." Her dig was not missed. "I had to renegotiate a few things to keep us on track."

"That's bullshit. Ms. Frost is getting more than enough compensation for her appearance." He bristled, regretting now she was receiving a year's VIP club membership to Black Light.

Jaxson was about to call Diva when Lola admitted, "The suite is in exchange for her agreeing to stay and hang out in the club for two weeks, so we are guaranteed to have celebrities for guests to hob-knob with."

Maxine scoffed. "Are you kidding me? She should be paying us for the publicity she'll get when she's here. She's a second-rate entertainer at best. I've already called in favors from several Runway regulars to make sure they're going to be making appearances in the first few weeks we are open."

For the first time, Lola's gaze turned to Maxine, her annoyance evident. "And just who the hell are you?"

Before Jaxson could make the introduction, Maxine stepped up, holding her hand out to Lola. Just before his PA took the hand, Maxine added, "I'm the manager of Runway."

Lola's hand pulled back, refusing to greet Maxine.

"What are you talking about? I didn't interview any candidates for club manager yet!"

"Yes, I understand that. Maybe you can explain why that is? I would have thought that would have been one of the first positions you'd have filled," Maxine added.

"Why the hell is that any of your business?"

Jaxson used her question as his re-entrance to the conversation. "Effective immediately, everything is Maxine's business." He paused until Lola's gaze met his, then added, "I've brought Maxine in to take charge of the opening and renovation project. As you've pointed out, I no longer have the time to be here twenty-four seven so I'm bringing in someone I trust explicitly to take charge."

"What the fuck? Like you can't trust me? I should be able to hire my own employees."

"Perhaps you misunderstood." Jaxson smiled. "You now report to Maxine. Not the other way around."

Maxine ignored the open-mouthed shock on Lola's make-up caked face as she added, "If you could be so kind, I'd like to gather all of the employees together so I can meet them. I'll be reviewing the hiring records to validate the hires myself. If you would also get me the job description you've posted for the club manager position, that will help me get started."

"Why? If you are the club manager. . ."

"Humor me."

"I don't know shit about you. Why should I drop everything to be at your beck and call? You have no idea how many details I'm managing with the opening."

Jaxson lifted a hand to make Lola shut up. "You know all you need to know. I told you Maxine is in charge. That is enough. And not that I owe you any explanations, but Maxine not only manages Runway East, but she was our project manager for the East Coast opening a year and a half ago. She's been through this with me once already."

"Ah," Lola looked relieved. "So you're just a temp."

Jaxson clarified, "I'll repeat. She is in charge."

"I don't like this," Lola complained.

Jaxson grinned while parroting her own words against her. "Like you said… if you can't handle a bit of change, maybe this isn't the right job for you."

Maxine ignored the drama, talking to Nalani. "You're absolutely right to focus on the public areas we will need for the opening. If Diva needs a place to stay, she can rent a room at a hotel. Do you have all of the tools you need to do your job?"

"I've started a list of things we'll need to order. Maybe we can go through that together?"

Lola growled. "I told you I ordered everything you'd need, Nalani. We don't have an unlimited budget."

Jaxson had had enough. It was time to let Lola go, but Maxine's calming hand on his arm stopped his words.

"Jaxson, I've changed my mind. You were telling me last night that you wanted to check on the progress at the pool house. Why don't you go check on that and let me handle things in here?"

His first reaction was to run from the room as fast as he could, but he glanced to Maxine first. "I thought you wanted to go through the action item list together."

"Let me spend a few hours getting the lay of the land first." She patted his arm reassuringly. "We can go through any questions I have later this afternoon."

Anxious to make a few calls of his own, Jaxson jumped at the offer, shedding a tiny bit of the stress he'd been carrying around for months, feeling better already that Maxine was on the case.

"I do have some calls I need to make. I'll be around. Text me if you need me."

"Will do." Maxine turned back towards the other occupants in the massive clubroom and started taking charge before he'd even gotten turned around.

He retreated quickly, walking quietly past the security office, hoping to avoid detection that might delay his escape. Once outside, he ambled down the stairs, heading to the left, finding the semi-hidden entrance to the walkway that was a shortcut to the back expanse of the property.

Tall evergreens lined the wide path, providing a secluded tunnel for the trip towards the backyard paradise. Small alcoves with benches surrounded by colorful flowerpots popped up every few dozen feet. In the distance, the sound of lawnmowers broke up the mid-morning peace.

I wonder how long I could hide in one of these spots without anyone finding me?

Once the final corner had been rounded, the walkway opened to a mammoth brick patio that stretched the entire length of the mansion. Several mature trees stretched to the sky, providing not only shade, but also helping to break the huge space into smaller entertainment areas. The huge grill with tables where they would host outdoor events. Lounge areas for relaxing, winding down the path to the mammoth bean shaped swimming pool surrounded by a brick pool deck where the rich and famous would sunbathe while sipping their mimosas.

In the distance, the one-story pool house caught his attention. He'd spent time in the building before they'd purchased the property, debating if they'd turn the space away from the mansion into Black Light. In the end, the huge windows and inability to protect the privacy of the patrons who would come and go to the kink club had forced him to build Black Light below Runway, just like they had in D.C.

Jax crossed the fifty feet of green lawn separating the pool deck and the pool house. He was surprised when the patio door to the two-story great room was unlocked.

A wave of heat hit him. They hadn't turned on the air in the unused space. Most of the furniture and belongings of the previous owners had been removed, but random pieces of furniture remained hidden under sheets and plastic to keep out the dust. Jaxson removed a sheet from what turned out to be a cream-colored leather lounge chair with a matching ottoman. Plopping down into the chair, feeling exhausted, he took a long breath.

They'd been under so much stress the last months. He felt guilty hiding out in the pool house, hidden away from everyone and everything, but he needed the quiet solitude to get his head on straight. Like it often did in the three days since he'd discovered Emma was pregnant, the news of him becoming a father hit him like a ton of bricks, making his chest tighten with anxiety.

In addition to worrying about Emma's health, he stressed about not knowing a fucking thing about being a father. How was he supposed to lead his family through this change when he felt like road kill when it came to knowing how to care for an infant?

As his anxiety escalated, he pulled his phone out and found Jonah 'Cash' Carter in his contact list. He hit CALL before he could second-guess his decision to confide in his friend.

"Jaxson! What's up, buddy?"

His old friend's voice calmed him. He didn't have a fucking clue where to start so he just laughed nervously.

"That bad, eh? I worried when I heard about the opening date that you might have bitten off more than you could chew. Anything I can do?" The sound of people talking in the background on Jonah's end of the line told him he'd probably interrupted his friend in the middle of something important.

Jax paused, unsure how to even say the words caught in his throat. Somehow saying them out loud would make it that much more real.

"You still there?" Jonah prodded.

Jax took a deep breath and plunged forward with the two words that had changed his life. "Emma's pregnant."

It was his turn to wait for a reply from the other end of the phone. He could tell Cash was moving to a more private location as the boisterous voices got softer just before the sound of a door slamming brought Jonah back to the call.

"You want to say that for me again? I was in a busy area and I think I might have misheard you."

"You didn't mishear."

A surprised whistle preceded Jonah's chuckle. "Welcome to fatherhood!"

"Thanks... I think."

"Let me guess. You're freaking out and you called me hoping I'd tell you it's the best thing since sliced bread."

"Something like that."

"You want me to blow smoke up your ass or tell you the truth?"

"I'm not a take it up the ass kinda guy, so I'll settle for the truth."

"Hey, with Chase in the picture, I didn't know."

"Smartass." Jaxson smiled in spite of himself.

"Wait a minute. How am I not hearing about this from Samantha? Has she been keeping this a secret from me?"

"Naw, I just found out myself a couple of days ago. We've been kinda sitting on the news, letting it sink in a bit before we told anyone. We'd better let Emma give her a call with the news, or we might both be in trouble."

"Roger that, but don't have her wait too long. Holding in a secret like this from Sami is gonna kill me."

"Yeah, keeping secrets from each other is a sonuvabitch."

"Why does it sound like you're speaking from experience?"

"She fucking found out on Valentine's Day. I don't know what makes me madder... her keeping a secret this big from us this whole time, or that I had my head so far up my ass with the new clubs, I didn't even figure it out on my own."

"Shit, that's a long time. I hope you roasted her ass for keeping it a secret that long."

"Excuse me? Did you miss the part where I told you she was carrying a baby? Ass-roasting is off the table for the next nine months."

"First, if she has known since Valentine's Day, it's probably more like six months, not nine months. Second, there are plenty of things that will be off the table for you, but ass-roasting isn't one of them. Sami was thrilled when her doctor told me as long as I kept it to just my hand or some other small implement like her hairbrush, I could discipline her up until late in her third trimester."

The information surprised Jax. "I don't know. I'd be too afraid to hurt her or the baby."

"I was too. It took me finding out that Sami had gotten a traffic ticket for driving twenty-five miles over the speed limit to finally test out the doctor's advice. I got my point across just fine with a heavy, wooden paddle brush."

"Emma hates the hairbrush."

"Then she better learn not to keep secrets, right?"

"I guess. That helps to know, but..." Jaxson paused, unsure how to express the swarm of doubts in his head. He finally finished with a simple question. "How do I keep from screwing this up?"

"Listen, I know where your head is right now."

"Why do you think I called you?"

"Right. Well, here's the thing. You're going to screw up. Everyone does, but it won't matter."

"What if I can't handle this? What the fuck do I know about being a father?"

"You know enough. You have Emma and Chase to help you and you're like me. You'll research the hell out of this to learn everything you need to know. In the end, it won't matter, because you'll take one look at the baby as soon as he or she is born and your heart will melt. Then the nurse will lay her in Emma's arms, and your fucking heart will explode with a new love you had no fucking idea could exist."

"That sounds painful," Jaxson muttered.

"It's not. The pain comes with the lack of sleep. Seriously, I thought babies slept most of the time and they may, but Tasha wakes up like every two hours hungry. It's impossible to get a good night's sleep. Poor Sami lives on naps. And forget sex most nights. You'll all fall into bed too exhausted to even think about fun."

"You aren't making me feel any better."

"I thought you wanted the truth."

"I do."

"So here is more truth. Take the damn birthing classes the hospital will offer. It will help you know what to expect in the delivery room. And hire a nanny, even if you guys want to do most everything on your own. You can afford it. A nanny will help relieve the stress a bit."

"Okay. Anything else?" Jaxson knew so little on the topic he didn't even know what else he should be asking.

"Where do you think you'll be delivering? Does Emma already have an OBGYN on the West Coast?"

"Not yet. Tracking one down is at the top of our to-do list. We need to get her in to be checked out."

"I'll text you the contact info for Sami's OBGYN when we hang up. We delivered in L.A. intentionally. Dr. Tipton handles a lot of high-profile cases practicing in Hollywood. With your unique relationship, this is bound to blow up big once she starts showing."

"Don't fucking remind me." Jax sighed when he heard someone yelling for Cash at the other end of the phone.

"Listen man, I'd love to chat longer, but our recording time just started. We're in the studio in New York laying down some new music. All of this downtime at home the last year to spend time with Sami and Tasha has been awesome for my creativity."

"Must be nice. I feel paralyzed since I found out."

"That will pass."

"Promise?"

"Yep. I'm telling you, other than the lack of sleep and the changing of dirty diapers, it's the best thing that ever happened to you, man. You'll see. Later."

The call ended, but it had done what Jaxson needed it to. He felt marginally better. If bad-boy rocker Cash could handle being a father, maybe he wouldn't totally fuck it up after all.

Jaxson enjoyed the solitude of the pool house, letting it sink in he would be turning this into his family's newest home. He got up, walking from room to room, visualizing bringing Chase, Emma, and the baby home from the hospital to the room next to the master suite. It would make a beautiful nursery. The master bedroom was huge. A customized bed for three would easily fit. The en suite bathroom was opulent, with a sauna, a whirlpool tub the trio would all fit in, and a shower the size of most bathrooms.

He had just returned to the great room when his phone vibrated in his pocket. He reluctantly pulled it out to see that it was Chase texting.

Better come home when you can. Robert called Emma today and she broke the news. It didn't go well.

And just like that, the stress was back, pressing on him as if an elephant had taken up residence on his chest. Closing up the pool house, he took off across the grounds towards the car hoping he'd think of something good to say by the time he got back to the rental.

CHAPTER NINE ~ EMMA

"*D*addy, you need to calm down. I was hoping you were going to be happy for me." Emma had been right to dread this phone call. They'd already spoken hours before when her father had actually hung up after receiving the news that his little girl was pregnant and not planning on getting married.

"Seriously?" her father asked.

"Yes. You know how much I love Jaxson and Chase, and even more importantly, how much they love me."

"I don't doubt that for one minute."

"Okay, then you just need to be happy for us."

"Put Davidson on the phone." It was the third time he'd demanded to speak with Jaxson.

"I told you, he's not here. He's at the club."

"How irresponsible. He should be there with you."

"Oh, for crying out loud, I'm pregnant, not dying. Do you really expect him to stay home and wrap me in bubble-wrap until the baby is born?"

"No, but I damn well expect him to stay home to start planning your wedding."

Emma took a deep breath, trying hard to not panic. "Like I told you this morning, there isn't going to be a wedding."

"Bullshit. I made it clear when you started this weird relationship that eventually I expected one of the men who are taking advantage of my innocent daughter to marry you."

"And we've told you from the beginning that wasn't ever going to happen. No one is taking advantage of me."

"Fine, Jaxson won't step up, then marry Chase. Two of the three of you need to get married."

His comment sparked her anger. She spat back the first thing that came to her mind. "Fine, maybe Jaxson and Chase will get married then. They are two of the three of us."

The sound of her father's angry growl corresponded with the front door slamming closed. Shit, one of the guys was home. She'd purposefully called her parents back after Chase had left for the grocery store. Jax and Chase had begun to look at Robert Fischer as a father figure in the years the trio had been together and she didn't want her father's promised anger to hurt their feelings.

"Put Mom back on, please," Emma urged, hoping to avoid more conflict.

Wonderful. Both of her lovers came into the kitchen, each carrying grocery bags and looking concerned when they saw her on the phone. Chase silently mouthed 'who' as he set his bags down.

She didn't get a chance to answer before she heard her mother's voice on the other end of the phone.

"That went well... not," her mother deadpanned.

"I know," she chose her words carefully, "but I'm not totally surprised."

Emma could hear a commotion on the other end of the phone before her mom added. "I'm sorry, Emma. I need to go. I'm happy for you, honey. I'll do my best to calm your father down. We'll call you later."

She held the phone to her ear for a few seconds after her mom hung up, trying to decide how much of the truth she was going to share with the men in her lives. As her eyes met a worried Chase's gaze, she knew she'd kept enough secrets for a lifetime. Nothing but the truth would do.

Emma threw her phone on the nearby kitchen counter before heading towards the men. When Chase threw his arms open, she rushed into them, comforted by his tight hug.

She was disappointed when Jaxson didn't sandwich her like normal. She loved their Emma sandwich hugs more than anything.

"I'll kick your father's ass if he hurt you," Jaxson growled. Of course he'd gone to check her phone to see who she'd been talking to.

"Mom is so excited for us," she offered against Chase's chest, her childish attempt at avoiding the coming conflict.

"Look at me, sweetheart."

Jaxson's use of one of her favorite endearments helped her release Chase. She was relieved when he let her turn to face their Dom, but then Chase hugged her again, pulling her back to his chest. Emma lifted her gaze to her Dom's to see his concern for her. She knew he was not-so-patiently waiting for her to fill him in.

"It's gonna take Dad a bit more time to be excited. I called them back hoping he'd have calmed down."

"He's pressuring you to get married, isn't he?"

"He's just old fashioned." She felt relief he already understood the dynamics at play. "Women are supposed to be married before they have kids."

"What did you tell him?"

Was he serious? "What do you mean? Of course, I told him none of us are getting married."

Chase hugged her supportively. "Good girl."

His words still hung in the air when Jaxson shocked them all. "You'll be marrying Chase."

She was spared having to figure out what to say by Chase exploding as he released her.

"Oh no you don't. We're not doing this."

"Are you refusing to listen to your Dom?" Jaxson challenged.

"Hell yes I'm refusing. We are not leaving you out just to appease Robert."

"It's not just Robert, and you know it."

Chase was furious, approaching Jaxson to make his point. "I don't give a shit who it's for. Until it's legal for us all to marry each other, there won't be any marriage ceremonies going on. We are a trio. We stay a trio."

Emma was relieved to see a small smile play at Jaxson's lips as he replied to Chase's demand. "Well alright then. I see you feel strongly about this."

"Damn straight I do," Chase declared, uncharacteristically serious.

Emma hugged him from behind. "I agree. My dad will get over it. If not before the baby is born, as soon as he sees her and holds her."

"You've referred to the baby as 'her' several times. Do you know something we don't know?" Jaxson asked.

Emma pulled out of the hug to place her palm over her tummy affectionately. "No. Nothing specific. In fact, I don't think I want to know ahead of time if it's going to be a boy or girl. Do you guys?"

"I don't want to know if it's a boy or girl either," Chase added.

"Okay, then it's unanimous. But... we do need to get you in to see the doctor to make sure that the baby is healthy."

"My doctor is in D.C. It will have to wait until after the clubs are open and we can go home for a long weekend or something."

Jaxson grabbed two bottles of beer and a bottled water out of the fridge and walked to hand them to his lovers as he added. "I talked to Cash today. He sent over the contact info for the doctor he and Samantha used for their delivery out here in Los Angeles. He's setup to handle high profile cases like ours."

"But I love Dr. Drummond back home."

Jaxson held her chin in his hand as he looked into her eyes. "This is our part-time home now too, baby. We'll keep doctors up to speed on both coasts so no matter where we are, we have someone who knows your case and is at the ready."

That made sense, even though she preferred they just go home to D.C. Then it hit her. "Wait, you told Cash about the baby? He isn't going to tell Sam, is he?"

"No, but he did warn me not to wait too long until you call her yourself."

"I'm going to go call her now!" Unlike calling her parents like she had dreaded, calling her good friend Samantha excited her. She grabbed her phone from the counter and headed back to their bedroom, looking for some privacy.

Chase called after her, "Tell Sam hi, baby."

Just twenty-four short hours later Emma found herself in the back seat of the Town Car the guys had ordered to pick them up for their drive to her new OBGYN, Dr. Tipton. Being celebrities had its perks, and getting an emergency appointment with next to no notice with one of the most sought-after doctors in the city was just one of those perks.

Jaxson's hand rested on her right thigh, Chase's on her left, as they sat silently linked in the mid-day Los Angeles traffic, each lost in their own thoughts. Her mind drifted to her father. She'd tried phoning him that morning after giving him a night to calm down, but the call had gone straight to voicemail. She knew he'd love his grandchild with all his heart down the road but hated the wedge the pregnancy drove between them in the meantime.

The driver had been briefed ahead of time to drop the trio at the back entrance to the modern medical building about a block away from Cedar-Sinai Medical Center. A uniformed security guard met them at the back door, ushering them down an empty corridor to a waiting elevator. The guard used one of the keys on his over-filled key ring to call the elevator and program the floor for them.

In tune with her inner nerves, Chase reached to his right to wrap his arm around her waist, pulling her close to him as they went to the top floor of the medical building. Jaxson reciprocated, wrapping his left arm around her back, linking the trio as each of them worked to quiet their nerves.

They exited the elevator as one, grateful the hallway was wide enough for them to remain connected as they approached the frosted-glass double doors to Dr. Paul Tipton's office. Jaxson reached to pull the door open, but found it locked.

A buzzing sound emanated from the nearby keypad as the door sprung open. Once inside, they found the waiting room to be different than any other she'd been in. Instead of a room full of chairs for patients, they found a wide hall with six openings to what looked like six small private waiting rooms. They weren't closed in, but it was impossible to see who, if anyone, was in each private space.

Relief she hadn't expected to feel overcame her as she realized they wouldn't have to worry about other mothers-to-be snapping her photo and selling it to the highest bidder. News would eventually get out about her pregnancy, but she wanted it to be on her own terms and only after her parents had gotten used to the idea.

She was given a clipboard with a thick stack of paperwork that needed to be filled out. An attractive RN ushered them into one of the empty waiting rooms, and Emma appreciated that unlike most women they met, she managed to keep her focus on Emma and not the hotties with her.

"The doctor is with another new patient, so it's a bit hard to know when he'll be free. Can I bring you anything to eat or drink while you wait?"

"No, I'm good," Emma responded just as Jaxson added, "Do you have any fruit juice for Emma?" She glared at him, but he didn't back down. "What? You threw up your entire breakfast. I want to at least get some juice in you."

The nurse patted her arm, somehow sizing up their family dynamic correctly when she agreed "I'll be right back with some juice."

Emma tackled the paperwork to avoid showing her annoyance with Jaxson's insistence on monitoring every calorie that entered her body. As she had promised herself, she refused to get upset by the men's hovering because it was infinitely better than how separated they had become when they had first moved to California.

The paperwork was routine until she dug deep enough to hit a questionnaire wanting to gather the medical history of the unborn child's father. She assumed it was to help with the screening for possible hereditary or genetic health problems, but the simple dilemma of not knowing which of her lovers had actually fathered her child brought unexpected tears to her eyes. Her father's words sprung forward, shaming her before she could consciously reject them.

Chase leaned closer. "You need some help, baby?"

Emma shot to her feet to avoid showing Chase what had her stumped. "I've completed all I need to. I'm going to take these back up to the nurse." She almost sprinted towards the opening to their small waiting room.

"Freeze." Jaxson's order had her screeching to a halt. "What's wrong?" he prodded her.

Still facing away from the men, she could have tried to lie that nothing was wrong but refused to hide things from them again so soon after promising not to.

"The rest of the paperwork is about the baby's father. Since I honestly don't know which of you is the father, and more importantly I don't care, I was going to just take the packet back up to the nurse," she answered with the most even voice she could muster.

The men paused long enough that she was about to proceed to the glass window when Jaxson spoke. "Bring it back. Let's look at it together."

Taking a calming breath, she turned towards the men. An awkward silence fell between them as both men leaned over her lap to review the pages of health history questions.

She was grateful when Chase spoke. "I'll go get another set of these forms. We'll both fill them out."

"Good idea," Jaxson added quietly.

It took another ten minutes to finish the questionnaires. When they were complete, Emma met the nurse waiting outside the entrance of the exclusive waiting area.

"Ah good. I'll take these. We have a room ready for you in the back."

"Okay, let me just go back and tell the guys…" Jaxson's arm around her waist cut her off.

"No need. We're coming back with you."

Emma should have expected this, but she'd truly been naive enough to think the men intended to stay seated in the waiting room, waiting for her.

"But, I'm sure he's going to want to examine me. Maybe the nurse can come get you when the appointment is ending and we are just talking."

Chase grinned a devilish smile. "Do you really think that lame excuse is going to work with us? I mean come on," he teased.

Emma looked back and forth between her lovers and knew there was no point in arguing. Their minds were made up.

"Fine. Let's go," she relented.

She'd been to visit doctors many times in her life, but this visit continued to progress unlike any other she'd had in the past, starting with the complete void of any other patients or even medical personnel for that matter.

They were ushered into a room that looked like a strange mix of traditional examination room to the right and a living room with a couch, several cushioned chairs and two end tables to the left. An attractive man in his fifties looked up from the iPad in his lap, turning his chair to face the door. He took off his reading glasses and stood tall, walking towards them with a hand offered towards Emma.

"Miss Fischer, it's wonderful to meet you." Only when he'd made eye contact with her, smiling kindly, did he turn to Jaxson, shaking hands as he introduced himself. "Mr. Davidson, I'm Dr. Tipton." He then turned to Chase and shook his hand as well. "Mr. Cartwright. Why don't you all join me over in the sitting area first so we can talk through Miss Fischer's medical history together before we get down to business."

Emma liked the doctor instantly. She'd intentionally chosen women doctors in the past, worried she'd feel awkward with a male doctor, but she appreciated Dr. Tipton's easy acceptance, at least outwardly, of their unusual relationship.

Once seated, the doctor asked the question of the hour. "So, what brings you here today?"

Jaxson had made the appointment. Emma had assumed he'd already covered the basics of their situation already. She looked to her Dom, uncertain. He reached to hold her hand before answering the doctor.

"We got your contact information as a referral from our good friends Cash and Samantha Carter."

The smile on the doctor's face broadened. "How is the beautiful Natasha doing?"

"Fine. Healthy. Still not sleeping through the night."

"Yes, well, these things can take some time." The doctor paused, waiting for Jaxson to continue.

"I called Cash because I wanted to find a doctor we can trust with our unique situation."

"You've come to the right place. Like many of my other patients, Mr. and Mrs. Carter received what I call my VIP service, offered to clients who are in need of additional privacy based on their occupations or simply their last name."

Jaxson started an interrogation. "Exactly how do you guarantee confidentiality?"

The kind doctor didn't seem upset at Jaxson's challenging tone. "You've already seen the beginning of how we differ from most of my peers. From your anticipated arrival and security escort through secured spaces to the private waiting rooms, to making sure patients never accidentally bump into each other… we make every effort to maintain your privacy. All of my nurses have worked for me for years. They have signed strict confidentiality clauses and legal non-disclosure agreements to ensure they never share the private information about our patients. This is over and above the normal HIPAA laws guaranteeing confidentiality. In other words, we recognize that many of our clients have more to protect than just their family medical history."

Jaxson nodded, seeming satisfied with the doctor's answers. He glanced to his right at Emma and Chase quickly before launching into a new question. "How familiar are you with our relationship?"

Dr. Tipton smiled as he answered. "I'd prefer you fill me in yourself. I've been at this long enough to know how much the press and social media can skew the truth. I tend not to believe half of what I read. All I ask is you are honest with me and give me all of the information I need to make informed decisions about Ms. Fischer's health."

If she hadn't already made up her mind she liked the doctor, his perfect answer would have sealed the deal. Jaxson proceeded, clearly satisfied with the doctor's answer as well.

"Chase, Emma, and I form a romantic trio. We live together and plan to spend the rest of our lives together. If it were legal, we would have already bound ourselves to each other in marriage. Unfortunately, that's not possible, and while I wish it were, it's irrelevant to the current situation."

"Which is?"

"Emma is pregnant."

Dr. Tipton turned her way again. "That's wonderful news. Congratulations to you all. Do you mind me asking a few questions?"

She liked that his question was directed at her, the patient, not the men. "Of course."

"Do you know for sure who the father of the child is?"

"No, sir. It could equally be either Jaxson or Chase."

"Okay, that's not a problem. I guess the bigger question is do you want to know who the father is?"

All three of them answered in unison, "No."

"Well okay then," the older man chuckled. "I'm sure you realize that with the visual differences between the men, it is likely you will be able to tell once the baby is born anyway, right?"

"Well, sure, but it doesn't matter to us at all." It was Chase's turn to answer that time.

The doctor glanced down at the pile of paperwork the nurse had left with him. "That will work as long as I don't see anything concerning in either of your medical histories that might have an impact on the pregnancy or the post-natal care of your child." He spent a few minutes looking over the paperwork before adding, "I see that heart disease runs in your family, Mr. Cartwright."

The news alarmed Emma. She turned to her lover, concerned. Chase grinned. "Don't look at me like that. I'm not dying here."

Jaxson groused, "No, but I've always worried about you knowing your father died of a heart attack at forty-two."

Emma felt like a total loser. She'd always known Chase's father had passed away years before, but she'd never bothered to ask the background of how that happened. She felt terrible.

"I'm so sorry. I should have known."

"How? I don't talk about it."

The doctor interrupted, "While that may be important down the road, this shouldn't make any difference with the pregnancy. My only caution to you is you might want to consult a lawyer with your unique scenario. I'm guessing you will not want to leave the father slot empty on the birth certificate. Establishing legal parental rights with one of you will be in both Ms. Fischer and your child's best interest."

Emma hadn't even started to worry about that hurdle yet. She was relieved when Jaxson replied, "I've been in contact with our lawyer to get his recommendation. He has practiced in both California and the District of Columbia, the two locations we would expect to deliver in. I'm confident he'll be able to guide us to the proper legal stance."

The doctor smiled widely. "It sounds like you've covered your bases. Just let me know if you decide you'd like to determine biological paternity prior to the delivery for purposes of the birth certificate. There are non-invasive tests we can administer."

Chase and Jaxson shared an uncomfortable staring contest until Chase finally assured the physician, "We'll let you know if we change our minds."

"Very well."

Emma was relieved until he turned and directed his next question to her.

"So how far along are you, young lady?"

"I'm not entirely sure," she answered truthfully.

The doctor made some notes on the iPad on his lap before asking, "Were you trying to get pregnant? Have you been on birth control in the last twelve months?"

Those were two different questions. "We weren't trying to get pregnant. It was a surprise."

"I see, well, that happens. What birth control were you on when you conceived, and when did you become aware you were pregnant?"

Jaxson answered for her. "She's been on the Depo-Provera shot, but then found out about the baby on Valentine's Day."

"Hmm, that was almost two months ago. Have you been to see another OBGYN in the meantime?"

"Just once." She felt Chase and Jaxson's incriminating stares as she answered. "I had an appointment with my doctor for my next shot on Valentine's Day when they discovered I was already pregnant."

"I see. So they performed a pregnancy test prior to administering the shot?"

"Exactly," Emma admitted.

She could tell Dr. Tipton was choosing his words carefully as he continued. "What was the cadence your physician had you on for your injections?"

Emma looked the kind doctor in his eyes as she answered, "Normally every twelve weeks."

"Interesting. The effectiveness of Depo at that interval is over 99%." He smiled as he asked the million-dollar question. "So you are either in that one percent or perhaps there was an interruption in your normal twelve-week cycle?"

She felt three pairs of eyes on her, waiting for her answer. The longer she took to speak, the more guilt she felt. "I missed my appointment in January. The Valentine's Day appointment was the make-up visit," she finally answered softly.

Emma felt the hand resting on her right thigh squeezing as Jaxson internalized her words and their implication. Why couldn't the damn doctor move on and just ask his next question?

Unable to stand the silence anymore, Emma whispered a soft, "I'm sorry." Her gaze dropped to her lap, unable to look any of the three men in the eye.

"So, you missed your appointment in January so you could go

visit Samantha and the baby in Colorado?" When Jaxson spoke, it wasn't in anger, but the question was delivered in the ice-cold tone she'd heard him use in business meetings with other alpha men. In that context, his voice had a way of melting her core, watching her alpha Dom control everyone and everything in his way. Him using that tone today... with her... when she was already feeling vulnerable... it hurt. Her hands in her lap swam through the tears pricking at her eyes.

"Answer me, young lady."

"Jax, don't do this. It doesn't matter how it happened," Chase defended her as he wrapped an arm around her shoulders supportively.

Jaxson didn't back down. "Eyes."

Oh God, why was he doing this here... now... in front of the doctor?

Because you didn't tell him the truth at any point over the last five days when you could have done it privately.

Relief was all she felt when she looked into her lover's gorgeous green eyes. Despite his clear displeasure at her actions, she could still see his love for her pouring from him.

"You're just full of secrets lately, aren't you, baby?"

Sweet relief came when he called her his baby. "I wanted to tell you," she admitted.

"And yet, you didn't."

"I told you now."

"A small consolation I'll take into consideration." Jaxson's eyes didn't leave hers as he addressed the doctor sitting across from them. "Dr. Tipton, there is another matter we need to discuss with you."

Oh no. He wouldn't.

"Of course. How can I help?" the elder man prompted.

Jaxson's lips curved up slightly, telling her that this conversation was part of her punishment for hiding the truth. "Are you familiar with the BDSM lifestyle?"

"I am. In fact, I have a few other clients that practice the lifestyle as well." Emma noted the doctor didn't name names, even though everyone in the room knew that at least one of those clients was Jonah and Samantha Carter. "Do you have specific questions I can answer for you?" he prompted.

Jaxson spoke for the trio. "Emma and the baby's safety is our top priority. I'm interested to know what aspects of the lifestyle should be put on hold during her pregnancy and which activities, specifically disciplinary sessions, can remain an option until after the baby is born."

Emma wanted to crawl under the long coffee table in front of the couch they were seated on. Her Dom was doing an excellent job of making her squirm in her seat. He knew damn well talking about punishments always did that to her. As much as she hated real discipline sessions, there was no denying not all parts of her body agreed. She was humiliated realizing the doctor would surely see the proof of her sudden arousal when she bared herself for the upcoming examination. The growing grin on Jaxson's face told her he knew that too.

"As a basic rule, most of the tamer portions of the lifestyle can remain safely unchanged throughout the pregnancy. Simple spankings, light bondage of wrists and ankles... anything that might be considered BDSM light is fine. Things to avoid are severe punishments or situations that will cause increased blood pressure. It goes without saying that at no time should any pressure of any kind, even light, be concentrated in the area of the baby. No breaking of the skin anywhere or activities considered on the advanced end of the BDSM lifestyle. Things like breath, blood, knife, or heavy impact play must wait until after Ms. Fischer recovers from her delivery."

Jaxson finally looked away from Emma to address the doctor. "It sounds like you've done your homework on the lifestyle."

Dr. Tipton's smile grew. "I've been known to dive into topics I would find it helpful to research for my rather specialized practice."

Jaxson reached into the back pocket of his jeans, pulling out his wallet. He took a black business card out that was blank on the front. On the back, Emma knew he had printed his cell phone. Nothing else.

"You might have heard we are opening a club here in Beverly Hills. We might have a more private area, one where you might like to do some research. That's my private number. Give me a call in a few weeks after we open if you'd like a tour."

The doctor got up to take the card. "Thanks. That sounds interesting and exactly like the kind of research my wife and I might be interested in checking out together."

Chase jumped into the conversation with his own cheery question. "What about sex?" He paused, glancing to his right at Emma, then Jaxson. "Things sometimes get a bit... vigorous between us. Can we hurt the baby having sex?"

"Normally I would say absolutely not, but as things can get a bit more intense in the BDSM lifestyle, my only caution is to use common sense. Intercourse is fine up until the final few weeks of pregnancy when the pressure of the baby may make it uncomfortable for the mother."

Emma could feel her cheeks turning a rosy red at the blunt talk in front of basically a stranger. And she had thought the actual exam would be the most embarrassing part of the doctor's visit. She didn't think she could be more mortified.

She was wrong.

"What about anal sex? Is that okay too?" Chase asked.

"With plenty of lubrication, I don't see that as a problem. Particularly if it's an activity that is within your normal lifestyle," Doctor Tipton answered with a smile playing on his lips, showing he was more than comfortable talking about personal sexual topics with his patients.

Emma groaned out loud when Jaxson asked her a pointed

question. "It definitely is part of your daily life, isn't it baby?" He squeezed her right thigh suggestively.

When it became clear no one in the room would say anything else until she answered her Dom, she squeaked out a quiet, "Yes, Sir."

Emma sighed with relief when the doctor finally turned the discussion back to her pregnancy.

"Based on the uncertainty of your date of conception, but knowing it could be as early as mid-December, I'd like to perform your first ultrasound today. It will help us pinpoint a bit better your due date. I'll have my nurse come in and draw blood and we'll do a full work-up on you. I don't suppose you're on prenatal vitamins?"

Emma answered with a simple, "No, sir."

"That's alright. Ideally you would have started on them before conception, but as this was a bit of a surprise, I'll prescribe some today. Take one daily. Have you had any physical symptoms?"

Again, Chase was happy to provide the doctor with a detailed report. "She's been puking every day. We've stopped having her around greasy food that seems to set her off, but we're worried she's not getting enough calories or nutrients, aren't we Jax?"

"Yes, we'd love it if you had dietary recommendations. Well, any recommendations on how to take care of her, really."

"For crying out loud, I'm not a puppy!"

"No, you're a hundred times more important than a puppy." Jaxson answered.

The doctor got up and crossed to the bookshelf next to the door. He took down a copy of a thick paperback book. He brought it over to hand to Jaxson. "This is one of the best resources on the market. It will walk you through everything on your journey from week to week, even the first few months post-delivery. I'd suggest you all read up and then ask any questions you still have on your next visit."

Jaxson seemed almost reluctant to take the thick book on

125

pregnancy, but he finally reached out to take it from the doctor, handing it as if it were a hot potato over to Chase who gladly held it.

"Okay, we just have one more question before we can move to the other side of the suite and begin your exam, young lady. I always ask parents if they'd like to know the sex of their baby. It's early in your pregnancy and there is a good chance I won't be able to tell today, but I'd like to know if we are sharing that information with you."

The men looked at Emma, letting her make the final call. "We've decided we don't want to know the sex of the baby before he or she is born."

"Fair enough. Many parents make that choice." He stood and placed his hands in the pockets of the white doctor's coat he wore over his dress clothes. "Are you ready to get your first peek at your baby?"

Emma placed her hand on her tummy, rubbing the little peanut too small to even show yet. Truthfully, she couldn't wait to see the baby. It might help make it all seem more real.

"Yes, sir."

"Okay, I'll leave you three alone while I run out to arrange your blood work. I'll be back in about five minutes. Take everything off from the waist down. Place the drape over your lap and take a seat at the end of the examination table."

The friendly doctor wasn't out of the room for two seconds before the men attacked Emma from both sides. She couldn't help but giggle.

"You guys, this isn't the time or the place for this! He'll be back in just a few minutes."

Jaxson kissed her neck as Chase groped her tender boobs through her top. "We could lock the door," Jax suggested.

"Oh for crying out loud, we are at the doctor, not Black Light. Don't you think he'll be able to tell we just had sex when he examines me?" she protested.

Chase looked up mischievously. "Why do you think we want to do it? You're extra adorable when you get embarrassed."

"Evil. That's what you are." She slapped both men away from her. They chuckled but let her push to her feet. Emma hustled to the padded exam table. A fitted white sheet covered the long table where disposable paper would be in most offices.

Emma picked up the soft folded sheet, noting it too was fabric and not scratchy paper — more of the VIP upgrades.

When she turned around her men were staring at her from the couch she'd just left. They had each crossed their arms, waiting for the show she was about to put on.

"You two should be ashamed of yourselves. There is nothing sexual about going to see a doctor."

"I'd have thought you would have realized that we have a gift." Jaxson grinned, letting his playful side come out. "We can turn anything sexual."

Chase grinned proudly, agreeing with their Dom. "I'm getting a boner just thinking about watching you put your feet in the stirrups. I think we're going to need to test out the new medical table back at the mansion when we get home."

Emma tried to stop her brain from picturing that scene, but it was too late. Playing doctor at Black Light in D.C. had been one of their favorite role-plays. It wasn't fair they were reminding her of that just as she had to strip for an exam by a near stranger.

Trying to stay focused, she turned to face away from the men and started taking off her shoes and socks before moving on to the slacks and panties she'd worn. She was well aware she was currently mooning the guys, but all things considered, it was a small thing.

She had just reached for the sheet at the end of the table when she felt four hands on her bared skin, palming her tummy, grazing her embarrassingly wet pussy, reaching under her shirt to squeeze her tender breasts through her bra. It felt so naughty sneaking in a sexual romp in the middle of a medical visit.

Her brain fought for control over her body's reaction, but she was a true sexual submissive. Her Doms were mastering her and it was so easy to turn herself over to them as she had hundreds of times before. The feel of a hard erection pressed against her left hip excited her almost as much as the thought of getting caught red-handed by the doctor.

"I wish we had time to do this right," Jaxson growled against her ear, "but I'll have to settle with watching you come and making sure the doctor has proof of just how well Chase and I take care of our girl when he examines you."

His words were accompanied with several fingers being thrust in her snatch. Different fingers pinched her swollen clit at exactly the same time what felt like a thumb was shoved in her ass.

It took less than a minute of their vigorous ministrations accompanied by filthy encouragement against her ear for Emma to go off like a firecracker. She collapsed like a wet noodle against her men, letting the wave of ecstasy wash over her, leaving her feeling a strange mix of satiated and embarrassed.

"Ah, I see you three got a bit distracted while I was out of the room. Would you like me to give you a few more minutes or are you about ready for us to start Ms. Fischer's examination?"

Emma wanted to crawl under the examination table and never come out. The men stepped back just enough to give the good doctor a front row seat as they extricated themselves from her body's cavities.

As if they had choreographed the scene ahead of time, both men leaned in to place platonic kisses on each of her cheeks as they had a thousand times before. A playful swat to her bare ass landed just as Jaxson answered, "No, I think the next round can wait until after you're finished with the exam."

"Very good. Let's get Ms. Fischer up on the exam table then, shall we? And you gentlemen can use the sink in the corner if you need to wash up."

It was the feel of the drop of wetness running down her inner thigh as she walked the few steps to the examination table when Emma lost the last remnants of embarrassment. She could choose to be mortified, but why? She was the luckiest woman on the planet. Loved by two amazing men who would do anything for her.

As she'd learned, *anything* included staking their claim on her body whenever and wherever they wanted, and today that meant in front of her newest doctor.

CHAPTER TEN ~ CHASE

Chase stood as close to the exam table as he could. Jaxson had taken up guard on the opposite side of their girl while the doctor stood at the end facing Emma.

"I'll be starting with a simple physical examination, then we'll perform the ultrasound. I prefer to perform a transvaginal ultrasound on my new mothers early in their pregnancy, just to make sure everything, not just the baby, is doing well in there."

"Um, okay," Emma answered, sounding as unsure of what that was as Chase.

The men tried to stay out of the way as the doctor called in his nurse to assist with recording Emma's vitals. Blood pressure. Checked. Eyes, ears, and throat. Checked. Heart rate and pulse oxygen level. Checked.

They got a nice view of her bare ass again as the doctor asked Emma to accompany him to the digital scale where he first checked her height against the measurement pole.

"Five feet, six inches," he exclaimed out-loud for the nurse to record.

As the doctor turned on the digital scale, Jaxson moved into action, stepping up close to Emma. "You've lost weight," he declared, displeasure in his voice as he saw her weight.

Before she could defend herself, Dr. Tipton came to her aide. "Many women lose weight in the first trimester as they battle morning sickness. Mr. Cartwright shared that she has been having troubling keeping food down." The doctor turned to Emma and asked, "Would you say you are feeling better or worse as the last few weeks went past?"

"Definitely worse. I used to just feel queasy but wouldn't actually get sick. Now I get sick at least once a day, sometimes more."

"Okay, it's probably nothing. Just normal pregnancy symptoms, but I'll want to watch this and if it continues, we'll test you for hyperemesis gravidarum."

"Excuse me?" Jaxson asked.

"It is a form of severe sickness that a small percentage of mothers experience. The good news is it doesn't usually impact the pregnancy directly. But it can lead to not getting enough nutrients and certainly puts the mother in danger of dehydration. I have a brochure on things you can do to battle nausea I'll give you to read at your leisure, and there is a chapter on this topic in the book I gave you. I find eating bland foods, frequently and in small quantities, while drinking as much water as you can is the best way to battle it."

Chase pulled out his phone and started tapping out notes. He didn't want to forget any of the important points they were learning. He'd be personally making sure Emma and the baby were getting all of the things they needed to be as healthy as possible.

"Are we ready to take a peek and find out just when we might be expecting the newest member of your family?"

Chase's heart swelled at the doctor's kind words. They had encountered so many judgmental people in the time they'd been together. It was a relief to have a doctor who not only accepted their unique trio, but who was doing all he could to support their complicated family situation.

"Gentlemen, can you help your lady back up on to the table? You can raise the end so she's at a small incline. I'll need her bottom at the end of the table and her feet in the stirrups."

Chase adored the pink blush that had returned to Emma's lovely face as they helped her into the vulnerable position. She attempted to drape the sheet over her lower half, but Jaxson confiscated it with a small shake of his head. Chase couldn't hold in his grin at Emma's pout.

Catching his eye, Jaxson nodded down towards their submissive as he took Emma's right hand in his own hand. Chase mirrored his Dom, holding Emma's left hand and linking the three of them intimately as the doctor took a seat on the rolling stool between Emma's open legs at the end of the examination table.

Chase suspected the doctor was playing along with the men, understanding and supporting their natural dominance over their submissive in small ways.

"I'll be performing an internal vaginal exam next and then I'll perform the transvaginal ultrasound."

Emma's gurgled embarrassment went straight to Chase's already hard cock. He tried his best to remember they were here for medical reasons, not sexual, but the sheer fact the trio's vigorous sex romps had led to the impregnation of their lovely submissive was ever present. Emma's body would soon be swelling with their child, and the thought filled him with obscene masculine pride he suspected linked him directly back to cavemen. His feminist, equality-loving self was at war with this new pro-patriarchy version of himself. One glance at Jaxson's repositioning of his masculine package through his slacks told him he wasn't the only one struggling to behave with propriety.

"When was your last pap-smear?"

"Last summer."

"Good." The doctor kept talking as he picked up the speculum from the rolling tray the nurse had supplied before she had quietly left the exam room. "This may be a bit cold going in, young lady."

Chase chose to watch Emma's face as the doctor inserted the medical device where his fingers had been just moments before. She closed her eyes. Had they been playing, he'd have asked her to open them so he could watch the emotions playing in her expressive violet eyes. The exam took several minutes with the doctor working in silence.

Emma exhaled with relief when the doctor removed the speculum.

"Everything is looking good so far." He pulled the latex glove off his right hand and wheeled to his left over to a machine in the corner of the room. The doctor unlocked a break on the wheel and started to pull the large machine with a huge flat-screen monitor and dozens of buttons and levers over to the examination table near Emma's raised feet.

The older man lifted what looked like a long, narrow dildo covered with a thin piece of plastic. The whole wand had a cord that attached it to the machine.

"As this is your first child, I want to explain what is about to happen. In the future, I'll perform a more traditional ultrasound on your visits to check on the baby's development. But today, I'll be inserting this wand into your vaginal canal. I'll be taking a look at your cervix, uterus, ovaries, fallopian tubes, and even bladder in addition to the baby, of course. I'll be able to glean a lot of information about how far along you are by measuring the size of the embryo as well as the thickness of the placenta. And this way, we will all breathe a bit easier knowing everything is in perfect working order in there for growing that baby of yours. Do you have any questions before we begin?"

The question was directed at Emma who shook her head no as

Jaxson spoke up. "Will the test be painful for her or hurt the baby?"

The doctor smiled. "Not at all. It shouldn't feel any more uncomfortable than vigorous sex and your baby is tiny at this point so I'm sure he or she won't mind sharing their space for a little bit."

Chase moved Emma's hand to his left and reached out with his right to stroke her thick hair. She loved when the men played with her hair. To be fair, she loved when they yanked it hard while they fucked her too, but that would come later.

"You're doing great, baby. I'm so proud of you."

"I'm just laying here," she deadpanned.

"Yes, but you're doing it beautifully."

"Okay, it's going in," the doctor warned.

Chase loved when Emma locked her gaze on him as he leaned over her. He smiled supportively, stroking her hair gently as the doctor worked in silence.

The first few minutes of silence were only broken by the occasional soft click of the machine he suspected was taking pictures of Emma's womb. When he finally broke his gaze with Emma to look up, he was fascinated to see the ultrasound picture of her on the large screen. He couldn't make heads or tails of anything he saw, but the doctor seemed engrossed in the exam, only uttering the occasional 'um' or 'oh.' It wasn't until he spoke his first word, "Interesting…" that the trio all looked his way expectantly.

Jaxson asked what they were all thinking. "Is there a problem, doctor?"

"A problem? No. No problem. I just need a few more minutes and I'll be happy to share what I'm finding with you."

Nothing on the screen looked even remotely like a baby to Chase. They all remained silent, letting the doctor do his work.

A full ten minutes went by before the doctor paused his

examination, finally looking up at the trio. "So, I have what I think will be a couple surprises for you."

Jaxson looked worried as he said, "I sure as hell hope they are good surprises."

The doctor smiled kindly. "Well, I think so, but we'll have to see what you all think. First, you are a bit farther along than you thought, Ms. Fischer. By my calculation, you are just over fifteen weeks pregnant which puts you already in your second trimester."

"What? How the hell?" Jaxson demanded.

"The calculation is showing you conceived somewhere between December twenty-eighth and January third. Did you have an extra fun New Year's Eve?"

Chase's mind raced to the NYE party they had attended at Black Light. As the threesome shared heated glances, he knew they were all remembering the epic night they'd had.

"You might say that." He grinned. "It was certainly one to remember."

"It looks like you'll have a souvenir to remind you of the fun you had since that night was in the heart of Ms. Fischer's fertile time based on my calculation."

"But wait. That means I would have gotten pregnant even if I hadn't missed my mid-January appointment?"

"It looks that way. Of course, this isn't an exact science. I could be off by a week or two. I'll check you again the next time you come in and we'll know more. But as of right now, I'm setting your due date as September twenty-second."

"September? That's only... a bit more than five months away." Jaxson was panicking. Chase could see it in his eyes.

"Hey, look at me." It was Chase's turn to play Dom. "It's gonna be fine. We have plenty of time." He loved the squeeze Emma gave his hand.

"What is the other surprise? You said you had a couple?" Emma asked, her forehead furrowed with concern.

The doctor got a bit more serious. "Perhaps you gentlemen might like to take a seat?"

"What the fuck? You promised it wasn't bad news!" Jaxson yelled, agitated.

The doctor refused to be intimidated, smiling instead as he calmly replied, "Nothing is wrong. I just find that many fathers feel a bit overwhelmed when I tell them they are about to have twins."

There was a sudden humming in Chase's ears. Had he heard the man correctly?

"Wait. Twins? As in two babies?" Emma squeaked.

"Yes. I'm certain. In fact, I was able to determine that each baby is in its own separate amniotic sac. They each have their own placenta and supporting structures. That means that you will be having…"

"Fraternal twins," Emma answered ahead of him.

"Most likely. Depending on when the egg split, it is still possible that they are identical, but unlikely."

Chase's heart rate had spiked. He was beginning to wish he'd taken the doctor's advice and taken a seat. One look at Jaxson and he knew his Dom felt the same way.

"Twins." Jaxson uttered randomly to the room, trying the word on for size.

"Twins," the doctor reassured them more forcefully.

"Two." Jaxson was staring off into the distance.

The doctor chuckled. "Like I warned, maybe you'd feel better taking a seat for a few minutes until the news sinks in."

"How did this happen?" Jaxson had turned pale. Chase was trying not to freak out at the news too, but seeing his Dom looking so lost helped Chase move into action. Only after he released Emma's hand did he realize how hard she'd been squeezing him. He rushed around the end of the exam table to hug Jaxson from behind.

"Hey, this is good news," he assured his lover.

"Since when is fucking up two kids instead of one good news?" Jaxson sounded almost manic.

"No one is going to be fucking up the kids. You're going to be an awesome father."

Jaxson's scoffing laugh only made Chase feel worse. It was Emma's calm voice that finally seemed to get through to their Dom. "Jaxson Davidson, you are going to be a wonderful father. Will you please stop comparing yourself to your father? You are nothing like him. I've seen you with kids in general and Natasha, specifically. Your face just lights up when you hold her."

"That's because I could give her back to her mother after a few minutes."

"Yeah, well then I guess we are all lucky there are three of us. Surely between the three of us, we'll be able to handle two babies," Chase reassured him.

"Would you feel better if I show you the first pictures of your babies?" the forgotten doctor interjected

"I'd love to." Emma answered for them. "I've been calling him or her peanut. I guess I'll need to come up with another nickname for the second baby."

"Well, they are a bit bigger than peanuts already. They are each a bit bigger than a lemon." He'd begun to move the wand inside Emma again, stopping to display an image that was unmistakably a baby on the screen. "This is baby A. I'm able to confirm everything looks perfectly healthy so far with this baby. You can even count five fingers on that hand right there."

He had to move the wand a bit more to display a second image on the screen.

"This is baby B. He or she is a bit more hidden, but so far everything looks perfectly normal. But..." He paused, waiting for the trio to look away from the screen and back at him. "There is nothing to worry about, but I like to treat all multiple births as higher risk. That means I'm going to want to see Ms. Fischer a bit more frequently. I want to keep a close eye on your morning sickness and make sure we keep you hydrated. I know I gave you the prescription for the vitamins, but they are more important than ever now that you are eating for three."

"I need to sit down." Jaxson had started to back into Chase who helped him to a nearby chair.

The doctor kept talking to Emma. "If you throw up within two hours of taking the vitamin, I'd like you to take a replacement. We need to keep the nutrients in you. If you find you're throwing up more frequently, call immediately. I might not be able to stop the sick feeling, but I can setup IV feedings to ensure you are staying hydrated."

"Yes, sir," Emma answered quietly.

"Do you have any questions for me?" the doctor asked as he pulled the wand from Emma and stood, pushing the machine away from the exam table.

Chase looked down at Jaxson. He knew they needed to leave and get some fresh air.

"I'm sure we'll come up with a million questions later, but right now, I think we just need to let the news sink in. When do you need to see Emma again?"

"I'd like you back in a week."

"A week? You sure everything is okay?" she asked.

"Just fine, young lady. I told you, this is a VIP service. I'm pretty sure your men are going to want me to keep an extra close eye on you and your babies. We'll be watching your progress closely, that way if anything does develop, we'll know about it right away and be able to take action."

"Thank you," Jaxson said softly. "Yes, you're right. That is exactly what we want. I don't care what it costs."

"Like I said. VIP service." The doctor grinned.

Chase suspected the bastard was making seven figures a year catering to the rich and famous of Southern California, but since he was putting the health of his family in the guy's hands, who was he to complain?

He moved to shake the doctor's hand. "Thanks again, Dr. Tipton. Should we make the appointment with your nurse?"

"Yes, and make sure she gives you one of my business cards. It has my home and mobile number on it. Call me anytime. Day or night."

"Let me guess. It goes with the VIP service?"

"You got it. If I don't answer, it's because I'm with another patient or in labor and delivery. My calls roll to my service twenty-four seven answering service and they'll get me the message the minute I'm available."

The doctor helped Emma sit up before turning to shake hands with the men. "Congratulations again on your happy news. I look forward to meeting those two babies in September."

After the door closed with his departure, the trio remained frozen, each lost in their own thoughts until Chase couldn't stand it anymore.

"That was unexpected."

"Understatement of the year," Jaxson mumbled.

Emma looked like she was about to cry. Chase went to her, needing to hold her... to touch her... the mother of his children. She fell into his arms from her sitting position at the end of the exam table.

When he felt her tears, he comforted her. "Hey, what's this? This was all good news, baby."

"My father is going to be doubly upset when he finds out."

"He just needs a bit more time. We'll let him cool off for a few weeks, then we'll fly to Wisconsin after the clubs open and get everything sorted out."

"You promise?"

"Of course. As long as Dr. Tipton says it's safe for you to travel."

He felt her relax in his arms, and glanced at Jaxson still seated in the chair a few feet away. Chase knew it was going to be a lot harder to help Jaxson come to terms with the news. He'd just started to not freak out about one baby. Lucky for them, he had figured out one sure-fire way to get their Dom to calm down over the years they'd been together.

Sex.

Chase moved from hugging Emma to massaging her. He moved his hands under her top to unsnap her bra.

"Hey, what are you..." Emma couldn't finish her question. He claimed her mouth in an open mouth kiss, thrusting his tongue into her mouth to dominate her as he let his hands fall to her bare thighs, pulling her legs wider.

They eventually had to come up for air. Chase was disappointed Jaxson still sat on the sidelines, but at least his frown had been replaced by an unreadable glare. If the kiss hadn't enticed Jax, he'd have to take things to the next level.

Chase stepped back, leaning down to grab Emma's ankles, spreading her legs wide until each foot was settled into the padded stirrup cups. His earlier hard-on had returned with a vengeance. As he pulled her legs up and out, Emma had to lie back onto the reclining table to keep her balance.

He fell to one knee on the now vacant stool before her, leaning forward to drag his tongue through Emma's wet folds, spending extra time on the nubbin of nerves that caused her to buck her ass off the table. Being an excellent multi-tasker, Chase was able to eat her out while reaching towards Jaxson with his left hand, his invitation to join them.

It wasn't until Chase stood to unbuckle his own pants and pull his cock out that Jaxson finally rose to his feet. The uncertainty in his lover's eyes had been replaced by vulnerable desire. Chase grasped his manhood, lightly stroking it to nurse the growing desire to come. The movement caught Jaxson's attention, and before the men were close enough to touch, Jaxson moved his attention lower to watch Chase squeezing his own dick.

Jaxson reached out to push Chase's hand away, taking over stroking duty just as Chase reciprocated, pulling Jaxson's cock free of his pants in a rush. The men fell into each other's arms, Jaxson claiming his own violent kiss from Chase while jacking each other off until Chase felt his balls tightening.

Chase pulled out of their kiss to grunt, "Gonna come. Need to be inside someone when I do."

He loved the naughty grin on Jaxson's face. "You'd better point that bad boy in Em's direction then."

Chase teased his lover, "Hey, we're going through a lot of changes. Maybe we should give you being on the receiving end a shot."

"You'd better turn around and get ready for my cock, or I might have to deliver my belt instead."

Chase grinned, relieved Jaxson was smiling again. "Yes, Sir."

His heart lurched when he turned towards Emma. Seeing her laid open and bare before him was better than presents under the tree on Christmas morning. The glisten of love in her eyes as she'd watched her men humbled him. She'd lifted her arms above her head, holding onto the edge of the table so she was properly presented for him.

Chase clumsily dragged his fingers through her open pussy to ensure she was still wet for them. Finding a pool of her juices, he lined up and fell into her, filling her in one stroke. He was so turned on he froze, buried in her until the urge to shoot his wad like an untried virgin passed.

Jaxson took advantage of Chase's stillness, spreading his ass cheeks enough to lather his anus with lube from the ultrasound tray. Within seconds, Jaxson's fingers were replaced by the head of his own erection.

The thrust that filled him was swift. The sudden fullness took his breath away. With each pump of Jaxson's cock, Chase came closer to shooting his wad and he hadn't even moved his hips yet. The desperation on Emma's face reminded him he had a job to do as well.

Like a fine-tuned piston, the trio fell into a dirty dance of push and pull, each chasing their happy place. As their Dom, Jaxson got to decide when they could come. Permission came in the form of Jaxson's grunted orgasm buried inside Chase who, in turn, pinched Emma's clit as he rammed into her and shouted, "Now, baby. Come for us."

Watching the mother of their babies come apart in front of him felt better than his own orgasm. The trio collapsed in a heap on top of Emma.

"You're squishing me," she complained.

"Well, we can't have that. Let's get you put back together and then we can take this home for round two."

Chase corrected their dominant. "You mean round three. Round one was in the shower."

The swat across his ass warmed him. "Keep it up and you'll find yourself plugged for the drive home."

Chase could only grin. "Promises, promises."

CHAPTER ELEVEN ~ JAXSON

"*S*he's asleep. We should talk about it." Chase spoke quietly in the back of the Town Car when they were almost back to the rental.

Jaxson stroked Emma's hair softly. She'd laid down across the back seat on the drive. Her feet were in Chase's lap, her head in his own.

And between them laid two tiny babies, safe inside their mother's womb, at least for the moment. But September wasn't nearly far enough away to get ready for the kind of change that he knew was about to rock the trio.

"There's nothing to talk about," he finally answered staring out his window at the Los Angeles traffic to avoid looking at his lover.

"The hell there's not. You're brooding."

"I don't brood," Jaxson defended.

"Ha! Right."

Jaxson turned to pin Chase with a warning glare. "This is not helping."

Chase let his smile slip as he answered. "I can see that. What will help?"

Jaxson looked back out the window as he answered simply with, "Silence."

"Too bad," was Chase's cheery answer. "We got into this by ignoring warning signs. I'm not going back there."

Anger flared. "No, we got into this because birth control failed. We got into this because Emma missed her appointment. If she'd gone in January, they might have detected the babies and we would have had options."

The cheery smile was gone from his lover's face in a heartbeat. In that same heartbeat he felt the crush of guilt press on his chest.

"Are you fucking kidding me? You'd better not be suggesting what I think you are, because if you are, we're going to have major problems."

Jaxson sighed, resigning himself to having the difficult conversation whether he wanted to or not. "I didn't mean that. I would never have wanted her to have an abortion. It's just…"

"Just what? I don't see the problem here. We've talked about having kids in the future. We all fell in love with Natasha when we've been around her, Cash, and Sam. So, it's a little earlier than we had planned, but I thought you wanted to have kids too."

Jaxson would have preferred Chase stay angry with him. It would have been easier to take that than the puppy-dog sad eyes he was getting from his lover now.

He moved his right hand, laying it on top of Chase's left that was resting on Emma's tummy. The small act somehow made him feel a bit better… more connected to his family.

His family.

He'd thought of his lovers as his family for a long time now, but this felt different. Not necessarily bad, just more permanent. But it wasn't the permanence that scared him.

Jaxson did not scare easy. He'd made it big in a cutthroat industry as a top model. He'd forged his own spot in the business world, playing with the rich and powerful. He'd even gone head to head with his formidable father and the senator's political cronies and come out the winner. They hadn't made him so much as flinch.

But fatherhood... twins... infants he would be responsible for? It scared the shit out of him.

"I'm scared." It was a whisper, barely audible. He closed his eyes to avoid making eye contact for fear his submissive would be disappointed in his weakness.

"Eyes." Chase shocked them both with his demand.

Jaxson couldn't help but open his eyes to see what the fuck was going on. The grin on Chase's face just angered him more. "Since when do you give the orders to me?"

Chase squeezed his hand as he replied. "Since you needed me to. Don't worry. I don't want the job full-time, but you don't have to carry the weight of our family's decisions all on your own. We're a team, remember? Where one goes, we all go. So prepared or not, you're coming along for the ride into parenthood. It's okay if you need me to take the lead every now and then until you get your feet under you again."

"It feels weird," Jaxson admitted. He left off the part that it didn't necessarily feel bad.

"I'm a switch. It doesn't feel so weird for me."

"Don't get used to it. I'll pull it together."

"Of course you will. And like I told you, I don't want the job full-time. I'm just suggesting that in this one small area of our lives you don't have to be Superman. Let me carry some of the load for a while. You focus on the clubs and getting the house ready for us. Let the news of the babies sink in slowly. Let me focus on Emma, the babies, and her health. Divide and conquer."

"Divide and conquer," Jaxson parroted, trying the idea on, feeling a bit of the weight lifting almost immediately.

The car came to a stop, and he looked up to find they had arrived in the driveway of the rental house.

He turned to look at Chase. "It might work. Let's get Emma

inside. I need to head back over to the mansion to check in with Maxine, but let's talk about this more tonight, okay?"

Chase looked relieved. "That sounds good. I'll stick with Emma and get her prescription filled and some food and drinks into her as soon as she wakes up from her nap."

"Divide and conquer," Jaxson said again, acknowledging they had already started the plan.

"I'll come around and carry her in. Can you open the front door?" Chase asked.

"Sure."

Chase came to Jaxson's door while he tried to maneuver the sleeping Emma into sitting in his lap. She stirred but was so tired she didn't wake. Not even as Jaxson handed her out to the waiting Chase who scooped her up in his arms, bride style.

She had just snuggled her face into the crook of Chase's neck when a man came running up behind Chase, shouting.

"What's wrong with her? Is she hurt?"

Fuck. Damn. Shit. Piss.

Jaxson exited quickly, stepping in between Robert Fischer and Chase. He had to place both hands on the older man's chest to hold him back. Jax had his back to his lover, but it didn't stop him from issuing instructions. "Go. Take her inside. I've got this."

He knew Chase had left because Robert was struggling to follow them. Jaxson had to use all of his strength to subdue Emma's father.

"Let me go, dammit! I need to see my daughter." The older man's voice cracked with emotion.

"You'll see her after you settle down."

"I'll settle down when you tell me her wedding date."

Double Fuck. Damn. Shit. Piss.

"Let's go grab a cup of coffee and talk about this like men."

"Not until I talk to Emma. I need to make sure she's okay."

"Are you fucking kidding me? You can be angry at me about

not marrying her, but you'd better not insinuate that she's not safe with Chase and me."

"Physically safe, sure. I'm talking about emotionally. She sounded so upset when we spoke yesterday."

"She was upset because you gave her shit instead of being happy for her."

The men stood in silence as the driver pulled the Town Car out and drove away down the street. At least the older man had stopped fighting to get past him.

Jax didn't know how he was going to get through to Robert Fischer. He didn't want there to be a wedge between Emma and her family any more than he wanted to disappoint the man he genuinely loved as a father figure in his life.

It was a long shot, but he had an idea. "Come with me. I want to show you something."

"I want to…"

"She fell asleep in the car. She gets tired easily these days. Let her rest. We won't be gone long. You can see her when we get back."

Robert waffled before reluctantly agreeing. "Fine. But just for a little bit."

Jaxson pulled his key ring from his pants pocket and nodded to the Audi parked in front of the garage. "We'll take my new car."

The ten-minute drive felt like it took an hour. The uncomfortable silence between the men stretched out until Jaxson couldn't wait to arrive. He pulled his keycard out that opened the private security gate they'd installed. In the near future, they would have guards checking IDs of all arrivals and departures. Until then, only those with security access could open the gate.

He drove down the winding tree lined driveway that helped hide the estate from passersby on the street. He normally took the two-lane main drive all the way to the front door of Runway, but today he turned left about a hundred feet early, taking the smaller one-lane through the thick trees, past a brand new twenty-car parking lot they'd installed where Black Light VIPs would park away from prying eyes.

He had kept the keycard out, hoping he'd need it again. He was relieved to find the security contractor had installed the newest security gate that would protect the private entrance to the pool house.

"What's with all the security? You have enemies after you?" Robert quipped, obviously concerned for his daughter's safety.

"Not really. Just a bunch of kooks out there and I want to make sure I can keep my family safe."

That seemed to satisfy Emma's father at least for a moment.

Jaxson pulled up to the attached garage that faced the driveway. The front of the pool house actually faced the estate with its walk out patios, fire pit, and private gardens that would separate them from the main mansion. He used his automatic garage-door opener to pull into the garage, closing the door behind them and turning off the engine.

They sat in silence in the dark for several long seconds before Robert prompted him. "You brought me to see an empty garage?"

Jax bit his tongue. It would be so easy to pick a fight with the older man. To take his pent-up frustrations out on him, but he had to acknowledge that both men had something in common — they were both freaking out about Emma's pregnancy. Maybe not for the same reason, but in the end it didn't matter. One of them was about to become a father, the other a grandfather — whether they wanted it yet or not. Realizing that helped Jaxson stay calm.

He opened the door, inviting Robert inside. "Come on in. I want to show you something."

He pulled a different card out of his wallet, using it to gain entry into the door separating the garage from the mudroom of the house. George and his security team would be upgrading the system to bio-entry in a few weeks, but this older system would have to do until then.

He wove through the house, making his way to the huge great

room that was linked to the state-of-the-art kitchen. Like he had a few days earlier on his visit to the house, he took a seat in one of the couches covered with a sheet, waving his arm to Robert in an invitation to sit.

"You want something to drink?" Jaxson asked, absentmindedly as he looked out the wall of floor-to-ceiling windows that offered a view of the expansive lawn and pool in the foreground and the three-story mansion beyond.

Robert hadn't sat yet. Instead he walked to the windows, looking out at the paradise of flowers, gardens and water features.

Jaxson let him stand in silence as he got back to his feet to cross to the refrigerator. He owed Maxine. She'd had Nalani stock the refrigerator with drinks as he'd asked. He grabbed two bottles of beer, popping the tops off before he crossed back to stand next to Robert.

Neither man spoke. Each sipped absent-mindedly on the beer, as they stood side-by-side, looking out into the California sun.

Jaxson broke the silence. "For what it's worth, I wasn't ready for this any more than you are."

"Then why the hell did you let it happen?" Robert answered, angry.

He was an asshole for doing it, but he chuckled. "Don't make me paint you a picture, man."

His candid comment threw Emma's dad off base. Jaxson felt, rather than saw, Robert looking at him. "That's not what I meant and you know it."

Jaxson turned to meet his gaze. "I do know. You'll have to forgive me. I'm a bit off my game these days."

"You?" Robert scoffed. "I don't believe it. I don't understand it, but I know you're always in control of yourself and everything around you, which includes my Emma."

"I'm not going to get into a pissing contest with you, Robert. We all love Emma. You, me, and Chase."

"I'm her father."

"And I'm not her father. What's your point?"

"My point is I went along with this crazy trio of yours when you were just dating Emma, but it's not natural. It's confusing. It upsets people." He paused, before admitting, "It upsets me."

Jaxson wanted to rail into the guy. To tell him it was none of his fucking business, but he resisted, in part because he genuinely knew Robert Fischer was a good man. But more importantly, because like it or not, they were now family, he and Robert. They would forever be linked. Emma would be miserable if she didn't have the support of her parents and that meant that Jaxson had to somehow get through to the guy standing in front of him looking like he was going to explode or cry… which ever burst out first.

"I'm sorry you're upset, Robert. I really am, but it's time you realize that Emma has not been dating Chase and me these last few years. We've lived together. Traveled the world together. Built several successful businesses together. Decorated several homes together. And yes, this month, we found out we created life together. The sooner you accept that Emma is my family now too, the sooner you'll be able to be happy for us."

"Happy? Are you kidding me? She's only twenty-four. She's too young…"

"Don't give me that shit. I happen to know for a fact you and Linda got married when she was twenty-two and Emma was born when Linda was twenty-four."

"You're missing the key part. We got married first."

"This is not nineteen-fifty, dammit. Are you really going to tell me you're going to dig in and break your daughter's heart by not accepting her relationship with the two men she loves? If you think I'm making her pick between Chase and me, you're nuts."

"Fine, I'm not saying you can't all stay together. All I'm asking is that one of you marry her. I don't even care which one."

Jaxson stepped a bit closer, leaning in to make sure Robert was paying attention. "There is no way two of us will get married and leave one person out. It would be the beginning of the end for us."

"Then what? She is a single mother?"

"Haven't you been paying attention at all? Emma does nothing alone. She has not one, but two men to stand by her... love her... protect her... support her."

"What happens when you get tired of this arrangement?"

"Do you honestly think I'd ever just desert Chase or Emma? If you do, it cuts me to the core. I thought I'd earned your respect by now."

The older man ran his fingers through his cropped hair nervously. "I just want to know she's set up for life. That her and my grandchild won't end up cast aside when you move on to something or someone else."

"Fuck you. When have I ever given you the impression I was only in this for the short term?" Jaxson was furious.

"Give me a break. Men like you..."

"Men like me? What kind of men are those?"

"Rich. Powerful." He paused before slicing the dagger into Jaxson's heart. "Men like your father."

"Jesus Christ, is that what this is about? My dear old dad?"

"It's only a matter of time. You're on the same path he took. Big business. Growing influence."

Jaxson let loose a maniacal laugh before tipping the beer back to take long swigs. He needed to numb himself for the bullshit conversation he was having. "I'm disappointed in you, Robert."

"In me?" Robert countered incredulously.

"You obviously haven't been paying attention to anything these last few years. Have you even met my father?"

"No, but..."

"You haven't met him because I haven't even seen him. Not once. Not since the fundraising event where we outed ourselves and took down his campaign. In case you haven't been paying attention, I loathe my father and everything he stands for. You can accuse me of many things because I'm far from perfect, but I draw the line at being compared to my father."

As he finished his impassioned speech, Jaxson was glad Chase wasn't there to hear it. He had to smile to himself. Chase had been trying for days to convince Jaxson that he was nothing like his father. He'd be gloating if he were there to know Jaxson was now agreeing with him.

"And for the record, I treated Emma better in the first weekend I met her than my father has ever treated my mother. I would give my life for her and Chase. Do you hear me? There is nothing I wouldn't do to keep them safe and happy."

Robert had turned to look back out over the lawns, thinking over Jaxson's words.

"Listen, if I thought for one minute having Chase and Emma get married would make things easier or better, I'd let it happen, but it would only drive a wedge into our relationship that we would never be able to overcome. It's time you realize you're stuck with both Chase and me as your unofficial sons-in-law. But if it makes you feel any better, I've already been in touch with my lawyer."

Robert turned to him again, looking concerned, but he kept quiet. "I've asked Connor to look into family law and come up with the best plan to make a legal arrangement that will setup Chase, Emma, and our children for life. I don't know what he'll come up with yet, but I can assure you that I will formalize a plan before the babies are born to make sure that no matter what happens in the future, Emma and the kids will never have to worry about their financial security ever again."

The worry lines around Robert's eyes seemed to relax ever so slightly as he internalized Jaxson's words. But then they returned with a vengeance. "Wait. You said babies. Plural."

The memory of Dr. Tipton telling them about the twins just hours before flooded back, bringing a fresh wave of panic. Jaxson stuttered through his response. "We just were coming back... Emma's doctor's appointment. He did tests... they showed...

two…" He took a deep breath and plunged ahead. "Twins. She's carrying twins."

Robert swayed. "I think I need to sit down." He turned to stumble towards the long couch that faced the windows.

"I know exactly how you feel. I think I'll join you." Jaxson collapsed into the lounge chair facing Robert.

The two men drank their beers in silence for a minute, each retreating to their own corners to regroup. Robert broke first.

"Twins run in Linda's family, you know."

Jaxson chuckled. "Naw, I didn't. That might have been helpful information before now."

"Would it have changed anything?" Robert probed.

Jaxson thought for a second and then answered truthfully. "Not a damn thing."

"So, my baby is really going to have twins?"

Jaxson was unsure why Robert was asking such a rudimentary question at this stage of the conversation, but he went along with it. "She really is. I saw pictures of them both today at the doctor's office. They are each about the size of a lemon, or at least that's what the doctor assured us."

"When is her due date?"

"September twenty-second"

"That means she's…"

"Yes, much farther along than we thought."

"I can't believe you all kept it a secret from me this long," he groused.

"You can thank you daughter for that. She only told Chase and me five days ago."

"I don't believe you. You guys share everything. How could she keep a secret like that for so long?"

"Believe me, I've been asking myself that question all week. If you figure it out, let me know."

"So why did you bring me here instead of talking back at your house? Which, I will tell you, I was a bit surprised you'd bought a pretty simple ranch. It didn't feel like your type of house."

Jaxson looked around the room before asking, "And what do you think of this place?"

Robert looked around, taking in the upscale details of the home. "Much closer to what I'd expect, but isn't this all part of the club?"

"Not any more. I've changed the plans. This is a four-bedroom private home that I'll be able to build a security net around. We'll still be on the same grounds as the club but have more privacy and safety for my family out here."

Robert looked nostalgic as he repeated, "Your family."

"That's what Emma and Chase are to me. I don't give a damn if we have an official document that says so or not."

The older man nodded, silently acknowledging Jaxson's claim before asking, "So, you haven't talked to your own family in years? That must be lonely for you."

The pressure on his chest returned like it did whenever people talked about his father. He forced a calm response. "I talk to my mother every once in a while. She's come to visit a time or two on her own, but…"

"But what?"

"Her visits always end in us arguing over why she stays with my father. I've tried, unsuccessfully, to get her to leave him."

"I'm sorry. I didn't know."

"I don't talk about it much. I guess I'm a bit surprised Emma hasn't mentioned it."

"Are you kidding me? She is so loyal to you and Chase, she wouldn't have shared anything she thought you wouldn't want us to know." Robert paused as if deciding what to say next before adding, "Maybe you should try calling your mom again. I'm sure she's going to be happy to hear she's going to be a grandmother."

Jaxson chuckled. "Yeah, I bet you're right about that."

The muffled sound of a cell phone ringing filled the quiet

space. Robert stood so he could dig the ringing phone out of his pocket.

"It's Linda. I'm guessing she's calling to chew my ass. I left her a note this morning when I left telling her where I was going."

"Ouch. You might want to get that before you end up in more trouble than you're already in."

"You might be right. You mind if I go out on the lawn to take this? I'd rather get my ass chewed in private if you don't mind."

Jaxson couldn't help but laugh. "Have at it and good luck."

"Thanks. I think I might need it." Robert was just sliding the glass door to the patio open as he answered the phone. "Hi honey." He closed the door before Jaxson could hear any more of his in-law's conversation.

He took the last swig of his now-warm beer before reaching to put the empty bottle on the glass top coffee table.

Jax looked around. He would need to talk to Ted, their interior decorator for the main building, to see if he'd be able to help them refresh the house and make it move-in ready. The sooner he could get them all settled into their new home, the sooner things might finally start to feel like normal again.

Normal. What the hell was that anymore?

He replayed the day's events over in his head again and again, trying to sort out his complicated emotions. It was damn confusing being thrilled and scared shitless at the same time. There were so many things he couldn't do shit about and he hated that.

As he thought through everything, he realized there was only one thing he had in his control at that moment that he could try to cross off his list. He fished his own cell phone out of his pocket and searched his contacts to find the number he'd probably have memorized if he were a better son.

Jaxson had started to make this call twice yesterday but had hung up before his mother had answered each time. While a big part of him longed to share his exciting news that he was about to become a father with his mother, he didn't know if he could trust her to keep the news a secret from his father. The last thing he needed was to add the stress of dealing with his father's bigoted opinion on their unusual relationship.

Like he'd shared with Robert, he hadn't spoken with the man directly in almost three years. Not since Jaxson had outed their trio at his father's campaign rally. That hadn't stopped the bastard from sending messages and veiled threats to Jaxson through intermediaries, the primary being his mother.

He pushed CALL again, this time holding his breath, refusing to hang up.

"Jaxson?" His mother's voice was so quiet he barely heard her.

"Mother?"

Only muffles could be heard at the other end of the line, so he asked, "Are you still there or did I lose you?"

"I'm here." Her volume had increased, but it only made it easier for Jaxson to hear the warble in her voice.

"Is everything okay, Mom?"

The ultimate southern politician's wife, he expected her normal bullshit assurance that life was grand in the Davidson household just as she always did. When it didn't come, he became alarmed.

"What's going on? Where are you?" he pressed.

A long sigh greeted him. "I'm in New York with your father."

"Where in New York?"

"Where is not important. It's the why you should be asking about."

"I'll bite." Alarm bells were going off. "Why are you in New York?"

He waited for her answer. It was almost a minute in coming. He could hear her sniffling on the other end of the phone, as if she had been crying. "Your father, against my wishes, is here to meet with the party leaders to explore the possibility of another run for the presidency next year."

Jaxson had been so sure he'd put the final nail in his father's dreams of living in the White House that it took him a few long seconds to understand what his mother was saying. "Who in their right mind would be encouraging him to run again?" Jaxson asked, incredulously.

His mom chuckled sadly. "Oh come on. You know how this works. As long as there is money to be stolen or deals to be made in backrooms, men like your father will flourish. Until the American people wake up and elect people who want to serve the country instead of their own personal interests, they will continue to get more of the same."

Jaxson had never heard his mother talk like this. While he agreed with her new sentiment completely, she had never broken her strict politician wife's code of unwavering support for her blowhard husband.

"Are you okay, Mom?" When she didn't answer, he added, "Has he hurt you?"

"He's hurt me every day for the last twenty years. Oh, not physically. He's too much of a gentleman to do something as unsavory as physically hurting a defenseless woman, well, unless you count forcing himself on me in the bedroom. The only good thing about his multiple affairs over the last few years is that he's finally stopped pretending to be attracted to me. No, he's moved on to forcing himself on innocent personal assistants, campaign volunteers, and cronies' wives."

"Mom, you need to get out of there. I'm going to buy you a plane ticket to come to California. You can stay with us and we'll figure out what comes next."

Her manic laughter frightened him. "Oh honey, it's too late for me. There is no saving me. Your father has made sure of that."

"I don't understand."

Her anger was dissolving. He heard her crying at the other end of the phone instead. He suddenly wished for her anger back instead. "He's a real bastard, you know that?"

"Yes, Mom. I've known that since I was eleven and I watched him throw grandmother into a nursing home against her wishes so he could sell off the family homestead to finance his first senate race."

"He broke her." She sobbed. "He broke me."

"That's it. You're leaving."

"I can't."

"Of course you can. You can start over. We'll help you."

"I tried to leave once already."

"You did? When? Why didn't you come to me?" Jaxson questioned.

"Because he is evil. He made sure to have dirt on me. His wife. Now he's blackmailing me into staying through the next damn election. The problem is, there will always be another election."

"Screw that. You're a saint. What could he have on you anyway?"

Silence.

"Mom?" he questioned.

"I was so lonely, Jaxson," she cried.

"Ah shit. Listen, who cares if he has proof that you cheated on him? We'll get proof that he cheated first. And anyway, you cheating looks worse on him than it does on you. He couldn't keep his wife happy. He'll never go public with that story."

"It's not that simple."

"Of course it is. Or what? Is the guy someone famous himself?"

Her answer was slow in coming. "It isn't a guy," she whispered.

"Then…" Jaxson's mind raced, trying to read between the lines of the disjointed story his mother was reluctantly sharing with him.

"I met Marjory at the country club. She's the tennis pro."

Mind blown. It was rare that Jaxson Davidson was left speechless. Ironically, it had happened several times on this super confusing day. "Okay, I admit. That was a bit unexpected, but I stand by my advice. Who cares if it comes out?"

"You aren't scandalized?" she asked incredulously.

"Mom, have you forgotten that I am in love with both a man and a woman and we are living our lives as a trio? If anyone can understand that love is love, it's me."

"Oh Jaxson, I don't know what to say. I've dreaded you finding out and being disappointed in me."

"Are you kidding me? This is the first smart thing you've done in years." He then realized what he'd said and hurried to add, "Sorry. No offense."

He relaxed a bit hearing his mother chuckle between her tears. "No offense taken. But, I still can't leave. He'll demonize me with this information. I'm not strong like you are. I can't take the negativity that would swirl around me if word ever got out."

"How does Marjory feel about it all?"

"I haven't a clue. We haven't spoke for over three months now. And before you get upset about that, I'm fine. She was just someone who helped me through a rough time in my life. We were good friends first and foremost. She needs to find someone permanent. And I need to play the role I signed up for when I married your father."

"Bullshit. You deserve your own happiness. And he deserves to go to jail."

"That will never happen and you know it. He has too many connections."

"You know what they say. The bigger they are, the harder they fall. If he makes it too hard on you, we'll just have to find something big enough on him to make him back off."

"I've dreamed of that day. I even have a few secrets tucked away in a safety deposit box in downtown D.C. just in case I ever needed it. But, I'm too old to change now."

Jaxson's mind raced for anything he could say in that moment to change his mother's mind. She'd never been this close to getting out before. He knew he only had a limited time before she'd get sucked back in fully again.

He smiled, realizing the universe had surely had a hand in all of the complex things in his life coming to a head all at the same perfect time. His mother would never leave his father for herself. Hell, she wouldn't even leave him for her son. But just maybe…

"I haven't told you yet why I called."

"It wasn't just to say hello?"

"Sorry, but no. We're in California and I'm buried trying to get the club ready to open on time next week."

"Then why call?" she asked sounding a bit brighter.

"I have some exciting news of my own."

"That's wonderful. I could stand some good news."

"What would you say if I told you that… you were going to be a grandmother?"

Jaxson had to hold the phone away from his ear. He'd never heard his mother squeal like a teenage girl before.

"You aren't teasing me, are you?"

"Why would I tease about something this important?"

"I don't know. To try to cheer me up?"

Jaxson chuckled. "Sorry. I love you but getting Emma pregnant wasn't on my radar for this year."

"Well planned or unplanned, it's no matter. It's wonderful news, Jaxson."

"Thanks, Mother. But there's more."

"More? Are you getting married to Emma too?" she guessed.

Why does the older generation think marriage is a requirement?

"No. That isn't in the cards for the three of us. But it looks like twins are."

"Oh my! Two babies? That's fabulous news."

"It's news, alright," he deadpanned.

"Jaxson Andrew Davidson, don't you dare make light of this. I remember the day I found out I was pregnant with you. It was one of the best days of my life."

It felt weird to talk about emotional things with his mother.

They'd never had that kind of touchy-feely relationship like most families.

"I have to admit. The last week has been pretty memorable for me too. I might have officially bit off more than I can chew." If there were anyone on the planet who would understand his fear of parenthood, surely his mother would get it. "I mean, with my old man as my role model, how the hell am I going to be a good father?"

"Jax, you are going to be a wonderful father. You know how I know?"

He could hear the passion in his mother's warbling voice. His own throat felt like it was closing up as his emotions threatened to get the best of him. He'd be damned if he was going to cry like a fucking pussy. He managed to grunt enough to encourage his mother to continue.

"You are the most honorable, loving man I've ever met. Sometimes I have to pinch myself when I realize I gave birth to a natural born leader like you. I couldn't possibly be more proud of you. Trust in yourself and learn to lean on Emma and Chase more."

Jaxson couldn't have answered her if he'd had a gun to his head. He swallowed again and again until the lump in his throat dissipated enough that he could finally grunt out, "Thanks, Mom."

A heavy sigh broke the silence. "I hate it, but I should probably get back inside before your father sends one of his lackeys to look for me."

He cleared his throat and spoke. "Pack a bag. Call a cab to take you to the airport. Get on a plane for Los Angeles. I'll pick you up at the airport. We have more than enough room for you here."

Even as he said it, he cringed, remembering how much having his mother around would inhibit their sexy times. But it didn't matter. If there was any possibility of getting his mother free of Gregory Davidson, he needed to help make that happen.

"I'll think about it," she waffled.

"I'm going to call you every day and badger you until you agree to leave."

"You do get that stubborn streak from your father you know."

"Don't remind me, please." He didn't want to have anything in common with his sperm donor.

The sliding door to the patio opened, letting the cool air-conditioned air out into the warm California afternoon. Robert let himself back into the house, looking a bit shell-shocked from the conversation with his wife.

"I need to run, Mom, but I'll call you tomorrow."

"Congratulations, daddy."

"Oh Christ, let's not start that already." But he smiled to himself when he realized instead of sounding sad or upset, he'd cheered his mother up. "Bye."

Robert collapsed back onto the couch like a deflating balloon.

Jaxson stifled the smile trying to erupt at the elder man's expense. "I take it that didn't go well."

"You could say that."

"Need another beer?" Jaxson offered.

"You have anything stronger?"

Jaxson chuckled. "Sorry. All the good stuff is up at the mansion waiting for opening day next week." When Robert didn't so much as smile, he got more serious. "You want to talk about it?"

"Not really, but since there is zero chance you aren't going to get dragged into this, I guess I better let you know that Linda found my note faster than I expected. She hopped a plane right behind me and is already back at the house with Emma and Chase."

It looked like they were about to have another unexpected houseguest.

"Okay. I guess that's a good thing, right? You both get to see Emma."

"Maybe. Maybe not."

"I don't understand."

Robert grimaced as if he had swallowed something sour. "Seems my lovely wife has forbidden me from stepping foot into your house or seeing Emma until I, and I quote, 'get my head out of my ass and apologize to all three of you.'"

Jaxson's first instinct was to rib his unofficial father-in-law for letting the woman in his life call and speak to him like that, but considering there was a pretty good chance he was going to fuck up fatherhood a time or two, who the hell was he to cast aspersions?

Instead, he pushed to his feet and offered an olive branch. "What do you say we head on up to the mansion? I'd love to show you around. I need to check in on a few things and we'll see about getting you a stiff drink."

"I'd say that sounds like the best idea of the day

CHAPTER TWELVE ~ EMMA

*E*mma woke to the incessant beep of an alarm clock. Exhausted, she hugged the torso she was presently using as her pillow while throwing her right hand up to cover her exposed ear.

The chest under her rumbled, "Poor baby. You don't like my alarm?"

Jaxson struggled to sit up enough to roll over Emma and reach his cell phone on the nightstand, finally getting the blasted noise to stop before plopping back down between his lovers. She snuggled back into the crook of Jax's arm as Chase threw his leg over them, weaving the trio together like a tight knot.

"I can only snooze one time and then I really do need to get up. You two can sleep in, though," Jaxson offered.

It was tempting, but Emma felt guilty. "It's still dark outside. You've been working so hard. You need to let us help more," she mumbled, secretly hoping he'd take her up on her offer, only later in the day. She was not a morning person.

"You are helping."

Chase was even less of a morning person than she was. "I thought we were gonna snooze again," he groused before adding, "And babysitting Emma's parents doesn't count as helping."

She should be offended by his description of the last three days, but considering how accurate it was, she couldn't object. Her parents were sleeping in the bedroom next door, but only after her father had spent one rather uncomfortable night on the couch. He'd finally relented and apologized to the trio for being so old-fashioned the next day, earning him a spot back in his wife's bed.

Jaxson disagreed. "Honestly, keeping them over here instead of underfoot at the mansion is a big help. Robert almost caught me heading down to Black Light to meet with the new dungeon master yesterday. I would prefer not to have to explain that to him. But don't forget, today is the day that Ted is ready to start on the pool house. I'd like you two to meet him over there at ten. I'm going to try to make it, but if I'm not there, start without me."

Emma hated that idea. "We'll wait for you. It's going to be your home too."

"I've got a meeting with Connor and I'm expecting it to go long. He flew in to finalize some things we've been working on. We have a shit-ton of topics to cover. And since he bills a goddamn fortune by the hour, it really is okay. I trust you guys with the decor completely. Get what you want."

"Now can we snooze?" Chase begged.

The room was still pitch dark. It had to be before six, and she was worried that Jax would be tired all day since they'd stayed up late, talking and groping into the wee hours.

"You two make it hard to get up, you know that?" Jax chuckled.

She could hear the smile in Chase's cheeky reply. "I can make it even harder."

Jaxson's tortured groan was followed by Chase's naughty addition, "Oh, I see you're already nice and hard. Need some help with this bad boy?"

Emma giggled, loving the easy banter between her lovers.

Jaxson's breath caught before he bucked his hips off the bed, taking Emma with him. "I don't have time."

"Of course you do. There's always time for a quick…"

Chase's last word was cut off by the hard cock that slammed into the back of his throat. Emma could just make out the shadow of his head bobbing up and down on their Dom's morning hard-on. Through experience, she knew that her men were usually hard as steel when they woke.

The gurgled choking mingled with Jaxson's grunts of satisfaction as he chased his orgasm was better than any alarm clock. Emma may be sleepy, but her girly parts were definitely waking up early. She couldn't resist latching onto Jaxson's right nipple, sucking on it as hard as she could. His instant groan as he bucked his hips off the bed made Emma feel powerful. Empowered, she groped his hard chest and found his other nipple, pinching it as her teeth grazed the nub in her mouth.

Chase and Emma knew every button to push on their Dom's body to propel him to the edge of ecstasy within minutes. As Jaxson's hips thrust higher off the bed, Chase had to reposition himself on his knees. As soon as he did, Jaxson reached out to grab onto his lover's shoulder-length hair, using it as a handle to control the action. Submitting to the face-fucking, Chase threw his arms behind his back and allowed Jaxson to use his mouth, controlling the depth and speed of the blowjob.

"Fuck, yeah. You're gonna get an early breakfast in about twenty seconds and I want you to slurp down every drop, you got it?"

Chase could only hum his approval around the flesh in his mouth.

"Christ, hum again. That's it." Low vibrations mingled with wet gags until Jaxson erupted in a loud release. Emma did her part to ride the wave with him until she felt her lover relax beneath her and the weight of Chase's body bounce slightly as he collapsed onto his side to recover. She wasn't sure which man was gasping for air harder after their impromptu exertion.

The threesome lay tangled together until Jaxson's alarm filled the room with the sharp beep Emma hated. As she was closest to the nightstand, she rolled to grab the offending gadget and hit snooze.

"That was an unexpected wake-up call," Jaxson chuckled.

"Yeah, well it's better than the damn alarm," Chase replied, his voice a bit scratchy thanks to his early morning fun. "Now can we snooze?"

Jaxson patted Emma as he extricated himself from their pile of limbs, maneuvering until he was able to stand. His departure made the bed feel too large. Like magnets, Chase and Emma rolled together until they were on their sides, spooning each other in the warm spot as Jaxson pulled the thin sheet they slept under over them. They had learned early on that three bodies could produce a lot of heat.

She felt Jaxson's lips on her head, kissing her as he tucked her back into bed. "I'm setting your alarm for nine. Don't be late to meet Ted at ten, you hear me?"

The sleepy duo replied in unison, "Yes, Sir."

Emma thought about getting up and making Jaxson some breakfast before he left. She felt guilty for not accompanying him into the shower to scrub his back as she often did and for not going with him to work on the backlog of accounting tasks that she needed to catch up on. But in the end, her tired body refused to budge until she drifted back to sleep in Chase's arms.

"You should drive faster. We're late," Emma urged Chase. She felt a not unpleasant tingle skitter across her bottom as she looked at the digital clock on the console of their new SUV. She prayed the time was wrong, because if not, they were already ten minutes late for their meeting with Ted at their new house.

It wasn't that she was that worried about the interior designer having to wait for them. In fact, she'd like to do many more things to inconvenience the man who kept hitting on Chase just to put the jerk in his place.

No. It was one of their longest standing rules that Jaxson had laid out for his often-tardy lovers. *Be on time or your ass will pay the price.*

The duo had learned many times over the years that the price was one stroke of punishment per minute late. They were still blocks away as she watched the clock flip to eleven after the hour. Her ass clenched, anticipating the paddling coming her way. Her only hope was that Jaxson was still stuck with Connor and would be too distracted to notice.

Chase pulled the car into the garage five minutes later. Ted's Range Rover was parked in the driveway, empty. He must have gone in ahead of them. Emma grabbed the bag of color swatches along with the iPad that had all of her notes and photos of the furniture she'd been admiring to show their designer.

She'd been to the house several times already with her parents and was getting excited to move in with Jaxson and Chase. She hadn't known how much she was dreading living on the top floor of the mansion until Jaxson had come up with the creative solution of confiscating the pool house.

"Sorry we're late," Chase offered up as they found Ted in the kitchen, blueprints of the house laid out on the marble counter. He was heading to the coffee maker to grab a cup of coffee as Emma put her stuff down near Ted. She had the perfect view of the designer's face as he spoke.

"I'm kinda glad you are. I happen to know the consequences. And since Jaxson is so busy I bet he'd appreciate me handling a bit of discipline for him, you naughty boy." The handsome designer had fixed Chase with a hungry stare.

Emma may be the submissive of their family, but that didn't mean she was submissive to anyone else. Ted Martin was about to understand his error.

Surprise registered on Chase's face. He'd been telling her she'd read Ted completely wrong. That he only saw Chase in a professional light. Before he could recover, Emma stepped into the few feet that separated the men, facing off with Ted.

"It's time you listen up. I've had enough of your sexual harassment of Chase. We hired you to do a professional job. Nothing more. Nothing less. From now on you will restrict all interactions to the business at hand that we are paying you good money to conduct. You will not speak to him sexually, look at him sexually, or most importantly, touch him in a sexual way, whether I'm here or not. Have I made myself clear?"

The interior designer stood frozen, eyes wide with shock at the normally reserved Emma's uncharacteristic outburst.

Without waiting for an answer, she continued. "Failure to do so will not only end up with you being fired, but I'm sure Jaxson has the kind of connections that can make working in this city impossible for you, got it?"

His pitiful, "Yes," was insufficient.

Emma was vibrating with pent up anger spilling out. "Yes, what?" she demanded.

"Yes, Ms. Fischer."

"Excellent. Now that we have an understanding, let's get to work."

The unusual confrontation had taken more out of her than she'd expected. Emma hated that when Chase hugged her from behind, she collapsed into his arms as if all the air had been let out of her. He held her tight, one steadying hand on her left hip while his right arm hugged her waist.

He leaned in to whisper against her ear, sending a ticklish shiver through her body. "I love watching you get uber protective, baby, you know that?"

She didn't answer him. She didn't need to. He knew her heart. They stood linked together until her speeding heart rate from her confrontation slowed to normal and Chase pulled her along with him back to the nearby refrigerator.

He was pulling a bottle of chilled apple juice out when she begged him, "I really need a cup of coffee today."

"Sorry baby, but no caffeine for you."

"That's not fair," she pouted.

"Maybe not, but you know the rules."

"Fine," she begrudgingly snatched the healthy beverage, silently remembering she was drinking for three. "Let's get to work then."

They spent a total of four hours walking from room to room, listening and talking with Ted on the plans for redecorating, without a single sexual comment or leer from the designer. They would end up with three bedrooms, four bathrooms, one home office, one gym, several huge walk-in closets, and one bedroom turned adorable nursery. With each room, she became more excited… and more hungry. When it was after two, she couldn't take it anymore.

"We need to take a break. I need to pee and get food, in that order."

Chase had brought up several kitchen supply sites on the iPad. "I thought we were going to pick out the kitchen stuff."

Emma's tummy growled loud enough for him to hear it and look up from the other side of the counter.

"But it sounds like it will need to wait. Let me call Jax and see if he's eaten yet or not. With any luck, he can take a break and go to lunch with us."

Emma was relieved when Ted wisely bowed out of their lunch break. "I'm gonna stay here and take more notes while they are fresh in my mind. Most of the changes we are making are easy enough that I should be able to get a crew in here and knock things out within a few days."

Now that she'd seen how awesome their new home was going to be, Emma was impatient to move in. Especially with sharing the small rental with her parents, she was sure the next few days were going to drag as she anticipated moving day.

"The sooner the better. I'm tired of feeling like everything is temporary. I can't wait to feel like we're at home again."

Chase hugged her from behind again as he reassured her. "With all of the work we still have to do for the clubs opening, I predict the next few days fly by, baby. Now, let's take a walk up to the big house."

They exited through the sliding patio door and headed across the lawn. When they reached the mansion, the patio door to the large ballroom that would soon be the main dance floor was already open. Today the space still hosted the pre-opening collaboration space. Emma could hear Lola even before they entered the building. She'd begun to think of the aggressive woman's grating voice as fingernails on a chalkboard.

"Emma and Chase! I've been watching for you two." Maxine's greeting was a welcome diversion from Lola's bossiness as she yelled at some unfortunate employee across the room.

Emma went to hug their friend and star employee from D.C. "Hi there! I can't believe I've missed you the last two times I've been here since you got to town."

Maxine hugged her back before answering. "Yeah, sorry I missed you, too. I was out both times picking up some supplies and making some decisions with Ted on the final pieces of furniture. Is Ted with you?" she questioned.

Chase answered, "Naw. He stayed out at the pool house."

Maxine huffed. "I told him to hustle back here as soon as he wrapped things up with you. We still have the main restrooms to make decisions on. We're about to run out of time and we can't very well open without a place for our guests to pee."

Emma felt guilty that they were taking Ted away from the main project to work on their house. She almost offered to divert him back to the mansion full-time but bit her tongue. They deserved their own place again.

"Where's Jaxson?" Chase inquired.

"He asked me to tell you to meet him in the kitchen. He's holding a staff meeting with some of the newest employees. It sounds like they were also going to be testing some of the new chef's menu items to give her practice with the menu before opening day next week."

Chase wrapped his arm around Emma's waist and started shuffling her towards the double doors that led to the main house. "That's perfect. We can help taste test too."

Emma chuckled as he pulled her along with him, calling out her goodbye to Maxine over her shoulder. Her friend shouted to her, "Remind Jaxson that the next candidate for the Runway manager job will be here in less than a half hour. He promised he'd sit in on the interview with me."

Chase had her almost out the door by the time she yelled her reply, "I'll tell him!"

He pulled her to the left when they exited the ballroom, taking the path along the back of the mansion weaving through several club areas that looked ready for opening day.

They had just passed the elevator and were about to enter the mammoth gourmet kitchen when a tall man dressed in black jeans, a black T-shirt, and a rugged black leather coat rounded the corner, almost mowing Emma down.

"Oh Christ, sorry about that." The apology came in a low, gravelly voice that sounded more like a reprimand than an apology.

Emma half expected Chase to pull her away protectively from the gruff looking man. Instead, he released her waist to reach out to shake the man's hand.

"I was hoping I'd get to say an official welcome. I heard you accepted our offer."

The weathered skin of the dangerously handsome man's face

172

broke into a broad smile. Only then did the laugh lines at the corner of his mouth and eyes light up his face. "I feel a bit like I just won the lottery. I still think you guys have lost touch with reality, but I'm gonna have fun while it lasts."

Emma was curious who the new employee was. He looked like he should be on the security detail, but they'd already hired Miguel for the head security position and there was no way this guy wasn't going to be in charge of something. She elbowed Chase lightly, trying to remind him of his manners.

Out of her peripheral view, she detected Chase's eyes on her. When he didn't catch on she finally turned to look into his eyes as she asked, "Aren't you going to introduce us?"

Chase looked nervous, glancing around the space before leaning in close. The guy in leather angled in as well, as if they were about to conspire on a top-secret mission.

"This is Elijah Keaton. He's going to be our Spencer of the West Coast."

Emma quickly understood the secrecy. It wasn't like they could go around talking about Black Light in the open at Runway. She reached out to take his offered hand. He had a firm grip as he greeted her.

"Nice to meet you, Miss Fischer."

"Thanks. You too, sir." She hadn't meant to use the respectful greeting. His intense masculinity and new job title of dungeon master just seemed to call for it. His wide smile proved he liked her salutation.

Emma was relieved when he released her hand. Not normally shy, her brain couldn't help but fast forward to a day coming soon that the alpha man in front of her would witness her naked and sexually dominated in the plethora of creative scenarios the men in her life would come up with. Her eyes took a sudden interest in her shoes as she felt the heat rising into her cheeks.

A gentleman would have given her a pass. Mr. Keaton was apparently not concerned with such niceties. "Ah, I see your sub blushes beautifully. I look forward to watching other parts of her body color, from a distance of course, after the club opens."

Chase hugged her closer, reassuring her. "Blushing is not all she does beautifully."

Despite the public location, Emma's pussy responded to her Dom's naughty implication by clenching. The last months had been the most vanilla of her entire relationship with the men in her lives. Between the babies, stress of opening the clubs, and distance from their private playground in D.C., they'd had few D/s encounters since arriving in California. It was in that moment Emma knew without a doubt that she'd missed it and couldn't wait until Black Light West opened the following week.

She forced her attention back to saying goodbye to the new dungeon master as he spoke. "I'll look forward to spending more time together in the future then. I just stopped by to pick up the newly printed business cards and membership invitations. I'm heading out to do a bit of networking to drum up some business for opening night with likeminded people."

The DM had moved around them and was already heading towards the front door when Chase called out, "Good luck with that! I hope you have the NDA's with you."

Elijah called back, "Yep, I have a big stack with me. Later."

After he'd gone, Emma expected Chase to pull her into motion again, but instead he leaned closer to talk close to her ear. "He was an excellent find."

"Why? Has he been the DM at other clubs?"

"Better. He just retired after twenty-five years as one of Hollywood's top stuntmen. He's lived his life on the edge and has built up connections with the most powerful people on the west coast. We hired him as much for his connections as we did his BDSM knowledge, which from what I can tell, is extensive."

Emma wasn't sure they should be having this conversation in the middle of a main thoroughfare of the mansion, but after glancing around it appeared they were still alone so she asked the question on her mind. "Why is he retiring? I mean he only looks to be in his forties."

"We asked him that. He didn't gc into a lot of detail, but it seems he had a pretty big accident about a year ago and his doctors have warned him that he's doing too much damage to his body to keep up with the dangerous career."

Emma tried to keep her voice calm as she replied, "He looked pretty healthy to me."

The grin on Chase's face reminded her that he knew her well. "My little subby was checking out the new DM, was she?"

"Not at all. I mean… he was right in front of me."

"Uh-ha," Chase teased.

"Knock it off. You know I only have eyes for you and Jax." Emma elbowed him in his ribs.

Chase's chuckle helped her relax. "Don't worry. I noticed too. He's smoking hot."

Emma elbowed him again, this time harder. "Yeah, well stop noticing."

"Jealous much?" Chased teased.

Emma admitted, "I didn't have these problems in D.C. It seems like everyone you meet is ready to jump your bones. The news anchors, Ted…"

He cut her off. "That's not true. Lola isn't hitting on me," Chase countered.

"No, she's hitting on Jaxson. It's like open season on my men out here."

Chase reached out to place his palm on Emma's stomach, cupping her rounded tummy lovingly. "You have absolutely nothing to worry about, baby. Just like you, I only have eyes for you and Jaxson. And I can't wait to meet these two little peanuts in a few months. I hope they have your beautiful eyes."

Emma leaned in for a proper hug, letting Chase's arms wrap her in a cocoon of love. They embraced quietly until her stomach growled loud enough that Maxine probably heard several rooms away.

"Let's see about getting that tummy of yours some lunch." Chase released her, reaching for her hand as he dragged them back into motion.

She heard the mild chaos in the mammoth gourmet kitchen before they entered. There had to be at least a dozen people seated at the U-shaped island in the center of the open space. In the middle of the U was their new chef, Avery Cross. Emma had met the redhead the week before when they'd gone through the food and beverage budget together. She'd been impressed with the woman's business sense at the time.

Jaxson called out to them from the far side of the island. "There you two are. I thought you got lost. Ted texted me that you'd left almost twenty minutes ago." He motioned to his right. "I saved you two seats."

Chase pulled her farther into the room as she tried to take in their newest employees, most of whom she hadn't met. The uniforms the men and women wore told her there was a mix of groundskeepers and security personnel chowing down on Avery's cooking. A beautiful woman with long, black hair sat alone at one of the three tables that separated the kitchen from the connected great room.

"Hey, Emma. Chase. Jax told me you were coming so I whipped you up a sampler platter to share. I hope that's okay." Avery slid a large oval plate in front of them before dramatically removing the warming lid to display the scrumptious looking food underneath.

"It smells awesome," Chase acknowledged. "I'm starving." He reached out to pick up a loaded potato skin and dip it in the bowl of sour cream before popping a bite in his mouth.

Emma chuckled. "I can see I'm going to have to fight for my half."

"Don't worry, I'll make you more if you don't get enough," Avery assured her.

Emma was reaching for a potsticker when Jaxson's arm wrapped around her waist, nearly pulling her off her tall stool as he leaned down to talk against her ear. "It's about time you guys got here. I've been waiting for you. Eat fast. We need to leave."

Something in his voice made her stop from taking the bite, turning to him instead. His potent glare threatened to swallow her, spiking her heart rate. Jaxson was an intense man on a good day. Today, his heated gaze knocked the air out of her lungs. He masked his emotions so well, she truly couldn't tell if he was happy or upset. All Emma knew was that something big had happened.

"What?" she whispered, almost afraid to ask for fear of getting bad news.

"Just eat. We only have a few minutes before we need to go."

"But... where are we going? We aren't done at the pool house."

"That can wait. This is more important."

For the first time, she noticed Jaxson's perfect lips turning up at the ends, giving a hint of levity. She relaxed slightly.

"Maxine needs you to interview a candidate for the Runway West manager position," she reminded him.

A proper scowl clouded Jaxson's handsome face. "Shit, I completely forgot about that."

Chase had been listening in, leaning in and talking with his mouth full. "Well she hasn't forgotten. Where are we going anyway?" he asked in his normal jovial cheer.

Jaxson's impatience showed as he groused, "You don't need to know yet." When Emma flinched from his abrupt response, he added on softly, "I want it to be a surprise." Pausing, he seemed to think through his options before he spoke. "Fine. It's gonna cost us a fortune to delay, but we'll leave as soon as the interview is done. I'm gonna go tell Maxine to text Madison and have her get here early if she can."

"Who's Madison?" Chase asked with his mouth full again.

"The woman who has Maxine and Lola ready to deck each other. I can't skip the interview if for no other reason than I need to be there to play referee."

Chase laughed out loud. "Oh this is going to be entertaining. Please tell me I can watch!"

Emma had snuck in a few bites while the men were chatting. She had enough stress in her life without needing to watch a catfight.

"You want to stay too, baby?" Jax asked.

"Honestly, I'd rather go back out to the house and lay down for a little bit. Can you guys just come out and get me when you're ready to go?"

Jaxson hugged her close again, placing a soft kiss on her forehead. "That's a fine plan. I want to make sure you and the peanuts get plenty of rest. Just make sure you get enough to eat, okay?"

He stood, ready to head out as Emma replied, "Yes, sir."

Only after Chase got up to head out with Jax did she realize she'd be going back out alone to where Ted was still working. When Avery offered second helpings on some of her favorites, Emma accepted, eating slowly in hopes of finding their house empty when she got back. She wasn't ready to go head to head with Ted solo yet.

CHAPTER THIRTEEN ~ CHASE

"Come on. You can tell me. I'll keep it a secret from Emma," Chase pressed Jaxson for the third time since they'd left Emma in the kitchen. He could tell the secret had to be something really big because Jaxson kept looking at his watch every two minutes, trying to make time go by faster.

Pop. The hard swat across his ass totally shocked Chase, coming out of nowhere. Everyone in the pre-opening office turned to look at him and Jaxson, curiosity on their faces.

"Ouch. What the hell was that for?" he asked, self-consciously reaching back to soothe the sudden discomfort.

"You know damn well what that was for. Ask me one more time to tell you the secret without Emma being here and we'll need to find a more private location and my belt will be coming off. Got it?" Jaxson turned to pin him with his most dominant stare.

It felt like every drop of blood below his waist had just rushed to his cock in the space of three seconds. Christ did he get turned on when Jaxson went all Dom on him. He was tempted to ask for the secret one more time, just so he could feel the heat of the wide leather kiss his bare ass. It had been far too long since they'd shared the intimacy of real discipline in their trio. Until that moment, Chase hadn't put together just how much he yearned for it.

Jaxson read him like a book, leaning in close to talk softly. "I know you need it, don't you, baby? I've been neglecting that ass of yours, haven't I? Well, I won't tell you the secret, but I can promise you that you'll go to bed with a warm bottom tonight if you'd like."

Chase swayed on his feet, leaning into the desk they were standing near to help steady himself and to also hide his raging hard-on that had to be visible through his tight jeans. He choked out his reply. "You know I won't ask for it, but if you feel that's what I need, then I'll submit."

"Damn straight you will."

Chase loved the possessive growl that told him that his Dom was as on edge as he was. It was in that exact moment that Maxine returned to the room with a petite blonde woman dressed in an outfit that looked straight off the runway. While most of the people working on opening the clubs were in jeans and T-shirts, or other informal work gear, the newcomer stood out conspicuously, and not just for her clothing choice.

The closer Chase looked her over the more he knew they'd been wasting their time waiting for the interview. Hell, the woman barely looked old enough to drive, let alone run their multi-million dollar business. The spiked heels were the only thing responsible for her topping five foot. Hell, she looked to be about twelve years old with her blonde hair pulled up into a messy, yet somehow elegant up-do. The severity of her black leather skirt was offset by the flirty softness of her powder-blue off-shoulder blouse. The huge Prada tote bag looked heavy enough to tip the wisp of a woman over.

Chase was leaning closer to Jax to ask if they could leave now when his lover moved forward, making his way around the desk to reach out and shake the young woman's hand. Chase followed, hoping they could wrap this up quickly since she was clearly not a Maxine caliber candidate.

"Thanks for coming in today, Ms. Taylor." Jaxson welcomed her just as Lola turned to notice their newest visitor.

Chase had just reached to shake the candidate's hand when Lola arrived next to them.

"Nice of you to join us five minutes late. I hope your tardiness isn't representative of your work performance," Lola drawled her sour accusation.

Chase was surprised that the small hand in his gripped back firmly before releasing him to turn and smile sweetly at Lola, her bubbly voice matching her look. "Hello again, Ms. Garcia. I can assure you that, like, I am never *ever* late. It seems that some unknown person added my name to the 'do not enter' list at the gate and, well, it took a couple of minutes for the boys down there to sort things out with Maxine here."

Chase had grown up in Southern California and he would bet his life that the spitfire of a woman in front of him had grown up in the valley. He knew it was a generalization, but if her accent didn't give her away, the glob of bubble gum she currently chewed was a dead giveaway.

Lola didn't back down. "Oh, I see that she's Maxine already. Isn't that a bit presumptuous of you to be on a first name basis?"

Madison Taylor smiled sweetly as she made Lola wait while she blew a tiny bubble with her gum. "I usually like to follow directions. Ms. Torres asked me to call her Maxine and so I will." The petite woman didn't back down one bit as she pressed, "Shall we get started? I'm anxious to hear more about the opening."

Before they could even sit, Jaxson asked the question Chase was thinking. "Before we get started, I'd like to make sure we aren't wasting each other's time. I don't know how to ask this gently so..."

Ms. Taylor cut him off, throwing up her hand like a stop sign. "I know. I look young, but I can assure you I'm considerably older.

Like, this position is the perfect fit for me and I'm not ditching you today until I convince you gentlemen that's the truth."

Once again, Lola interrupted. "I'd be trying to impress me if I were you, young lady. I am the one who makes the employment decisions around here."

Maxine scoffed. "Not so fast, Lola. Jaxson asked me to take charge of filling this position and you know it."

All three women turned to pin Jaxson with expectant glares. Chase would have wilted, but his Dom held up admirably under the pressure.

"Ladies, I've put Maxine in charge of finding the right candidate for the demanding manager position. She assures me you are that person, Ms. Taylor, but I'll be making my own decision on that subject this afternoon."

Lola stomped her foot like a spoiled child whose mother had just taken her favorite toy away, crossing her arms over her chest in a huff. Chase had already had enough of her dramatics. It was time for them to fire her. He'd be talking to Jaxson about it later.

"I'm sure you have more important things to work on this afternoon, Lola. You're excused," Jaxson said with an authority that dared her to argue back.

Chase relaxed when she spun on her heel and stomped back towards her desk.

Maxine took charge. "Let's head on into the dining room where we'll have a bit more privacy, shall we?"

The men fell in behind the women, following them as they weaved through the mansion. Chase was in the perfect position to hear the women's conversation.

"Did you bring your portfolio?" Maxine asked.

"You bet." Madison had barely answered when she ground to a halt to exclaim, "O.M.G. Is that a genuine Granville Redmond?" She had stopped to admire an impressionist piece that the previous owners had left behind on the large expanse of wall in the dining room. The men had liked the piece, so they kept it.

Maxine looked at Jaxson for help.

"I'm not sure. We hadn't got around to having an appraiser come in yet. I'm pretty sure there are several other pieces by the same artist throughout the club."

Madison leaned in to take a closer look before answering, "I'd love to take a peek if you don't mind."

"That's fine, but may I ask how you know so much about the artist?"

She reached into her Prada bag and came out with a sheet of paper. "It's all on my resume. I graduated with honors from USC with a degree in art and design."

"Not cinematic art?" Chase asked. That was the major many of his southern California friends had chosen as they chased roles in nearby Hollywood."

"Oh hell no! I did a few commercials when I was a kid. That was enough to tell me there was no way I wanted to compete in that rat race my whole life."

Chase chuckled at her candor, wondering what Khloe would think of the spitfire.

Jaxson brought them back to the topic at hand. "Well, let's see how the interview goes. If we hire you, you'll be able to explore the artwork to your heart's content. Shall we?" He waved his arm towards the grand table that could seat up to twenty.

Only after the foursome were seated at one end of the table did Maxine continue the interview. "It's no secret that I've already made up my mind. The reason I had you come back today is that we need to convince the owners that you are the right lady for the job. Why don't we start by showing them your portfolio," Maxine prompted.

Chase leaned back, crossing his left leg over his right, ankle on his thigh. He watched as Madison reached down into her Prada bag, expecting her to come out with an iPad or a sleek portfolio. Instead, she pulled out a three-inch thick, huge book that looked to be bursting at the seams with papers and edges of photos sticking out of what seemed like a scrapbook.

Madison heaved the weighty book up to the table, letting it land heavy against the wood. On the cover was a handwritten *Madison's Portfolio* with colorful swirls of design hand drawn around the title to decorate the book. Chase grinned, remembering his sister's high school scrapbook that had been decorated in a similar fashion.

He glanced at Jaxson who seemed to be having trouble keeping a straight face. His Dom opened his mouth as if he were about to put a stop to the interview when Maxine asked her first question. "Why don't you start by telling Mr. Davidson and Mr. Cartwright about your last job?"

"Sure thing. For the last few years I've been running events and meetings for a varied portfolio of customers." She paused and Chase was underwhelmed until she added. "I've loved my job, I really have, but I'll be honest, the traveling has gotten to be a bit much. I'm stoked to be able to stay in one place again for a little bit."

Having traveled the world themselves for their job, Chase and Jaxson could understand the need to grow roots, but just because she wanted to work in one place didn't make her qualified for the job. Jax finally asked the million-dollar question. "That's understandable, but I'm afraid we need someone who can run a multi-million dollar business. Someone who can book big name celebrities as entertainers and run intricate multi-day events for hundreds of people. We need someone who is both business and people savvy and who can also manage a staff of several dozen employees. I'm sorry, but you just…"

He didn't get to finish his sentence. Ms. Taylor had opened her book and started flipping through the early pages of her scrapbook. "Like I said, I did a few commercials when I was a kid. That was because my dad is Burt Taylor. You might recognize his name. He's kinda a bigwig over at Universal. Through my father, I have hundreds of powerful and influential contacts in the business. Actors, directors, musicians... exactly the clientele you are hoping will gravitate to Runway's unique offerings."

Okay. She had his attention.

She barged ahead, flipping through her book until she opened it again on a page labeled 'Master's Tournament.'

"This is one of the first big events I ran. I specialized in golfing events at first. As you described, several day affairs that included coordinating rooms, food and beverage, and heavy scheduling, not to mention entertainment, gifts, transportation, and staffing."

She flipped through several pages of pictures showing famous golfers and celebrities to land on a page with handwritten numbers. "You'll see my budget was three million on this particular project."

Flipping a few pages deeper in her book, she stopped at a page labeled 'Sundance.'

"This project was one of my more challenging. For two years I was the project manager in charge of transportation and the press relations for the ten-day film festival in January. This last year was especially a killer because they cut my budget by a quarter, but the attendance was up by thirty percent. It was a real bullshit move on their part and I told them so."

Jaxson chuckled next to him at her candor. "I just bet you did. That certainly is an impressive event, but what do you know about running a dance club?"

"Management is management, right?"

"That depends. If I called one of your previous bosses, how would they describe your work habits, Ms. Taylor?"

"Call me Madison, and that depends on who you call, I guess. If you call Martin Porter, he'll tell you I'm a spoiled brat because I refused to work in the hundred-degree Palm Beach desert sun without an air-conditioned RV. He was a cheap bastard who tried to save a buck and make the event team work in the heat for three days straight. I had two employees rushed to the hospital that weekend with heat stroke. I told him to shove it up his ass the next year when he called me to come back."

Again, Chase sensed Jaxson fighting to hold a straight face as the young wisp of a woman surprised them all with her spunk and honesty.

"But if you call Mrs. Rutherford up in San Francisco, you'll hear how she begged me to work for her full time at her exclusive bed and breakfast and spa in Carmel."

"Why did you turn down her offer?"

"Well for starters, the space was much too small to hold any events larger than fifty guests. More importantly, I had just started dating a hot drummer from a band down in San Diego and I didn't want to be that far away from him."

"And how did that relationship turn out?" Chase asked.

"Not surprising, he was a cheating bastard like most guys I've met who are into music. That's why I've made a new rule to only date guys outside of the arts." She blew a huge bubble with her gum, letting it pop as she moved a bit deeper into her portfolio.

"Here, this is the one I wanted to show you the most. I know you two earned your creds on the runway. I'm not sure, but I think you were at this event a couple of years ago in New York City. It was the charity event held at the Met that Bruce Springsteen headlined."

"Hey, I do remember that event," Chase added. "Isn't that the party where the Chinese gymnasts and trapeze artists were part of the entertainment?"

"Yep. That was my idea." She flipped through several pages of pictures, finally stopping on a group shot of people looking up at the ceiling. "There! Isn't this you?"

The men leaned in to take a closer look, almost bumping heads. Jaxson confirmed, "Yes, that was us. That burgundy dress right there is Emma. Christ she looked hot that night."

Chase agreed, "I remember." He left off how much fun they'd

had in the limo on the way back to their town house that night. It had been a memorable ride to be sure.

Jaxson cleared his throat, trying to get refocused on the interview. "So I'm confused. It's clear you have a lot of experience and connections. Tell me again why you want to settle down and work for us here at Runway? You have to have been making bank with all of these high-profile jobs."

Madison smiled as she chewed her gum harder. "I don't want to freak you out or anything, and I sure as hell don't want to work for free, but I don't need to work for money. I have enough."

"Excuse me?" Jaxson asked incredulously. The men were rich, but never once did they want to take on any projects that wouldn't increase their bottom line.

"Let me explain. I recently lost my grandpa. He left me his house and an extensive portfolio. My own mom has been battling breast cancer on and off for a few years now and I just don't want to be away from home as much anymore. My house is only a few blocks from here. The club will only be open four days a week. I'll get to use all of my talents, but still be able to spend time with friends and family."

"Why not just retire? If you don't need the..."

"Stop! I love working. I'm good at it. I'll be damned if I'll stay home and turn into the air headed blonde California girl that everyone assumes I am when they meet me." She pinned them with an accusatory glare, but wisely stopped short of calling them out verbally.

The men shifted uncomfortably in their chairs having been caught red-handed jumping to the conclusions they were being accused of.

Madison smiled. "It's okay. I get it. I've had to scratch myself to the top over and over because of the way I look. I'm not afraid to do it again with you guys. Now, what else can I tell you that will convince you that I'm the best person for this job?"

A pregnant pause fell on the room as all eyes fell to Jaxson. It was clear the decision was now his. She'd convinced Chase.

"So exactly how much is it going to cost me to lock you into the position? And more importantly, how can I lock you in for at least a year?"

"Well, now, that's my kind of question!" She laughed as she slammed her scrapbook closed and pulled an iPad out of her bag next. Chase glanced at Maxine who had her own iPad in front of her. He guessed the women had more in common than he'd noticed on the surface.

Madison moved her chair around closer to the men and laid the tablet on the table where they could see it. "You'll see I took the liberty of making up a proposal for you. I assume you've had to sink a major investment into both the property and renovations to get things ready for opening. Because of my unique situation, I'd like to propose a rather low base salary, but I'd like a cut of gross revenue. That way you only pay me if I'm making bank for you."

"That sounds generous of you, but I'll have to pass on gross revenue. Now, if you make it a cut of net profit, we might have a deal," Jaxson negotiated.

"Interesting. That puts a lot more pressure on me. Risky."

"True, but profit is all we really care about. We need to see a return on our investment or we won't be in business for long. As a businesswoman, I'm sure you understand," he added.

"Yes, indeed I do. But there are many things that I'll need to be able to control in order to sign up for that deal. After all, if you refuse to give me the budget to accomplish what I need to, I won't be able to effect change. I mean, what if you make boneheaded decisions that I don't agree with?"

The tiny woman was fearless, facing off with the dominant man that intimidated many, including Chase at times. Jaxson crossed his arms over his chest, holding her stare until she parroted his stance. The two remained in a silent stare down. Chase glanced at Maxine who was grinning from ear to ear.

Unbelievably, Jaxson caved first. "I see why Maxine likes you so much. Are you sure you two aren't related?" Jaxson deadpanned before finally smiling. The other two people seated at the table sighed as the tension seeped out of the room. "Here is my counter proposal. We'll start you with a full six-figure annual salary we had planned to pay our manager. You'll agree to stay a minimum of six months after which we'll sit down and renegotiate. By then you'll know that you can trust me to do the right thing by the business, and I'll know for sure that you're the right person for the job long term. If so, we can talk profit sharing. Deal?"

Madison hesitated, chewing her gum extra hard as she appeared to weigh her options before thrusting out her tiny hand with meticulously painted and pointed long fingernails. "You have yourself a deal, Mr. Davidson."

The two shook hands to seal the deal before Jaxson spoke again. "I hope you can start right away. Maxine has been doing a fabulous job, but I've promised her husband that I won't keep her out here away from her family for too long after the club is open."

"I just need tomorrow off, but then I'll be all yours."

Jaxson turned to Maxine and asked, "I assume you've covered all of the NDA and security topics with her, including the more private purchasing we'll want her oversight in, correct?"

"Of course." Maxine sounded insulted that he'd even asked. "She even consented to a background check which Miguel finished already. Obviously, she wouldn't have been selected as the front runner if we'd found any problems."

"Excellent." Jaxson pushed to his feet, bringing the interview to an abrupt end.

"It was nice meeting you Ms. Taylor... Madison. I look forward to working with you as we turn Runway West into the premier club on this coast."

The pint-sized woman stood to shake Jaxson's hand once more. She was over a foot shorter than him, even with her high heels. "You won't regret hiring me. I promise you that. I'm so stoked to get started."

"That's good. We have some long weeks ahead of us until we get everything running smoothly. I hope you're up for that."

"You bet I am."

"Excellent." Jaxson then turned to Maxine to add, "Chase and I need to head out. We're going to pick up Emma and then we'll be out of pocket until mid-day tomorrow. Text me with emergencies only, okay?"

"You got it. I need to track Ted down and get the restroom situation straightened out. That's the last major obstacle that could mess us up, but with five days left until the grand opening, we should get across the finish line just in the nick of time."

Jaxson paused and then surprised them all. "I already talked to Avery and she's on board with a slight change in plans."

"Oh no, I don't like changes this close to the finish line," Maxine grumbled.

"Then you're going to hate this." Jaxson glanced nervously at Chase and then back at Maxine and Madison. "I've booked a small private party for some good friends for the day before the grand opening so we are down to four days, not five."

The women both started to argue with Jaxson about it being impossible, but he cut them off.

"Stop. It's too late. I'm committed to this plan. It will be for less than fifty guests. Avery is onboard for the food and beverage. The grounds are close to ready. Security and music are ready. I know it is a bit of a hassle but look at this as a practice opening with an intimate group."

Chase hadn't a clue who Jaxson had made the promise to, but whoever it was had snuck in under the radar. Madison surprised them all by supporting the idea.

"I like it. As long as the guests understand they will be our guinea pigs, it should be fine."

"Yep, don't worry about that. You ladies just work towards a Wednesday mid-afternoon party around the pool and then a sit-down dinner for around fifty in the ballroom. It should wrap up early enough to get things reset for the next day's fashion show during the day and concert in the evening. I'll share more details tomorrow after we get back."

Jaxson stopped long enough to take his Ray-Ban sunglasses out and put them on, making him look like the celebrity he was. "Now, Chase and I are running late. Later."

Chase took his cue from Jaxson who nodded towards the back of the house. The men walked silently side by side through the great room, avoiding the still half-full kitchen and exited through the sliding doors onto the back deck of the mansion. The afternoon sun beat down on the men as they made their way down to the lawn to skirt around the pool towards their house.

They were almost there when Chase finally spoke. "So who the hell did you promise a party to for next week? That seems pretty risky scheduling something earlier rather than later with the deadlines we're under."

Jaxson avoided answering the question until they were in the shade of the back patio. He stopped just before opening the sliding glass door and turned to Chase to answer. "You'll find out soon enough and then you'll understand. Right now we need to wake up Emma and head to the car."

"But…"

Jaxson cut him off, placing his fingers over Chase's lips. He couldn't resist sucking the quieting fingers into his mouth in a filthy emulation of sucking on other body parts.

An almost feral groan came from deep in his Dom's throat. "Shit, the things you do to me. We don't have time for that right now."

Chase bit down just hard enough to nip the fingers as Jaxson

191

retracted them, causing them both to break out into an easy laughter. Chase's heart swelled with the love he felt for the man he hoped to spend the rest of his life with. He wasn't sure which version of Jaxson he loved more. The ultra-bossy, take charge, alpha dominant or this mischievous, easygoing lover. When Jaxson swatted his ass playfully as they entered the air-conditioned house, Chase decided it was this light-hearted version he loved more, if only because it was reserved for only Emma and him. They had to share dominant Jaxson with the world.

The men stopped just inside the door when he noticed Emma asleep on the couch. She'd curled up around a throw pillow.

"She looks so peaceful. I hate to wake her," Chase bemoaned.

Jaxson peeked at his watch before answering. "We're already thirty minutes later than I'd planned. We can't delay, so we'll have to wake her." He moved towards Emma, but Chase reached to hold him back.

"Let me go start the car in the garage. Maybe you could carry her out and she could sleep a bit longer."

"Yeah, okay, we can try that. I'll follow in a few minutes."

Chase jogged to the kitchen, grabbing the keys to his new SUV from the counter and dashing out to start the car just in time for Jaxson to carry a sleeping Emma out. He helped his lovers get settled in the back seat before taking the driver's seat and putting on his own sunglasses.

"Thanks for joining us, Mr. Davidson. My name is Chase and I'll be your driver today. What address, please?" Chase tipped his imaginary hat at the rear-view mirror.

"Smartass. Just head towards the 405 and then go south."

They were a few blocks away when Chase prodded him again. "When are you going to tell me where we're going?"

"It's a surprise."

"So you've said. Don't you think I might need to know since I'm driving?"

"You'll find out soon enough. I'm not going to tell you without Emma."

Chase detected a nervous vibe rolling off his Dom, which was so unusual that it put him on edge. With each mile they put behind them, Chase's anticipation grew until he wanted to scream to wake up Emma in the hopes Jaxson would finally spill his big secret.

"Okay, take the next exit and head west."

"You do realize we are eventually going to hit the ocean, right?" Chase sassed.

"Just drive towards the marina, will ya?"

A spark of excitement helped Chase speed up. They'd talked about renting a boat to go out on the ocean for a day but had agreed that they were just too busy with the club openings to fit that into their schedule for a few months. If Jaxson had rented them a boat, he had really messed up though since it was already late in the day.

"Emma, baby. It's time to wake up. We're almost there."

Chase looked into the rearview mirror to watch Jaxson trying to rouse their girl who stretched and yawned as she tried to get her bearings.

"Turn into the next driveway and stop at the guard shack," Jaxson instructed.

Chase went along with the game of follow directions they were playing. Once he was stopped at the entrance, he rolled his window down, unsure what he was going to say to the uniformed guard who approached the SUV's window.

To his surprise, the guy welcomed him by name. "Mr. Cartwright, we've been expecting you." The guard stuck his head into the window to glance into the back seat before adding. "Mr. Davidson. Ms. Fischer. Welcome to the marina. You can meet your party in the slip next to the California Yacht Club. Just take this main street around as it curves to the left and follow the signs. You can't miss it. I'll phone ahead so they know you're coming."

Chase didn't have a damn clue who 'they' were that the guard was talking about, but he followed directions, pointing the SUV in what he hoped was the right direction. Several blocks in he saw the sign he was looking for and turned, weaving through crowded parking lots and narrowing streets until he came to a dead-end at the club.

"Go ahead and park in the lot behind the yacht club," Jaxson instructed.

Chase played along, his curiosity piqued.

It was Emma's turn to question Jaxson. "Why are we here?"

Only after the car was locked up did Jax reach to grab Chase with one hand and Emma with the other. "You'll see in just a few minutes. Let's go."

The trio made a wide swath that filled the sidewalk leading towards the water. In the distance Chase saw slip after slip filled with boats. Some were motorboats, others sailboats and at the end of the pier were several opulent yachts. They passed boat after boat, narrowing down the selection for their final destination until the only boat left was the biggest yacht they'd seen. He was about to turn and ask Jaxson what was up when Connor Lambert, their lawyer, stuck his head out of the interior cabin to make his way to the back of the ship where it was docked.

"There you are! I was beginning to think you were ditching me," their lawyer observed.

"Naw, we had to finish up an interview before we could head out."

"Suit yourself. I'm glad my flight doesn't leave until tomorrow though."

Connor reached out to help steady Emma as she climbed aboard, followed by Jaxson, and Chase brought up the rear. He was distracted trying to think about why Jax had kept it a secret that they would be seeing their lawyer and why the hell the meeting was on a boat instead of dry land.

Once they were all onboard, Connor invited them inside. "Come on in. I'll show you around."

Chase couldn't help but comment. "I know you lawyers bill a pretty penny per hour, but we are seriously paying too much if this is your yacht."

Their lawyer chuckled. "I wish. But it's nice to have friends in high places. I think I'm going to bring Gabriella out next visit and we can take a trip out to Catalina Island."

After they crossed the back deck, the trio triggered an auto sliding glass door that opened into the opulent main cabin. Unlike most boats he had been on before, the interior was high enough for even the tall men to stand upright without fear of bumping their heads on the crystal chandelier style lamp in the center of the spacious cabin.

Once his eyes adjusted to the closed space after the bright sunlight, Chase glanced around to find an older couple standing at attention on the far side of the room near what looked like a fully stocked bar.

Connor waved the couple closer to the new arrivals.

"I'd like to introduce you guys to Captain Thomas Burrows and his wife, Camille. The Burrows are going to be your hosts and will be taking very good care of you on your journey today."

Chase didn't know what the hell was going on, but Jaxson stepped forward to shake the captain's hand while nodding at the middle-aged woman next to him.

"Captain. Mrs. Burrows. Thanks for agreeing to sail with us today at such short notice. I assume Mr. Lambert has brought you up to speed on why you are here?"

The older man nodded. "Of course. We're honored to play a small role in such an exciting event."

Chase couldn't hold his tongue. "It's nice someone knows what the hell is going on around here since I haven't a clue."

Jaxson didn't turn to look at Chase as he scolded him. "You'll know when I want you to know and not a minute before. Got it?"

Chase could feel the blood rushing to his face, embarrassed at the admonishment. His "Yes, sir," was reflexive.

Jaxson continued his conversation with the older couple. "And the paperwork? All signed?"

Mrs. Burrows answered, a twinge of indignation in her voice. "All signed, but we have worked for Judge McDonald for years. I resent the implication that we would…"

"Camille that will be enough." Her husband reached for her arm, squeezing as he pulled his wife closer as he addressed Jaxson. "I'm sorry, sir. My wife takes her role rather seriously. What she means to say is that it's our honor to be trusted with such an important event and we will ensure not only your privacy, but the confidentiality that you deserve."

"Thank you, Captain. We do appreciate it." Jaxson acknowledged before adding. "We just need to wrap up a bit of paperwork before Mr. Lambert will be disembarking and then we can head out."

"Very good, sir. We'll go up to the bridge. Just ring the bell when you're ready for us to shove off."

"Will do, and thanks." Jaxson nodded and watched them go towards the front of the boat through a narrow hallway and a door at the far end before turning toward Chase and Emma.

Chase wasn't prepared for the uncertainty on Jaxson's face as he stumbled for his next words. "So… I…" Jaxson paused, taking a deep breath before plunging forward. "Connor has some paperwork I need you both to sign."

Emma sounded as confused next to him as Chase felt. "Paperwork? Now? Why would we have to come out here for this? Connor could have just met us at the club if it's club business."

Connor looked like he was about to speak, but Jaxson held his hand up to quiet him.

"It isn't club business." Jaxson took a nervous breath before adding, "It's personal."

Chase parroted his words. "Personal in what way?"

"You'll find out soon. But for now. ." Jaxson glanced back and forth between Emma and him before asking a strange question. "Do you two trust me?"

Emma's "What?" sounded incredulous.

Chase couldn't hold in his chuckle. "Seriously? I think that's the stupidest question you've ever asked us."

"Don't get cheeky. This is serious."

The men were in a stare down. Chase didn't have a clue what the hell was going on, but whatever it was, it had Jaxson on edge. It truly pissed him off that Jaxson had the nerve to ask him such a stupid question, let alone stand in front of him looking like he was worried Emma and Chase could possibly say no.

It was Emma who bridged the awkward standoff between her men by walking between them, reaching up to stroke Jaxson's chiseled jaw gently until he looked down into her eyes. "I trust you with my life. With the life of our children." She glanced over her shoulder at Chase to prompt him. "Just like Chase does."

His lovers both pegged him with an expectant glare until Chase stepped forward to close around Emma's back to touch Jaxson's other cheek. "There is no one on this earth I trust more than you and Emma," he added.

He could feel Jaxson's jaw relax under his fingers, as if he hadn't known for sure how his lovers would answer the ridiculous question.

Chase foolishly thought they were past the silly conversation when Jaxson gave his next instruction to his submissives. "Then both of you sit down at the table. You're going to sign a package of legal paperwork that Connor has for you."

Emma prodded. "What kind of paperwork?"

"That's the rub. I'll tell you, but when we are out at sea."

Chase was starting to understand how serious things were

getting. "You want us to sign legal paperwork without even knowing what we are signing?"

He had hoped he had misunderstood so Jaxson's firm, "Yes," surprised him.

Connor spoke up from behind him, "I'm not sure I'm comfortable with this, Jax."

"Tough shit. I have a plan."

"But…"

Jaxson broke their eye contact to throw a glare at their lawyer. "I get it. I'll have them phone you after we talk about it. You'll be able to abort if you aren't satisfied they are onboard with the plan, but I'll be damned if we're going to do this like a business transaction."

"Isn't that exactly what it is?" Lambert asked.

"Fuck you. You know it's a thousand times more important than that," Jaxson argued.

Connor relented. "Of course. You're right."

Jaxson turned back to them and asked the question again. "So, do you trust me?" The question didn't seem quite as silly this time knowing that his lover expected them to sign legal paperwork without even knowing what they were signing.

He felt Emma place her hand into his and squeeze. He looked down at her to see tears in her beautiful lavender eyes.

She was waiting for him to answer for them both. One glance back at Jaxson's vulnerable face and the answer was absurdly easy.

"I'll sign anything you need me to," Chase responded.

Jaxson rushed forward to pull them both into his arms for a tight hug. Chase could feel the tension rolling off his Dom. He pulled out of the embrace, suddenly anxious to get the details taken care of so Connor could leave them. Only once they were out at sea would he get the answers to the plethora of questions running through his head.

CHAPTER FOURTEEN ~ JAXSON

*J*axson watched from the far side of the room as Chase and Emma sat at the dining table with Connor as he led them through the huge stack of paperwork in front of each of them. He understood why the lawyer wasn't crazy about his idea, but that was too fucking bad. Once they'd made the plan, he couldn't wait to make it a reality.

He didn't really believe in divine intervention, but there was no denying there was some higher power at work these last few days as solutions to all of his problems seemed to present themselves like magic. Things were falling into place even better than he could have hoped.

With each page signed, Jaxson relaxed for many valid reasons — and tensed for a whole different purpose. He reached in to touch the contents of his left pocket for the hundredth time that day. Feeling the small objects brought him comfort in a way he never thought would be possible.

"Okay, that about does it." Connor straightened the packets of paperwork, placing a clip on each stack before reaching to put them into his briefcase and pushing to stand. "I'm heading over to get this all filed before the office closes for the day.

Please give me a call if anything changes after…" he paused looking up at Jaxson who threw him his best 'keep your fucking mouth shut' look. "After you get back on dry land," their lawyer finished.

"Will do. And you give me a call tomorrow if you run into problems."

"The only problem is that it's the weekend so I'm having to pull in a lot of extra favors. You're absolutely sure about the timeline?"

Jaxson wanted to wring his neck. "No," he blurted. Connor had started to smile when Jax added, "Can you make things go any faster?"

Connor didn't bother answering. Instead he stalked past the trio towards the door leading to the aft deck.

"I'll expect a call tomorrow when you're back, sooner if there is a problem." He threw his right hand up in a short wave and was gone.

Emma asked quietly. "We're going to be gone overnight? I didn't pack a bag."

Jaxson turned towards the loves of his life, relieved they were finally alone. It happened so rarely these days, especially with Emma's parents staying with them.

"Don't worry about it. I brought everything we'll need. It's just one night."

Then he remembered the small crew was still onboard. He pushed the button to call for assistance and the Burrows rejoined them right away.

"Mr. Lambert has left. We're ready to shove off."

"Very well, sir. It will only take us about five minutes to finish our final departure checklist. My wife and I will stay on the bridge until you call her down to prepare dinner. Is that satisfactory?"

Jaxson was relieved. His instructions were being followed to a T. "That would be perfect." He made one deviation from his previous instructions. "Just one thing before you go. I'd like to open a bottle of champagne for our departure."

"Of course," Mrs. Burrows assured him. "I have several bottles already chilling."

"Excellent." He glanced at Emma as he asked. "We'll need that apple juice I requested as well."

"Yes, sir."

The trio stood silent, watching as the elderly lady bustled around gathering the supplies she needed. She was about to open the bottle of bubbly when Jaxson stopped her. "Go join your husband. I'll take care of that."

"Of course, sir."

Once they were alone, Jaxson crossed to the table to grab the champagne and begin peeling the foil and muselet away from the bottle. He filled all three flutes before turning and carrying two to his lovers who were watching him curiously.

"Wait. You're letting me drink alcohol?" Emma asked incredulously as he handed her a glass.

"Just one. I didn't fill it very full."

"Okay, what the hell is going on? I went along with the whole signing my life away without much of a problem, but since when do we let the mother of our children drink alcohol while pregnant?" Chase complained.

Jaxson had returned for his own glass. He turned, taking in the sight of the two people that he loved more than anything else in the world.

A foreign wave of insecurity invaded. It wasn't often that Jaxson Davidson was unsure of himself, but in that moment as Chase and Emma looked at him expectantly, he felt a vulnerability that humbled him. He may be their dominant, but at the core of their relationship, he knew they held all of the power in their partnership. Their submission was a gift that he wasn't entirely sure he deserved. Their happiness was more important to him than all the money in his considerable bank account.

Chase smiled the impish smirk that Jaxson loved so damn much. "I love seeing you nervous. It happens so rarely."

"I'm not nervous," he protested defensively.

"Yeah. Right. That's why you look like you want to run to the railing to puke overboard."

"Don't be melodramatic," he groused. "Let's go out on deck and watch as we pull out of the marina."

Jaxson followed them out into the Southern California sunlight. It was getting late enough that the sun was lowering in the western sky casting gorgeous streaks of reds, yellows, and oranges across the blue horizon. It was the perfect backdrop for their special night.

The trio stood silently at the railing as the captain expertly navigated the large yacht through the congested marina. As soon as they cleared the final port markings about fifteen minutes later the captain increased their speed and they headed out into the Pacific Ocean.

He felt Chase's gaze turn towards him instead of the majestic scenic view. It was time. Jaxson took a deep breath and stood tall, turning towards Emma and Chase who were both watching him with intense interest.

Jax opened his mouth to speak, but he was suddenly parched. He self-consciously threw back his glass of expensive French wine like it was a shot, in part to whet his whistle, but more to give him a bit of liquid courage.

He finally got his first words out. "Let's sit." He waved his arm in a grand gesture towards the white leather couches that formed a half circle across the middle of the aft deck. As the boat picked up speed, the wake behind them grew. He turned his back on it to sit in the middle between his lovers, but quickly hated the position because he couldn't see both of their faces at the same time.

Jaxson shot back to his feet like a Jack-in-the-box within

seconds after sitting, drawing a chuckle from Chase. So far the only thing he was succeeding in was making a fool of himself.

Unlike Chase, Emma was beaming up at him, her lavender eyes bright with love... or pity. He wasn't sure which.

"You two sit closer together," he instructed, recognizing he was stalling.

Once they were close and holding hands, Jaxson took a deep breath and barged ahead before he did anything else foolish.

"So... you know I've been working with Connor to try to figure out a way to setup our holdings in the best way to ensure financial security, not only for each of us, but for the kids after they are born."

Emma's smile dimmed. "You mean that's what all of this is about? Business? Money?"

Anyone who had ever met her would have been able to pick up on the disappointment in her voice. Jax pushed down his panic. He'd known this was how she'd react... at least at first.

"It's part of what this is about, yes. A big part, I guess." He paused before throwing her a bone. "But it's not everything."

Chase had been sitting on the edge of the couch, looking excited. As Jaxson's words sunk in, he slumped back. Jaxson bit the inside of his cheek to keep from smiling at the petulant move. He hadn't expected this reaction, but he had an idea of how to make it work in his favor.

Chase sipped at the champagne before he complained. "We could have just stayed at the club for this conversation. I thought you told us it was personal."

Jaxson explained. "I disagree. There are too many nosey people hanging around there. And while I adore your parents, Em, we don't have much privacy at the rental. The new house isn't ready. When I mentioned to Lambert I was going to book us into a suite at a downtown hotel, he was the one that mentioned us using the yacht."

Emma took a tiny sip of her drink, no doubt trying to make it last as long as possible. Then she asked, "So, whose boat is this, really?"

"It belongs to one of the silent investors he hooked us up with. An investor I'll be introducing you to properly soon."

It was Chase that started putting things together first. "Properly? I know all of the investors. Mrs. Burrows mentioned Judge McDonald." He paused, looking as if he were trying to remember something. "We met him once in D.C., right? If I remember he was…" He paused again, this time a grin coming to his face that lit up his caramel brown eyes with mischief. "He was Naughty Boy the night of Roulette."

Jaxson lifted his empty glass in a silent toast to their absent host. "The very same. Seems the judge has done well for himself both politically and financially. He was so impressed with Black Light after that night that he begged to become a minority partner in the west coast club. He's a federal judge in the Southern California district. That's where the connection with Lambert, Urbanski, and Reed comes in."

"Okay, so that makes sense I guess." Chase pinned Jaxson with a pointed glare as he added, "It still doesn't explain why we needed to set sail just to get some privacy."

"No, it doesn't," Jaxson agreed, wishing he'd brought the rest of the bottle of booze out with him. He could use a refill.

He'd planned out what he wanted to say, so the fact that he was feeling tongue-tied made Jaxson feel uncharacteristically vulnerable.

What if they think I've made a mistake?

Being in control was something Jaxson Davidson was very comfortable with, so the racing of his heart as he tried to say the most important words he may ever say felt foreign to him.

He was grateful for the patient smiles reflecting back at him from both Emma and Chase as they waited for him to pull his shit together. He grasped the contents of his left pocket in his closed fist and barged forward.

"Judge McDonald has agreed to make a special visit to the mansion next Wednesday. Technically, he won't be there in any official capacity, but his presence is important to me."

"Next Wednesday? Is he the person you agreed to host a party for the day before the official opening? I still can't believe you agreed to anything that accelerated the opening deadlines," Chase replied.

"The judge is actually just a guest. He'll be officiating at the wedding that we will be hosting on the lawns near the pool."

Emma's face shined with excitement. "A wedding? Oh how fun! Who's getting married?"

Just say it.

Jaxson stepped forward until he was just in front of his lovers sitting on the couch, and then he went down on one knee. Pulling his hand out of his left pocket, he held the contents out in front of him as he answered her question. "I'm hoping we are."

He'd expected some confusion... maybe a few questions... crying... laughter... He hadn't expected silence.

"Say something," Jaxson urged, hating the warble he heard in his voice.

Emma and Chase looked nervously at each other before turning back towards him. Chase finally spoke. "Exactly which one of us are you asking to marry you?"

Duh.

"Neither. I mean both! All three of us."

"But, that's not legal," Emma added, still confused.

"Of course not, but that doesn't mean that we can't have a commitment ceremony where we pledge our love to each other publicly in front of our closest friends and family. I know your father wants the real thing, but this is the next best thing."

Emma looked uncomfortable. "We don't need to do this just for my father. He will get over it eventually."

This wasn't going like he'd planned it in his head at all. Jaxson pushed down his insecurities as he tried to recover.

"I'm not just doing this for Robert. I'm not doing it for anyone really, other than ourselves." Jaxson spoke from his heart as he finally got out the words he'd been planning. "You two are my life. My family. I want us all to spend the rest of our lives together. I know we don't need a piece of paper to legitimize our family, but now that we're going to bring the twins into this world, I want more than anything for us to stand in front of each other and those we love and pledge our lifetime commitment to each other and our children."

It was tenderhearted Chase who started crying first, but Emma's happy tears weren't far behind. Jax had to close his fist quickly to avoid dropping the contents as Chase and Emma catapulted as one from the couch, knocking him on his back to the deck of the yacht as they pelted him with hugs and kisses through their laughter and tears.

Jaxson laughed. "Okay, this is a little closer to the response I was hoping for."

Chase pushed up so he could peer down at Jaxson as he asked, "How long have you been planning this?"

"A few days."

"So it's *our* wedding that is the event next Wednesday?"

"If you'll have me."

Emma had collapsed against him, hugging him tight, her answer muffled against the shirt she was presently wetting with her tears, "Yes!"

Chase's answer came in the form of an almost violent open-mouthed kiss. The triad lay sprawled on the back deck of the boat, letting their passion for each other weld them together as surely as any legal marriage could have.

By the time Chase came up for air, all three of them were short of breath, lying in a heap as the yacht rocked gently the farther and farther away they sailed from the coastline. No one spoke for a long time, just enjoying the promise of their future together.

It was Emma who finally broke the silence. "I get that it can't be legal and that's fine, but then what was all of that paperwork you had us sign?"

Jax patted each of them, silently signaling for them to all sit up. Despite being only a few feet away from the couch, the trio chose to stay seated on the deck where they could form a tight circle.

Only once they were settled where they could see each other again did Jaxson answer. "With Connor's help, we've drawn up incorporation papers for our new official partnership. Up until now, Chase and I have been individual investors, in business together as half owners of the East Coast clubs. He's helped us set things up to not only join our assets into our new family business, but he also made sure to do it in a way to help us minimize taxes and future inheritance concerns. I'll let him answer any legal questions you have, but in short, we are now all equal partners. We are also starting a trust fund for each baby as soon as they are born that they will get control of when they turn twenty-five. This will make sure they are taken care of, no matter what else happens with our business."

The spark of anger in Emma's violet eyes surprised him. "Don't get me wrong. I'm thrilled to stand in front of our friends and family and declare our love and commitment, but I don't need a piece of paper to prove anything, and I sure as hell am not in this for a slice of your money."

Chase turned to her, grinning. "Which is just one of the million things we both love about you, but Jaxson is right to do this. It will help protect you and the kids just in case something happens to Jax or me, or God forbid, both."

"Don't say such a thing!" Emma cried out.

Jaxson stroked her arm gently trying to keep her calm. "Nothing is going to happen. We are just being cautious. It's the responsible thing to do to make sure you and the babies are taken care of. I'd never even finalized a will before now for crying out loud! And since we can't legally marry, the courts would get to decide what to do with my assets if I died today." He paused before adding on his number one concern. "Don't for one minute think that my father wouldn't swoop in and try to make a grab for everything. He'd love nothing more than to get the last laugh over what he sees as our sinful way of life by stealing everything from both of you."

The threat wasn't some idle long shot. He knew with every fiber of his being that his father would love nothing more than stealing everything from Chase, and even Emma and the kids, should anything happen to him. It would have been bad enough before, but he would never let that happen to his children.

Chase nodded seriously. "I hadn't even thought about him, but you're absolutely right. He'd love to stick it to me after how we came out so publicly. And, I hate to say it, but he'll never accept the babies."

He could see Emma mulling their words over, still not convinced.

Jaxson reached for her hands and waited for her to look into his eyes to speak from his heart. "I love that you don't want our money, baby, but like it or not, we need to make sure we do all we can to protect ourselves and the kids. If it were just two of the three of us, you wouldn't be giving it another thought. Married couples combine assets all the time."

"Or they have pre-nup agreements," she answered quietly.

"Fuck that! You are an equal partner. I'm convinced that without you, Chase and I would still be on the road, unfocused and gallivanting from photo shoot to photo shoot. I'd have just kept getting more angry and distant. You and Chase together helped me focus on the important things in life. You're the catalyst for me wanting to step up my game."

Chase grinned. "Jax is right. You should have seen how surly he was getting before we met you."

"Thanks for the help, Chase," he deadpanned.

"Anytime, babe," Chase teased.

The trio chuckled in unison. As usual, Chase provided the good-natured lightness that Jaxson loved so very much.

He thrust his left hand forward into the center of their intimate circle and waited until he had his lovers' attention before turning his hand and opening his fist, palm up, to reveal his next surprise. He'd picked the contents up just that morning on the way into the mansion.

Chase and Emma leaned in to get a closer look, but neither of them dared to touch the rings now glittering in the late afternoon sunshine.

Jaxson picked up the smallest of the three identical rings, holding it up for their inspection.

"I had them specially designed. I hope you both like them. And aren't disappointed that I didn't buy you a big diamond, Emma. I wanted us to all wear the same rings though, since they are so symbolic of our relationship."

"Don't be ridiculous, they're beautiful!" Fresh tears were streaming down Emma's cheeks as she reverently reached to touch the ring he held up.

"Hold out your left hand, baby. Let's see if I got the size right."

Emma complied. Jax could see a slight tremble in her hand as he slowly placed the trinity ring on her left ring finger.

She glowed as she exclaimed, "It's perfect! I love it so much."

Jaxson turned to Chase next who already had his left hand out, waiting for his own ring. As he took Chase's hand, he explained what was probably obvious to them. "I had the jeweler design the three smaller rings linked together into one wedding band. The black onyx band is for me since we all know I'm the darkest one of the three of us. Like in real life, the white gold band is for you Chase, because it's lightness balances me. Dark and light."

Tears glistened in Chase's eyes as Jaxson seated the ring lovingly on Chase's ring finger. Only then did he explain, "The diamond encrusted band in the middle is for you, Em, because you are the sparkle that lit up our lives. And we are all at our best when we are intertwined together."

Emma leaned forward to hug Jaxson. "It is the most beautiful piece of jewelry I've ever seen. I would have been so upset if you got me something different. It is absolutely perfect for us. Thank you."

"So you're going to wear a wedding band too?" Chase asked.

Jaxson pulled Emma to sit in his lap so they could look at Chase. "Of course. Why wouldn't I?"

"I don't know. Sometimes husbands don't always wear a wedding ring."

"Well this husband is going to. It never even occurred to me not to. I love that we will all share this." Jaxson slid the last ring on his finger.

"I agree completely," Emma added.

"That's not all that I think we should all share." Jaxson looked between them.

Chase grinned. "I think we are extremely good at sharing lots of things already, unless you're trying to tell us you're going to take your share of sleeping on the wet spot after all these years."

They all chuckled. "Nope. I'm still your Dom and as such, I draw the line at sleeping in the wet spot." He waited for the levity to pass before adding more seriously. "I was actually hoping we could all share the same last name, like most other married people."

Emma squealed, agreeing easily. "Emma Davidson! It is a bit like a dream come true. I've never been one of those liberated women who insist on keeping their own last name."

Chase was a bit slower to answer, just as Jaxson had expected. Chase Cartwright was a brand. It wasn't just who he was as a man, but it was the name he'd got famous with... made his millions with. Only Jaxson could truly understand what he was asking of his lover and friend.

"Chase Davidson. It does have a nice ring to it and God knows

I love the idea of sharing your name, Jax. Please don't be angry, but it may take me a bit more time than Emma to get used to the idea since men don't normally plan for changing their name."

"I totally understand. In fact, the more I thought about it, I just couldn't feel right about asking you to lose the Cartwright name... so that's why I had Connor fill it out to have your legal name changed to Chase Michael Cartwright-Davidson."

"That's nice, but I'd rather just have the same last name as you and Emma."

"Oh, you will. He is filing Emma's legal name as Emma Nicole Cartwright-Davidson."

It was Emma that complained. "No! I agree with Chase. We want to all three have the same last name. That's important."

"I couldn't agree more." He grinned before adding, "That's why I'm changing my legal name to Jaxson Andrew Cartwright-Davidson."

He had never seen Chase look more surprised. Not in the almost ten years they had known each other.

"You did WHAT?" Chase screeched.

"You heard me. I'm officially changing my last name, too."

"But... you're Jaxson Davidson," Chase uttered with awe in his voice.

Jax chuckled. "Yep, and I'll still be the same Jaxson, but as soon as Lambert gets the paperwork filed and approved, that will be Jaxson Cartwright-Davidson." Jaxson turned to Emma in his lap and teased her. "I hope you understand why I didn't make it Fischer-Cartwright-Davidson. That would have been ridiculously long."

Emma hugged him so hard it almost hurt. "You are absolutely the most romantic man in the whole wide world. What an awesome surprise!"

Jax hugged her close as she wrapped her legs around him, clinging to him like a monkey. He was able to watch Chase over her shoulder. His heart swelled with the love he felt for the handsome blond with the sexy as fuck hair he loved to pull as he fucked him from behind. When Chase turned his expressive eyes to meet Jaxson's, the love he felt shining back at him would have turned his knees weak if he'd been standing.

Jaxson reached out with his left hand, his own trinity ring shimmering in the sunlight as he silently beckoned his lover to join them. Chase leaned in reverently, sandwiching Emma between the men, exactly where she belonged.

Chase's voice warbled when he spoke softly. "You don't need to do this. I'll happily change my name to Davidson."

The men's eyes locked as Jaxson reassured him. "I know you would, but it's done. I love you, and in my heart I know this is the right thing for us."

Chase leaned in, placing his forehead against Jaxson's, intimately linking their trio as he repeated the mantra they had come up with years before. "Where you go, we all go."

"Hell yes. And right now I think we should all go find our stateroom and do a bit of celebrating before we have Mrs. Burrows make us dinner."

His heart warmed when Chase and Emma answered in unison, "Yes, sir."

It was that moment he was absolutely certain he was the luckiest bastard on the planet.

CHAPTER FIFTEEN ~ EMMA

"*I* always knew you'd be the most beautiful bride I'd ever see."

Emma had been lost in thought and missed that her mom had let herself into the bedroom on the second floor of the mansion they were using as their staging area for their big day. Looking up into the mirror from her chair, she saw the reflection of her parents standing just inside the door.

"Thanks, but you might be a bit biased, Mom. It all feels a bit surreal to be honest."

"Well that's probably because Davidson only gave you a few days warning to try to pull off the impossible. I don't know why he's hell-bent to do this so fast," her father grumbled.

"Daddy, I can't believe you. First you complain that no one is going to marry me and make me an honest woman. Now you're complaining that they are marrying me too fast. Make up your mind!"

Emma's mom globbed on. "Robert, we talked about this. Today is their special day. A day you pushed for, I might add. You should be thrilled for them."

"I'm just speaking the truth. And this isn't going to be a legal ceremony anyway."

Emma had been floating on cloud nine for the last few days as she rushed to plan one of the best days of her life. She'd been coddling her father along the way, giving him the time he needed to adjust to the big changes. Listening to him complain yet again was the final straw.

She pushed to her feet, and rounded to face her parents, letting the long, white designer gown flow to the floor. Jaxson and Chase's old modeling contacts had magically produced the gown of her dreams from a top designer in just a few days. The deep breath she drew in and expelled was the only warning for her father. "I love you so much, Daddy. I really do. And I used to think you were just worried about me because you had my best interest in mind. That you don't want me to get hurt." Emma paused and the older man nodded in agreement, a relieved smile starting to grace is lips.

Too bad it wouldn't be there for long.

"But I don't think that's true anymore. Jaxson and Chase have done everything you've asked for and more. If you can't see how much we all love each other and how insanely happy I am today, then maybe you shouldn't be here."

"Wh-what?"

"I mean it. This is a very special day for me, and I don't want anyone to attend that is going to be uncomfortable with the unique nature of our relationship. This isn't just a phase I'm going through. We aren't just dating or goofing around until something better comes along. These are the men I am lucky enough to love with all my heart and I thank God every single day that they love me back.

"I'm sorry we don't fit your mold of what a proper *couple* is supposed to look like. We've done everything in our power to give you the time you needed to get used to things — years even — but time is up. Today I am going to stand in front of our closest friends and family and declare my love openly for both men and they will do the same, and I don't want anyone even watching that isn't one-hundred percent happy for us, and that includes you."

"But, you don't understand…"

"I understand perfectly. Our trio isn't how you define marriage. I get it, but here's the thing. They make me happy. They love and protect me. They take care of me and are going to be wonderful fathers for your grandchildren. This, today, is how Jaxson, Chase, and I define our marriage and, honestly, our opinion is the only one that counts now. Just like when you and mom got married your parents were no longer the primary people you had to make happy because you had mom. The same is true for me. I beg you, please don't make me choose between you and the guys, because you will lose and it will break my heart."

Emma had practiced this little speech in her head a hundred times over the last few years, perfecting it in the last week as she discovered her father was still dug in despite all her men had done to prove their love to their future father-in-law. It would truly break her heart to have to hurt her father, but she could no longer allow him to hold a grudge against her unique relationship.

"I don't… I mean… I actually like Jaxson and Chase very much. This isn't about them."

"Then what the hell is it about?" Emma demanded, not backing down.

She could sense his panic as he lifted his hand to drag his fingers nervously through his short hair, and she had to bite her tongue to keep from adding on more. As uncomfortable as the silence was that stretched between them, she knew it was necessary. Emma and her father needed to face his final objections, whatever the hell they were, head on so they could leave them behind once and for all.

Her father's eyes darted to his wife, silently begging her to jump in and defend him, but Linda Fischer stood still exactly like her daughter, waiting for Robert to finally string a reply together.

LIVIA GRANT

It took almost two long minutes, which felt like an eternity, for him to finally speak.

"We've never discussed it, and I don't know for sure, but... when I'm around the three of you, you are different. More..." He struggled for a word before finishing with, "submissive. You never say 'yes, sir' to me or any other man that I've noticed. You've always been a strong, independent young woman, but when you are with them, you defer to them for almost everything. It's like they have you brainwashed. Like you have to ask permission to do the most simple things. I worry that you've fallen under their spell in some way and that one day you'll wake up and regret letting them smother the real you."

It was Emma's turn to fall into an awkward silence, unsure how she could possibly explain the true nature of her relationship with the men, her dominants. Her mind raced for some way to help her father understand without actually spelling things out in embarrassing detail. Sex in general was a topic to be avoided between most women and their fathers. Talking about the kinky activities the trio was into, well, that just couldn't happen.

She had to fight to hold her father's eye contact. She'd be damned if she'd look away as if she had something to be ashamed of. She loved her life, including, and especially, her choice of submission. And it was a choice.

The truth would have to do.

"You're not wrong about that. I choose to be submissive to them intentionally. It makes them happy, but more importantly, it makes me happy."

"How can you be happy when you have no power in your relationship?"

Her chuckle broke the tension.

"What's so funny?" her father questioned.

"You're gonna have to trust me, Dad. I hold plenty of the power. I just choose not to wield it often."

"Like never."

"That's not true at all."

"There is no way you could influence them to do something they didn't want to do on the timeline they want. From where I sit, they make all of the important decisions for you."

"Name one thing they've forced me to do that I didn't want to. One thing. In our almost three years together."

"Move to California. You don't like it here."

Emma shot a dirty look at her mother, regretting sharing those particular feelings with her mom in confidence several weeks before. At least Linda Fischer looked sheepish.

"That was before. Things are getting so much better."

"Oh. And why's that?" her father pressed her, his accusation heavy in his tone.

"I wasn't unhappy because of California. I was unhappy because I had fucked up! I was keeping the mother of all secrets from them and it was eating me alive from the inside with guilt. I was unhappy because I wasn't feeling well and yet I didn't want to make a big deal about it because they were working so damn hard to get the club off the ground. I didn't like the temporary housing situation or living out of suitcases. All of those things are behind us now."

"That doesn't explain the almost reckless growth of the clubs. Jaxson dragged you into this business venture and from what I can see, he is overextended both in time and money."

"Are you kidding me? Did you forget that I'm in charge of our finances, not just for the clubs, but also for Jaxson and Chase's entire portfolio? Do you understand the level of trust that took for them considering I brought nothing but big-ass student loans into our relationship financially?

"And I can assure you that we are not overextended. But more importantly, to your earlier concern that I have no voice in this relationship, I'll have you know that I got the final vote on proceeding with the clubs or not. They were prepared to walk away from the deal if I didn't think it was a good idea, either personally or professionally. Does that sound like them bowling me over and not letting me have any input in our future?"

Her answer frustrated her father further. His complexion growing red and splotchy like it did when he got hot under the collar, literally. Anger bubbled up in her.

"Why today? You've had days to talk to me about this shit. Today is my wedding day. The only one I'm ever going to have. It's supposed to be the happiest day of my life."

Her father tried to smooth things over. "And it will be. Just chalk my reservations up to being an overprotective old man."

"No! I meant it. I don't want you there if you can't truly be happy for me. Not if you can't look at Jaxson and Chase and know with every fiber of your being that they are the only men who can make your little girl happy. Because they do... they make me so happy."

Robert sighed. "I think you think you're happy, but one day you'll wake up and realize you have no voice of your own."

"What will it take to convince you you're wrong once and for all? How can we put this behind us forever so you can just be happy for all three of us?"

"It's not that simple, honey. I don't expect you to change how you interact with them now. It's too late."

"You don't have a damn clue what you're talking about, you know that?"

"I know better than you think I do."

"Really?" Emma paused, unsure of what her father was trying to say.

His face got a shade redder, but this time from embarrassment. "The walls at the rental are pretty thin."

She could no longer maintain eye contact with her father. Frustration made the already awkward conversation worse. The right words escaped her long enough that she finally asked softly, "Do you really want to have this conversation?"

"Not really. You pushed."

"No, Dad. You pushed by refusing to believe me when I told you that I've never been happier and that I can't imagine living my life any other way."

"I just have to ask one thing and then we won't talk about it again." He paused and waited until she finally looked back into his eyes. She was relieved to see love and concern where moments ago there had been frustrations.

"Okay, ask away. I promise to tell you the truth, whatever it is."

He came to her then, placing his hands on her elbows and pulling her closer until they embraced. She could smell the cologne he always wore for important occasions. It reminded her of so many other events she'd been to with her parents over the years and in that moment, all she could think about was how important it was that she share the future milestones with them as well. The birth of the twins, their christening, birthdays, and more. They had to get this disagreement sorted out once and for all or it would forever overshadow her most important relationships.

"I need to know that they don't hurt you."

"Hurt me? Why would..." She paused, finishing with a simple, "Oh."

"Like I said, the walls are thin. I don't want details, but your mother has tried to assure me that you're in no danger and my brain agrees, but... well... there is just so much about this whole relationship of yours that I just don't understand. I need to know they haven't changed the real you. I need to know that my baby girl is safe and happy."

A small part of her wanted to go hide in the closet until her father left, but she was an adult. A woman. A *pregnant* woman. She had done nothing to be ashamed of and to try to hide or act embarrassed would only cheapen the depth of their unique relationship.

"I promise you, Dad. They never ever hurt me in a way that I don't like. It's so complicated, I don't know if I can find the right words to explain it, but the closest I've ever come up with is that we are like a three-piece puzzle. We each have our role to play in holding the puzzle together. Jaxson is our leader at the top. He is fierce and smart and he keeps Chase and I below him safe and protected. Chase has the hardest job in the middle, switching back and forth between protecting me and submitting to Jaxson's lead, but he does it with charm and a levity that brightens all our lives so much.

"And it's true, I may be submissive to them, but it doesn't mean they push me down. It means they protect me and love me. They call me the glue that holds us together, but in this analogy I'm the foundation. Without me, they would crumble. Without any one of us, we wouldn't be whole."

"You didn't answer my question," her father persisted.

"They didn't change me, Dad. They saw the real me. I know it is confusing. On the one hand, our relationship is modern and enlightened. We never could have been open in a bisexual trio in the past. On the other hand, we are pretty old fashioned. More like marriages from the fifties — they lead, and I follow.

"I love every single solitary minute of my life with them, and yes, that includes when they discipline me because they do it because they love me. I'm not going to get into our unique personal relationship dynamics but know that I have a safe word. I can use it at any time I feel uncomfortable and whatever we are doing stops. Nothing will ever happen to me that I don't want to happen."

Tears filled her father's eyes, and Emma held her breath, hoping she'd found the right words to put her father's concerns to rest once and for all.

"It's always been my job to protect you, Emma, and I can't just turn that instinct off because I know you're in love." He looked towards her mom before returning his gaze to hers. "But if you tell me that this is what you want, that you're safe in whatever you choose to do with them, then that's good enough for me. Anyone who is around you for a few minutes can see how much you love each other and how happy you are. I just... I worry that they've been together longer and that... never mind. It was silly."

"Listen, I wish I had a crystal ball and could see into the future. I don't get to know what is in our future any more than other couples do on their wedding day. But I know this. I'm having their babies. We are going to be a family and they are going to be awesome fathers. Your grandchildren are going to adore both of them as much as I do. I just hope you'll be there to be happy for us."

"I will be. As hard as this conversation has been, how *really* hard it's been... I'm glad we talked before the wedding."

"So, you agree that it is a wedding, even if it isn't legal?" she pressed.

"I do. Like you explained, it is a commitment ceremony and Davidson has put the paperwork in motion to back up his responsibility to you and the kids."

"Okay, dad, then let's put this behind us for good. Can you finally just be happy for me?"

"I was always happy for you. It was your future I was worried about."

Jaxson's voice boomed from the doorway. "And now you know she has nothing to worry about in her future. I'll spend my last breath making sure she is safe and happy."

Emma had her back to the door, but her father's gaze left hers to look at the new arrivals. He didn't release his daughter as he spoke. "Emma and I were just making sure we had talked through a few things. She didn't want me to walk her down the aisle with anything left unsaid."

"She's smart like that," Chase answered.

Robert Fischer looked down into his daughter's eyes as he agreed. "Yes, thank goodness she seems to be smarter than her old man."

Emma's mom had been quietly watching the drama from the

sidelines, but with the arrival of the men, she joined the group in the center of the room.

"Now that we have all of that sorted out, I think it's almost time to head on downstairs." She turned to her soon-to-be sons-in-laws and asked, "Are you two supposed to see the bride before the ceremony?"

Jaxson groused, "We already saw her this morning, and anyway, I don't believe in silly superstitions like that. The club photographer is here. He'll be taking the only sanctioned video and still photos from the event. I was hoping we could have him come in and start getting some pre-ceremony shots."

"That's a great idea," Linda answered for the group. "I'm so relieved you took care of it. I remembered with a panic this morning and worried we wouldn't have any good photos."

Emma's dad released her after leaning in to give her a kiss on her forehead. She turned to the door in time to see a good-looking man with dark tanned skin and short, cropped black hair stepping into the room. He was dressed in a classic black suit and looked like he could be on the runway instead of photographing models there.

"Emma, this is Peyton Wade. He's a photographer we've worked with in Europe the past. He's settling down here in L.A. and has graciously agreed to work with us for a bit while we look for a permanent photographer for the clubs."

Robert was the one that picked up on Jaxson's flub. "Clubs? You mean he'll be doing photo shoots in D.C. too?"

Jaxson didn't miss a beat with his prompt reply. "No. I misspoke. Just club. Runway West."

Emma suspected her father knew more than he was letting on about the second more private club two floors beneath them, but he wisely kept his guess to himself.

"Nice to meet you Peyton. Thanks for being here for our special day," Emma said, smiling. His handshake was as soft as the brown of his eyes as they greeted each other.

"I'm honored Jaxson and Chase trust me for such an important assignment. It's nice to meet the woman who got them off the road and settling down. I don't need to tell you there were more than a few broken-hearted models missing them from the fashion circuit last season."

Emma chuckled. "I traveled with them for almost two full seasons and I don't doubt that one bit. Not one day went by that I didn't see someone, men and women, hitting on them."

"That doesn't surprise me one bit." He pulled his expensive camera from the bag he was carrying before adding, "Are we ready to get started? I know it's still early but the first guests have started to arrive and we don't want them down there with the open bar for too long before you make your appearance or we may have guests falling into the pool before the day is over."

The group chuckled as they followed Peyton's instructions to set up for their first of many photos of the day.

"I can't believe almost everyone we invited was able to be here on such short notice," Emma said in wonder as she looked down on the pool venue where the people closest to the trio were assembling to witness the unusual ceremony that would soon begin.

Chase stood next to her, wrapping his right arm around her waist as he looked down on the growing crowd and added, "I'm pleasantly surprised as well. Considering the insane schedule most of them have, I was worried we might not have anyone show up."

Jaxson didn't answer. She'd noticed him becoming increasingly distracted the more photos they had taken. He'd been glancing at his watch repeatedly as if the time were going by too fast... or too slow. Now he was looking out over the guests, looking for something... or someone.

Emma went to him, wrapping her arms around his waist, happy they had a few minutes alone before the men would go downstairs ahead of her.

"Is everything okay, sir?" she asked as she looked up at his drop-dead gorgeous face.

She was relieved at his smile.

"I love being your sir, you know that, right?" Jaxson observed.

"I do."

He hesitated. "I heard what you said to your father this morning. I was just getting ready to burst in the room to give him hell for upsetting you today. Chase stopped me just in time." He gazed down into her eyes. "You handled him perfectly. I am so damn proud of you, Emma."

Her heart skipped at his loving praise. "I've been preparing for that showdown. I knew he'd been having trouble holding back and I wanted it all out before the wedding."

"Well you did good. I just wish…" His voice trailed off as he looked away from her. She hated how sad he looked and knew what he was thinking of.

"You still haven't heard from her then?" she asked, hopeful he'd just forgotten to tell her that his mother was going to make it to their important day after all.

"I'm sure my bastard father found out and prevented her from coming. She sounded so happy when I talked to her, both about the babies and then a few days later about the wedding. I really did think—" He didn't finish his sentence. It probably hurt too much to admit that he had got his hopes up that his mother, for once, might have chosen her son over her asshole husband.

Chase joined them, trying to cheer their Dom up. "I have an awesome wedding gift for you and I need to give it to you before we go downstairs."

"That's not fair. I thought we agreed not to get each other gifts since we had so little time!" Emma complained playfully, trying to lighten Jaxson's mood.

"I think you'll agree with this one once you see what I have. To be honest, it's a present for all of us in a way."

Jaxson thrust his hands in his pockets, looking impatient. "We should get going. Are you sure it can't wait?"

"I'm sure. I left it out in the hallway. I'll be right back."

Jax shot Emma a dirty look. "Are you in on this? He's been acting suspiciously secretive all day."

Emma answered truthfully, "Sorry, he didn't tell me either. I'm sure it must be something awesome though if he is this excited."

The door opening drew Jaxson and Emma's attention. They turned as one expecting to see Chase carrying in a gift, but instead found Jaxson's mother standing in the doorway with a grinning Chase right behind her.

"My flight was delayed and then I had to make a stop on the way over. I was so afraid I might be too late," she spoke excitedly. "I'm sure Chase was getting worried that he might need to stall."

Jaxson stood in stunned silence. It was in that moment that Emma realized that he truly hadn't expected his mother to come. She had let him down so many times in the past that he hadn't dared to hope she'd come through for his important day.

Emma rushed forward to hug her soon-to-be mother-in-law. "Miranda, I am absolutely thrilled that you made it. It wouldn't have been the same without you here."

As the women hugged, Emma could feel how frail the older woman had become since the last time they'd seen each other. The already thin matriarch had lost a dangerous amount of weight.

As they pulled out of their hug, all of Miranda's attention was on her son who stood stalk-still across the room. The mother-son couple were in a stare down until Jaxson finally spoke. "Did you leave him?"

"We can talk about..."

"Did. You. Leave. Him?" Just talking about his father had

Jaxson heading into his dark place. Emma wished he could just be thrilled his mother had arrived.

It was Chase who crossed the room and went to their Dom, pulling him into his arms and leaning up to whisper something into his Jax's ear that the other occupants of the room couldn't hear. While they waited for Jaxson's response, Emma felt his mom's hand latching onto her own, squeezing her so tight it almost hurt.

Jaxson took several deep breaths as he let Chase calm him enough to speak again. "I'm sorry. I don't mean to attack you the second you got here. I was just worried about you is all."

Emma squeezed Miranda's hand back and walked her across the room towards the men as his mother answered him. "We should talk about it all tonight, after the wedding and the dinner. I don't want to get upset now when we have so much to be celebrating."

"That isn't an answer," Jax groused.

"Of course it is. It's just not the answer you were hoping for."

They were close enough for Chase to get out of the way so that Jaxson could give his mother a hug. Emma stepped back, enjoying the reunion between mother and son.

She elbowed Chase next to her. "I can't believe you kept this a secret from me, too," she grumbled with a smile.

"Well believe it. I'm a good secret keeper. In fact, I have another even more surprising secret."

Emma turned, placing her hands on her hips. "And just when do I get to find out this big surprise?"

Chase leaned in close to speak softly. "You won't have to wait long. Watch Jaxson, though. He's going to flip."

Emma turned her attention back to Jaxson and his mom when a knock interrupted and Maxine let herself into the room. "Excellent! I heard that you'd made it here, Mrs. Davidson. I was worried we'd need to send a search party out for you."

"Thanks for accommodating my delay. I just couldn't come to the wedding without my date, though."

Emma watched Jaxson as he internalized his mother's words.

"You stopped to pick up a date? I mean, don't get me wrong, anyone is a step up from the old man, but shouldn't you at least get a divorce before you start stepping out in public? He's going to skewer you in the courts if he catches wind of you dating already."

Something was fishy. The longer her son admonished her, the broader his mother's smile got until she was grinning.

"Oh, I'm sure your father is going to use every trick to get even with me for leaving him, but this is one secret I'm pretty sure he'll be keeping."

"And why is that?"

"Because my date is someone he wants to keep his distance from at all costs."

Maxine opened the door and started waving to someone in the hall. As the door swung open, an older man with leathery, tan skin and a goofy grin stepped into the room. Emma had never seen the gentleman before so she had absolutely no clue why he was there. All she knew for sure was that there was no way in hell that Miranda Davidson would be dating him. He looked completely out of place in his simple khaki pants and worn golf shirt.

When she turned to ask Jaxson if he even knew the man, she was almost floored by the tears in her dominant's eyes. She held her breath understanding something special was happening.

The older man spoke first. His Spanish accent was so thick that Emma had trouble understanding him. "I am luckiest man in Mexico. I hope you are not angry that I am here on your special day, mijo."

Jaxson finally moved, rushing to pull the older, shorter man into a hug. "Tio Juan! It is so good to see you. You are always welcome."

Emma was truly confused. It was Miranda who filled her in. "Juan was with our family for many years, taking care of our properties as if they were his own. As a kid, Jaxson used to spend countless hours outdoors helping Juan, learning from him. They have always had a close friendship that my husband was, of course, jealous of.

"I'm ashamed that when my husband banned Juan and his family, getting them deported back to Mexico, that I wasn't strong enough to stand up to the bully. Once I decided to leave Gregory, I knew finding Juan and making sure he and his family were taken care of was high on my list of mistakes I needed to correct."

"Mijo, your mother has hired a lawyer for me. Can you believe such a thing?"

Jaxson pulled back to look at his mother. "I do believe such a thing. She's a good woman, especially when she is not being corrupted by the man she made the mistake of marrying."

Miranda waved her hand. "Enough about that for now. Today is a day to celebrate you and the loves of your life."

His mom stopped, as if she suddenly remembered the unseen additions to the family. She turned to Emma and reached out to place her palm on her rounded tummy in awe. "It's true? My grandchildren are growing here, even now?"

Emma placed her hand over her mother-in-law's as she reassured her. "They are, and they can't wait to meet their grandma."

Miranda chuckled. "I hope you aren't going to have them call me granny. It makes me sound so damn old."

Emma reassured her, "My mom already said the same thing. We still have a few months to come up with fun nicknames for each of you that you can approve."

Chase piped in, "I'm anxious for you to meet my mom and sister today, Miranda. My nieces and nephews already call her granny so she'll be happy to keep that nickname."

Mrs. Davidson smiled at Chase. "Please call me Mom." She turned her attention to Emma to add, "Both of you."

"I'll be happy to," Emma reassured her.

Maxine jumped back into the conversation. "We are running incredibly late and while I know this is somewhat an informal affair with only your closest friends and family, I do want to keep things moving or Chef Avery is going to have my head when her appetizers get ruined because we ran long."

Jaxson linked his mother's hand into the crook of his arm, inviting her to join him. "It's time for us all to go down. I'll escort you and Juan to your seats." He then turned to Emma and added, "I'll send your dad back in to escort you down the aisle, okay baby?"

Emma's heart lurched, realizing the moment was upon them. She was about to marry the men of her dreams. "Thank you, sir. I'm more than ready."

CHAPTER SIXTEEN ~ CHASE

"What the hell is that newswoman doing here?" Jaxson leaned in close to talk against Chase's ear as the two men stood at the front of their makeshift outdoor wedding chapel, looking out on the intimate grouping of their best friends and closest family. Chase scanned the crowd and agreed that Brandi Wittman, his old babysitter, stood out as the one person in attendance that did not belong.

"I have no idea who let her in," he whispered back. "I sure as hell didn't invite her, and I'd bet my life that Emma didn't either."

Jaxson growled softly next to him. "Now what the fuck do I do? Emma and her dad are on the walkway and will be here in one minute."

Chase changed his focus from the seated group dispersed around the pool deck to the flower-lined path stretching between the pool and the main club. His pulse quickened seeing Emma in her gorgeous gown, slowly walking towards her men, taking steps to the beat of the romantic music being provided by the Grammy award-winning string quartet they'd hired.

He finally leaned in to his Dom to answer with their only option.

"It's too late to throw her out without making a major scene. I don't think Emma will notice she's here and then we can have Miguel get her out of here as soon as he can without making a commotion."

"I'll text him now to make sure he's on it," Jaxson added.

The clearing of a throat right behind them cut the men's quiet conversation short. It was Judge McDonald's veiled way of telling the men to quiet down now that the ceremony had begun. Chase felt rather than saw Jaxson throw a warning glance to the submissive judge to stay out of their discussion.

It had been awkward for the first few minutes of being reacquainted, but the three men had simultaneously agreed to ignore their previous meeting in February at the Roulette Redux event where the judge had been dominated by one of Black Light's most active dominatrixes.

Emma and Robert were almost to the brick patio deck where the wedding guests were standing and turning to watch the bride walking down the pseudo aisle. Jaxson put his phone back into his pocket and added, "I sent a text to Miguel and told him to keep an eye on her and get rid of her as soon as he can."

Just as Jaxson finished his sentence, the overcast sun decided to make an overdue appearance, showering the entire wedding venue in bright sunlight. The golden glow shone a spotlight on Emma, creating a halo around her that seemed to shift the ground beneath him.

She was fucking perfect in every way. As if he could read his mind, Jaxson reached out and grabbed Chase's hand, linking their fingers intimately as they leaned against each other, anxious to touch as they shared what was arguably one of the most important days of their lives together.

The rest of their closest friends and family faded away when his eyes locked with Emma's as she and her father got closer to him and Jaxson. The grip on his hand got stronger as Emma turned her love-filled gaze on Jaxson next. It reminded Chase that his strong Dom was not immune to the more emotional aspects of their complicated love.

They hadn't had any practice for the day so Chase didn't know exactly what to expect when Emma stopped directly in front of her men, her father next to her. The foursome hesitated until the judge took charge.

"Please be seated." He paused while the guests took their seats before continuing. "We are gathered here today as witnesses to the commitment ceremony between three extraordinary people who are fortunate enough to have found each other as they traveled through the vast world. Just like each and every one of you, their closest friends and family, I have had the privilege to witness the depths of the love that Jaxson, Chase, and Emma have for each other. While their relationship may be unconventional in the eyes of many, no one who meets them can doubt for one minute the deep level of commitment they have for each other."

Chase had to force himself to focus on the words the judge was saying. The whole afternoon was beginning to feel surreal. For years, as their unique trio grew closer, he had been coming to terms with the idea that he would never get married as there was no way two of the three of them would have married and left the third person out. Yet as he looked past Emma to see his mom, sister, brother-in-law, nieces, and nephews in the front row, it registered that today he was the groom.

At least one of them, anyway.

The judge's words faded to the background as Chase watched the beaming faces of their best friends — Khloe and Ryder, Jonah and Samantha, Spencer and Klara, and even their lawyer and friend Connor and his new girlfriend, Gabriella. Their old agent Roberta had flown in from London as had Emma's grandmother from Wisconsin. The women were sitting next to Jaxson's mom. Even Emma's four roommates from the University of Wisconsin who had been supportive at the start of their unique relationship had been able to fly in with little warning and were watching from the last row of chairs. Every single person there, with the exception of the uninvited newswoman, was so important to the trio.

A squeeze from Jaxson's hand brought Chase out of his contemplative thoughts and back to the judge's comments.

"While this ceremony may not be a legal marriage in the eyes of the State of California, I would argue it is more binding because it is the love and respect the trio has for each other that forms the glue that will unite them as one, not some piece of paper.

"As with a traditional marriage, before Jaxson, Chase, and Emma exchange their promises to each other, I'd like to ask who gives this lovely woman's hand in marriage?"

Chase hadn't expected for Robert Fischer to have an active role to play in the service. As the group gathered were the people closest to them in the world, all eyes pinned Emma's father expectantly, knowing how vocal he'd been regarding the unique relationship his only daughter was in.

He wasn't surprised when Robert entered into a stare down with Jaxson. As the head of their family, Robert knew that it would be Jaxson who would take the lead for making sure Robert Fischer's daughter was happy and loved. After several long seconds of the tense showdown, Robert spoke loud and clear for all present to hear. "It is not a secret that I haven't always understood the complicated relationship the three of you have formed..."

"Daddy, please. Don't..." Emma had turned towards her father, ready to beg him not to make a scene by publicly denouncing their relationship.

Her father cut her off. "Don't worry, honey. I promise, you'll want to hear what I have to say."

Chase sincerely doubted that, considering the conversation he'd overheard just over an hour earlier. Jaxson was squeezing his hand harder than ever, giving Chase a hint that his Dom had the same worry as Chase.

Robert continued on. "As I was saying, I know I've not been as supportive as I maybe could have, or should have, been over these last few years, but I want to assure all three of you that my reservations were never aimed at either of the men that my baby has fallen in love with. On the contrary, I have the utmost respect for each of you. My reservations have always been because I was trying to protect my little girl from being hurt. What I didn't understand until recently is that instead of Emma somehow getting less of either of you because she was having to share, I can see that you each love her with all of your heart. She lost her own heart to you both years ago, and for that reason it's an honor for her mother and I to give our blessings to your marriage."

Chase watched Emma as her father spoke, not quite sure if the moment was real or imagined, but the small squeak Emma released as she suddenly hugged her dad confirmed it. They'd actually received the older man's blessing, and when Chase turned to look at Jax he saw the same warmth he felt in his chest.

"Thank you, Robert," Jax said, offering his free hand to shake as Emma tried to compose herself. She looked even cuter with her nose turning red, and her violet eyes more vibrant from her happy tears.

It took another well-timed squeeze of his hand from Jax for him to turn his gaze back to her father. Caught staring at one of the loves of his life only made him smile and shrug a shoulder. "Sorry, she's a bit distracting when she looks so beautiful."

His new father-in-law smiled kindly as he answered. "I agree. Her mother looked just as beautiful the day I married her."

"Thank you for your blessing, I know it means the world to Emma... to all of us." Unwilling to release Jaxson's hand, he opened his left arm for a hug and was surprised when Robert stepped forward to pat him on the shoulder and squeeze.

"Just take care of my baby girl, all right?"

"Always," Chase replied just as Jax promised, "We will."

"If you'll take your seat Mr. Fischer, we'll move forward with the ceremony," the judge spoke softly. a smile playing on his lips, and Robert gave Emma one last kiss on the cheek before he offered her forward.

That was the moment when Jax released his hand to take Emma's right, and Chase stepped around to stand on her left. Almost like their favorite position, but a little more publicly appropriate.

He must have smirked, because Jax had a devilish look in his eye for a moment just before his Dom reached across Emma's belly, his fingers resting over the bundle that she was keeping safe and sound for now. It was the perfect option, to reach across Emma and entwine his fingers with Jax's over her tummy, and the soft sniffle from her as she squeezed his hand told Chase that Emma loved it too.

"We're ready," Jax spoke, nodding to the judge.

Judge McDonald faced them, and the small crowd, and opened the portfolio with his notes before he continued. "We will start with each of you declaring your promises to each other first and then I understand each of you would like to deliver your personal vows."

The judge paused long enough for Jaxson to nod before continuing.

"Wonderful, first the promises." Chase felt the heat of the judge's gaze as the older man turned to him to ask, "Chase, will you have this man and woman as your husband and wife; to live together in dedicated marriage? Will you love, honor, comfort, and keep them, in sickness and in health; and forsaking all others, be faithful unto them as long as you all shall live? If so, please respond with 'I will.'"

Chase stood a bit taller as he answered confidently, "I will."

It was ridiculous that two such simple words could hold such important meaning, yet he felt better... more complete as soon as the promise left his mouth.

The next time the judge asked, the questions were directed at Emma. She responded with her own confident, "I will."

It was while the judge was asking the vows for the third time that Chase heard the first buzzing sound in the distance. Jaxson was able to get his own "I will," out before the noise became loud enough to distract the judge as well as the guests. Whispers and side conversations could be heard as the trio looked around trying to figure out where the high-pitched racket was coming from.

When Miguel, their head of security, came bursting onto the scene from the small satellite security office near the pool house, Chase suspected there might be something bigger going on than just a plane flying a bit too close to the ground. Miguel was followed by two of their newly hired guards dressed professionally in black suits and ties. All three men were jogging towards the wedding party.

Chase was still trying to figure out what was happening when Jaxson released both his lovers and rushed to meet Miguel halfway down the aisle. The noise continued to grow louder and he knew it was some motorized vehicle of some sort. Knowing they were in the center of the huge, several acre property, Chase was confused as to what vehicle could possibly be getting this close to the pool.

"Code Blue!" Miguel shouted, escalating whatever the hell was going on to an official security event. Chase racked his brain to remember what the code blue indicated. Having not opened yet, he hadn't had the time needed to learn all of different procedures their new security team had put into place. The only thing he knew for sure was that he needed to protect Emma and the babies while Jaxson conferred with Miguel.

Chase pulled Emma into his arms protectively, watching over her shoulder as things turned from confusing to chaos. Ryder stood, running to Miguel and Jaxson just before all three men started looking up, scouring the sky. In unison all of their guests turned their attention to sky as well. When Chase followed their lead, he immediately knew what was happening.

Two large drones were converging on their location. One had come from the direction of the main club while the second, lower flying drone had snuck in from over their future home in the opposite direction. They were flying low enough to the ground that Chase could easily see the high-powered cameras on each pointed in the direction of the wedding.

Instinctively, Chase released Emma just long enough to rush to the edge of the pool deck, pulling a huge umbrella they would use as shade in the future from the center of the glass table it was attached to, pulling as hard as he could until the heavy umbrella lifted up. Chase rushed back to Emma, shielding the two of them under the camouflage as he rushed her towards the overhang of the nearby outdoor bar for better protection.

Irrational anger started to bubble up inside of him that someone, one of their trusted friends or family, had clearly blabbed about their special ceremony. He couldn't think of any other way the owners of the drones had known the exact date, time, and location of their unusual wedding. Any hope of it being accidental was gone when the unmanned flying devices moved even lower, hovering just feet above the venue. The click of the onboard cameras could be heard over the high-pitched whir of the machines as they got low enough to get pictures of the entire location.

Emma clung to him, shaking as she asked. "Who would do this to us?"

"I don't know, baby, but I guess we should be glad they are only taking pictures and not doing something more dangerous."

As soon as the words left his mouth he regretted them.

"What do you mean, more dangerous?" Emma pressed him.

"Never mind. Forget I mentioned it," he reassured her, not wanting to tell her he'd been in one meeting where security had discussed the possibility of weapons being flown into their private airspace by drones to escape the ground security detection.

The judge had joined them in the protected area. Khloe, Jonah, and Samantha, holding their infant Natasha, were rushing their way as well. As celebrities, they were all used to the crazy things the paparazzi would do to get the scoop on a hot story. That was when Chase remembered Brandi, a journalist, was in attendance.

Out of instinct, as soon as Jonah arrived next to him, Chase pulled Emma out of his embrace and stepped forward to meet the rock star.

"Will you stay with Emma and protect her from any bullshit going down? I need to go help Jaxson and security figure out what the hell is going on."

"Sure thing, man," Cash answered. "I'll stick here with the ladies."

Emma clung to his arm. "Don't go!"

Chase turned back to her, placing a small kiss on her forehead. "You'll be safe here. I just want to go see what's happening and how I can help."

Tears threatened to fall down her cheeks as Emma begged him not to go. With a nod to Jonah, Chase left the cover of the bar area and jogged back to the chaotic poolside crowd in time to see one of Miguel's security guards running up with a titanium looking briefcase. It was the kind of top-secret case that might be handcuffed to a guy in mirrored sunglasses.

Chase didn't look closely at the contents of the suitcase as he passed, but he could see technical equipment inside that he hoped would bring down the drones. Knowing there was nothing he could do to help with that effort, he instead got busy looking for Brandi.

The seat towards the back of the venue that she'd been in just minutes before was now empty. Chase scanned the area, observing the confusion on the faces of most of their friends and family. Several asked him what was going on as he passed and he truthfully told them he didn't know yet, either.

He caught sight of their new club manager, Madison, barking orders to several servers who had seemed to come out of the woodwork. Maxine's husband had come in for the wedding as well, and she had left him to go assist Madison. It looked like they were moving the guests in the direction of the overhangs and umbrellas as one of the drones got so brave that is was only a mere twenty feet above the scattering guests.

There were two people conspicuously missing from the small crowd. Not only was Brandi missing, but so was Lola. She'd been in the main house seeing to the reception details before they had come down for the ceremony. She could still be there, of course... oblivious to all of the commotion happening outdoors, but something in Chase's gut told him to seek out the employee they had already decided to let go as soon as the clubs were successfully opened.

He was about to start sprinting across the lawn to the main house when Jaxson's mother stopped him, placing her frail hand on his tuxedo-covered forearm.

"I swear to you, Chase. I didn't tell Gregory about the wedding. I'd never do that because I knew he'd love to disrupt the ceremony if for no other reason than to make Jaxson angry."

Chase stopped long enough to reassure his new mother-in-law. "This isn't your fault. Even if you had told the senator, you wouldn't be responsible for his devious actions today any more than you have been in the past."

He could see she didn't believe him. The creases of wrinkles on her forehead as she frowned made Miranda look a decade older than she was. He quickly hugged her, trying to reassure her before extricating himself and resuming his trek in search of the missing women.

The sound of the chaos got softer the farther away Chase got from the pool. By the time he had crossed the lawn and climbed the stone steps of the huge balcony, it was almost quiet. Certainly quiet enough for the sound of heated arguing to make it to his ears.

Chase slowed down, careful not to make any noise as he neared the final row of eight-foot hedges meant to camouflage the under-construction portion of the huge deck. He pulled to a dead stop when he realized that at least one of the raised voices belonged to his old babysitter.

"You lied to me, you bitch! There is no way I was invited to this event. It's downright intimate."

Lola answered, clearly trying to keep their voice lower. "Relax. They put me in charge of sending out the invitations and since I'm also in charge of the marketing and advertising for the club opening tomorrow, it only made sense to get some mileage out of the wedding with the press."

Chase's blood had started to boil with anger as he listened to the employee they had known was a total bitch spell out how she'd purposefully sabotaged their important day. Before he confronted her, he pulled out his phone and shot off a text to Jaxson with the new information.

"Where the hell did the drones come from?" Brandi's voice cracked with panic.

"You and your TV station ordered them to get the aerial shots to go with your story, of course," Lola snapped.

"You bitch! I never intended to write a story and you know it! You invited me here just to try to pin this whole debacle on me," Brandi defended. "How much did you get paid for this little stunt?"

"I don't know what you're talking about. I invited one of Chase's oldest friends to his wedding. If you decided to capitalize on that invitation by getting the inside scoop on the celebrity wedding of the year… well, I can't be responsible for the actions of one of the guests."

Jaxson and Miguel arrived just as Lola finished her over-the-top pronouncement of innocence that Chase knew was total bullshit.

He leaned in to whisper to the new arrivals. "It was Lola. She set this up and probably got paid a pretty penny for it, too."

Two burley guards had arrived next to Miguel as Chase spoke. Their head of security tried to reassure them. "Ryder has a lot of experience with neutralizing drones. He's who I consulted with before purchasing the detection and bring-down equipment. He should be able to destroy any photos the drones did take. The police are on the way. Let me and my guys take care of detaining Ms. Garcia."

"Fuck that. I'm the one who's going to handle this, and, believe me, we won't be doing much talking." Jaxson's voice was ice cold. His eyes were as dark as Chase had ever seen them.

Miguel tried to reason with his new boss. "You hired me to handle shit like this."

Jaxson was having none of it. Chase knew he was the only one who had a chance of getting through to him. Stepping up to his tall Dom, he hugged Jaxson's stiff torso and leaned up to talk calmly against his ear.

"Take a deep breath, baby. You need to let security handle this. No good will come out of you confronting Lola."

"Fuck that. She needs to go down hard."

"And she will go down, but if you confront her right now, the police will be taking you in on manslaughter charges. I might be wrong, but it will be a bit difficult to help Emma and me raise our kids if you're in prison."

Jaxson's muscles tensed as he tried to yank away from Chase's strong hug. He wasn't listening to reason. Chase held him tighter, refusing to let his Dom loose to charge the final distance to Lola.

Chase softly begged him then. "Please, baby. For me and Emma, for the twins, let Miguel handle this."

In seconds he knew that his pleading and reasoning were not getting through to Jaxson. His Dom was on the edge, ready to explode with anger that the paparazzi had ruined their special day. Chase knew it was because Jax deemed the invasion to their privacy as a direct threat to the people he loved the most. He was in Papa Bear protector mode.

On instinct, Chase did the only thing he could think to do.

He was a switch.

So he switched.

He pulled out of their hug to pin the taller man with his best glare. "Jaxson Cartwright-Davidson, stop it right now. Miguel is going to handle this while you and I stay here. You will not end our wedding day in the back of a police car. Do you hear me?"

The surprise in Jaxson's green eyes almost made Chase laugh... almost. The moment was too serious for that. The men stayed in a silent showdown. The raised voices of Lola and Brandi arguing on the balcony above them were the soundtrack to the intense showdown.

It was Miguel who eased the tension, stepping up to the men and leaning in. "Mr. Cartwright is right. Let my men and I handle this. I promise you, she will regret her actions."

Jaxson refused to look away as he answered Miguel. "Detain her. Question her. But she doesn't leave until I have a chance to confront her as well, got it?"

Miguel hesitated, glancing from Jaxson back to Chase, unsure in that moment whom he was supposed to be taking his orders from.

Jaxson raised one eyebrow in that adorable way he always did when he chastised his submissives. For some it might make him look scarier, but for Chase, it just turned him on since he most often saw that raised eyebrow just before he was to be punished for some infraction. And since his Dom loved to fuck him right after every punishment, his body had been trained, like Pavlov's dogs, to love that raised eyebrow.

Chase finally answered Miguel. "Let's see how things play out, shall we? The most important thing is to secure the area first and foremost and then to make sure those responsible for the unforgivable disruption are detained."

"Yes, sir." Miguel stepped back and turned to head up the nearby steps with the additional security guards following.

Only when Jaxson and Chase were relatively alone did Jaxson finally speak. "That was pretty brave of you. Or stupid. I'm not entirely sure which yet."

Chase finally let the smile he'd been holding in spread across his face as he answered. "I'd like to think of it as smart, actually. Not only did I hopefully stop you from doing something stupid, but with any luck, I got myself signed up for a sexy punishment on our wedding night."

"I see. So you're trying to top from the bottom? I'll have to take that into consideration when I'm deciding how to best punish you." The first hint of a smirk had appeared at the corners of Jaxson's lips as he struggled to maintain control. "Do you consider that tone of voice you just used with me to be properly submissive?"

"No, Sir. It was very naughty of me."

"Yes. It was." Jaxson leaned in close to speak against the shell of Chase's ear, sending threads of electricity through him. "That bare ass of yours is going to be bright red when it gets fucked later."

The dirty promise melted Chase from the inside out. Blood rushed to his cock, engorging it until it tented the front of his pants, and he could feel Jaxson's erection rubbing against him through their tuxedos. He had to swallow several times before he could speak. "I'll look forward to it, sir."

"Oh, I wouldn't if I were you. I'm pretty sure you're going to hate me in the middle of your discipline session."

Chase went to his toes to brush his lips against his Dom's. The light kiss ignited into an open mouth devouring of each other. Only when both men were out of breath did Chase finally answer. "I am certain I could never hate you. In fact, I love every single thing you do to me."

"I'll remind you when you're begging me to stop tonight."

Only the sound of a scream above them on the balcony could drag them out of their sexual tryst. Lola's loud voice could be heard screaming at Miguel to get his filthy hands off of her and that she'd done nothing wrong.

Chase was surprised that Jaxson didn't resume trying to join their security team and instead took out his phone to send off a text.

"Who are you texting now? Everyone we know is here already."

"I sent a note to Connor to come join us. He drafted the specific language in the NDA that Lola signed. If anyone can make sure Lola understands exactly how much legal trouble she's in, it's Connor."

"That's a wonderful idea. He should bring Judge McDonald too. I'm sure the two of them can scare the shit out of her."

They had to wait at the bottom of the stairs for several minutes until Connor and the judge arrived. Chase was confused when Connor arrived grinning. "What's so damn funny?" he asked.

Connor leaned close so the women above them wouldn't hear them. "Ryder used a new technology to bring down the drones with a net. It's illegal to shoot them down, but there is no legal precedent against just forcing them to land when they are low enough to the ground to be caught by the net. The cocky idiots would have probably got away with it if they'd flown higher."

Jaxson growled. "I still can't believe we can't shoot the fuckers out of the sky."

Chase remembered the debate they'd had in a recent meeting about the topic, knowing that rampant drone usage in nearby Hollywood was a hot topic.

"Well, believe it. It seems your team invested in the right prevention though." It was the judge who weighed in this time.

Jaxson was impatient to confront the traitor among them. "Let's get upstairs."

Connor shook his head. "Let me handle this. I'll text you..."

"Not a chance in hell," his Dom argued.

The newcomers spent several long moments trying to convince Jaxson and Chase to remain behind, but Jaxson would hear none of it. Instead, he reached out for Chase's hand.

"You two go first, but Chase and I are coming behind you," Jaxson asserted, finally putting the discussion to a rest.

Lola's screeching got louder the closer they got to the wide balcony overlook. By the time Jaxson and Chase got their first visual of the scene, the two guards who'd been with Miguel had Lola subdued, her arms behind her back presumably in handcuffs. Miguel had stepped up to tower over her, doing his best to intimidate her into silence without actually touching her.

"I suggest you quiet down, Ms. Garcia. Your hollering is not helping your case."

She stopped her yelling to utter her first bitter words since the men's arrival. "You can't do this to me. I've done nothing wrong, you barbarians! She's the one responsible! She wasn't even invited!" Lola nodded towards Brandi.

The men couldn't see Miguel's face, but they could hear the menace in his voice as he leaned only inches from her shocked face. "You are too stupid to understand just how much trouble you're in, aren't you?"

Lola's eyes widened at his harsh words. "Me, stupid? That's funny. You can't have me arrested. I've done nothing illegal."

Miguel chuckled. "Oh honey, don't worry. We didn't call the police."

Chase felt Jaxson moving forward in protest. Chase pulled him back, whispering. "Let it play out. He's up to something."

"Fuck that. I want her behind bars," Jaxson groused.

Connor stepped forward next to Miguel, but Judge McDonald

leaned into Jaxson and Chase to clarify, "Your security guard is right. So far I haven't seen any laws broken."

Jaxson started to argue back, but Chase dared to cut him off. "Shush, I want to hear."

He felt Jaxson's hand squeezing his ass cheek through his tailored tuxedo pants just before his Dom advised him, "This ass of yours is going to be beet red before bed tonight if you keep it up."

Chase's knees actually felt weak under him with the wave of sexual tension that hit him as Jaxson pulled his hand away and swatted his ass hard, a preview of what was to come.

He managed to choke out a groaned, "I look forward to it, sir," as the judge chuckled at his expense next to them.

Brandi's crying brought their attention back to the spectacle in front of them. Chase looked up to see his old babysitter staring at him as tears poured down her face.

"I swear to you, Chase. I didn't know today was going to be such a private event. I got this invitation for a grand opening party hand delivered to the station two days ago and I thought you had sent it. I never would have come here had I known how private… that it would be your wedding ceremony…"

Connor was the one who answered her. "Exactly why did you come? Did your station send the drones?"

"I came because… I thought… maybe Chase wanted… it was stupid." She paused, turning red before tacking on, "I was never going to write a story. I travel with a news crew and van when I'm doing a story. You can check. I drove my own car. I came alone."

"Let me see the invitation you got," Madison asked briskly.

The new Runway West manager had snuck up on them, joining the growing crowd, approaching the newswoman to snatch the invitation out of her hand as soon as it was out of her small, jeweled clutch purse. The men watched Madison turn the invitation over and look at the back of the paper instead of reading the actual invitation.

Lola's manic ramblings were the only soundtrack at the moment. "There is no proof whatsoever that I had anything to do with sending that invitation. It's printed, not handwritten."

Miguel squeezed her upper arm to hold her stationary when it seemed Lola had thoughts of walking backwards.

"Oh, and how do you know that? I thought you hadn't even seen it before." Miguel taunted her.

That shut Lola up.

When the petite Madison looked up from examining the paper, her eyes sought out Lola's. "I know without a shadow of a doubt that Lola printed this invitation, not only against the orders she had received from any of us regarding the guest list, but more importantly, in direct violation of the non-disclosure agreement she signed when she became an employee."

"There is no way you can pin this on me, you bitch! You have no proof," Lola spat.

Madison stepped closer. "This isn't my first rodeo, you idiot. I've worked many VIP events where invitations have to be managed carefully or every Tom, Dick, and Harry will show up with false invitations.

"When the paper stock arrived for the wedding invitations, I marked each of them on the back with a small number and tracked each and every invitation, by number. I am certain that we only used invitations 1-17. I distinctly remember handing you the remaining paper stock and telling you to shred it to avoid this exact kind of scenario."

Lola's eyes widened. "That doesn't prove anything. And even if I did send out another invitation, which I'm not saying I did, I still didn't do anything wrong. She's the one who works for the press. She's the one responsible for…"

Ryder was the next one to break into the growing crowd, cutting Lola's speech off.

"The drones aren't registered to Ms. Whittman's TV station," he announced.

Brandi sighed. "I told you so," she said, her voice still shaky.

Ryder continued. "My source with access to the FAA database confirmed they're registered to the parent company of TMZ." He paused, pinning Lola with his scariest interrogator glare. "How much were you paid for the information on the wedding, Ms. Garcia?"

"I don't know…"

Ryder approached Lola, cutting her off. "Oh come on. You can tell us the truth." He jeered. "You were just trying to get a bit of publicity going for the opening of Runway West, right?"

His question made her pause as she considered her options. Chase could see Ryder was giving her a bit of rope, and he suspected Lola was about to hang herself.

"Well, I was in charge of advertising for the club opening. Not that I did anything wrong, but you have to admit this is going to get a big buzz going ahead of the opening tomorrow."

She'd taken the bait.

Connor took over. "There's only one problem with that, Ms. Garcia. You signed an ironclad non-disclosure agreement. Today's wedding is not a club event, and even if it was, your advising the press of the nature of today's event along with the exact location and time is a direct violation of that NDA."

"What do you know about this? I've never even seen you before," Lola snapped, still defensive.

"I know everything there is about this. I'm the lawyer who wrote the NDA you signed."

Judge McDonald stepped up next. "As a sitting judge for the State of California, I can tell you with certainty that you will be found in violation."

"Oh so what! Even if I did it, and I'm not saying I did, breaking an NDA isn't a crime."

"Not in a criminal court, no. But fortunately for us, my firm and I handle multi-million dollar civil law suits as our bread and butter. I hope you're ready to lose every single possession that is important to you, Ms. Garcia. When I finish with you, you'll be lucky to be able to afford a bicycle and a studio apartment on Skid Row."

Finally realizing the gravity of her situation, hard-as-nails Lola turned on the water works. Chase almost felt sorry for Lola. *Almost.* Then he remembered that she had tried to ruin the only wedding day he would ever have.

Jaxson stepped forward, edging past Connor, Ryder, and Miguel to stand in front of the now crying woman. Lola was stupid enough to take his arrival as a reprieve.

"You believe me, don't you, Jaxson? All I've ever done has been for you."

Jaxson took a deep breath. When he spoke, he barely contained his anger. "I should have fired you weeks ago like Chase and Emma asked me to. I will always regret giving you the opportunity to almost ruin my wedding day. And for the record, you do nothing for anyone but yourself. We're going to dig into your financials. Not only will you lose when we sue you for breach of the NDA contract, but we're going to uncover every piece of dirt you'd rather keep hidden and we'll shine a nice big spotlight on it. I'll make it my life's mission to make sure you won't work in this state ever again. And we'll have a restraining order within twenty-four hours to make sure you can't come anywhere close to the property ever again." He paused, stepping even closer until they were only an inch apart. "Consider yourself lucky you aren't leaving here in the back of a police car, Ms. Garcia."

Jax had turned to tell Miguel to escort her off the property when Lola pulled her head back and threw her head forward, trying to head butt Jaxson. Chase shouted out to his new husband and Jaxson was able to move enough that Lola's head rammed against his shoulder instead. Instead of stopping her, she fought to free herself from the handcuffs security had put her in, flailing while screaming with fury.

Miguel and his men made easy work out of regaining control. All her temper tantrum had done was seal her fate.

Connor spoke loudly. "Jaxson, the ball is in your court. Would you like to press charges for assault? We have over a half dozen witnesses that she attacked you. We could turn this civil case into a criminal case now."

"What?" Lola shrieked. "I'm handcuffed. I didn't hurt him."

Ryder grinned. "I don't know. Davidson can be a real pretty boy at times. I bet you could have done some damage."

Jaxson's side glance shot daggers at their friend. "Helms, you can be a real asshole, you know that?"

Ryder chuckled. "Yeah, but you like me anyway."

Lola was crying in earnest now, realizing she'd made a major mistake getting physical with so many hostile witnesses.

Jaxson got in her face again, almost daring her to head-butt him again. When she didn't, he gave the final orders. "As much as I would love seeing you driven away in the back of a police car, I don't need the kind of scrutiny that a public police report would bring. So consider this your severance package. I'm going to let Miguel's team escort you to your car and then drive you to the gate. You will never again come within a mile of this property. Connor and his firm will be in touch with details on the consequences of breaking the NDA. If you're lucky, it will just cost you the money you took to sell out my family and me. Be warned. If you continue to shop our secrets to the highest bidder, we won't stop until you have nothing left to lose." He never took his eyes off Lola as he added, "Get her the hell out of here."

After Lola and the security team were gone, the remaining occupants of the balcony took a moment to take a collective deep breath. As their leader, everyone waited for Jaxson to turn. When he did, he glanced from person to person, nodding his silent thanks for how they'd helped handle the explosive situation.

"Thank you, all. Truly. As angry as I am that her actions interrupted our wedding, I couldn't be happier with how quickly everyone took action to make things right. Chase, Emma, and I... well... we owe you."

Ryder stepped forward, never afraid to go head to head with anyone, not even Jaxson. "Yeah, well, being a pretty boy and all, we all knew you'd need a little help."

Jax gave Ryder his best glare. "Pretty boy, eh? You're a real prick, you know that, Helms?"

Ryder chuckled. "Yep, guilty as charged. Now, are we going to finish this wedding or are you gonna use this interruption as your get out of jail free card?"

Chase used that as his cue to link his arm through Jaxson's and start pulling him back towards the stairs. "Believe me, he's not getting away from Emma and me. He's stuck with us. Now let's go finish the ceremony so we can get the party started."

CHAPTER SEVENTEEN ~ JAXSON

"My feet are killing me. I can't wait to get upstairs and take my shoes off." Emma winced as the newlyweds walked the long corridor from the ballroom, winding through the ground floor of the mansion, heading towards the grand foyer. After the disruption in the wedding, the rest of the ceremony, dinner, and reception had been picture perfect.

Jaxson smiled inwardly. Both Chase and Emma thought they were heading towards the grand staircase that would wind them upstairs to one of the newly renovated guest rooms that would soon be available for rent by their VIP guests… for a tidy profit of course. Jaxson had one final surprise gift for his new husband and wife.

When they got to the front foyer, Jaxson stopped them from heading upstairs. "We're not going upstairs. Let's go outside instead."

He didn't miss the disappointment on Emma's face. He knew she had to be exhausted. Even though it wasn't that late, it had been a long and eventful day. Not wanting her to overexert herself, Jaxson moved forward, scooping her up into his arms as she squealed.

"Put me down! I'm too heavy!" she cried out as she squirmed to be put down.

The men's eyes met as they both recognized her broken rule. With his arms full, Jaxson couldn't do anything about it. Luckily, Chase could. He moved closer and quickly deposited three fast swats to their wife's wedding-gown-covered ass.

"I can't believe you put yourself down on your wedding day," Chase admonished. "You are a gorgeous bride who is absolutely perfect."

"Owie. I can't believe you did that in the middle of the foyer where anyone can see us," she complained.

Jaxson smiled down at her adorable pout. "Honey, that argument might fly tomorrow, but absolutely every person on the property at this moment knows the true nature of our relationship so you don't get to play the innocent tonight."

"Fine, but I really am tired." She paused, a naughty smile on her lips. "I thought you guys would be as anxious to get upstairs to go to bed as I am. I mean it is our wedding night, after all."

Jaxson agreed, "Oh, baby, I'm more than ready to get behind closed doors with just the three of us. I just have one more small surprise is all."

Chase had opened the door for Jaxson to step out onto the front porch, still carrying Emma in his arms, bride style. The driver was there waiting at the bottom of the stairs with a black Town Car just as he'd ordered.

It was Chase who questioned him next. "We're actually gonna drive somewhere tonight?"

"Just get in, will you? You are both taking all the fun out of my surprise with your complaining."

Once they were all seated in the back seat, the driver took off, rounding the massive circular drive and heading towards the exit to the property.

Emma's yawn made Jaxson grateful the trip would be short.

Chase pulled their bride into his lap. "Come here, Em. You can use my shoulder as a pillow until we get wherever Jax is taking us. I just hope it isn't back to the rental. It's going to be a little hard to have any playtime fun with your parents in the room next to ours."

Jaxson smiled when both his lovers closed their eyes for the drive. About half way back to the main gate of the property, the driver turned down the private one-lane road that jutted off the grand drive. He stopped to insert the security card Jaxson had given him into the electronic gate and a minute later, the driver pulled the car up to the back entrance to their new house.

"Okay, we're here," Jaxson announced, unable to hide his excitement.

He watched Chase and Emma as their eyes flew open. "Already? We barely…"

Jaxson reached his hand out to them. "We're home. Ted brought in an extra crew to get the house ready to move in tonight so we could spend our wedding night in our new bedroom."

The driver exited the car and came to the door next to Chase. As the door opened, the interior of the car was washed with light and Jaxson got a good look at the love shining his way from both Chase and Emma.

He was surprised to see tears in Emma's eyes, as she asked, "So no more rental? We really are home?"

Jaxson had known she was unhappy in the temporary housing. She wasn't a diva when it came to physical possessions so he hadn't figured out why she hadn't been happy in the small house a few miles away. But if the joy in her eyes was any indication, she was truly thrilled to be moving into their new home.

Jaxson reached out to take her hand, loving the feel of her wedding ring on her fourth finger.

"We really are home, baby. Well, just one of our homes anyway. I just hope you are happier here than you were at the rental."

She swished the one tear from her cheek that got away from her.

The men stayed seated, sensing that they needed Emma to finally explain to them why she was so anxious to get settled. It took her a few long seconds before she could put her feelings into words.

"There's nothing wrong with the rental. Not really. It's just... I stupidly associated that house with the start of all of our communication problems. I know it's silly. But we moved there within a couple days of me finding out about the pregnancy. We all made so many mistakes. We fell apart there. Maybe it's superstitious, but I'm anxious to move into our new home together and have things get back to normal again."

Her reasoning was sound, yet Jaxson was a bit more of a realist. He knew the ranch house had jack-shit to do with their problems. He'd taken his eye off what as most important and that was to blame for their brief breakdown in communication. Like he promised in the ceremony in front of their closest friends and family that afternoon, he would spend the rest of his life making sure he never let something like that happen again to his family.

He smiled, reaching up to cup her cheek softly as he reassured her, "Baby, that's what today is all about... fresh starts... as a real family. Now let's go inside and get our wedding night started, shall we?"

Chase pulled Emma away from Jaxson as he turned to exit the open car door, calling back to Jaxson, "Enough talk! We have a date with our new bed."

Jaxson chuckled at his new husband's apparent glee. He got out his side of the car and met his lovers as he reached for the keycard to unlock the door. The lighting was dim so he couldn't see Chase's face as he reminded his husband, "You have a date with my paddle first, young man, before you're going to make it to our bed."

Chase's tortured groan at the reminder was one part dread and two parts sexual excitement. "Yes, sir."

His submissive reply revved up Jaxson's libido a notch higher as he opened the door and the ambient lighting automatically came on.

The trio stopped just inside the door to look around the space.

The sexual tension was growing, each of them anxious for the consummation of the vows they'd made to each other earlier that day. Jaxson used his best Dom voice to take charge. "Ted warned not everything is completely move in ready, but our bedroom and the master bath is ready to go. You two go ahead of me. I'm going to grab some food and drinks for us from the kitchen and I'll be there in five minutes. When I arrive, I want you both still fully dressed, standing at the end of the bed and waiting for your next instructions."

Their practiced "Yes, sir," was in unison. Like always, their submission warmed him from the inside out. His heart physically ached as he watched the two people he loved more than anything else in the world walking hand-in-hand towards their bedroom.

It only took a couple of minutes to fill the tray he assumed Ted had left on the counter with chilled water, several bottles of craft beers, apple juice, and the cheese and cracker tray with a bow on it in the refrigerator. He knew their housekeeper, Nalani, was responsible for the delivery of the limited food items. They'd need to find a grocery store the next day, but he was grateful for her thoughtfulness.

A fission of excitement coursed through Jaxson as he approached their new master suite. The day was flying by too fast. He wanted this special day… and night… to last. It would be the only wedding night they'd ever have. And as tired as they all were, he didn't want to rush the planned scene he'd been looking forward to all day.

Pushing the door open with the wooden tray, the sight that met him took his breath away. Jax paused, watching undetected as

Emma and Chase swayed to non-existent music as they held each other close, slow-dancing, letting their hands roam over each other's bodies as they waited for Jaxson.

"I see you've started without me," he teased as he moved farther into the room.

His lovers didn't stop swaying. Chase simply lifted his right hand from Emma's lower back and used it to beckon to Jaxson to join them. It was such a simple gesture, but in that moment, Jaxson recognized how damn lucky they all were that they had found a way to form this complicated love into something that was somehow perfectly balanced. They may have lost their way for a few weeks, but they'd come through it stronger than ever before.

Jax put the tray down on top of the bed's white comforter before joining Chase and Emma. Like puzzle pieces that had been assembled many times, their bodies molded together in a tangled embrace.

No one spoke for several long minutes. No words were needed. Their embrace spoke for itself. The small caresses, increasingly assertive gropes, shortening of breaths, and occasional sighs were all the best kind of foreplay. After a wonderfully chaotic day, it was exactly what each of them needed.

Jaxson knew it was time to move to the next phase of their wedding night when Emma started to fade on them. She had thankfully not felt nauseous all day, but he knew she hadn't eaten right and that she wouldn't be up for a long play session.

Pulling their embrace apart, Jax stepped back, taking a moment to look around the room. It was in better order than he'd hoped. Ted may be an asshole in many ways, but he genuinely did understand the style the trio had been looking for and he'd delivered on it. Jax glanced back at the oversized king bed, noting the unique head and footboards that would double as restraint equipment on future nights.

The long backless couch at the end of the bed was even better than he'd hoped. The white leather would be easy to clean and the extra tall padded armrests at each end were the perfect height to bend a naughty submissive over to receive a punishment. Adding the hidden straps that would also restrain an errant sub had cost a pretty penny, but he planned on getting a lot of use out of the unique piece of furniture, starting tonight.

Looking back at the loves of his life, he barked his first order. "You both have too many clothes on." He sat down on the bench at the end of the bed and added, "Stand over by the fireplace and start undressing each other. I want to watch."

Chase pulled Emma the few feet away and did a bit of his own dominating. Spinning her to face the stone fireplace, he instructed, "Hands up on the mantle, baby."

Once she was stretched out, he slowly started to unzip her long dress, leaning in to place sexy kisses down her back as her milky skin came into view. Jaxson had to hand it to Chase. He was doing an excellent job of unwrapping their best wedding present of the day.

As the two halves of Emma's designer gown fell apart, Chase slipped his hands in her dress, reaching around to cup her full breasts, squeezing hard enough to get a pained moan.

"Let's get this bra off next, shall we?"

Jax watched Chase undress Emma, his own cock thickening with each new body part exposed in front of him. He popped open a bottle of beer, taking a drag as he lounged, watching the show as Chase pulled Emma back so that he could push the dress off her shoulders to pool at their feet. The white lacy bra hit the floor seconds later. Her white hose and garter belt showcased her perfectly curvy ass that was barely covered by the tiny French cut panties.

When Chase reached to undo Emma's garter belts Jaxson intervened. "Leave on the hose and heels," he instructed before moving on to give Chase his next orders. "Hands back on the mantle, Em. Chase is going to spank that beautiful ass of yours to give it a bit of color."

Jaxson's erection ached for attention inside his tuxedo pants. With steely self-control, he leaned back to leisurely swig his beer and enjoy one of his favorite forms of foreplay... watching Chase dominate Emma. As expected, the spanking was light enough to draw mews of arousal from their girl while tenting the front of Chase's tuxedo pants with his own growing length.

"I'm not sure which turns me on more. The pink of Emma's ass peeking out from below her panties or that bad boy perfectly filling out your pants, Chase."

Chase glanced back at Jaxson, for the first time showing a fission of anxiety. "I'm just glad it isn't the thought of my coming punishment that has you the most turned on."

Jaxson reached to cup his family jewels through his pants, trying to relieve the ache Chase's words caused between his own legs. It took all of his self-control to keep from rushing to his lovers and sticking his rock-hard shaft into the first available hole he found.

"Emma, your turn to undress Chase. I want him naked when his ass meets my paddle."

Jax didn't miss Chase biting his lower lip nervously as he often did before a real discipline session. Little did Chase know, tonight wouldn't be a real punishment. Not really As angry as Jaxson had been that afternoon immediately after the drones had interrupted the ceremony, none of what happened was Chase's fault. He had enough perspective now that the crisis was over to admit that Chase's intervention had prevented Jaxson from doing something stupid and for that, he would be rewarded with a good-boy funishment.

But he wouldn't tell Chase that just yet. He knew the anticipation of not knowing what Jaxson had planned added to his lover's excitement.

Off came Chase's cufflinks, black bow tie, and white tuxedo

shirt. When Emma hesitated, Jaxson helped her by barking his next instructions to her. "Stalling isn't going to prevent the inevitable, baby. Off with his shoes and socks. Unbuckle his belt. Pull down his pants."

Jaxson had a front row seat to another of his favorite shows — watching his two submissives slipping deeper into their sexual submission. Anticipation for the unknown of what they may be asked to do. Desire for a brush of pain they'd learned could enhance their joint pleasure.

As Emma obediently slipped to her knees to take off Chase's shoes and socks, her body softened, tension from the exciting day slipping to the floor along with pieces of clothing, shed almost as easily, allowing her to sink into a place where only the three of them existed.

And like the Dominant that he was, his lover's submission fed him, chasing away his own tension, quieting his mind from all other distractions.

When Emma pulled Chase's boxer briefs off his hips, his thick rod sprang free, jutting out proudly, notching up the heat level in the room.

"Suck him, Emma. I want to see that whole cock disappear down your throat."

Her "Yes, sir," was cut off by Chase's lunge forward, anxious for the wet tightness the order promised.

Like a perfect submissive, she had thrust her arms behind her back, turning over control of the blow job to Chase who had thrust his hands into her thick, flowing hair, using it as a handle to control the action.

The wet suction and gagging sounds as Emma bobbed back and forth almost made Jaxson change his plans. He had the perfect vantage point to watch that thick shaft he loved so much disappearing again and again down her throat. A glance up to Chase and he instructed, "Enough. Stop!"

Chase's disappointed groan coincided with Emma's gasp for

air. When Chase grasped his own erection and started to stroke himself in hopes to finish what Emma had started, Jaxson chuckled.

"Nice try. Hands behind your back, baby. No coming for you until we get the business of your punishment taken care of."

Chase turned those caramel brown eyes on him with anticipation. "Can't we..."

Jaxson wouldn't let him off the hook just yet. "Come. We're going to try out this new piece of furniture I ordered."

He stood from the backless couch, motioning for Chase to join him. Like a good girl, Emma waited on her knees for instructions.

Jax pulled Chase in for an open mouth kiss as soon as he was within arm's length. He couldn't wait to wrap his right hand around that fat erection, stroking Chase just hard enough to edge him higher, but stopping before allowing his sub the satisfaction of a release.

He ended the kiss abruptly, using his cock like a leash to lead Chase to the left end of the leather couch, pulling him into place before pressing on his lower back with his other hand, motioning for his new husband to bend over the waist-high, padded arm rest.

"Palms flat on the seat. They don't come off until I give you permission to move them. There are restraints under the seat. Don't make me use them tonight," he ordered.

"Yes, sir," Chase acquiesced quietly.

Jaxson moved behind him, using his foot to tap at the insides of Chase's feet, forcing him to shuffle his stance wider until Jaxson could step back and admire the view of Chase's heavy cock and balls, swinging down below his legs. *Christ, what a beautiful sight.*

Jax reached forward to palm Chase's ass, squeezing and kneading the tight muscle until he felt his lover relaxing. That's when he delivered a spray of spanks to the same butt cheek, warming it nicely. Not to be forgotten, he moved his hand to the other side and repeated his attention.

Back and forth for several long minutes, Jax edged Chase higher with the exact kind of sweet pain he knew the switch craved. The rock-hard erection swaying was Jaxson's barometer to know he was on the right track, stopping several times to squeeze the velvety hardness.

A glance at Emma, still on her knees watching her lovers, but now rocking as her own sexual need grew, gave Jaxson an inspired idea.

"Time to test out to see if this couch is going to work like I'd hoped it would. Emma, crawl over here, baby. I want you to lay at the other end of the couch facing us."

She scrambled to comply, her long hair starting to fall out of the beautiful updo she'd worn at the wedding. Jax watched her as she got closer, loving the smeared makeup and streaks of black mascara around where her eyes had watered during her face fucking. This was the face only the men in her life got to see.

Jax helped her crawl onto the couch, adjusting a decorative pillow behind her to make her comfortable as she laid back.

"Legs bent, feet flat on the couch. Open wide. Chase and I want to get a good look at those soaking wet panties."

After all their years together, he loved that his words brought a blush to her cheeks. Even as a now married, pregnant woman, there was an innocence about Emma that Jaxson treasured. Years of living in luxury hadn't changed her at her core. She'd found a way to remain the same perfection inside as that wholesome co-ed they'd found in France.

"You two stay right where you are, keeping a close eye on each other. I'm going to go grab a few things we're going to need."

Jax wasn't gone long. He'd asked Nalani to have a suitcase he'd packed brought out from the mansion. He found it in the walk-in closet as he'd requested. He quickly dug through the change of clothes for each of them and a few other needed items to get to the heavy wooden paddle with three large holes drilled in it. He also grabbed the bottle of lube and the one final sex toy he'd had the clairvoyance to throw in at the last minute.

The sight that met him as he returned to the bedroom almost made him throw away his plans. Technically Emma and Chase had followed his directions, holding their positions apart from each other. But each being desperate for the other, they were both thrusting their hips in the air in a dirty rhythm. It had Chase's cock and balls crashing into the side of the couch again and again, the contact clearly giving him some satisfaction. Emma's panties had only got more wet as she thrust her hips off the couch emulating getting fucked.

All he had to do was clear his throat to bring their rocking to a tortured stop. He went to Emma first, holding out the contents of his right hand. Her eyes lit up when she saw her favorite vibrator. She greedily grabbed the sex toy from him.

"Let's get these panties out of the way."

He knew with her garters and hose, it would be hard to get the scrap of clothing off her. But being lacy and delicate, Jaxson just tore the fabric at each hip, allowing him to pull the panties away to discard them to the floor, unwanted.

"No penetration until I tell you. Just lie there and play with yourself as you enjoy watching Chase receive his punishment. You'll get to be a bit of entertainment for us as well."

Her blush deepened, realizing her bald, swollen pussy would be on display for her men.

Jaxson held out the heavy paddle for Chase to see. Anxious fear warred with excitement in those brown eyes he loved so much. This particular device had brought agony and ecstasy in the past.

Moving behind Chase, he used the dense wood to playfully tap the cock and balls hanging heavy between his legs. The taps were light, but unexpected, and Chase shot bolt upright, breaking his position. The immediate crack of the paddle against the center of his ass punished him for his mistake.

"Hands on the seat of the couch," Jaxson demanded, enjoying the wide-eyed surprise on Emma's face at his stern rebuff. The fast rubbing of the vibrator through her wet folds betrayed how much she loved to watch their lover be disciplined.

It had only been one stroke, but Chase mewed with relief when the next thing to touch his ass was Jaxson's palm, squeezing and kneading.

Smack.

Another connection of wood and flesh as cocks grew harder and her sweet pussy grew wetter.

Again, a tad harder.

Hips now swayed, anticipation of the reward coming to each of them soon.

The next swat drew a grunt from his submissive. Jax tempered the pain he'd delivered with a squeeze to Chase's balls, bringing a torture of a different kind.

Emma had closed her eyes. He knew she was close to coming.

"Eyes, Emma. You do not have permission to come yet. Use that free hand to play with your tits. Put on a nice show for us."

Her pout was perfection. The pinch to her left nipple demonstrated her love for a touch of pain. They were close enough to her core to smell her arousal, adding to the perfection of the scene.

Crack.

The next swat to Chase's ass was lower across the crease between butt and thighs. It was Emma who groaned, though.

Chase broke the silence to tease their wife. "I just remembered how turned on you got that first time Jaxson spanked us in Paris that first weekend together. I think that was the moment I knew how perfect you were for us, Em."

"I wasn't turned on, I was scared to death," Emma countered breathlessly.

Jaxson added his own memory of the life-changing event. "You were scared and turned on, baby. Chase is right. We loved our time with you, but realizing you had a deep seeded desire for the submission was a huge turn on for us."

It was Chase who put new puzzle pieces together for them. "And that you liked to watch. I think that's something we all have in common. It's such an important part to us not getting jealous when we watch the other two playing without us. We all know we love each other and can enjoy watching almost as much as participating."

"Nice observation, sub. How would you like a reward for your insightful reflection?"

"I would like that very much, sir," Chase groaned at the fresh squeeze to his family jewels.

"Emma put the toy down and scooch down here to this end under Chase." It took a minute for her to get into position at their end of the couch before he added, "Lift your feet up to me, baby." As soon as she did, Jaxson pulled her legs up to wrap around Chase's back and added, "Push your hips up off the couch, Em. We're going to let Chase quench his thirst a bit on that river you have flowing between those legs of yours."

With her shoulders pressed into the couch, her hands on her hips and using her leg muscles, Emma contorted herself to lift her pussy to Chase's waiting mouth. Like a parched man, he got to eating her out with gusto.

It took all of his will power to step back from them. Knowing how it affected both of his submissives, Jax undid his wide belt buckle, and with one swift yank pulled the belt from the loops of his pants, letting the tip snap loudly in the air, announcing to Chase that the leather would soon be connecting with his already red bottom.

Jax had a lot of practice with this particular punishment device. He could make Chase hate it, but tonight, he used his skill to only stoke the heat of their tryst higher and higher. Jaxson delivered a steady stream of belt strokes to paint the entirety of Chase's bottom with two-inch wide overlapping stripes. The harder he administered the belt, the faster his lovers ground together until he heard the distinctive sounds of Emma crying out her orgasm.

Jaxson smiled inwardly. He'd counted on her not being able to hold off indefinitely.

"Tsk, tsk, baby. I didn't give you permission to come. That was extra naughty of you." Her eyes that had been closed with ecstasy shot open, searching out his gaze to see how much trouble she was in. He hoped his face told her she wasn't in any real trouble at all.

He hadn't punished Emma at all since the disastrous night she confessed she was pregnant after safe wording. Jaxson admitted to being a bit terrified to add any physical discipline back into their sexual life where Emma was concerned. Thoughts of the two tiny babies safely nestled inside their mommy's belly brought a bout of anxiety to Jaxson that he had to push down.

He'd had another conversation with the doctor when they'd returned for further paternity testing the week before. His brain knew that delivering swats to Emma's bottom could not possibly harm the kids, but he couldn't shake how wrong it felt to strike her. He was determined to try to push through his reticence.

"Up on your feet, Emma. It's time for you to take the same position as Chase at the opposite end of the couch. This time he's going to get to play voyeur to your punishment."

If he'd doubted he was doing the right thing, the sexual heat that had jumped into Emma's violet eyes reassured him that she really did want to feel the leather of his belt on her bottom. He helped her extricate herself from the somewhat awkward position she'd been in and then move to her feet, leading her to the end of the couch and pressing her into her prone position.

"Legs wider, baby. Let's see if we can get that pussy to drip juices onto this new carpet on our first night in the new house."

Her embarrassed groan brought a grin to Chase who looked all too excited for the show about to begin. Jaxson took up his position behind her and forced himself to proceed before he could think too hard about the fact that he was about to strike the mother of his children.

It was a spanking, not a beating.

He was making her feel good, not bad.

He had to repeat the words in his head on auto-loop as the first two-inch wide stripe of pink colored her milky white ass. Pushing through his own hang-ups, he landed the second strike just below the first.

Emma shocked him by speaking to him with an angry tone. "You're going easy on me. You aren't going to hurt me, Jaxson."

Her assertive rebuff was so out of place for their scene it shocked them all. Leave it to Chase to lighten things up again. "Oh, I can't wait to see how hard you're gonna get it for that sassy outburst, baby."

Jaxson pushed down his nerves and delivered a belt stroke every bit as hard as he'd delivered to Chase minutes before. The difference of the strength was evident to all of them as the crack of leather on flesh was forceful, bringing tears to Emma's eyes, yet she didn't call out for him to stop.

The next stripe was to her sit-spot and brought a sexy whimper from his submissive as she wiggled her butt as if that could ease the sting. His cock felt like it would soon rip a hole in the front of his pants, where his erection had turned to weighty steel. Admitting a small defeat in his self-control, Jaxson unzipped his fly, fighting to navigate his shaft until it sprang free, jutting proudly towards his lovers.

"Oh, God. Please, give me that bad-boy. I need it so bad," Chase begged.

Not to be outdone, Emma countered, "He's working on me right now. I think he should start with me."

The banter was playful, or at least as playful as they could be in their hyper horny state.

Jaxson delivered one final belt stroke to Emma's curvy bottom, crisscrossing all of his previous lines of heat, hoping she'd feel the spots where the belt had connected multiple times when she was sitting at breakfast the next morning.

Their foreplay had to come to an end. They each deserved their marriage consummation and he knew the best way to make that happen.

"Chase, come to Emma's end. You're going to fuck that pretty pussy of hers while I fuck your ass. You proved yourself the perfect switch today in how you handled me at the mansion and tonight, your reward is fucking and being fucked at the same time."

The sexy blond didn't need to be instructed twice. He moved like a sleek animal of prey, gracefully changing positions as he sandwiched himself between his lovers. Like the trained sub that he was, Chase lined his cock up with Emma's pussy, rubbing the tip of his cock up and down to make sure it was plenty wet for the fast insertion that was coming.

Jax pressed on his shoulders lightly, silently asking Chase to angle his torso while kicking his legs wider than even Emma's. It took all of Jax's will power to take the time to grab the tube of lube and dribble several drops on the now visible pucker of Chase's tight ass. Then he added a few drops to his cock, appreciating the coldness that failed to squelch his burning heat.

He didn't need to give Chase the order. The second Jaxson pressed the tip of his cock into the ring of Chase's anus Jax felt Chase moving forward to pierce Emma's core. That one stroke, each moving slowly, making sure it felt good, but then like a practiced orchestra, the men moved to the main chorus of their dirty dance. Jaxson pulling out first and then Chase pulling out to thrust back again as Jax crashed forward, filling Chase's ass completely as Emma felt empty.

Back and forth like synchronized pistons, each lover giving and receiving the pleasure they'd only found with each other. Harder... faster... deeper... until they lost their rhythm. It signaled they were so close to exploding that they could no longer keep up the even pace, erratically chasing the elusive high that was their favorite drug.

"Now! Come with me," he shouted, knowing none of them would be able to stave off the climax about to strike for much longer.

The wet slurping of body parts pounding together was the soundtrack to their final release, all three of them crying out as each shattered into a shuddering orgasm, the men depositing copious ropes of cum deep inside their lovers.

The trio lay collapsed in a heap of sweaty body parts as they tried to catch their breath. Only Emma's complaint, "I can't breathe," got the men extricating themselves from the tangle of limbs.

A manly pride consumed him at the sight of his cum dribbling out of Chase's asshole. That was doubled when Chase pulled out of Emma and huge glob of his cum dropped to the carpet between Emma's feet. That Chase could focus on coming while getting drilled hard always amazed Jaxson.

Chase helped to scoop a shaky Emma up from the couch, yelling back to Jaxson when he was half way to the master bath. "Time to try out the huge shower! You're a bit overdressed, sir. Follow us and we'll get you ready for round two."

Only then did Jaxson realize he was still in his tuxedo. He'd undone his pants and lowered his boxer briefs for their tryst, but every other stitch of clothing was still in place.

He chuckled as he loosened his tie and followed his new husband and wife to their brand new shower. They were going to have so much damn fun christening every room and piece of furniture in their new home in the coming weeks.

He couldn't wait.

CHAPTER EIGHTEEN ~ EMMA

"*I* think you should stay home tonight, baby. You look exhausted."

Emma didn't disagree with Chase. She was pretty tired. The last three days had been some of the busiest of her life and that was saying something. At least she'd seen her parents and grandma off at the airport that morning so that was one less thing to juggle.

She looked up at her blond husband's reflection in the mirror she was sitting in front of, applying her makeup for the evening. Chase was so handsome that she had to pinch herself at times when she realized he was just one of her husbands.

Seeing he was waiting for an answer, she responded, "I won't stay long, but there's no way I'm going to miss tonight. It's the grand opening of Black Light West."

Chase smiled at her in the reflection. "You aren't fooling me. You're only going because Cash and Samantha will be there tonight."

She finished applying her favorite pink shimmery lipstick before smiling back. "And what if it is? I barely got to talk to them at our wedding on Wednesday and then they had other appearances keeping them from the opening of Runway West yesterday. They're flying out to New York tomorrow. I don't want to miss my chance to catch up with Sam more."

Chase was buttoning his dress shirt, finishing his own preparations as he let her know, "I took a peek at the VIP list for tonight's opening. It is going to be a lot of fun. We got confirmation that Ryder and Khloe are coming."

"See! No way do I want to miss tonight."

"Well I'm going to be keeping an extra close eye on you. I have it on good authority that Ken Cruisie will be there. He's old friends with Elijah."

"Holy shit! Maybe I need to add more makeup if I'm going to meet one of Hollywood's hottest actors tonight," Emma taunted.

Chase placed his hands on her shoulders, standing above her and squeezing. "I hate to tell you, but you're a married woman now. No gallivanting around with famous actors," he teased back.

"I would never gallivant. Look, maybe. But I'm more than satisfied with my not one, but two, gorgeous husbands. I hardly think I need to add a third man to the mix."

"I should think not. Let's get you in your dress. Jaxson texted. He's wondering where we are."

Emma made her way to the walk-in closet. They'd had a mover bring over the rest of their belongings from the rental property the day after the wedding. That was another relief to be moved out of there. Still, most of their belongings were in D.C. so the closet was relatively empty.

The deep purple silk gown hanging from a rack in the middle of the room raised her heart rate. It was gorgeous, and downright scandalous. Spaghetti straps would barely keep the deep cut neckline covering her heavy breasts. The back was cut so low that the upper curve of her rounded ass was on display. Two tiny crisscrossing straps were the only thing holding the fabric together in the back.

Had it been a full-length gown, it might have been okay, but the men had insisted on the skirt being a jagged cut with the lowest points of the fabric falling mid-thigh and the highest points at the joint where her leg and hip met. The skirt was thankfully full with plenty of fabric, but anyone paying close enough attention would get glimpses of her bare pussy as she walked if she wasn't careful. She begged her men to let her wear panties, but as was the rule on the East Coast, she wasn't allowed anything to prevent them from touching her pussy at their whim while inside Black Light.

She'd had a seamstress come earlier in the week to do the final fitting for all of her opening outfits along with her wedding dress. Unfortunately, she hadn't tried the dress on after the alterations and as she lifted the dress over her head, she found the bodice was much tighter than she remembered. She wouldn't be wearing a bra and now the dress's expensive fabric hugged her boobs like a second skin.

She was about to look for something else to wear when Chase stepped behind her, reaching around to pinch both of her tender nipples, exclaiming, "The dress is perfect! I can't wait to show your hot body off to all of the new members we'll be meeting tonight."

"No way! This is scandalous. I need to change."

"Excuse me, sub?" His words were accompanied with a strong swat to her ass. "Considering you will often be completely naked in the club, I hardly see the problem with this dress that showcases all of your attributes in the best possible way."

She wasn't in the right frame of mind for this night. She was too stressed. Focused on the hundreds of details she'd been working on for the wedding and openings. Emma tried to wiggle out of his arms, ready to scour her meager belongings to find something, anything, more appropriate.

Recognizing that she was about to argue with her Dom, which was never a good thing to do before heading out to a BDSM club, Chase took charge. "I can see we have a bit of a problem. Let's see if I can get you in the right frame of mind for the night," he said as he grabbed her hand and started pulling her into motion.

"My mind is perfectly fine. It is my growing body and this tiny scrap of fabric that is the problem," she retorted sharply. *Too* sharply for her husband because he stopped pulling and turned to face her, his trademark smile wiped from his face.

He released her hand to place his palm over her rounded tummy. "This growing body is perfect in every single way. You had better not be putting yourself down, baby, or you're going to find yourself getting a real punishment on opening night."

Chase was always so jovial that it was easy to pick up on the signs when he was truly angry and the man in front of her was upset.

"I'm sorry. I'm not trying to pick a fight. I'm really not. I'm just feeling extra self-conscious is all. We're going to be meeting a lot of new people... VIP's... and I don't want to feel out of place is all."

The tension drained from his face, as his smile was back. "Honey, you're forgetting something. This," he waved his hand in the air back and forth, "all of this is yours."

"Ours."

"Yes, ours. These people are our guests. I don't give a flying fuck what they think. They need to be trying to impress us, not the other way around."

She knew Chase meant his words, but she had to remind him. "We aren't inviting them to a private party. We are running a business. We need them to join and pay our exorbitant membership fees. That means they need to feel comfortable that we've built a place they can see themselves relaxing enough to perform the most intimate sexual acts. So, like it or not, they will be judging us."

Her answer frustrated Chase. He wasn't having any of it.

"I'm putting my foot down. You're wearing this dress. It is perfect and you look fucking amazing. Now... if you'd like me to convince you over my knee, I'd be happy to do that."

Her core clenched at the mention of a spanking. The light belting on their wedding night had reignited her deep desire for her men's physical domination of her body. For a brief moment she thought about staying dug in on the dress if for no other reason than to find herself with a hot bottom for the night. But knowing they were already running late, she acquiesced.

"Fine, I'll wear this, sir."

"Good girl. Now, let's go find our Dom, shall we?"

"EMMA!"

She heard Samantha calling her name before she caught sight of her good friend. Jaxson, Chase, and Emma had formed a short receiving line about a dozen feet inside the main entrance to Black Light. They'd been personally greeting each new arrival for the last hour — welcoming new members, honored guests and several members she recognized from the original Black Light, joining in for the celebration. Her friend would have to wait her turn to make it to the trio.

Emma was having trouble focusing on the portly man in a suit Jaxson was currently talking business with. She took the opportunity to glance around the open space. In almost every way, the club was so different from Black Light in D.C. Where the original was one huge club space with a few smaller rooms on the fringe of the club, the new club was much more intimate. There were several sectioned off areas, each with its own purpose and rules. She hadn't gotten to take the final tour yet since the renovations had been completed. All she could see from their vantage point near the main entrance was the social gathering space where sex and full nudity were prohibited.

Whether guests arrived from Runway directly above them, winding down a hidden staircase behind the bar, or if they came through the back entry to Black Light from the secret parking lot, everyone would go through security and start in the social room. The mammoth bar with its glass, and neon and black lights was similar to the original bar except this club had more tables, chairs, and high-tops for mingling customers to visit. From where she stood, the club looked like any high-end bar.

She knew that hidden behind the purple velvet curtains to the left of the bar was where the atmosphere changed drastically from social to sexual.

Chase's introduction to a movie producer brought her attention back to the line. Samantha was next and her friend was not too patiently jumping on the balls of her high-heeled shoes.

"Emma! I didn't think we'd ever make it to you guys. I love your dress," Sam cheered eagerly as her husband grinned behind her, shaking his head.

Samantha's hug was so tight, Emma squeaked. Sam's bad boy rocker husband leaned in, pulling his wife gently away.

"Let's not suffocate Emma now. I'm sure Davidson would kick my ass if you hurt his pregnant wife," Jonah 'Cash' Carter chastised.

"That's Cartwright-Davidson now, for the record," Jaxson corrected their friend.

Jonah chuckled. "Christ, it's gonna take me some time to get used to that."

Jaxson stepped closer to shake their friend's hand. "You and me both."

Emma was still beyond shocked that Jaxson was legally changing his last name. She hadn't been surprised that he'd ask her and Chase to change theirs. But never in a million years had she expected her Dom and the head of their family to change his infamous last name. More than the ceremony or identical rings, their new shared last name made her feel like they were one family. She was grateful that it would also make it easier for their children, not having different last names than some of their parents.

"Earth to Emma. You okay, baby?" Jaxson and their good friends were all staring at her.

"Sorry. I guess I zoned out there for a minute. Can you repeat the question?"

Chase must have overheard because he took a break from his discussion with another new member to lean in and add, "I tried to get her to stay home. She's exhausted."

She argued back quickly. "I told you, I wanted a chance to see Sam and Jonah and take one of the tours of the club. I haven't even seen most of the changes yet."

Jaxson looked concerned. "Emma, you live here. You can take a tour any goddamn time you want. Let's get you…"

"Please, sir. I just want to stay for a little while longer," she implored. Emma batted her eyes in her best pout, hoping to sway her Dom.

"Oh no you don't. Your begging isn't going to work tonight. I'll take you…"

He didn't get to finish his sentence because Ryder and Khloe, who had arrived without them noticing, had come up behind Jaxson. In typical fashion, Ryder took the opportunity to give Jaxson some good-natured ribbing. "You having more problems with your sub there, Davidson? I think you're losing your touch."

Emma saw the annoyance in Jaxson's eyes as he answered without turning to face the newcomers. "My touch is just fine, thank you. And like I was just reminding Carter here, it's Cartwright-Davidson to you. Need me to make you a sign?" The corner of Jaxson's sexy lips curled up in a slight smile, obviously having fun sparring with his friend.

Ryder chuckled, happy to be getting under his fellow Dom's skin. Emma had to smile. The two alpha men were a bit like sand paper, always rubbing against each other hoping to scratch the other.

"Naw. That won't be necessary. I'm just happy to know you're finally making an honest woman out of this beauty." Ryder stepped closer to Emma, reaching out to pull her into a loose hug. "I didn't get a chance to talk to you after the wedding on Wednesday." He pulled out of the hug to turn his icy blue eyes on her before continuing. "You were a beautiful bride. Khloe and I were honored to be there to see you tie yourself down with these two."

Emma's heart raced. Ryder Helms was an intense man. He rarely spoke directly to her and when he did, she always felt like he had x-ray vision, able to see deep inside anyone and everyone he encountered. She somehow strung together a short reply. "Thank you, sir. I'm so happy you could both be there."

Elijah, the new Dungeon Master, was just returning to the bar area with a small group of new members following behind him. Jaxson waved him over. "Chase and I are going to take the Carters, Emma, Ryder, and Khloe on a tour of the club. You okay holding down the reception line for a bit on your own?"

"I can take them if you'd prefer," Elijah offered.

"I'd like to take them myself. You can stay and help get new arrivals oriented. We shouldn't be gone long."

Chase interjected. "As much as I hate to say it, I do think on opening night one of the three of us should be here to greet guests. Why don't you guys go ahead and I'll stay with Elijah."

"Are you sure?" Jaxson glanced his way.

"Yeah, but on one condition." A naughty grin lit up his face. "You'll give me a call if you decide to play. I don't want to miss out on any fun."

"Deal."

Jaxson grabbed Emma's hand and started walking in the wrong direction.

Ryder didn't miss his opportunity to give him shit. "Eh… maybe I'd rather have a different tour guide. Even I can tell the club is that way," he teased, thumbing in the opposite direction.

"Fuck off, Helms," Jaxson said with a good-natured grin. Emma knew the men both enjoyed their sparring.

Only when Jaxson opened one of the double doors in the far corner of the social room did she remember that they had planned to install a theater in the club. They moved about a dozen feet into the room where the half-dozen rows of plush couches and reclining seats started, all facing the mammoth screen at the far end of the room.

The lighting was dimmed and the movie Secretary was playing on the screen. Several couples were seated, paying more attention to each other than the movie or the new arrivals in the room.

"We'll be streaming movies in here. The plan is that the later in the night we get, we'll start switching over to BDSM porn. We also plan on recording our educational sessions on some of the edgier kinks and can play them here for members who weren't able to make the training in person."

"Smart," Jonah added.

"Don't tell him that. He'll get a big head," Ryder added.

Jaxson pinned him with a glare, asking, "You about done?"

"Not quite," Ryder retorted, a sly smile gracing his lips.

They retraced their steps back out to the social area where Jaxson stopped again to explain. "We've set up the club in zones. The deeper you go inside, the more kink you'll see. We purposefully made this reception area nudity and sex free. Members need to at least be in robes here in the bar area. The lighting is dim, but bright enough to see those you're talking with. The music is also softer here with a lot of seating so members who aren't in the mood to play can still stop by for a night cap in a safe environment."

It was Jonah who seemed most impressed. "Shit, I love this idea, man. There are so many times Ryan and I have wanted to grab a beer after a recording session or some appearance, but we don't because it's not worth the hassle of being swarmed by fans."

"Exactly. No electronics also ensures no one is taking your photo and since it's past security, there should be no groupies down here like upstairs," Jaxson added.

Samantha leaned into Emma to complain. "Great, now he'll never come home when we're in L.A."

Jonah overheard his wife, popping her on the ass playfully as he answered, "Or I'll call you and tell you to get your adorable, sassy ass over here so I can light it up for an audience."

Sam's eyes widened as her cheeks turned pink at her husband's chastisement in front of their friends. She wisely sunk back into her submissive role, "Yes, sir."

Jaxson started walking again, past where they had been before, around the busy bar that had both bartenders on duty hopping, and towards the velvet curtains Emma knew were the entrance to the next zone.

A security guard Emma hadn't met yet stood guard at the curtain, keeping order as members came and went between zones.

"How are things going Dimitri?" Jaxson asked.

"Exactly as planned, sir. No problems," the dark-skinned man with bulging muscles answered politely.

"Very good. I'm taking this group back myself. Any chance we can reserve the last studio for a half hour in the near future?"

Only then did Emma notice the tablet the guard had in his hand. He took a minute to press the screen several times before confirming, "You're in luck. It is due to be free in twenty minutes. I've booked you for the following thirty-minute block."

"Excellent. I appreciate it."

"Of course, sir. Have fun."

"Oh, I'm sure we will."

Emma didn't know exactly what to expect, but knowing her husband like she did, her pussy clenched with excitement, suspecting it was going to get a little attention soon.

The transition was dramatic behind the curtain. Almost all ambient lighting was gone, replaced by darkness. The only source of lighting in the eight-foot wide long hallway was black lights that lit up strategic items and artwork along the walls and floor.

A one-inch strip of purple light lined the corner where the

walls met the floor, laying out a pathway for members. A few feet in, they arrived at the first glass case lining the right wall. A quick glance at the lit up artifacts inside the case found sex toys and punishment devices, all painted with the reflective paint that shone bright in the black lights shining down from spotlights above.

On the left wall were several pieces of framed artwork, all sexy scenes painted with the neon colors that shone bright in the unique black lighting.

It was Khloe who commented first, "This is a genius way to do the lighting!"

"You can thank Chase. The original plan called for different lighting, but he reminded me of a rave we went to once in Amsterdam. It was where we got the name Black Light from in the first place, but we decided to take it to the next level here on the West Coast."

"Well, it totally works."

They arrived at the first of three doors that Emma could see in the long hallway. The painted 'MEN' sign on the door was lit up in a neon blue.

Jaxson explained from the lead as he kept walking down the hall, "Like in D.C., there are men's and women's locker rooms with showers. The bigger locker room in the middle is co-ed. Playing is only allowed in the co-ed space since some guests who are only visiting the social area may want to use the men's or women's room without being exposed to the kink levels in the rest of the club."

At the end of the hall was the painted door of the VIP elevator. Emma had taken it the week before and knew that it was the same elevator that was near the entrance to the kitchen on the main floor. She'd had to use her biometric eye scan in order to make the elevator move, just another way they were keeping Black Light secure from Runway patrons.

The door at the end of the hall past the elevator opened into an open area about half the size of the social bar area. Like the hallway, the room was dim with most light sources coming from the brightly colored items that lit up in a rainbow of neon under the black lights across the ceiling.

The pounding beat of the music was louder, but not loud enough to drown out the sounds of several couples having sex around the room. Like in D.C., Emma noticed three raised platforms spread out in a triangle of sorts, with several couches and seating arrangements interspersed throughout the space. Only one of the platforms was occupied by a redheaded submissive secured to a whipping post and being flogged by a shirtless older man. Across the room in the distance was the long lap pool they'd turned into their own version of a Roman bathhouse.

Jaxson explained, "The previous owners installed the indoor pool. We had planned to remove it, but our interior decorator convinced us to turn it into a cooling off pool. We did convert half of it to a hot tub and we also kept the extra-large sauna."

Ryder exhaled a high pitch whistle. "Impressive."

Jaxson answered dryly, "Of course it is."

Emma and Khloe both chuckled at their Dom's continued snark.

Jaxson ignored them and continued his tour. "Pretty much anything goes in this area. There's a shower over in the corner we ask everyone to rinse off under before they get in the pool." He nodded to the area closest to the door they'd come through and added, "We installed two small cool-down rooms here for couples to go after a scene if they need to. There's a small juice bar along with energy snacks in each room along with places to lay out or sit to wind down before heading back to the locker rooms."

Ryder decided to tease Khloe instead of Jaxson next. "Hear that, baby? You'll be able to eat healthy even when we come here to play. No excuse to starve yourself."

"Oh goody," Khloe groused, wisely not saying any more.

Samantha snuggled against her husband while watching the flogging in action with intense interest. "It's a lot smaller than the club in D.C., isn't it?"

Jaxson turned to answer her. "Actually, the square footage is only about twenty percent less than the D.C. Club. It's just laid out in a lot of more intimate zones. We haven't got to the third and most exclusive zone yet."

Everything had changed so much since the last time Emma had been in the club that she didn't know what to expect when Jaxson pulled the curtain aside on the far left of the room near where they'd come past the locker room. It exposed yet another wide hallway. In fact, with the lighting lining the path, the whole club was starting to feel a bit like a big maze or labyrinth, all lit by the same neon florescent lighting under the namesake black lights.

As soon as they turned the first corner, she was transported back to their trip several years before to the Red Light district of Amsterdam. A nearly naked woman was on display on a raised platform behind a floor to ceiling wall of windows. Her olive skin was painted with an almost gold paint that shone iridescent as she humped the dance pole in the middle of her display window.

"We're calling this our store window. We have a lot of fun things planned for this space. Some will just be exhibits for members to enjoy watching, but the window retracts into the ceiling so members can interact with our entertainment when appropriate."

Emma was trying to listen to her Dom but was totally distracted by the man just past the window dancer who seemed to be fucking the bare wall. Jaxson noticed he'd lost her attention, and when he noticed where she was staring, he waved their small group forward a few feet until she could read the sign about eye level on the wall. It read, 'Enjoy the Glory Holes.'

No explanation was needed. They were close enough now to see a man she'd never seen before was in the process of getting a blowjob by a phantom person on the other side of the wall. The small group kept to the right side of the hall as they passed, trying not to disturb him.

Only when they were past the grunting man did the naked ass sticking out of a small hole in the wall come into view. Even in the dim lighting, it was easy to see that both the asshole and pussy of the hidden submissive had been thoroughly used at least once already.

Jaxson stepped closer to the ass, turning to talk with his friends and wife. "Submissives can sign up for a shift in either the glory hole or what we are calling our 'free fuck' booth. Only the staff will know the identity of the hidden submissives and each of them are given a panic button that they can press if they need to be released or want to stop a scene."

"Shit, this is genius," Jonah observed.

Samantha swatted Cash. "Don't act so excited. It's not like you're ever going to partake in this fun, husband."

Jonah hugged his submissive, grabbing her long dark hair as he threatened her. "Maybe I was planning on offering you up for a shift. I mean, your oral skills are epic."

Jaxson called his bluff. "Right. Like any of the three of us would let another man's cock anywhere near our women."

Ryder growled, "Damn straight. Only one cock gets to choke this beautiful throat." He reached out to lightly strangle Khloe, making his point.

Jaxson wrapped his arm around Emma and she leaned into him, loving feeling him close. All of the sexy scenes had it getting pretty damp under her silky dress.

They'd come to a ninety-degree right turn in the hallway. In front of them was a much longer hall, so long that she couldn't see the other end in the dim lighting. More lit up kinky artwork and cases of taboo sex toys lined the right wall of the wide hallway. Under the artwork were several padded long benches, setup as observation seats to the wall of windows that made up most of the left wall of the hall.

Jaxson led them a few feet into the hall before stopping and turning to watch the scene going on behind glass in the first room. He explained the space while they all enjoyed watching the kink scene playing out.

"There are four rooms down this hall, each one with its own theme. We have props and costumes to support each theme in a closet in each room and all four rooms have the basic BDSM equipment like spanking benches and other sex furniture for more general play. The observation windows are one-way mirrors. The occupants won't know if they're being observed or not. We had a few heated debates, but finally decided not to include any audio. While I'm sure voyeurs will miss hearing the lovely sounds of sex and discipline, our founding principle of being a safe haven for celebrities to come and have a degree of privacy won the day.

"You'll see that there's an iPad next to each door. Members can reserve the rooms in thirty-minute intervals in advance if they'd like or can just grab an open room or share the space when no one has it exclusively reserved. Only their membership ID will show on the reservation, helping to protect identities. Members also have the option of paying an up charge to black out the room so they can't be observed if that is important to them."

Emma asked quietly, "So that couple in there right now doesn't know we're watching them?"

"Nope. They just know that anyone can walk by at anytime and stop to watch. If they don't want that, they'll have to pay a premium for exclusivity."

Ryder laughed, slapping Jax on his back. "You bastard. You've found the perfect way to keep upcharging us poor members."

Jaxson grinned, clearly happy with himself. "Hey, this is a business. We're in this to make a profit."

"In other words, you found a way to stick it to those of us who carry around cash." The rocker who got his nickname Cash Carter honestly, pulled out his trademark wad of hundred-dollar bills from the pocket of his perfectly tight jeans.

Jaxson was having fun with his friends. "No cash needed, buddy. All you'll need to do is swipe your membership card on the iPad inside. We'll throw the charge on your next monthly statement, just like we do your bar bill or if you purchase merchandise."

Emma was only half paying attention. She was having too much fun watching the submissive woman in the tight schoolgirl uniform on the other side of the glass. Her Dom was clearly playing the role of her professor or principal and was in the process of caning her bare ass as she leaned over the top of the wide desk at the front of the room. The words 'Sex Education' were written in neon chalk on the blackboard above her prone body. Even in the dim lighting Emma could see the lines of raised welts painting her butt from top to bottom.

Jaxson leaned down to whisper to her softly. "You'd better be a good girl or we might need to pay a visit to the principal's office for a naughty girl caning."

Emma had a true love-hate relationship with their cane and her husband knew it. She protested, softly, "Oh please. I hate the cane."

He stepped behind her, pulling her tight against him, her back to his chest as they both watched the next strike of the cane cutting into the sobbing woman on the other side of the glass.

"The jury is still out on that, baby. You may hate it while I'm caning you, but I think you love the ache that sticks with you for a few days."

He wasn't wrong about that. For days after a caning, Emma was hyperaware of her choice of submission. The tenderness as she'd sit or even brush against something would shoot sparks of sexual excitement through her, reigniting her ache to submit to her men. She didn't contradict Jaxson's observation since he was spot on.

The three couples silently played the role of voyeur to the classroom scene, watching the final six strokes of the cane doing its job just before the alpha man delivering the punishment whipped out his hard cock and reamed the upturned ass in one swift thrust. Emma felt Jaxson stiffen as they watched the Dom almost violently fucking the raw ass of his sobbing submissive. She was sure he was thinking the same thing she was.

He had just released her to wave down the dungeon monitor several feet farther down the corridor when the sobbing woman started screaming loud enough for them to hear her in the hall, "Yes, fuck me, sir!"

Emma relaxed, relieved that the submissive was clearly enjoying the intense scene. When the DM got close, Jaxson instructed him, "Keep an eye on this one, will you, Eric? We don't know our members well yet and I'd like to make sure the ambassador doesn't take things too far."

"Yes, sir. I…" Eric paused, unsure if he should continue.

"Spit it out, man."

"It's just that I noticed his submissive had some bruising when they arrived. I was already trying to keep tabs on them."

"I've given Chase and Emma bruises a few times so that…"

"They were on her face," he added quickly.

That shut her husband up. Emma watched Jax's eyes go the almost black they got when he was at his most angry.

"Keep close tabs on him and let's flag his membership card to disallow him from making a session private. I want eyes on him until we know we can trust him to maintain our consent rules."

"Yes, sir."

With a final look back at the fucking couple they'd been talking about, Jaxson turned and kept moving down the long hallway.

The next room was empty, but they stopped for Jaxson to

describe the plans for this room. "This is our brothel room. You'll see we have several tables setup in the center of the room. The plan is to run some poker games in here. We'll have servers dressed like hookers in old-fashioned saloons. We're still sorting out the rules on the number of drinks allowed while in a game. There'll be sex breaks in between games."

Cash spoke up. "I can't wait to let River know about this. He's totally gotten into the whole poker scene lately, even participating in a few celebrity tournaments. He'll love combining his love of poker and kinky sex together."

Jaxson knew Ryan 'River' Trubach well. "Tell him to let us know when he'll be in. We'll make sure we have servers working who love anal on the nights he's gonna be in town and arrange for games."

The third themed room had the glass smoked out, making it impossible to see what was going on inside. Jaxson had to just describe the decor to his tour.

"There is a dual theme to this room. It is both our medical room as well as a station setup for the most taboo of kinks. Doms will have to pass a certification before being given free reign in this room since we have the materials for knife, needle, and blood play along with fire and electro kinks among other edgier things."

"So who the hell did you certify before opening night?" Ryder asked.

Jaxson didn't look happy. "I was just thinking the same thing." He pulled a cell phone out of his pocket and dialed someone."

"Must be nice getting to keep your phone in here," Ryder groused under his breath just as Jaxson started talking to someone on the other end of the phone.

"Who's in the medical room right now?" He waited a few seconds and added, "Did you certify them for a private session?" A few long seconds of silence again before he added, "Excellent. Well done."

He hung up the call without saying goodbye before filling

them in. "One of the dungeon monitors is in there observing. Let's keep going."

Jax squeezed Emma's hand as they moved forward towards the final room. A couple was sitting on the bench outside, making out as the woman bounced on the lap of the man, each of them too engrossed in their fucking to notice their small group passing by.

Emma's pulse shot up as soon as the final room came into view. A couple was just cleaning the equipment inside, having finished their scene. She watched as the Dom wiped down the St. Andrew's cross on the far wall. She scanned the space, recognizing several pieces that reminded her of the dungeon in the D.C. club.

"Now this is my kinda room," Ryder commented, pulling Khloe tight against him. It was no secret that even on the night they'd first met at Black Light during the Valentine Roulette event, they'd spent a lot of their time in the dungeon. It had been their favorite play space on each of their visits.

They let the couple that was vacating the space leave with a short nod of acknowledgment before Jaxson held the door open for them all to pass.

"I've got the room reserved for the next thirty minutes. I'm pretty sure we can come up with a few fun things to keep us busy."

As tired as Emma had been earlier in the evening, a spike of adrenaline at the thought of the kinky scene they were about to share with their best friends got her pulse going. They had all witnessed each other having sex, and in any number of intimate sexual encounters, but they'd never intentionally shared a scene together. Just the thought of what was coming had Emma's mind running wild with possibilities.

She knew it was a figment of her imagination, but she could swear she felt the skin of her bottom tingling in anticipation. All it took was that sexy as hell heated glare from Jaxson, full of promises and the debauched ideas he was coming up with.

When the three Doms put their heads together, literally, the women moved closer together too. The thrill of what was to come had the three women slipping into their submission, holding hands quietly, all experienced enough to know they needed to wait for instructions from the men they trusted to dominate them.

It didn't take the guys long to make their plan. When they separated, Jaxson and Jonah moved to the sides of the room to gather up the things they'd need while Ryder stalked towards the submissives like a predator. He was in dangerous interrogator mode, edging up Emma's nerves another notch. She couldn't help squeezing Khloe's hand harder as he got so close she could smell his aftershave.

"Strip. All of you. We know you've been keeping secrets from us. We're going to have some fun seeing how long you can keep your secrets once we start our interrogation."

"Oh shit." Emma didn't mean for her nervous reply to be audible.

Ryder's dominant glare turned on her as he leaned even closer. "I see I have your attention, young lady. I don't believe your Dom has properly punished you for keeping the mother of all secrets from him for weeks."

"Double shit."

"I see you understand your predicament perfectly," Ryder growled.

CHAPTER NINETEEN ~ JAXSON

*J*axson knew he should be ashamed of himself for letting Ryder take the lead with their joint scene but seeing Emma's wide eyes as she internalized Ryder's words had all of the blood from above his waist racing to the growing erection in his suddenly too tight pants.

He knew it made him a prick, but he had to acknowledge he loved the twinge of danger that Helms added to any interrogation scene. The edge of fear emanating from all three submissives as Ryder barked orders to strip fed the sadist in him. He kept his face expressionless as Emma glanced nervously at him to see if he was going to save her. When he didn't contradict Ryder's instructions, she bit her lower lip nervously and reached for the hem of her sexy dress to pull it over her head.

Jax resisted reaching down to reposition his aching cock as Emma's naked body was revealed in one quick movement. As required while at the club, she was nude under the dress. She hadn't even worn hose, so she stood on display in only her high-heeled sandals.

When she moved her arms to cover her breasts, Jaxson gave

his first command of the scene. "Hands down, sub. Don't cover up what's mine."

Her hands flew to her side, eyes trained on the floor. Emma flexing her fingers nervously was the only hint of how anxious his new wife was. He let his gaze wash over her soft body, loving each and every sexy curve, including the slightly larger tummy where two tiny peanuts were nestled.

Jaxson shook his head, determined to shake the thoughts of their coming children from his brain for the next thirty minutes. This was not the time or place to be thinking of parenthood. There would be no faster way to put a damper on their fun.

Jonah had gotten the three pieces of furniture into place by the time Khloe and Sam stood naked next to Emma. All three submissives were well trained, keeping their eyes lowered, giving the three men in the room the opportunity to ogle them. Three gorgeous and sexy women, each in their own unique way. Jaxson knew they were three very lucky Doms.

It was that thought that had him pulling his phone out of his pocket. Despite the dirty look Ryder cast his way, he didn't feel the least bit guilty for giving himself and Chase the exception to the no electronics rule. They'd purchased devices to use exclusively at the club that had no cameras or recording capabilities to minimize any risk, but he was at least able to shoot off a text to Chase, telling him to get his ass back to the dungeon as soon as he could.

Ryder maintained the lead over the scene, allowing Jaxson the opportunity to stand back and enjoy playing the voyeur for a few minutes. "Enough stalling. Time for each of you to choose one of the spanking benches and climb on. We don't have all day."

Jaxson had to hand it to Helms. He sounded like a scary sonofabitch, and Jax was relieved that in spite of their verbal wars, the alpha men had always been on the same side. He'd hate to have Ryder Helms as an enemy.

Emma and Samantha, unaccustomed to Ryder's intensity,

scrambled into motion, heading to the first two benches that had been set up in a semi-circle.

Khloe, on the other hand, was less inclined to make things easy on her Dom. If they were going to play out an interrogation scene, the actress appeared ready to play her role a bit more convincingly. "You're not going to get shit out of me, asshole. I demand we be released immediately."

The dark smirk on Ryder's face told Jaxson he and his sub had played this particular game before. "You demand? Really. And who the fuck do you think you are?"

Khloe's face lit up in a naughty grin. "I'm the Princess, of course."

Despite the serious scene, all occupants in the room burst out laughing, recognizing Princess as Khloe's code name from the game of roulette on the fateful night the couple had met.

Even Ryder couldn't maintain his interrogator cover. He grinned, reaching out to yank the petite blonde against his chest, holding her tight. "Oh baby, you sure as hell are my naughty little princess, aren't you?"

Knowing she'd succeeded in forcing her Dom to uncharacteristically lose his control in a scene brought a bright smile as she looked up into his eyes, teasing him back. "Guilty as charged, sir."

Ryder pounced like the predator he was, devouring Khloe's lips in an almost violent kiss. The other four occupants of the room waited for several long seconds and when they showed no signs of wrapping things up, Jaxson stepped in and took charge.

"It seems we've lost our chief interrogator to a bout of kissy face. Don't you two think this means you're getting out of your deserved discipline."

Ryder finally pulled out of their kiss and took Khloe along with him to the final bench in the room. Emma didn't take her eyes off the actress as she kneeled up on the padded ledges on the outside of the unique piece of furniture. Ryder adjusted the height of the top padded bar lower so that it hit his sub at stomach level. He then guided her hands lower towards the handgrips that would put her in a prone position. Like the other two subs, her legs were spread wide, held firmly apart by the wood brace. It exposed not only their pussies, but their puckered ass, bare back, and thighs to be used in any devious way the alpha men desired.

Seeing the wetness already gathered between Emma's nether lips reminded him of how lucky he was to have her in his life. She was subconsciously wiggling her bottom, already anticipating what was to come.

"We aren't going to tie you naughty girls down. Don't make me regret it. The first one of you that lets go of the hand grips and tries to either get up or reach back will not only be restrained, but will also receive an added six of the best with the cane I know you all hate."

Jaxson watched the women look at each other nervously, each determined not to feel the hated cane.

"Damn, you guys started without me." Chase had snuck into the room when Jax wasn't looking.

The men's eyes met. The switch of their family was looking for instructions on the role Jaxson wanted him to play in the scene.

"You're just in time. We were about to start. Mr. Helms is going first."

Jaxson nodded at Ryder who moved to a side cabinet to gather a few supplies before stepping behind Khloe's upturned ass. His sub couldn't see what he held, but the rest of the occupants of the room had a front row seat to Ryder drizzling heated lube onto a fat butt plug that would create a burn over time, using his index finger to lather it up nicely before wiping his hand on the towel at the top of the tall stack of linen provided in each room.

He waited until the fat end of the bulging toy touched Khloe's pucker, making her jump, before he resumed his role in their game. "Hold still. I've covered this helpful tool with a truth serum.

In just a few minutes, you'll be ready to answer any question I ask you, Princess."

The actress closed her eyes as she struggled to take the oversized sex toy into her anal cavity. Based on how quickly her tightest ring expanded to allow the intruder, Jaxson guessed her bottom was accustomed to taking objects deep. Even so, she grunted under the strain of Ryder's constant push and pull, stretching the puckered hole again and again until he finally shoved the plug deep, drawing a short cry of discomfort from the prone woman.

Jax knew when the cream had reached an uncomfortable heat level because Khloe's eyes sprang open, her initial surprise quickly replaced with panic.

"It's too hot! It burns bad." She jerked her bare ass back and forth, trying her best not to let go of the handgrips, and losing her battle.

Khloe shot upright, kneeling up and throwing her hands back, trying to pull the hot plug from her body. Ryder was ready for her, hugging her tight to his body from behind and leaning in to growl against her ear. "That didn't take long. Looks like we'll be starting with the cane today."

His submissive was struggling to escape his iron grip. Being an actress, Jaxson was unsure exactly how much of what they were observing was part of the scene. Her distress seemed genuine and as much as the sadist in him loved a good punishment scene, he had just started to worry when Ryder reminded his sub with tears streaming down her cheeks. "I haven't heard a safeword, baby. Use it if you need to. Until I hear *red* from those pouting lips of yours, you'll hold that bad boy exactly where it is. Understood?"

His words were harsh, but Ryder was holding her, gently stroking her hair, helping her get the pain under control. It took almost a minute of deep breaths before Khloe adjusted and answered with a quiet, "Yes, sir."

"That's my good girl. Now… let's get you back into position."

As soon as she was holding onto the handgrips like Emma and Sam, Ryder let loose with his next surprise.

"If you thought we were just playing at a scene tonight, Princess, you're going to be disappointed. I have a few questions for you. If you answer truthfully, the rest of your night is going to improve. If you try to lie to me... or hide the truth... well then, let's just say that the heat you're feeling in your ass will be the least of your worries."

The other five occupants of the room had a front row seat as Ryder landed the first stern cane stripe across both globes of Khloe's ass, drawing a lovely scream from her.

The second she stopped screaming, Ryder crouched in front of her, putting himself at eye level with his submissive as he asked, "Exactly when were you going to tell me that you've started purging again?"

Khloe's eyes widened, surprise registering at her Dom's question. "How did...?"

"How did I know? I know everything where you're concerned, Khloe."

"Trevor. What a fucking blabbermouth."

"More like a fucking friend," Ryder deadpanned. Jax knew the older man well enough to recognize that he was working hard at containing his anger.

"Your friend, maybe. I liked it better when he was on my side."

"Baby, don't you see he is on your side?" He sighed. "Now, how much weight have you lost?"

"How should I know? Maybe I've gained..."

Like a predator pouncing on prey, Ryder reached out to grab Khloe's long hair with both hands, holding her head in a vice grip as he got within an inch of her face.

"Do not lie to me. Do I need to take every scale out of the house again? You only got them back a few months ago."

"No! Don't. Please," Khloe begged.

"This isn't a joke. You're hurting yourself with this starvation routine. Am I going to have to close down my new business venture just so I can stay home to babysit your eating?"

Khloe tried to push up, but he was too strong. "Ryder, you're overreacting. I'm sure I haven't lost any weight."

Despite Khloe seeming genuinely truthful, Ryder demanded again, "How many pounds?"

She hesitated, trying to wait him out, before finally answering quietly. "Six."

"Six too many. It will also be the number of cane strokes coming your way, young lady. That and we lose the scales again. You just can't help yourself."

"No, not that! You don't understand. It's for my job."

"No, it's not. It's for this." Ryder used his pointer finger to tap lightly at Khloe's temple. "I get it. You can't help yourself. So, I'm going to help you by removing temptation."

"That's crazy!" Khloe continued to protest.

"This isn't up for discussion."

"The hell it's not. It's my career!" Khloe had become outright antagonistic; not a wise thing to do in her current prone position.

Ryder pounced, gripping her face in an iron clasp as he shouted, "I don't give a flying fuck about your career. It's your life I care about. Let the next six strokes remind you I don't take kindly to you hurting this body that I love so much."

He released Khloe as fast as he'd grabbed her, standing and stalking back behind her, swishing the heavy cane through the air for several practice swings giving Khloe time to kneel up again. She at least wisely stopped her arguing.

The second cane stroke landed a half inch below the first, forming two perfectly parallel marks on Khloe's pale ass.

Ryder made easy work of pressing on her back, forcing her back into the prone position. She was still trying to get a handle on the intense pain when his third cane stroke landed another inch lower. By now, the first two marks had turned a crimson red and Jaxson knew if the lighting was better, he'd be able to see them rising into welts.

Helms was delivering a genuine punishment to his submissive. Jaxson wasn't entirely sure that corporal discipline was the best way to tackle Khloe's long-standing eating disorder, but then again, who the fuck was he to second guess Ryder's tactics?

The scene had turned too real. Emma and Sam both looked distressed, wanting to comfort the sobbing Khloe as she stayed in position for the fourth slice of the cane.

Ryder took a break then, stepping up to lightly squeeze the marked bottom of his woman. Despite his harsh punishment, Khloe calmed slightly at his touch.

"Am I making myself clear, Khloe? You are beautiful exactly as you are. No more starving yourself. No more purging. No more obsessive checking of your weight."

"Please…"

Jaxson couldn't believe she was still resisting the inevitable. He noted the determined clench of Ryder's jaw as he stepped back from his sub to deliver his strongest strike of the night, this fifth line crisscrossing at a perfect angle to intersect with the previous four lines of pain.

"Red!" Her scream of the house safeword brought the caning to an end, but one look at Ryder's face and Jaxson knew the showdown between their friends was far from over.

Ryder admitted as much when he threw the cane to the floor, stepping close to talk to the sobbing Khloe. "This isn't over, Princess. You can safeword out of a punishment, but you'll be taking better care of this body of yours, if I have to handcuff McLean to you when I'm not home."

It took her several deep gasps of air to catch her breath before Khloe could finally speak. "I'm sorry. I made a mistake." Her voice shook with emotion.

"Damn straight you did. Luckily, it can still be fixed."

"I don't see how," she lamented.

"You leave that to me, baby. Now... I think we've used up more than our share of the time. We'll resume this discussion at home."

Cash tried to lighten the heavy vibe in the room. "Shit, that was intense. I was going to try to get to the bottom of why my Cuban cigars keep disappearing, but I somehow don't think that's going to be a riveting secret to get to the bottom of after that scene."

Samantha agreed, not even trying to hide the truth. "They're bad for you, and they make you smell terrible. I don't want that around Natasha."

Jaxson teased, "That was easy. You broke her down in seconds."

"We'll talk about this later, Samantha."

Chase teased. "Yeah, he doesn't like looking henpecked in the dungeon."

"I'm not henpecked, dammit. I'm married. You two better watch it. You're in the same boat now."

Jaxson had to admit how many things had changed in just the few short weeks since they'd found out they had the twins on the way. The tiny lives growing inside Emma had changed everything.

Speaking of which, he moved into motion, taking up position behind Emma while nodding to Chase to move in front of her.

Their scene may not be as intense as Khloe and Ryder's, thankfully, but he had decided that he did need to discipline Emma for her epic secret keeping skills.

"Emma, we've already established that Chase and I share equally in the blame for the three of us falling out of sync earlier this year, putting our entire relationship in danger. We've all apologized to each other for letting ourselves get so distracted and not following our own rules that have kept us happy for years."

Jaxson paused, looking up at Chase who nodded slightly, urging Jaxson to proceed. "But Chase and I have decided that you took secret keeping to a whole new level in keeping the babies hidden from us for almost two full months. It isn't just that you didn't tell us. It's more that you put your own health, and that of the twins, at risk by not letting us know what was going on. More importantly, you weren't being seen by a doctor as you should."

As Jaxson paused, Chase took over the lecture. "While everything may have turned out okay in the end, we need to make sure you understand the gravity of your mistake in order to make sure it never happens again."

Jaxson reached for the leather tawse with its split tail that would be delivering his message loud and clear to the bottom of his new wife. He knew she couldn't see what implement he held, but she would feel it soon enough.

Pushing down his reservations regarding disciplining his pregnant wife, he adjusted his grip. The doctor, and even Cash in the room, had reassured him that what he was about to do would not harm Emma or the babies. Their sexy session on their wedding night had gone well, bolstering his decision to proceed on their first night in their new club. It was a christening of sorts.

Emma jolted forward as the bite of the leather connected with her pale bottom. Even knowing it was coming, he could tell the sharp pain had taken her breath away. He was grateful when Chase knelt in front of their wife, stroking her hair away from her face gently, balancing the discipline with a dose of love.

Jaxson and Chase balanced their roles perfectly as Jaxson delivered the painful lesson and Chase delivered the lecture. "Never again, Emma. Do you hear me? No more secrets."

He was proud of Chase, normally the softy of their family, for staying strong as their girl finally started crying out on the eighth strapping of leather against reddening skin. He was sure his message was being heard loud and clear.

"I'm sorry!" she cried out, no doubt hoping to bring her punishment to an end.

Chase wiped the tears from her face as he comforted her, even while urging Jaxson to continue. "We know you are, baby. We aren't mad. We were just scared for you. You made so many questionable decisions putting yourself at risk. The slate will be clean after tonight. Everything forgiven and you'll know how serious we are about you keeping secrets from us in the future."

Crack. Jaxson landed another stroke of leather a bit lower, laying down a new line of misery for their girl. He knew the pain was real, but he could also smell the musky scent of the juices making her spread pussy slick. Emma was perfect for the men because she loved all of the kinky shit they did together as much as they did.

The men's eyes met. At this point in their relationship, they could often communicate volumes with just a glare. It was time to wrap up the punishment and move on to more fun activities. In fact, out of the corner of his eye, he could see that their friends had already started that portion of their scene without them. Cash was in front of Samantha, getting a blowjob from his submissive wife. Ryder had taken his erection out and was about to pierce Khloe's pussy.

Jaxson finished with three fast strokes, one after the other, driving home the final lesson to his wife. Her bottom was a splotchy red by the time he finished and threw the tawse back to the table as he reached to touch the crying Emma.

"Shhhh, it's all over now, baby. All's forgiven. Time for a little reward," he added as he ran his fingers through the river flowing between her legs, concentrating on her clit. Chase leaned in to steal a passionate kiss as Jaxson pinched her swollen nub. Within seconds, her whimpers of pain had morphed to cries of pleasure.

Khloe cried out as Ryder filled her with a double penetration since the huge toy was still shoved in her ass. Jonah had moved behind Samantha, taking her in one quick thrust.

Jax and Chase may be falling behind, but they would catch up quickly as they each pointed their rock-hard cocks in the direction of their wife; Chase in her mouth, Jaxson her pussy.

Chase filled Emma's throat with his erection. Her gurgle as she struggled to accommodate Chase's girth was sexy as hell. Their husband was not a small man, but she swallowed him like a pro.

Three couples, all doing the dirty dance, each chasing their own orgasm as their submissives took what the men gave, enjoying every minute of the domination.

Having gotten an early start, Jonah and Samantha finished first, each groaning as they climaxed.

Chase and Jaxson were next, calling out to Emma to come with them as the trio fucked hard and fast until they were all three panting, coming, before they were able to begin recovering from the explosive orgasms.

Even when Jaxson had caught his breath again, he found Ryder still pounding Khloe like a goddamn machine. From her mews and groans, it sounded like she was enjoying the intimate attention. Jonah, Chase, and Jax cleaned themselves and their subs up, and had pulled the women into comforting embraces when Ryder's steady pace finally grew erratic.

Jaxson couldn't resist. "You gonna finish any time soon, old man, or should I reserve the room for another half hour to give you time to get your rocks off?"

Ryder pulled Khloe's hair, forcing her to arch her back as he rode her to her third screaming orgasm before finally shouting out his own finale.

Through the older man's labored breathing he retorted. "You're just jealous of my staying power. I didn't see you giving your lady three orgasms and there are two of you for Christ's sake. You should be ashamed," he teased.

They took a few minutes to get the women into the plush Black Light robes hanging in the closet, there for the complimentary use of members who wished to wear robes back to the locker room.

With all of the equipment they'd used wiped down and ready for the next occupants, Jaxson opened the door to find a small crowd had gathered outside of the dungeon, no doubt curious to watch the infamous trio and their famous friends christening the dungeon.

"Show's over, folks. I hope you all have as much fun in there as we did," Jaxson offered to a smattering of applause as the group started to disperse.

Only when most of the crowd was gone did Jaxson notice that Dr. Tipton and a woman he assumed was the doctor's wife remained, waiting to talk with their hosts. His wife was a good-looking woman in her fifties. Like he'd insinuated during their office visits, the choker collar with the leash leading back to her husband's hand confirmed that the doctor was indeed practicing the BDSM lifestyle.

Jax reached out to offer his hand. "Welcome. I'm glad to see you were able to make it to opening night."

Chase and Emma were next to him and he felt Emma stiffen, no doubt feeling uncomfortable with their doctor getting this intimate peek into their complicated sexual relationship. Considering what he did for a living, though, Jaxson just couldn't be embarrassed at literally being caught with his pants down.

Only after their handshake ended did Jaxson pick up on the fact that the doctor seemed uncomfortable as well, surprising him. "We were just about to head back to the bar area. How would you two like to join us for a night cap?"

Dr. Tipton glanced around the dim hallway, nervously checking to see who was nearby. Jaxson's sixth sense had alarm bells going off.

He didn't waste time beating around the bush. "Something is wrong, isn't it? Is it something with the twins?"

The older man tried to dismiss Jaxson's concern. "I'm sorry. We shouldn't have come tonight. It was silly of me to want to talk to you here. It can wait until your next appointment."

The fuck it could.

Jaxson stepped closer, towering over the shorter man. "Something's wrong. Did the tests find a problem?"

Emma swayed on her feet, leaning heavy on Jaxson. He turned, pulling her into his arms just as her knees seemed to give out under her. Jaxson scooped her into his arms, shouting for Chase and the doctor to follow him.

He turned to go down the final bit of hallway they had left before turning to his right and coming out of the hall into the playroom near the pool. Jaxson weaved through the members gathered in the seating areas and around the raised platforms, beelining it to the closest cool down room, praying no one was already using the space. They needed privacy.

They were in luck, the room was empty. He passed by the couches and chairs close to the door to lay Emma on the padded table at the far end of the narrow room. Even in the dim lighting, he could see how pale she was. He hated the fear he saw in her eyes as she glanced around, looking for the doctor.

Chase arrived with a cold bottle of orange juice, and helped their wife sit up enough to get a few swallows of the juice before laying her back down.

Dr. Tipton made his way to Emma's side, reaching out to take her pulse before trying to put them all at ease. "I'm so sorry to have worried you. I don't have bad news. On the contrary, I think I have good news, but still, it should have waited until you came in for your next appointment."

"Well too late now. There's no way we can wait now," Chase countered. Jax could hear the apprehension in his voice as well. They were all on edge.

Ryder, Khloe, and the Carters had followed them into the room. Sensing that the doctor was going to talk about the pregnancy, their friends started to back out of the room.

"We'll catch you later," Ryder spoke for the group.

Jaxson stopped them. "No, you guys can stay."

The doctor looked even more uncomfortable than he had

before. "This was a mistake. We should talk about this in my office… in private."

"As you just witnessed, we pretty consistently share our most intimate moments with these friends. There is nothing you're going to tell us that they aren't going to find out about from us anyway, so spill it. There is no fucking way we are waiting a week to find out what you know. Not now that we know you have news."

Emma looked like she was going to cry. Her hand lying over her tummy, gently patting where their children were tucked away.

Dr. Tipton looked between the three of them and finally started to talk. "I normally follow my patient's requests to a T. I know you told me you didn't really want to know the sex of the babies. When you came in for paternal testing last week, you explained it was so you'd have more information to help you fill out the birth certificates as well as line up your business trust."

"You warned that the tests could take several weeks or even months. Are you saying you got the results back already?"

"I did. Consider it part of my VIP service." The doctor tried to make light of his comment, but the trio was way too tense to find anything he was saying funny. He cleared his throat awkwardly before continuing. "Anyway, I thought you'd want the results as soon as they came in. I should have called, or waited, but you'd invited me to the opening so I stupidly thought…" he trailed off.

Jaxson and Chase looked at each other, each of them realizing that one of them was about to find out they were going to be the biological father to the twins, and the other, that they were not going to be blood related to the children that they would love no matter what. Jaxson truly didn't know which outcome terrified him more. In the end, the fear of passing on his father's asshole gene had him reassuring Chase. "I pray they are yours, baby. I can't wait to see their sunshine smiles."

Chase looked shell shocked. This was all coming out of nowhere. They hadn't had time to prepare for big news. But as long as the babies were healthy, Jaxson knew that the rest didn't matter--not really.

Emma sat up between them, reaching for each man's hand, linking them together as they turned to the doctor to await the news.

"I'll start by letting you know that you are expecting one girl and one boy."

That brought smiles to all of them. "That's awesome. That way we can always decide to have more kids in the future if we want, but if we don't, we'll still get to have a son and a daughter," Chase reasoned, still looking nervous enough for all of them.

Jaxson steeled himself to be strong, no matter the doctor's next words.

Dr. Tipton turned to Chase, a broad smile on his face. "Chase, you are the biological father..."

A loud hum in Jaxson's ears bleated out the rest of the doctor's words. He saw the man's mouth moving... smiling even. This is what he'd wanted. Chase was the biological father. The kids would escape the asshole gene, after all. It was a good thing. Jaxson loved Chase and Emma with every fiber of his being, so loving their babies would be as easy as breathing.

Emma and Chase were jumping around... animated... excited. They were hugging each other, happily laughing with the news.

For the first time in their three years together, Jaxson felt like an outsider. It hadn't even taken twenty seconds and the impossible had happened. He was jealous and he fucking hated it. His brain raced to tell him he was being stupid, that better he feel this way than tenderhearted Chase feeling left out. He was the Dom. He'd power through.

Jaxson spoke to Chase. "Congratulations, man. They're going to be adorable with Emma's lavender eyes and your infectious smile." Jaxson forced the comforting words out, determined to pull his shit together. He was being a pussy.

Chase hadn't answered him yet. In fact, both Emma and Chase

were staring at him strangely. The small smile on Chase's handsome face slowly grew into his best smile — the one that reminded Jaxson of pure sunshine. It comforted Jaxson.

"You didn't hear a word he said, did you?" Chase questioned.

"Sure I did. He said you're the biological father. It's what we wanted, right? No chance of my father's bullshit DNA contaminating our kids."

Chase crossed his arms, pinning Jaxson with the dominant glare he usually reserved for Emma. "Jaxson Cartwright-Davidson, that's the very last time you're going to put yourself or your DNA down, is that understood?"

"Excuse me?"

"You heard me. Never again."

"Why the hell do you care if I label my family as the jerks they are?" Jaxson spat defensively.

"Well, for starters, I happen to love you even when you act like a jerk, which you happen to be doing a spectacular job of at this very moment."

"Did you just call me a jerk?" Jaxson countered, truly not understanding why Chase was trying to kick him while he was down.

"I call it like I see it."

Emma intervened, reaching out to each of them. "You aren't helping, Chase." She smiled at Jaxson then, her unique eyes he loved so much twinkling with excitement. "Jaxson, Dr. Tipton did say that Chase was the biological father of our son."

"I heard… wait, of our son? You mean of our twins."

"No, I mean our son. *You* are the biological father of our little girl. So, if it's all the same to you, I'd really like it if you'd stop referring to yourself and our daughter as assholes."

"Wait." Jaxson looked between his husband and wife and then turned to pin the doctor with an expectant glare. "I zoned out. How is this possible? I mean, I never even dreamed…"

"It's not as rare as you'd think. Emma's eggs were fertile for two to three days. If you each had sex with her during that same time period, you had equal chances at being the father. The fact that the twins are fraternal tells me she released at least two eggs. It looks like you each had a winning horse in the race, so to speak."

"We are each... I mean both..." Jaxson was uncharacteristically tongue-tied. The news stunned him.

Chase walked around to Jaxson's side of the padded table, pulling him into perhaps the most important embrace of his life.

It was a miracle. He hadn't even known such a thing was possible. Until this exact minute, Jaxson had refused to admit even to himself how important the outcome of the paternity tests were to the fragile balance of their complicated relationship. It shocked him to realize how easily he'd been figuratively knocked on his ass.

He let himself be wrapped in Emma and Chase's love as they hugged him close, humbling him with their easy forgiveness. Taller than his lovers, he was able to see over their heads as the doctor and his wife slipped quietly from the room, leaving the trio and their closest friends to celebrate the news.

Jaxson released Chase and Emma, giving them up to the wave of hugs and well wishes from their friends. And that was the moment that he knew as surely as he was standing there that he was the luckiest bastard on the planet.

In one perfect moment, Chase and Emma turned as one, looking at him with the most adoring gaze as they waited for their Dom to lead them.

They'd managed the impossible. In four short months, they'd bought and renovated the massive property and had not one, but two successful grand openings. They'd found out they were going to be parents, planned and pulled off a wedding, convinced his mother to finally leave his father, and managed to renovate and move into their new home.

They deserved a vacation.

"Let's go home." He paused making them wait before adding, "We need to get some rest. Our flight leaves tomorrow afternoon."

Neither of his loves looked happy with his comment. He didn't blame them. They were as exhausted as he was.

Emma asked hopefully, "Are we going back to D.C?"

"Not this time. Now that we have the clubs open, I thought it was time that we go on a honeymoon. By this time tomorrow, we'll be relaxing in our private cabana in Hawaii."

That brought a smile to their faces.

Chase pressed him, "How the hell did you pull that off without me finding out?"

Jaxson grinned. "Emma isn't the only secret keeper in this family. Let's go home and pack."

(Not) The End

Because Jaxson, Chase and Emma own the clubs, readers will be lucky enough to get glimpses of our infamous trio in other upcoming Black Light books.

NEED MORE BLACK LIGHT?

Did you miss Jaxson, Chase, and Emma meeting? Catch the beginning of their story and the Black Light World in *Infamous Love*

Blurb:
A private car on a train to Paris.

One penniless, language-challenged, curvaceous grad student.

Two A-list male models with a penchant for dominance; for each other, and a stranded young woman.

Emma Fischer begins her journey a girl, but ends it a woman in the commanding arms of Jaxson Davidson and Chase Cartwright.

Does what happens on the train have to stay on the train, or can it bloom into something real? Find out in this sexy, exciting menage romance.

And Coming August 1st, 2018
Black Light: Suspicion by Measha Stone

Blurb:

Detective Sophie Nelson wants just a taste of her fantasies. She's been burned enough times to know it's not going to happen for her in the real world, so the sexual playground, Black Light, is the best place to turn. She never suspects to find her partner not only at the club but wanting to have her for himself.

Scott shouldn't be involving himself in Sophie's exploration of her submissive side. They're partners after all, and mixing work and sexual relationships rarely ends well. But a stern dominant knows when it's time to bend a rule. An even better one knows when to make his sub toe the line.

While solving the puzzle of how to make their relationship work, they have a criminal case to solve. A dead body, a videotaped crime, and no solid leads. As the investigation and their off-duty kinky activities intensify, suspicions rise. Can they work through all the twists and turns and come out together on the other side?

Chapter One - *Black Light: Suspicion* by Measha Stone

DID PEOPLE GET FOOD POISONING FROM BOTTLED WATER?

Sophie Nelson rubbed her stomach as she inched her way through the crush of the crowd. She'd traded in her daily meals for large bottles of water in anticipation of the evening's events. Knowing nerves would finally show their ugly head at exactly the wrong moment, she wasn't taking any chances on getting sick because of them.

Except, her stomach still twisted and turned. Though she was pretty sure she'd be able to hold it together. She had waited too long to finally go for it—no way she was letting a little nervousness get in her way.

A quarter of D.C. showed up at Black Light for the Valentine Roulette. Or rather it just felt that way with everyone crowding around, waiting for the event to begin.

She'd joined the club only a month ago, so it seemed like the perfect way to start down this new path of hers. Go to the party, get paired with someone, and fall to her knees in servitude. Of course, she knew it didn't really happen that way, but a girl could dream.

Even though she'd become a member, she hadn't actually set foot in the club until the night of the roulette game. She considered the wasted money a down payment on her future bliss.

If this worked and she actually met someone.

She made her way to the bar and ordered another water. A bourbon straight sounded better, but on an empty stomach it was like lighting a match near an open gas line. She'd never make it back to work in the morning.

"Sophia?" A deep voice, a familiar voice, a spine-tingling familiar voice, called her name from behind her.

Placing the bottle of water back on the bar, she pushed on a smile and turned around.

Fuck.

"Scott! Hi." She forced lightness, while her toes scrunched up in her flats.

"What are you doing here?" He maneuvered through a small group of women and stopped right in front of her.

The odds of her new partner showing up at the same BDSM

club, at the same event on the same night as her? Shouldn't it have been an impossibility?

Her face heated, but with the dark ambiance and the neon lighting, she could find some comfort in that he probably couldn't see how deep her blush burned.

"Same as you, probably." She gripped the end of the bar, pushing the edge into her palm.

"By yourself?" he asked, surveying behind her.

"I didn't think this was really a plus one event." She tilted her head and bit down on her lower lip.

He took half a step back and looked her over. The ground could open up any time now to swallow her up. She'd gone with a pair of black leggings, a white tunic, and a thick black belt to accentuate her waist. His stare paused but didn't linger where she'd left the top two buttons of the low neckline unbuttoned, showcasing cleavage but more importantly the purple lace bralette she'd picked up for the evening.

"You're rolling?" he asked with a furrowed brow. He'd shaved. He must have gone after their shift; his beard was trimmed, his hair neater and styled. The sandy blonde hair paired beautifully with his light brown eyes.

She cleared her throat to pull herself out of her trance. "Yes. Of course... Are you?" What could be more awkward?

He laughed. "Yeah. What are the odds, huh?" He leaned one elbow against the bar, his casual smile tore right through her.

After transferring from the second district to the third within the Metropolitan Police Department, she'd been paired with Scott. As a partner, he was efficient, smart, and completely easy to work with. They'd already managed to get two closed cases under their belts. And while on duty, when she had the badge strapped to her belt, she could forget how handsome he was, how enticing his rock-hard body could be. She forced her libido to chill out. But now, in this lounge where his tight black T-shirt rode up his arm, showing off the tribal band she hadn't known he had, and his lazy smile occupied all the room in her brain—she couldn't function.

"You okay?" he asked, placing his hand on hers.

"What? Yeah. Of course." She pulled away, his touch too warm, too tingling. Her head spun, a little tilt at first, but then it really took a nose dive, and she latched onto his arm to keep from falling over.

"You sure?" His eyebrows knitted together.

Blinking a few times and grabbing a few more sips of her water, she nodded. "Yep. Just got a little lightheaded. Must be all the people. It's really crowded in here tonight." She turned, pushing her back against the bar, wishing it had more of a bite. The rounded edges didn't do much for a distraction.

"How long have you been a member?" He tilted his head. She knew that look. He'd given the same one to the suspect they'd questioned in an armed robbery case last week. Casual tone, but serious eyes. He was fishing.

"Recently enrolled. Really hoping for the free month though, right?" She laughed then cleared her throat again. When the hell were they going to get the party started?

"Uh, huh. So, you've been here, how many times exactly?" He took the water bottle from her hands when the plastic crinkled.

"What about you, new or veteran member?" Turn the questions on to him and maybe he'd drop it. She didn't need to explain her complete lack of experience. It was nerve-racking enough being a complete newb in the presence of so many people who looked every bit like they belonged there. A neon light over her head pointing her out how virginal she was in their realm would only make her nerves heighten.

Her stomach swirled, and she swallowed. The lightheadedness from a moment ago increased. The crowd moved forward.

"Looks like they're starting." She pointed, moving forward along with the crowd. Scott followed, standing behind her.

Another couple appeared beside him, talking with each other.

The low murmur in the room rose in volume. Chattering, laughing, a squeal from a microphone. She touched her forehead to steady her mind.

She was actually going to go through with it. She was going to be paired up with a man, who would spend the next three hours dominating her. Finally, she'd know what it was like. All the fantasizing, all the horrible attempts with previous boyfriends who placated her would finally be worth something. Those experiences brought her to where she stood.

What if she couldn't do it? What happened if she had her turn to spin the wheel for an activity that sounded perfectly hot when she'd filled out the application, but once in the middle of it, she needed to cry red. She wouldn't only be blowing her own chance at a free month's membership, but her partner's as well. It would be her fault. He'd hate her. He'd tell everyone in the club how much of a pussy she was, and she'd never find anyone. She'd be stuck in the vanilla world forever.

Her chest constricted. Air became harder to take in as the crowd moved again, closer. Too close to her. She tried to turn to her side, to give her chest more room to expand. Nothing. Maybe it was the bralette; maybe she had it too tight.

"This was dumb," she muttered to herself. Scott moved behind her. She could feel him shift from one foot to the other.

Again, her mind lurched, spinning off its axis. She needed air. She needed to get a grip.

"I- I can't do this," she said and turned to push her way out of the crowd. Instead of taking a step, she fell into darkness.

***

He glared at her.

When Sophie opened her eyes, the dim lighting didn't hide his hard stare. Scott sat beside the medical cot she lay on, leaning over her with a fierce frown planted on his face.

"You're awake," he said, although it sounded more like an accusation.

Of course, she was awake. Her eyes were open, weren't they?

"Hey." She smiled, pushing her hands against the cot and trying to get up.

"No." He shook his head and put a hand on her shoulder, putting her right back down on the cot. "Not until Garreth looks at you again and tells me you're okay."

"Can't I tell you I'm okay?" She pressed the heels of her hands to her eyes. She'd fainted. Fuck. She hadn't fainted since high school. Her head fogged up, and a headache wasn't too far off.

"No, but you can tell me what you ate today." No more lighthearted questions.

She sighed. "Nothing. I ate nothing. Which is probably what made my blood sugar drop and made me faint." No sense in lying. "Why are you here? You should be out there." She jerked a finger at the door. "They're going to start soon."

"They already did." He sat back in his chair, folding his arms over his chest.

"Oh." She closed her eyes again. She'd ruined her night, and his. No wonder he was pissed.

"You didn't need to stay with me. I'm fine."

"Hey, you're up. Good. How do you feel?" Garreth walked up to her with an open bottle of water and some sugar cookies.

"Like an idiot." She swung her legs over the side of the cot and sat up. Scott didn't move from his position, so she had to scoot down to make room for herself. "I'm really sorry."

"Not a problem. It happens. Nerves are normal when you're trying something for the first time. And tonight is a big event." Garreth handed her the cookies. "As long as you're doing okay, I'm going back to the floor. There's a medical scene I want to be near tonight."

"Yeah. I'm fine. A few cookies, and I'll be good to go."

Garreth looked her over again. "Okay. If you need anything, Scott can come get me." He slapped Scott on his back.

"Will do," Scott answered, but continued to grind his glare into Sophie as she nibbled on her cookies.

"Okay, then," Garreth said and left.

"Don't look at me like that." She pointed a finger at him and shoved the last cookie into her mouth. The buttery sugary crumbles melted on her tongue. Her stomach growled.

"Like what?"

"Like I'm the asshole sitting across the table from you in an interrogation room. So, I'm a new member, never been here before. I was nervous, so I didn't eat today. And now I've ruined my night, and yours. I'm sorrier about ruining yours." Her shoulders drooped. Humiliation could be handled, but tanking someone else's fun just plain sucked.

She focused her attention on the bottle of water in her hands. He should be saying something. Anything would be good. The silence stretching out made her ears throb.

"Did you drive?" he asked after a heavy sigh.

"No. I cabbed it. Wasn't sure if I'd be—"She stopped herself from finishing her sentence. She wasn't about to tell her partner, her very hot partner, that she'd hoped to go home with someone that night.

Ugh. What a whore she'd sound like. She capped the water and placed it on a nearby table.

"I'll drive you." He stood from his chair and offered his hand to help her up.

"You don't have to do that," she argued. "Maybe you can still get a partner? Maybe they'll let you still roll? Or someone from the audience will want to join and take my place?"

He shook his head and wrapped his hand around hers when she didn't take his offer.

"I'm getting you a burger then taking you home and putting you to bed."

She didn't put up a fight when he pulled her to her feet. He didn't back up, either, making her breasts brush against his chest. She didn't match him in height, but he didn't dwarf her either. She stared at his chin in silence. He'd never been so close to her before, although they'd shared a car since being paired up.

Hell, he smelled good. Like musk and leather.

"A burger sounds perfect."

"Let's go." He laced his fingers with hers and pulled her along. "Before I change my mind and give you the ass whipping you deserve."

She heard him, but it had been said so soft, without a glance in her direction, she figured it hadn't been meant for her ears.

ABOUT THE AUTHOR

USA Today bestselling author Livia Grant lives in Chicago with her husband and furry rescue dog named Max. She is fortunate to have been able to travel extensively and as much as she loves to visit places around the globe, the Midwest and its changing seasons will always be home. Livia's readers appreciate her riveting stories filled with deep, character driven plots, often spiced with elements of BDSM.

~

Connect with Livia!
www.liviagrant.com
lb.grant@yahoo.com

Sting of Lust

Hero to Obey

Royally Mine

Stand Alone Books

Blessed Betrayal

Call Sign: Thunder

Don't miss Livia's next book!

Sign-up for Livia's Newsletter

Follow Livia on Amazon

Follow Livia on BookBub

BLACK COLLAR PRESS

Did you enjoy your visit to Black Light? Have you read the other books in the series?

Infamous Love, A Black Light Prequel by Livia Grant
Black Light: Rocked by Livia Grant
Black Light: Exposed by Jennifer Bene
Black Light: Valentine Roulette by Various Authors
Black Light: Suspended by Maggie Ryan
Black Light: Cuffed by Measha Stone
Black Light: Rescued by Livia Grant
Black Light: Roulette Redux by Various Authors
Complicated Love, A Black Light Novel

Black Collar Press is a small publishing house started by authors Livia Grant and Jennifer Bene in late 2016. The purpose was simple - to create a place where the erotic, kinky, and exciting worlds they love to explore could thrive and be joined by other like-minded authors.

If this is something that interests you, please go to the Black Collar Press website and read through the FAQs. If your questions are not answered there, please contact us directly at: blackcollarpress@gmail.com.

Where to find Black Collar Press:

- Website: http://www.blackcollarpress.com/
- Facebook: https://www.facebook.com/blackcollarpress/
- Twitter: https://twitter.com/BlackCollarPres

THANK YOU FROM LIVIA

Like most authors, I love to hear from my readers. The art of writing can be a lonely activity at times. Authors sit alone, pouring our hearts into our stories, hoping readers will connect with our words and fall in love with our characters. It's easy to get discouraged at times.

And that's where you come in.

I'd sure appreciate it if you'd take a few minutes to drop me a line or better yet, leave a review to let me know what you thought of the book you just finished. Reader feedback, good and bad, is what helps me continue to grow stronger as an author.

Happy reading!

Livia

Manufactured by Amazon.ca
Bolton, ON

13916175R00181